Acclaim for Jay McInerney and

MODEL BEHAVIOR

"[McInerney] has an effortless knack for the cadences of dialogue and the pacing of scenes. His portraiture is quick, vivid and often very funny."
—*The New York Times Book Review*

"No one who truly loves Manhattan in all its soiled beauty and shopworn glamour can fail to derive pleasure from this book."
—*New York Post*

"McInerney is a gifted comic writer, capable of lines that drip with wit and scenes that percolate with hilarity."
—*St. Petersburg Times*

"[*Model Behavior* is] very funny, and full of rakish, old-fashioned literary elegance that McInerney always manages to mix into the slangy idioms of his characters."
—*The New York Review of Books*

"*Model Behavior* is written with style, wit, and considerable depth."
—*Fort Lauderdale Sun-Sentinel*

"Uncommonly resourceful . . . [McInerney is] a gifted social observer."
—*Chicago Tribune*

"McInerney is the real thing, a writer of undeniable flair and charm."
—*Entertainment Weekly*

Jay McInerney
MODEL BEHAVIOR

Jay McInerney lives with his wife
and their two children in New York
and Williamson County, Tennessee.

Model Behavior

Model Behavior
A Novel and Seven Stories

Jay McInerney

VINTAGE CONTEMPORARIES

Vintage Books

A Division of Random House, Inc.

New York

FIRST VINTAGE OPEN MARKET EDITION, JULY 1999

Copyright © 1998 by Bright Lights, Big City, Inc.

The stories in this book were previously published as follows:
The Atlantic Monthly: "Smoke"
Esquire: "Reunion"
Granta: "The Business" and "Getting in Touch with Lonnie"
The New Yorker: A portion of "Model Behavior" (originally titled "Philomena,"
December 25, 1995, and January 1, 1996)
Playboy: "Con Doctor" and "How It Ended"
"The Queen and I" was originally published in *Spin* and as a
Bloomsbury Quid paperback original by Bloomsbury Publishing Plc., London.

The Library of Congress has cataloged the Alfred A. Knopf edition
as follows:
McInerney, Jay.
Model behavior : a novel and stories / Jay McInerney. — 1st ed.
p.   cm.
ISBN 0-679-42846-1
1. United States—Social life and customs—20th century—Fiction.
I. Title.
PS3563.C3694M6   1998
813'.54—dc21   98-27859
CIP

Vintage ISBN: 0-375-70644-5

www.vintagebooks.com

Printed in Canada
10 9 8 7 6 5 4 3 2 1

For Scott Sommer

CONTENTS

Model Behavior   3

STORIES

The Business   179
Con Doctor   194
Smoke   205
Getting in Touch with Lonnie   224
How It Ended   234
The Queen and I   246
Reunion   257

Acknowledgments   271

Model Behavior

MODEL COUPLE

When Philomena looks in the mirror she sees a creature fat and unattractive. This despite the fact that she is a woman whose photographic image is expensively employed to arouse desire in conjunction with certain consumer goods. Or rather, *because* of that fact. Toxic body consciousness being the black lung of her profession. Dressing for the party, she screams that she's bloated and has nothing to wear.

I'm clutching a preparty martini when she makes this declaration. "You look terrific," I say.

She seizes my glass and hurls it at the mirror, shattering both.

It's all right, really. I drink too much anyway.

THE PARTY

The name of the party is the Party You Have Been to Six Hundred Times Already. Everybody is here. "All your friends," Philomena states in what can only be described as a citric tone. It seems to me that they are *her* friends, that *she* is the reason we grace this fabulous gala, which takes place in the Waiting Room of Grand Central, presumably evicting dozens of homeless people for the night. We're supposedly on hand for the benefit of a disease, but we were comped, as was everyone else we know. "I'm sick of all this pointless glamour," my glamorous girlfriend says. "I want the simple life." This has become a theme. Weariness with metropolitan life in all its colonoscopic intricacy. I wonder if this ennui is somehow related to that other unstated domestic theme: sex, infrequency thereof.

We are accosted by Belinda, the popular transvestite, whom I am nearly certain is a friend of my girlfriend's, as opposed to one of my very own. I can't exactly remember if I know him from the gossip columns or if I know him personally, from events like these. Belinda is with an actual, ageless woman with striking dark eyebrows and buzzcut white hair, a woman who is always here at the party and whom I always sort of recognize. One of those women with three names: Hi Howareyou Goodtoseeyou. All the women lately have either three names or just one. Even the impersonators.

"Oh God, hide me," says the woman whose name I always forget, "there's Tommy Kroger, I had a bad date with him about five thousand years ago."

"Did you sleep with him?" Philomena asks, raising one of her perfectly defined eyebrows, which looks like a crow in flight in the far distance of a painting by van Gogh.

"God, who can remember?"

"If you can't, then you did," says Belinda. "That's the rule."

Ah, so *that's* the rule.

"Hello, darlings." Who could it be but Delia McFaggen, the famous designer, streaking toward Belinda, blowing kisses all over everyone. I retreat, slaloming through the thick crowd to find beverages, the first of many trips.

A FRIENDLY FACE

At the bar I encounter Jeremy Green, an unlikely and conspicuous figure at this venue, his golden locks falling superabundantly across the square shoulders of his rented tux—which juxtaposition suggests a flock of begowned angels camped atop the Seagram Building. He is an actual friend, my best friend, in fact, though he ignores my repeated greetings. Not until I pour vodka on his shirt does he deign to acknowledge my existence.

"Fuck off."

"Excuse me. Aren't you Jeremy Green, the famous short story writer?"

"That's an oxymoron. Same category as *living poet, French rock star, German cuisine.*"

"How about Chekhov?"

"Dead." Jeremy pronounces this verdict with a poète maudit manner that seems tinged more than faintly with envy. He doesn't quite add *Lucky bastard,* but you can see that's what he's thinking.

"Carver?"

"Ditto. Plus, you think the guy who read his gas meter knew who Carver was? You think this bartender knows?"

The bartender, an aspiring model, says *"Shortcuts"* in mid-pour. "I saw the movie."

"I think," Jeremy says, "that proves my point. And don't even think about saying *Hemingway.*"

"Wouldn't dream of it. Any particular reason you're ignoring me?"

"I just think I'll feel better about myself if I pretend I don't know anybody at this hideous ratfuck." Finally he turns his wrathful gaze upon me. "Besides, if memory serves, you're the slimy lowlife who talked me into attending this fetid fete."

"Your *editor* talked you into it," I remind him. "I merely encouraged you by way of saying that *I,* personally, would be happier and less chagrined if you were among the throng."

Why, I wonder, are all the boys and girls blaming *me* tonight? Jeremy has a book coming out, and his editor, Blaine Forrestal, thought it would be good for him to be seen. Blaine is part of this world. She wears terrific suits, has a Radcliffe degree and a house in Sag Harbor; Jeremy is the least commercial of the writers she publishes. In fact, one might surmise that she is publishing Jeremy as a kind of penance for the frothy, wildly successful stuff she generally dispenses—memoirs by disgraced politicians, autobiographies by Emmy-winning TV stars. Jeremy's stories tend to appear in *Antaeus* and the *Iowa Review* and frequently are set in mental institutions.

"I feel," he says, "like a whore."

"Now you know how the rest of us feel."

"I'm sure this will really boost my lit cred, showing all the media elite that I swim in the same sewer they do."

"Don't worry, I think the media elite's swimming in some other sewer tonight." Indeed, excepting a few young black-clad Voguettes and self, I don't see much in the way of the Fourth Estate.

"Who's that fucking midget over there who told me he 'rather liked' my first book."

Following Jeremy's aquiline nose, I spot Kevin Shipley, book assassin for *Beau Monde*, in conversation with the *New York Post*.

"Jesus, I hope you didn't insult him. That's Kevin Shipley."

"He told me he bought it on the remainder table at Barnes and Noble and I said I was deeply honored that he felt he'd gotten his buck ninety-five's worth."

"Just pray he doesn't review the new one. His keyboard's made out of human teeth."

"Yeah, but how does he reach it?"

Finally *I* have reached the bar, where I request several cosmopolitans, one of which I hand to Jeremy. "Your problem," I say, "is that you don't drink enough. Where's Blaine, anyway?"

"Last I knew she was kissing Hollywood butt. Some fucking troll from Sony Pictures."

"Let's go find Phil," I suggest. "Maybe you can cheer her up."

WHAT'S WITH PHILOMENA?

The love of my life has been decidedly edgy and nervous. I would ask her why, except I'm not entirely certain I want to know. What we need is some ecstasy therapy, drop a few tabs, have a long night of truth and touch. There has been too little rapture of late. Not to mention the touching part.

Fortunately, by the time I find her again, she seems to have undergone a mood transplant. Delighted to see Jeremy, she kisses him and then, for good measure, me.

I introduce myself to the attractive young woman of color with whom Phil has been conversing, whose name sounds familiar.

"Do I know you?" I ask.

"We've never met," she says. "I'm Chip Ralston's personal assistant."

"Well," says Jeremy, "bully for you."

"I was just telling Cherie," Phil tells me, "that you're doing the profile for *CiaoBella!*"

A photographer suddenly appears: "Philomena, let's get a shot."

My statuesque soulmate breaks into autosmile and gamely reaches for my arm, but, shy guy that I am, I say, "Do a shot with Jeremy, we're trying to get him noticed." Shoving them together, I chase after the retreating personal assistant.

"Is Chip *here*," I ask.

"You just missed him," she says. "He's flying back to L.A. tonight, but I gave him your message. I'm sure he'll check in with you next week."

I'd press her harder, I've got to talk to the bastard, but soon, then I suddenly see that she's edging directly into the path of Jillian Crowe, my formidably glamorous boss; and while I admire Jillian's fashion sense and editorial skills, I'd just as soon avoid her at present. Backtracking, I find Philomena teasing Jeremy about the career that awaits him in modeling. She is more vivacious than I've seen her in days, Jeremy being such a Jeremiah that he tends to spur his companions to sparkle and shine.

Fueled by several uncharacteristic cocktails, Philomena's high spirits last well into the morning; she surprises me by agreeing to join an expedition of fashion folk down to the Baby Doll Lounge, a low strip joint in TriBeCa.

Cabbing down with three revelers—satellites of Planet Fashion—she sits on my lap and sips from a drink she managed to smuggle out of the party. "I have a joke," she suddenly announces.

TOPLESS MODEL IN HEADLESS BAR

At the Baby Doll, Philomena orders another cosmopolitan and, not unkindly, critiques the bodies of the dancing girls.

With the body God gave Phil, she can afford to be generous. Finally the guy named Ralph, whom Philomena introduced as "genius with hair," suggests that Philomena show us her tits. The cry is taken up by Alonzo—who introduced himself as "a powder fairy," which Philomena annotated as "makeup guy"—and then by the adjoining tables. To my astonishment, she jumps on the bar and pulls her dress down to her waist, giving us a liberal flash of lunar breast. And it is a measure of their excellence of form that I nearly swoon—if indeed one can *nearly* swoon—despite having seen them nearly every day for the past three years of my life. Tumid with desire, I try to coax Philomena home the minute she jumps down from the bar. But she's on a roll. Wants to dance. Wants another cosmopolitan.

For the third time I try the men's room and it's still locked.

SHIPS IN THE NIGHT

We continue to have an uproarious time, but by now I have lost the feeling of being in the moment, and stand as if on the sidelines watching Philomena entertain her friends, though I dance and drink with the best of them. I don't mind, it's good to see her like this. Alonzo, feeling no pain either, slips me his phone number and says we ought to get together sometime. I explain to him that while I appreciate the thought, he is barking up the wrong telephone pole. He raises a skeptical eyebrow, then plants a hand voguishly on his hip. Working as I do for a young women's magazine with a strong emphasis on fashion, I often encounter this suspicion.

Philomena's mood slips away when I'm not looking, possibly around the time that Ralph's giving me his card and telling me that I have to do something about my haircut immediately, for the sake of the nation. "They actually let you into the offices of *CiaoBella!* with that do?"

"Maybe he really *is* straight," says Ralph.

By the time we get in the cab my love is silent and pensive. As we undress for bed, she announces preemptively that she's exhausted.

No nookie for you, buckaroo.

AT LONG LAST, SEX

The narrator, slightly hungover now, the day after the party, helps Philomena choose the outfits for her trip—a versatile taupe suit from Jil Sander, a Versace jacket and ripped jeans for the plane, a fetching little sheath from Nicole Miller for the audition, as well as an extra pair of ripped, faded jeans plus three immaculate white T-shirts. And some nice clunky boots suitable for heavy construction or light shopping in SoHo. If he were more attentive it's possible the narrator would pick up certain clues from the packing, or from her behavior, indications that this trip might be something more than advertised, but he is not a suspicious person by nature, and his powers of observation are swamped by a surge of hormones. When, after trying on the sheath, she slips out of it and asks him to fetch some panties from her dainties drawer, he is overcome with desire for the taut, tawny flesh beneath her teddy.

"Please," he pleads. "Just a little slice." He reminds her that it has been five days, nine hours, and thirty-six minutes. And they're not even married yet.

"No we're not, are we?" Oh, dear, a tactical mistake on his part, this allusion to matrimony. This is a sore point, something he has been meaning to get around to addressing for the last couple of years. While she has been waiting for the big question, he is waiting to be worthy of such an honor; he does not believe that anyone, let alone Philomena, could really want to hitch her shining carriage to his lame gelding. Yet for some reason she seems to want to do so. As long as he is only a boyfriend, he believes that his fortunes are still fluid, that his lowly station is merely a stage of gestation. Whereas she believes that the actual obstacle is his sense of superiority. Luckily she doesn't pursue the subject, though perhaps with the absence of a marriage proposal in mind she makes him kneel and beg for it.

Craven, genuflective begging ensues, as per standard form. But heartfelt and genuine on his part. PLEASE PLEASE PLEASE. Feeling like the target audience for the recent beer commercial in which she appeared, oiled and glistening in a bikini, he tells her he will do anything. He will bark like any species of canine she can name and, if necessary, roll over. Finally she peels off the teddy and lies back on the bed like Manet's *Olympia*, ripe and haughty, a bored odalisque.

"Fast," she commands, "and no sweating."

The narrator takes what he can get, a grateful consumer.

AFTERGLOW

Afterward, lying in bed, a single gemlike tear appears on Philomena's cheek. When I ask what's wrong, she concocts a smile and shakes her head.

"Don't worry," I say, although I have no idea what I mean by this hollow formula. While I am full of doubt as to the future, my job, I feel, is to reassure her, my consort, my lost little girl.

Later, a moment of perfect melancholy: watching Philomena gather her cosmetics at her vanity in front of the cracked mirror, the dusky dimness infiltrated with pulsing red light that strobes through the window slats of our half-basement bedroom. This lurid glow likely signifying a more permanent death than the one I have just experienced; across the street is a nursing home where ambulances call with some regularity.

"Don't go," I say in a sudden swoon of dread.

"It's just for a few days," she says, brushing her hair.

"I love you," I say—a too-rare declaration.

She smiles at me from a shard of mirror.

LOCATION, LOCATION, LOCATION

We live in the West Village, near the river, on the southern edge of the Meat District, far enough west that we are largely spared the Visigoth invasions of provincial teens with boom boxes. Of a summer's evening the breeze is frequently infused with the stench of decaying flesh wafting from the scrap heaps of the warehouses; after dark, the streets outside the butcheries are taken over by transvestites and the cruising vehicles of their johns; many nights we will be awakened by thick whispers and carnal grunts from the stairwell just outside the bedroom windows. Love and death. "It's always a trade-off with Manhattan real estate," our agent cheerfully informed us, just before she demanded seventeen percent of our first year's rent.

POSTCOITAL REFLECTIONS

Meditating on the strange fact that while you were making love to Philomena you were actually fantasizing about a previous fucking. With Philomena—so she has no real grounds for complaint, though even so you don't propose to share this insight. This has become almost a habit, conjuring a previous sexual episode in the commission of a current one, as if the memory possessed a vivacity somehow lacking in the physical present. As if, say, the breast of Philomena, delectable as it might seem in the flesh, was only truly eroticized in the imagination. But why isn't the flesh enough?

You have a repertoire of sexual memories, and in time this latest act might be added to it, but while happening it was experienced through the scrim of a recycled midsummer encounter behind a beach house in Amagansett. Sex itself becoming, according to this model, merely the raw material for an aesthetic event.

IMMEDIATE FAMILY

My sister, Brooke, has a tiny rent-controlled apartment in the Geritol Zone off Beekman Place. Not long after putting Philomena in a car for the airport I call, but she will not pick up her phone. I know she's there, listening to the messages. I know because I am my sister's keeper. Maybe it's my hangover, or perhaps the ambulance has made me jumpy and morbid; nonetheless I'm filled with a sense of the fragility of life, love and the social contract. That something bad is about to happen feels as palpable as rain in the air. I consider calling the airline, to see if Phil's plane is okay. Except come to think of it, I don't know which airline, which flight.

Instead I walk out to Hudson beneath the yellowing stingko trees. Wait for a cab, sharing the sidewalk with nocturnal pigeons who waddle uptown like portly tourists.

At the door of Brooke's building, trying to flush her out of her lair, which takes longer than the cab ride uptown. Finally the intercom crackles to life. She beams me up after I identify myself as her only sibling. Pushing through the cracked door, I find her in bed, reading, bones poking through the sheets, her beautiful strawberry-blond hair unwashed. When I kiss her, her breath has the hollow keloid stench of starvation, of the body consuming itself. I try not to look alarmed.

"They made separate piles of the body parts," she says in greeting. "Legs in one pile, arms in another. Living torsos on a pile of other torsos six feet high. Their neighbors. People they had lived with for years."

"Bosnia?"

"Rwanda."

Brooke is reading transcripts from the UN War Crimes Tribunal. On the headboard of her sleigh bed she has taped a map of the former Yugoslavia. Sarajevo, Mostar, Srebrenica and other unfortunate cities are circled in red ink. Lately she has taken up the study of the recent atrocities in Central Africa.

Searching the kitchen cupboards, I discover an inch of Orville Redenbacher's popcorn in the bottom of a jar and a half inch of olive oil in another. I fire up a bowl, bring it back to the bedroom, casually placing it within reach of her delicate, freckled hand on the bed.

"How's Mad Dog," I ask, this being my ironic appellation for Doug Halliwell, M.D., her current would-be consort. Doug is a trauma surgeon whose acquaintance Brooke made in the ER at New York Hospital after she tumbled down a set of stairs at Rockefeller University. To me he does not seem worthy of my sister's attention, let alone any of her now-mended body parts. Not that I really imagine Doug has actually gotten hold of any of them just yet. Brooke's on the rebound from a colorful marriage, hence this sudden tolerance for beige.

"I wish you'd stop calling him that. Doug's fine. And how's the mannequin? Has she mastered the alphabet yet?"

"She's in San Francisco on a shoot," I say. "And for your information she took *Anna Karenina* on the plane."

"You enjoy saying that don't you? *On a shoot. On location.* The jargon of the glamour industry."

"Well, let's just say she's on a business trip."

"Do you know that one of the reasons the Hutus hated the Tutsis is because the Tutsis were considered more attractive? Tall, thin noses, lighter skin."

"Are you suggesting that the secretaries at Ford and Click might rise up and kill all the models?"

"Seems like she's been traveling a lot lately."

"Why wouldn't she?"

"Hmmmm," she hums.

Brooke is not a fan of Philomena's. And vice versa. Phil calls Brooke the scrambled egghead. Which goes to show that she's far sharper than Brooke would ever concede. Staying loyal to both has been difficult. While I'm used to Brooke's skepticism vis-à-vis my squeeze, tonight it makes me anxious. My ribs shrink around my lungs. What does Brooke know that I don't?

Why do I always feel that everyone has more information than me? Actually, Brooke knows a great deal that I don't know: the difference between natural and unnatural numbers, the significance of Heisenberg's indeterminacy principle, Gödel's incompleteness theorem, the probable casualties from Banja Luka and environs. Until recently Brooke was doing postgraduate work in physics at Rockefeller University, but she is on an extended hiatus, crippled by depression and an acute sensitivity to human suffering. My sister resembles one of those bubble children who are born without an immune system; she does not possess that protective membrane that filters out the noise and pain of other creatures. She is utterly porous.

Mom and Dad think it has to do with witnessing a murder at age seven. And while that would be enough to fuck most of us up, Brooke decidedly is not most of us.

"So how was *your* day?" I ask, fishing. *Something* must have gone wrong, whether on a global or personal level.

"My day? Well, let's see . . . it started with Jerry on the *Today Show* explaining the proton accelerator to a grateful nation."

Ah, yes. Here's the pea under the mattress, the fly in the K-Y. Until recently Brooke was married to a prodigious young Harvard professor, Jerry Sakoloff, who wrote an improbable best-seller about quantum physics and who frequently appears on television to explain subatomic phenomena. Brooke had been Jerry's student when their romance commenced; the problem was that Jerry continued to sleep with other students after he and Brooke were married. Or rather, the problem was that he didn't at all see why he shouldn't and in fact insisted on bringing them home to befriend his wife. It's hard to say which upset Brooke more, the infidelity or the television appearances.

"How was he?"

"Charming. Quotable. Hair and tie askew for that authentic, absentminded professorial look. Before those shows he'd work on the tie for twenty minutes so the knot would hang just low enough that it looked like he'd forgotten to pull it up all the way. And brush his hair within an inch of its life, then muss it up with his fingers—you know, as if he'd been tearing at it while pondering the great problems of the universe."

"If I'd been here instead of Japan I never would've let you marry him."

"You wouldn't have let me marry anybody."

"I do think you might consider the life of a nun. Lord knows, the Church could certainly use you." This an allusion to the discarded but indelible faith of our forefathers.

I pretend to look aimlessly around the room while attempting to will her to eat the popcorn. EAT EAT EAT EAT.

"How are the beautiful people," she asks, reaching down and tweezing a kernel of popcorn between thumb and forefinger.

"They're fabulous, by definition," I answer, watching out of the corner of my eye as she inserts the popped kernel between her lips. CHEW CHEW SWALLOW SWALLOW.

"What about that young actor who died? The one with the weird hippie name." Her hand is in the bowl again, and she's actually chewing! "Did you know him?"

"You mean River Phoenix? Brooke, that was, like, years ago. This is 1996."

"So, excuse me, I'm not a big maven of popular culture."

"Okay, so I spent a few hours with him at the Olive, which was this club in West Hollywood, when I was doing a piece on his girlfriend. Let's just say it's a wonder he lasted as long as he did."

LISTEN TO YOURSELF

Lord, listen to you. How embarrassing that you even know this shit. How pathetic, the offhand manner in which you exhale this little toxic cloud of inside dope.

Meanwhile you are worrying that Philomena *does* seem to be taking a lot of trips lately. And why wouldn't she know where she was staying? Or if she did know, why wouldn't she leave you her number?

But hey, wait a minute—this is ridiculous. You trust her. Right? Well, yes, basically, although you can't quite ignore the merest tingle of suspicion, of dread, that animates the hairs at the base of your neck.

ANOREXIA STRIKES DEEP

Once Brooke is fully engaged with the popcorn I repair to the kitchen to warm a can of Campbell's chicken noodle soup. *"Um-um good,"* I call out. "Just like Mom used to heat." No, actually, come to think of it, Mom would ask the housekeeper, Daisy, to do the heavy lifting. Anyway. I pour the nourishing liquid into a big Harvard mug and carry it in on a plastic tray, treading cautiously so as not to frighten the prey. In her approach to eating my sister is rather like a stray dog we adopted as children who was so used to stealing food that he couldn't eat while anyone was looking. Any direct reference to nutrition will scare her off for days. Neither, of course, are we allowed to speak the name of her illness. Several years ago, at the nadir of her emaciation, she told me that the average weight loss among adult residents of Sarajevo after a thousand days of siege was twenty-five pounds, thereby giving her fast a symbolic dimension, but the siege is long over, and anyway she's been starving herself on and off since the Vietnam War.

Toward the end of her marriage to Jerry she began to cut herself—small, razored incisions on her arms and legs.

IMMEDIATE FOREBEARS

"Talked to the 'rents lately?" I ask. Although not actually eating the soup, Brooke is blowing at it, a hopeful sign.

"Dad called a few days ago," Brooke says.

"How was that?"

"I find it strangely reassuring—the sound of ice cubes against glass."

"Crystal," I correct.

"You have to give them credit, though—our parents—for being the only couple in America still together after forty-odd years."

"Indeed." Our father inherited orange groves in Central Florida from his father, who at the age of fifty sold his seat on the New York Stock Exchange and followed the sun. The property produces just enough income to keep my father in bourbon, Brooks Brothers shirts and Book-of-the-Month Club Main Selections for life. Exactly enough to kill any ambition he might have had to actually work for a living. Not enough that there will be anything left for us after estate taxes. Every few years Dad sells off five acres to finance a trip to Europe. So don't worry about a looming inheritance spoiling me. Dad reads the classics—Grisham, Clancy and Crichton—plays tennis and keeps a fond paternal eye on the oranges. Mom reads poetry, paints landscapes and sips her drinkie. Cummings is her favorite poet, Bonnard her painterly hero, Pernod her current preferred tipple.

Oranges are not exactly labor-intensive. They grow while you sleep, while you drink, while you play tennis, while you paint, while you nap. And they are still growing when you wake up to stir another cocktail. Twice a year the migrant laborers come to pick them, and sometimes a frost blowing down from the North will necessitate the application of smudge pots and extra-strength cocktails. Conveniently, oranges are monoecious, containing both sex organs in the same blossom—the laziest of fruit.

Unlike Brooke my parents don't worry enough. The worry muscles are thoroughly atrophied. Every fall they spend a week in New York. In just a few days, they will arrive to celebrate Thanksgiving with us here in the city. Gobble gobble gobble.

"How can people live together for years and suddenly start to butcher their neighbors," Brooke asks. "What happens to them? Is there a fucking light switch on the moral faculty?"

"Are we talking Rwanda here?"

"*That's* what's so depressing. The situation was identical in both places."

Devoid of insight, I hold the mug to her lips, tilting it toward her. One tries to distract her from these idées fixes, even at the best of times. When my sister isn't depressed, she talks about Boolean binary lattices and icosahedral symmetries with an enthusiasm that calls for a gag order.

My sister, my beautiful tomboy sibling with an IQ like the surface temperature of the planet Venus.

MOUNT OLYMPUS

I slip away while Brooke is watching a special war crimes edition of *Nightline*, stopping at a cash machine to draw out two hundred dollars, which leaves a residue of three hundred seventy-one dollars and change. Must get a draw from the magazine. From the street I decide to call Jeremy as a possible accomplice for whatever comes next. The message on his machine says: "Hi, I'm either out or I'm sitting here listening to see who you are before I pick up. So if you're willing to risk rejection, go ahead and leave a message after the beep."

I identify myself as a member of the committee distributing the MacArthur genius awards. "If you pick up within the next ten seconds you will receive a grant of sixty thousand tax-free dollars a year for five years in recognition of your services to literature, but only if you answer the phone immediately."

What does it mean when your friends and relatives won't take your calls?

Thus, a cab to Mount Olympus, where, at least, the tuxe-doed doorgent appears delighted to see me. "How are *you*, sir?" His bonhomie is such that I feel obliged to give him five dollars on top of the fifteen for admission.

I enter a universe of twinned spheres, silicone heaven. In ancient times, you may recall, blocks of marble were cleaved from the earth in the vicinity of Carrara and coaxed into the likeness of deities; now it is living flesh which is sculpted into goddess form at the hands of surgeons and personal trainers. Look, there's Cassandra, of the wine-dark hair, dancing nipples to nose with a baldie. And Demeter, shaking her booty for three mesmerized Japanese businessmen. *Kirei, desu ne?* But where is my own personal goddess, the celestial Pallas? A hostess in white garters with whom I am unacquainted greets me and brings me to a table. Squeezing past the Japanese businessmen—oops, bumping *into* the Japanese businessman, who spills his drink all over his navy-blue suit. *Domo summi-masen.*

At last I spot her, three tables away, table dancing for an aging mortal in a chalk-striped suit. From this distance his skin appears scaly, beneath patchy tufts of hair, and I am nearly certain he has horns. I watch in horror as Pallas shimmies closer and closer, her rare, all-natural breasts dipping within inches of the foul creature. Suddenly my view is eclipsed by a field of blue sequins. "Hi, I'm Isis. Would you like a dance?" She is very pretty, a light brown woman with long, straight obsidian hair—not cornrows, as you might expect in a fertility goddess. It makes me feel bad that I have to turn her down, though I know she makes about a thousand dollars a night and is unlikely to take it personally. That is the principle at work here: to make it *seem* personal. How could you say no to a beautiful girl who wants to dance naked for you and you alone? A fairly effective principle all in all. But if I fail to conserve my funds, at twenty a dance, I could be busted in ten minutes, and I am sworn to wait for the divine Pallas. Whatever happened to "Ten Cents a Dance"?

The hostess relieves me of my credit card. Thanks, that was

getting heavy in my pocket. Low on cash or no, I would still give a hundred bucks if someone would promise to destroy every single recorded copy of Rod Stewart's "Do Ya Think I'm Sexy?" which is now playing, animating some dozen pelvi and two dozen pendant glands in parabolas of simulated seduction.

Watching the other men. Sorry bastards. In groups they are emboldened, leering and winking at each other, tossing their horned heads with exaggerated nonchalance, but the singles are as shy and solemn as Japanese rock fans, not quite sure what to do with their hands or facial muscles. They look, in a word, ridiculous. And I am one of them. Sitting at our tables naked with yearning, inappropriately dressed for the party. We are penises trussed up in wool suits and silk ties. Blind voyeurs, we dimly suspect that the joke is on us. Can you imagine how they talk about us, the dancers? Thank God our drink has arrived. We gulp half of it before it touches the table. Another dancer shimmies up. "Hi, I'm Dawn, what's your name?"

CURRICULUM VITAE

The narrator's name is Connor McKnight. That's me. Hello. Connor here. Thirty-two and two-thirds years old and not really happy about it. Still waiting for his adult life to begin. Is this *his* fault, or *life's* fault? He could blame his parents, perhaps; that would be novel. Or perhaps the real problem was the seven years he spent in Japan. First in Kyoto studying Japanese literature, a large and highly speculative investment of time whose dubious value plummeted the moment he decided to stop short of his Ph.D. Then in a Zen monastery in Kamakura, counting his breaths.

I do think I missed something while turning Japanese. In fact, that was what brought me back, the suspicion that I was missing something back here. Still waiting to find out what it was, exactly. Not Rod Stewart's "Do Ya Think I'm Sexy?"—nope, that was practically the fucking soundtrack of my sojourn in Nippon, playing in the hidden upstairs "snacks" of

Roppongi and the pubs of Shinjuku and the ward office where I renewed my alien registration every six months, an abiding whine like a mosquito in the dark of a musty summer bedroom or like the tune in a Warner Bros. cartoon which cannot be stilled even after Elmer Fudd or Sylvester the Cat smashes the radio to smithereens with a sledgehammer, demolishes the still-singing speaker tweeter and drops it down a well . . . even then, you can still hear the faint adenoidal bad-hair voice of the Rodster.

I have a job, of sorts. The name of my job is Paying the Rent Until I Write My Original Screenplay About Truth and Beauty. Specifically: writing articles about celebrities for *CiaoBella!*—a lifestyle magazine for young women. Much of the magazine is devoted to telling our readers what to wear and how to snare boyfriends. I am hagiographer to their saints—those men and women who, in simulating real life on large and small screen, are transubstantiated into beings who are far more real than those who watch them.

THE NEW ONTOLOGY

In the new ontology, nothing exists until it has been reproduced on film stock. (Or videotape.)

CONNOR McKNIGHT, ONTOLOGIST

I can't claim that it's hard work, verifying the reality of the new idols, describing their diets and dating rituals. In fact, I'm planning to develop a computer program which will spit these things out with the touch of a few keys, freeing me up to squander even more time than I do now. It would be a simple program, since this genre offers very few variables. Already my word-processing program contains macro keystrokes which instantly call up such phrases as "shuns the Hollywood limelight in favor of spending quality time with his family at his sprawling ranch outside of Livingston, Montana" (CTRL, *Mont*). And: "There's nothing like being a parent to teach you what really matters in life. The fame, the money, the limos—

you can keep it. I mean, being a father/mother is more important to me than any movie role could ever be" (ALT, *baby*). And the ever popular "Actually, I've always been really insecure about my looks. I definitely don't think of myself as a sex symbol. When I look in a mirror I'm like—*Oh, God, what a mess*" (SHIFT, *What, me sexy?*). This is pretty basic stuff, though. What's needed is a program employing a spin factor with numerical values from, say, 20 (ax murder) to 1 (blow job, swallow). Journalism by the numbers. For my purposes, and that of most other high-sheen magazines, number one would be the default setting. ("Despite his tough guy image, ——— likes nothing better than a quiet night at home with a volume of poetry.")

I'm always amused when someone asks me about some actor I have interviewed: "What's he really like?" To which the only honest response is "What's he *like*? He's an *actor*, for Christ's sake."

Right now I'm trying to write a profile of Chip Ralston, boy movie star, but I cannot seem to track him down. Although he allegedly agreed to the piece, his agent, his business manager *and* his personal assistant are all behaving somewhat evasively, while his publicist is being an unmitigated bitch. Is it possible he remembers a rather negative—all right, way negative (18.5)—review I wrote a few years back in the *Tokyo Business Journal* about his second movie in which I said the best acting was done by his car, a British racing-green Austin Healy with sexy wire wheels and a deep throaty voice? Scuttlebutt, however, has it that Chip can't read.

When I mentioned the proposed interview to Philomena, she said, "I hear he's kind of a jerk."

To which I responded, "Phil, honey, he's an *actor*."

Forgetting that Philomena is herself an aspiring thespian.

PALLAS

"Wow, that must be really interesting, getting to meet all those famous people," says Dawn, rosy fingered from handling ice-cold beverages here on the slopes of Mount Olympus.

"Yeah, well," I say. "I'm also writing a book about Akira

Kurosawa. The film director," I add helpfully. This is true almost, though at present I'm mired in the early middle of the first chapter.

"We get a lot of Japanese gentlemen here."

At last—I see Pallas gliding toward me, a vision in gold sequins and matching hair. "Hey, Connor." The sound of my name on her lips makes me weak. "Want me to dance for you?" She is so lovely it hurts my teeth to look at her.

"Not yet," I gasp. "Let's have a drink first." I know the rules: she lifts the hem of her long form-fitting one-piece sequin dress up her sinuous calf, over her knee, and I deposit two twenties in her garter, hoping that will hold her for a while.

Pallas sits down beside me. "What do you know?" This is her customary greeting, a locution she seems to have imported from her native Kentucky.

"I know the ending of *The Charterhouse of Parma*," I say, "but I wouldn't want to spoil it for you."

She smiles, impervious to my lame attempt at equalizing the balance of power.

"More properly known as *La Chartreuse de Parme*," I explain, "by Stendhal, not to be confused with *The Porterhouse of Chartres*, a book I might soon write about the role of medieval nutrition in the development of flying buttresses, or with *The Porter of Chartreux*, by Gervaise Latouche, which I commend to you as a very filthy, dirty book indeed."

I always have a different answer, and she always listens and smiles like a doctor in the presence of a colorful but harmless lunatic.

"Come to the theater with me tomorrow," I suggest. "I have tickets to the new Nicky Silver play."

"I'm working," she says. "Is he the guy who does the *Lethal Weapon* movies?"

"Not exactly."

"Chip Ralston was in here a few nights ago," she says, eyes aglow.

"*Chip Ralston?*" Imagine me all agog. "I've been looking for that bastard for two weeks. Are you sure it was Chip Ralston?"

"He was really nice."

"Then it was probably somebody else."

"No, really. He was . . ." She pauses to refine her impressions. "Nice."

"Nice? What's that supposed to mean?"

"He was, you know, like a regular guy."

"*Like* is the operative word in that sentence. Physically he *resembles* a human being—in fact he often plays one—but he's a nasty little shit with lifts in his shoes and a silicone-enhanced ego. You noticed, I hope, that he's shorter than you? He didn't leave his phone number by any chance, did he?"

"What are you so mad about?" Pallas asks. "What did Chip Ralston ever do to you?"

WHERE DO YOU START?

"What did he do to me? Everything. Right off the bat, I'm mad at him because he's making my life difficult by not returning my calls. In the larger scheme, he is sucking up all the fame and money and adulation of women which might, in a more just universe, accrue to a more worthy party. Generally speaking it's not worth liking or disliking movie stars—they're like the weather, for God's sake—but this guy is really beginning to piss me off."

WHAT CHIP IS LIKE

I try to pump her for information, anecdotes, dirt, scandal—anything I could use for my piece. But Pallas is as vague as a bowl of rice. Could she be a secret Buddhist, attuned to the oneness of the many? She keeps repeating that he was nice, as if he were a glowing, fragrant gas. "I read somewhere he has a ranch in Montana," she offers.

"Did he come on to you?"

Pallas shrugs. "I think he was, you know, into me."

"Did you make a date with him?"

"His bodyguard told me to, like, call him." She doesn't seem surprised by this invitation, but neither is she displeased.

"You called his *bodyguard*?"

"No, his bodyguard told me to call Chip."

"So you *do* have his phone number?" Torn between jealousy and professional zeal.

"It's at home somewhere. Anyway, who knows if it's really his right number?"

"Did you meet him after work?" I demand. "You did, didn't you?" I put my head down on the table, distraught. Pallas strokes my head maternally.

"Connor, what do you want from me?"

WHAT HE WANTS FROM PALLAS

What he wants is not exactly sex, although it is surely coextensive with sex. What he wants almost certainly doesn't even exist: the Platonic essence of Pallas. Like goddesses of screen and runway, her inaccessibility is the key to her allure. She is part of his current spiritual crisis—his perverse need to prove himself worthy of Philomena even as he behaves in unworthy fashion. In reflective moments he tells himself that he wants to prove to Pallas that love exists, that there is another model besides the purely mercenary one she subscribes to, in which case he might be able to believe that Philomena could love him in spite of his own negligible market value.

According to Plato, love is the desire for the good; yet it's hard to see how his desire for Pallas can lead to anything but trouble. In *The Symposium*, Aristophanes defines us, qua lovers, as human sores seeking to be healed. Connor has not yet quite determined how to remain true to Philomena even as he yearns for something else. Neither Brooke, with all her powers of reasoning, nor even the great Sophists Protagoras and Gorgias, might be able to crack this one.

WHAT YOU SETTLE FOR

"Would you like me to dance," she asks, still stroking your hair. You answer by thumping your head against the table. It's the best you can do, for now. She rises and slowly shimmies her dress down over her shoulders, down the articulate ridge of her clavicles and up the rising slope of her chest until are revealed those breasts which, even here in this Mammary Hall of Fame, are to your mind among the chief wonders of the modern world, not least because they were shaped by nature and gravity. No little scars underneath. In addition to her current employment at Mount Olympus, Pallas is also a breast model for several prominent cosmetic surgeons. Once she begins to dance you see illustrated in the most striking fashion various laws of physics which, of all your wide acquaintance, only Brooke could identify by name.

THE MOLE PEOPLE

There are people who live underground, in the pipes and tunnels beneath the city. Thousands of them—their children growing up in the dark, their childish eyes becoming weaker, their noses and nostril hairs longer, afraid of the bright surface light. Life became too complicated on the surface. Broken water mains create subterranean oases. Perhaps this is what Philomena means by the simple life.

WHY THE JAPANESE MAKE SUCH
GOOD CARS AND SELDOM KILL
EACH OTHER

One of the things that you admire about the Japanese, collectively, is that it hardly occurs to them to ask *why*. But, whatever you might once have thought, back in Kyoto in your snug little *uchi*, wearing your woolen *hakata*, wooden geta on your feet, you are not, nor will you ever be, Japanese. You arrived with the teleological itch already in place.

Your sister could learn plenty from the Japanese.

THE WRITER AT HOME

Finding myself on the Upper West Side the following after-noon—having interviewed an actress on Central Park West (boring, please, don't ask)—I decide to drop in on Jeremy. (Well, all right, you slavering sluts, I'll treat you to one quote that's going straight into my programming bank: "I don't con-sider myself a star. I'm just proud to be part of an artistic com-munity" (SHIFT, *Bloomsbury*).

Jeremy buzzes me in, watches me through the slot of the stairwell as I trudge up five flights.

"Dude ascending a staircase," he says, his long blond hair hanging halfway to the fourth floor. He nods grimly, precedes me inside, then collapses on the chaise in his impeccably neat, plant-infested living room. I sense wintry gloom amidst the verdure.

"You must be the man from the suicide hotline."

"Nope. President of the Jeremy Green Fan Club."

"You lie. It disbanded shortly after *Slender Mercies* was remaindered. Two of its members went into group therapy and the other one ditched me for the Dennis Johnson Fan Club." Jeremy sighs and squirms; though you might think a hand-some writer sprawled on a chaise would evoke the young Tru-man Capote, Jeremy calls to mind a man being stretched and tortured on the rack by invisible inquisitors.

"Look at this," he demands, shoving a copy of the *Daily News* under my nose. There, in the "On the Town" section, is a photo of a glowering Jeremy and a beaming Philomena at the benefit.

"Congratulations," I say.

"I'm fucking mortified."

"Is that a comment on my girlfriend?"

"She's a model. Fine for her to stand around grinning at the camera—that's her job. I'm a *writer*, for Christ's sake."

"One picture in the paper doesn't necessarily compromise your artistic integrity."

"They'll never review me seriously again."

Jeremy is so fastidious and fearful of seeming to promote

himself at the expense of the words on the page that he has
refused his editor's offer of a publication party. He professes a
horror of the wet kiss of popular taste, although he bitterly
resents his obscurity vis-à-vis certain writers he considers far
less talented. Favorably reviewed in the Sunday *Times Book
Review*, and *The New Yorker* (in brief), his debut collection
sold some forty-five hundred copies in hardcover, respectable
numbers for a story collection in which suicide is a major
theme; and while he likes to say there are only five thousand
serious readers of fiction in the entire Republic, I have also
heard him speak libelously about the sales force of his former
publishing house. His forthcoming collection is called
Walled-In, a gloss on Thoreau—with a nod to Poe's "Cask of
Amontillado"—in which the island of Manhattan serves as a
dystopian mirror for the pond of Walden, a septic ecosystem
which drives its inhabitants to despair and suicide. I keep asking for a galley, but he insists that I wait for the finished book.

Standing up, he paces the room and sighs eloquently. "Is
there something they tell everybody else about how to wake
up in the morning and actually *want* to get out of bed? Something I missed at the portal of this last incarnation? Is there
some reward that I don't know about for not just killing yourself?"

"I think it's called sex."

"Easy for you to say. You live with the cover girl, you bastard. Me, I can't even get my fucking dog back." Jeremy sticks
his finger in one of the numerous flowerpots, frowns, walks to
the kitchen. Actually, Philomena has never been on the cover
of anything—has in fact semiretired from the modeling profession to become an actress—and Jeremy has women heaving themselves across his path, clutching his ankles, weeping
at the sight of him, begging for his phone number, a lock of
hair, a drive-by sperm deposit. Imagine a rock star with great
skin and teeth and an astounding vocabulary to boot. Most
men walking around inside of Jeremy's epidermis would find
multiple reasons to be happy. As for Jeremy's former canine
companion, it's a long, sad story. He emerges with a watering
can, which he applies to the ficus.

"I thought you were getting the beast back last week."

Uh-oh, sorry I asked. Jeremy appears ready to burst into tears. Turning from me, paying particular attention to the thirsty ficus.

A BOY AND HIS DOG

Sean was a spirited Irish terrier who liked to chew shoes and bark at the roaches which have the free run of Jeremy's apartment. Sean was purchased after the demise of Mulligan, Jeremy's beloved companion of thirteen years. After nearly a year with Sean, Jeremy decided he hadn't recovered from the death of Mulligan, and that it was not fair to treat Sean as a surrogate. Moreover, he concluded that it was a crime to keep a dog, particularly one as feisty and energetic as Sean—who could perform a triple axel on hardwood—walled in, as it were, in a one-bedroom apartment in New York City. So he took out ads in *Newsday* and the *Bergen County Record* soliciting a good country home for Sean, envisioning a New Jersey farm with rolling fields to run and rabbits to harass. Waiting for the responses to pour in, he debated the relative chemical toxicity of New Jersey versus Long Island. Finally, after interviewing all three callers, and visiting homes in Patchogue and Nyack, Jeremy selected the Jamisons, a childless couple living near Flemington, New Jersey. The Jamisons—Bob and Edie—agreed that Jeremy could visit once a month.

Returning home on the New Jersey Turnpike, Jeremy realized the enormity of his mistake. Distraught, he pulled over on the shoulder of the Pike to catch his breath and scarf a Klonopin. But he sucked it up and tried to convince himself that Sean was better off, waiting three whole days before calling, whereupon he asked the Jamisons to put the phone to Sean's ear. The following Sunday he drove out to Flemington and stayed for two hours, in spite of the three-week hiatus specified by the original agreement. When he returned again the following Sunday, it is to be imagined that the Jamisons thought they were seeing rather more of Jeremy than they'd prefer. All I have is Jeremy's testimony: that he couldn't sleep, couldn't write, missed Sean and wanted him back. Moreover, on one of his visits he had discovered, having perused the reading matter displayed on the coffee table, that Mr. Jamison was an ardent firearms enthusiast and hunter. He told the Jamisons he'd changed his mind, which fact did not seem relevant to them, a deal being a deal. Sensing he had their number, Jeremy offered money. They agreed to five hundred dollars and then demurred. He raised his offer to a thousand. They promised they'd get back to him.

This began almost six months ago. Ongoing negotiations reveal—if Jeremy is to be believed, and let me say right now that my best friend gives new depth and resonance to the concept of an unreliable narrator—that Mrs. Jamison is quite a brilliant sadist. The husband professes himself willing to surrender the dog, but leaves the details to the little woman, who seems to delight in tortured, elaborate negotiations that somehow break down at the last minute. Only the combined ministrations of Jeremy's shrink and his guru have kept him intact, and perhaps preserved Mrs. Jamison's life. But in truth she is sorely testing Jeremy's credo of nonviolence.

The watering can empty, Jeremy walks over to his answering machine, rewinds the tape, presses REPLAY:

MESSAGE FROM THE DOG MOTHER

"Hello, this is Edie Jamison. I know you sit there and listen to people talking into your machine. You're probably there right now, with your ridiculous self-important hair, listening to me. Does it make you feel superior to have people talk while you pretend not to be there, like that writer in your story? That's just the kind of thing someone like you would do, isn't it? You think people don't see through you but they do. Oh yes, they certainly do. I read your so-called book, you know. What do your poor parents feel about what you write? How do they feel about that sewage? I bet they're ashamed to walk down the street. If I were your mother, I'd be disgusted with myself for raising a spoiled know-it-all ungrateful brat who can't even take care of his dog, who gives his poor dog away and who thinks he can just walk into people's lives and offer them some money to make everything the way he wants. Well, let me tell you something, my husband may be a pushover, but I'm not. You think you're so superior—"

Enraged afresh, Jeremy jerks the plug out of the answering machine.

"What," I ask, "was your latest offer?"

"Two grand."

"Hell, *I'll* be your dog for that."

Jeremy's face clearly expresses the information that he does not find this even a little bit amusing.

THE BUDDHA OF WEST SIXTY-NINTH

Jeremy does have an unreliable sense of humor. Perhaps partly because he is as acutely sensitive to his own suffering as my sister is to that of others. Whatever residual sympathy Jeremy can spare is donated not to humans but to other life-forms—from mammals to insects—a fact which I try to keep in mind when I am tempted to reach out and squash the roaches that roam the apartment as freely and abundantly as buffalo in the Old West. Jeremy not only refuses to kill them himself, but he also bars the landlord's exterminator, with the result that all the roaches in the building, knowing a good deal when they smell one, have migrated up here to the top floor.

"What does your swami say?"

"Swami say—'It sometimes veddy veddy tricky to tell dog from man. Also, veddy veddy hard to justify ways of dog to man.' " Jeremy's fluent ability to ridicule his swami even as he reveres him, even as he arranges his life in accordance with the master's gnomic instructions, has always puzzled me. The swami actually convinced him once to take a vow of celibacy for six months. Maybe Philomena has been consulting the old fraud.

I am unable to persuade him to come out for lunch. Not even the invocation of lentils and kasha and other vile fibrous fare at the nearby hippie vegetarian boîte can turn the trick. When I pull the door behind me, Jeremy is once again sprawled over the chaise, as if on a bed of nails.

THE IMPORTANCE OF JOHN GALLIANO

Back home, strangely, no message from Philomena, but one from Connor's boss, Jillian Crowe, asking for an update on the Chip Ralston situation. Chip was Jillian's idea of an idea. She had seen him, the young thespian, a few weeks ago at the Bryant Park fashion shows, checking out the models. The notion of a profile came as an afterthought during an editorial meeting at which Jillian declared that John Galliano might well be the most important artist of the latter half of the century. And this at a meeting of the Features Department, as opposed to Fashion. Beautifully tonsured heads, Jillian's courtiers, bobbing assent all around the conference room table. In the realm of fashion, where breathless enthusiasm sings harmony with toxic ennui, Jillian has perfect pitch; she's like a publicist on smack, and cannot for the life of her understand why she has not yet been tapped to edit *Vogue* or *Harper's Bazaar*.

CONNOR AMONG THE PLUTOCRATS

There was a moment when Connor seemed to have the knack of pleasing Princess Jillian, a twinkling when he detected an almost girlish interest in both his person and his so-called work, culminating when he escorted her—a last-minute substitute for Boaz Mazor, but an escort nonetheless—to the Costume Institute Ball at the Metropolitan Museum. This was the metropolis as it was meant to be seen, in the flattering aphrodisiac light of eminence, a brilliant oligarchy compounded of wealth, power, accomplishment and beauty. The atmosphere of festive mutual regard extended even to tourists, such as Connor, on the happy assumption that their applications for full-fledged citizenship were pending. He was with Jillian Crowe, therefore he was. If he'd first taken the whole thing more or less as a joke, secure in his self-knowledge as a flunky and a last-minute, anomalous, heterosexual walker—toward the end of the night he was nevertheless beginning to feel remarkably comfortable in this new role.

Infected with a desire to please and fortified with half a dozen glasses of champagne, he regaled the table with colorful anecdotes about Japanese sexual practices and the untold story behind a recent celebrity interview. He expounded his theory that there are exactly two kinds of movie star, the Solipsist and the Seducer: one speaks only of himself, not believing in the existence of anyone else; the other still seems not to believe in his or her own existence at all and has to seek constant verification from every possible fan in the room, working it like a politician, looking into the great round mirrors of our eyes, trying to seduce us all one at a time. Al Pacino was sitting at the adjacent table, and Jillian was apparently offended on his behalf, which was silly, in Connor's view, since he wasn't remotely listening to anything anyone else said anyway, at his own table or elsewhere.

Connor doesn't think Jillian appreciated this performance quite as much as he'd hoped she might. Truthfully, he doesn't exactly remember. Perhaps—it's possible—he drank too much. He does recall her saying "Darling, when I offer to show you the *ropes*, do try to pick up more than *just* enough to hang yourself."

And then came Philomena's reaction: irate at the datelike aspects of what Connor tried to present as a tedious professional obligation. Strictly a court eunuch, Connor assured her.

"Why don't you ask Jillian to fuck you" became a late-night refrain in their bedroom for quite some time. "I'm sure she'd be happy to oblige—if she hasn't already."

It seemed to Connor that he paid dearly for this little outing on both fronts, at home and at work. Re the latter: perhaps his novelty simply wore off, novelty being the cardinal virtue in the value system of the magazine; or perhaps Jillian realized he despised his job. At any rate, after that night, the frisson fizzled between Connor and Jillian Crowe. Short of assassinating Anna Wintour, he can't quite imagine how to regain Jillian's esteem.

AN OMEN?

Also, besides the Crowe call, a message from Mrs. Combes, ancient West Village bohemian landlady who used to hang out with Edna St. Vincent Millay: "Hello? Hello? Is this working? Oh, dear, I hate these things. Well, if anyone can hear me, this is Sharon Combes. Mr. McKnight, I've been calling your, uh, Miss Briggs on the number I have for her but she hasn't, uh, called me back. I'm sure there's some mistake, but her rent is almost a month overdue. It's the twenty-third today. And she's always been so prompt, I usually get her check the last day of the month, sometimes on the first or second, which I really appreciate since it takes five days for the check to clear and I've got the heating bill and the mortgage and . . ."

Pouring yourself a large tumbler of Jack Daniel's in order to drown the rambunctious colony of moths in your belly.

YELLOW

Jeremy calls, furious with John Cheever. In his journal, a portion of which has just been published in the *Paris Review*, Cheever had some unkind things to say about bitterness, and Jeremy is taking it personally, although the offending remarks are actually directed at J. D. Salinger.

"Listen to this," Jeremy shouts into the phone. " 'His prose is excellent and supple but he seems very close to crazy. I am reminded of the bitterness in my own work, that bitterness that is not art but that is its opposite. So I would like to write a story that is all yellow, yellow, yellow, the brightest yellow.' " Jeremy is indignant. "Where's all this goddamned bitterness in Cheever? A little bitterness would have been welcome."

Cheever has slandered one of Jeremy's favorite emotions. He tends to read all literary criticism as thinly veiled commentary on his own work. Salinger is one of his secret totems, and when Cheever assails him, however mildly, he might just as well kick Jeremy Green directly in the balls.

"Yellow, yellow, yellow," Jeremy sneers. "What is he—a

fucking Nip? Give me a break. Céline should have felt *less bitter*? Would that have made him a greater artist? What about Evelyn Waugh?"

"Foreigners," I point out. "Euros always do cynicism better."

MILAN, ITALY, FALL '95

Re: Yellow. There exists a mustardy, light-starved, paradoxical, melancholy shade of this most cheerful hue found only in Milan. Connor once went there with Philomena, during the spring collections, to write a profile of an actress who just had to get a sneak preview of the new Versaces. Business. And pleasure. Oh, yes. One night after drinks in the Four Seasons, Philomena had challenged him to take her right there, in the Via Gesù, against the yellow stucco palazzo. *Come on, do me.* Leaning against the wall, her tongue in his ear. The street momentarily deserted. Bittersweet Campari on her lips. "Come on," she said, licking his ear. "Pretend I'm a hooker. A streetwalker." Earlier, in the bathroom of the Four Seasons, she'd encountered two Russian prostitutes, just off the plane, changing into their best and painting their faces, comparing notes on the men in the bar. Returning to their table with the tale, she could see that it excited him.

Now, on the street, this was her challenge: "Right here, right now."

"Here?" But he was already lifting her skirt, lowering his fly, enfolding her in the tent of his camel's hair coat, cradling her cool ass and scraping his knuckles raw against the stucco. A couple passed, hugging the far side of the narrow street, but by then Connor didn't care. He wasn't there. He was somewhere far more beautiful than Milan by then.

Venice, at the very least.

GOTHAM, FALL '96

When I ask Jeremy to dinner, he claims he's too bummed out. (You might even color him bitter.) In desperation I offer to submit to culinary high-fiber horror on the Upper West Side, but he is still engaged in the World Wrestling Federation's Short Story title bout. Cheever in tights, yanking Jeremy's long blond mane. Jeremy tagging Salinger, who leaps into the ring and stubs out his cigarette on Cheever's backside. Updike in a rabbit suit outside the ropes, waiting to spell Cheever.

Did I mention that Jeremy's still trying to get over the revelation of Cheever's bisexuality? For him it was not a moral question, but a personal one: he wondered if he might be missing out on some crucial component of literary experience by virtue of not sleeping with men. We spent many nights parsing this subject; also, the subject of whether he should try heroin. Because I'd snorted it a couple of times he considered me an authority. I didn't try to dissuade him with the notion that it was dangerous, which after all was the whole point, the authenticating virtue. The real problem, I told him, was that it was so damn fashionable—the cool recreational choice of young Hollywood's hottest—knowing this would chill his Shaker heart.

"As a fiction writer," I say, "it behooves you to get out in the world more, fill up the old well. Coming out to dinner with me is a good start."

"I'm too depressed to face a room full of masticating yuppies. And I can't handle a night of staring across the table at your girlfriend. It's too fucking depressing looking at her across the table, thinking *you're* going home with her."

"*Pas de* sweat. She's in San Francisco on an audition."

"Are you crazy? Don't you have any idea what goes on around movie sets?"

"She's not on a set. She's just auditioning. Or maybe a shoot." Suddenly I realize that the actual nature of the trip was never quite specified.

"So I guess you've never heard of the casting couch."

"I trust her, okay?"

"Don't say I didn't warn you. Sex is the medium and the currency of that racket. That's what she's selling. I mean, being a model is, like, acceptable on a certain level if you're a beautiful girl like Philomena and you just sort of slide into it while you're figuring out what to do with your life. But a model who aspires to be an actress—that's a premeditated cliché. That's culpable."

"It's not exactly up to me, Jeremy. She's a grown-up."

"Anyway, I think she's moving against the flow of the culture. Models are the apex of consumer society. Pure image. Actors have to speak. They have to simulate personality. They have to actually *do* something. Pater said that poetry aspires to the condition of music. I think modern celebrity aspires to the condition of pure image. Modeling is the purest kind of performance, uncomplicated by content."

"I think Phil," I say, "is *looking* for a little content in her life. As aren't we all?"

"Just don't come crying to me after she's started fucking the director."

And so my best friend succeeds in darkening my night. I dial in some Vietnamese spring rolls, so as not to be away from the phone when Philomena calls from San Francisco. Which, now that I think about it, is far too picturesque and foggy and sung about for its own good—or for mine.

A red light flashes through the slats of the shades from the nursing home. A sign? Of what, precisely? Eventually I check the ringer on the phone, call my own number from Philomena's to make sure it's working, then check the dial tone—a high and lonesome sound that echoes through all of the empty spaces inside of me.

ONANISTIC INTERLUDE

Connor masturbates, replaying the previous day's erotic encounter—a fresh entry in the memory bank—as an act of magic, perhaps, to bring her closer, to conjure her back. This is his own special form of fidelity—the fact that Philomena is his exclusive muse in this department. It must be love, he reasons, if after three years you still, and only, beat off to the image of your girlfriend. Though embarrassment has prevented him from sharing this information with the object of his desire. When she returns, he decides, he will tell her. He will open his heart, amend his life, strive to be the man for her that he has so far failed to be.

Amen.

EXTERIOR

No phone messages when I awake. Outside, a trio of old folks bundled against the cold in their wheelchairs, optimistically facing the silver November sun. Gingerly venturing outside for cappuccino and a chocolate croissant to help me face the day, I sidestep a giant pink-and-white bone with pendant flesh outside the bakery—the thigh of a mastodon by the look of it.

On the corner, waiting for the light, babe in a wheelchair; very chic, black coat and skirt, tiger-striped black-and-gold hair under a beret, Doc Martens perched on the silver footrests. The first love of the morning. Fall in love at least twelve times a day. But you, my dear, are absolutely my first love on wheels. . . .

Across the street two cops loitering.

"Matthew Broderick."

"I didn't see that one."

"No, that was him. Just now."

"No shit?"

E-MAIL

Congratulations, Mr. McKnight. *"You've got mail!"* My computer talks to me.

To: Scribbler
From: Lawgirl
Subject: Lazy White Folks
Dear Connor:
What's with Brooke? She wigging out on us again? Can't get the girl to return my calls or e Mail. Will you *please* tell her to check in ASAP? Or am I gonna have to come down and beat the shit out of you both? Tell her I don't think I can make Christmas this year, cause Uncle Errol's real sick in Freeport and I got to go see the old bastard whiles I still can. Gotta go. Loved your insightful, sensitive piece on Judd Nelson.
Your loving sister,
Corvetta

Nice to see that the fine art of personal correspondence isn't dead yet. Have I mentioned Corvetta? Her Bahamian parents worked the orange groves as migrant pickers, until her father sliced her mother's stomach open with a cane knife. It happened right in front of Brooke and Corvetta, who were playing outside the trailer at the time. I don't remember any of this, but my parents tend to date Brooke's almost pathological sense of empathy from this event. Corvetta, on the other hand, having so violently lost her mother, grew up tough as . . . well let's just say she grew up to be a lawyer. As though, in that moment when the blade flashed and disappeared into Corvetta's mother, Brooke conveyed all of her own psychic armor to her friend.

Brooke could never understand why my parents didn't adopt Corvetta. A few days after the murder, in an attempt to persuade them, she conducted her first hunger strike. Corvetta was eventually raised by relatives, but she spent summers and Christmas holidays with us, and my parents paid for her education. With Brooke's fierce encouragement she eventually graduated from Harvard, where they roomed together, and went on to distinguish herself at the law school. Brooke's best friend from age three to this very day, she now practices criminal law in Oakland, having turned out better than her friends in the big house, Brooke and me, casualties of privilege.

MORE E-MAIL

To: Scribbler@aol.com
From: Jenrod@inch.com
Subject: A Fan!
Dear Connor:
Is it okay if I call U Connor, Mr. Scribbler? I got your address from the "Contributor's Notes" at the front of the magazine. Have you noticed how most of the good E mail names are already taken? My actual name is Jennifer Rodriguez but I'm thinking about changing it. That's one of the things I want to ask you about. But first before you start thinking who is this crazy grrrl and

why is she e mailing me let me just say I am a HUGE
FAN! (That doesn't mean I'm FAT on the contrary I'm
quite slim!) I don't know if writers have "fans" or not
but in your case they should! I mean, writing could be
considered a talent just like acting or singing. Maybe I
could start a Connor McKnight "fan club." Except I'd
rather keep you to myself for now. (Just kidding!) I
especially loved your interview last month on Jennifer
Lopez, not just because we share the same first name
and are both Latinas (Half, anyway, my Mom is Irish). I
really felt like you got inside her head. Anyway it must
be really cool getting to meet so many interesting stars
and celebs and spending "quality time" with them.
Some articles you don't really know what that person is
really like, it just sounds like HYPE with a capital H!
but your articles really make me feel like I get to know
the people. But I bet you're just as interesting yourself.
It's not just the Stars who have fascinating personalities
although we might not all be famous! Your "head shot"
in front of the magazine last month was really cute, I
bet you could be a movie star yourself! Believe it or not
people say that to me! And not just my mother. (Ha
Ha!) Maybe I will send U my picture anyway. I caught
the "acting bug" playing Molly in "The Unsinkable
Molly Brown" in junior high and since then I have
taken classes and my teachers say I have real potential.
One of the things that interests me about reading about
the stars is how they got their big breaks. I'm still waiting for my big break it seems like its all about "who
you know" and "connexions" instead of natural born
talent. Plus which being half Dominican which I use to
think was against me but now with Jennifer Lopez and
Daisy Fuentes and whoever I feel like may be I have a
chance. I have also noticed that modelling is a "stepping stone" to an acting career certainly in the case of
Rene Russo that is true although after seeing Cindy
Crawford in that movie with Billy Baldwin I am not so
sure! (Two thumbs down from Jennie Rodriguez.) May
be we could meet some time for coffee. I can come to

Manhattan anytime except for Tues and Thurs nights which are my acting class. Have you heard of Don Garrison? He's my teacher he had a part on "Saved by the Bell" as well as several major theatrical productions. Oh well guess I have been rambling on enough about me. What about you? E me! PS Don't worry, nobody reads my E mail except me, myself and I.

FALL

Yellow leaves fluttering down the face of the building across the street, like messages from a princess in a high tower. The putrid, wino-vomit smell of gingko leaves underfoot in the Village. Another year sliding past.

DEMI-TASSE

Demi Moore on the cover of *Beau Monde* again. But, hey, it's a whole new twist—she's wearing clothes. Although her head is naked this time, shorn stubbly for a movie she's shooting. For those of you who have just immigrated from Kigali, Demi Moore is a person who is paid twelve million dollars a pop to impersonate fictional characters on-screen. *Beau Monde* is a late-twentieth-century glossy magazine devoted to naked pictures of Demi Moore as well as articles about:

1. International affairs
2. Demi: the woman behind the mask
3. La Dolce Vita
4. What it's like when two international superstars (Demi and Bruce Willis, her famously temperamental former-bartender hubby) share the same house!
5. The Literary Life
6. How Demi knew from the time she was a little girl that she would someday be a star
7. Sex Lives of the Saints

8. Demi's body: how she *feels* about it
9. The British Royal Family and the lesser peerage
10. How *everybody* knew from the time she was a little girl that she would someday be a star, despite her *childhood demons*
11. Lives of the Supermodels
12. How Motherhood is more important to Demi than anything (CTRL, *baby*). Well, almost anything
13. The Media
14. Demi's opinion of narrative modalities in *The Charterhouse of Parma*
15. The beau monde
16. Demi's opinions on the prospects for long-term peace in the Balkans
17. Madonna
18. Demi's body: how we *feel* about it
19. Glowing profiles of fashion designers who happen to be major advertisers
20. Meta Demi: learned asides about the way in which previously published photographs of and articles about Demi in *Beau Monde* have modified and amplified her legend

RELEVANT DISCLOSURE

Your commentator has twice been turned down for a job at *Beau Monde*. But this does not, in his own opinion, unduly prejudice his comments on this particular subject: he's been turned down by practically every publication in town from *Sassy* to *Foreign Affairs*.

PERSONAL DEMONS

Hard to shake the feeling that Demi Moore is following me around. I saw her at Mount Olympus just a few weeks ago. Once there were guardian angels and patron saints; now we have Celebrity Nemeses. Come on now, it's not just me. You have one, surely. Some celeb whose accomplishments, fame, riches and choice of sleeping partners affront you in a deeply personal way, who makes you hurl your copy of *People* magazine across the room in anger. "Basically, I just think of myself as an ordinary person whose job happens to be acting/singing/getting my picture taken" (ALT, *unglam*).

And where the hell is Chip Ralston, boy movie star, goddamnit? His demon publicist, Judith Viertel, will not return my calls. I have actually succeeded in finding the unlisted number at Chip's beach house in Malibu, but all I get is a machine with a viscous, groin-tingling female voice. "No one is here to take your call right now, please leave a message and someone will get back to you real soon. Have an excellent day." For some reason I imagine this to be the voice of my new e-mail correspondent.

SUSPICIOUS INFORMATION

Connor calls his girlfriend's modeling agency to ask for the name of her hotel in San Francisco.

"San Francisco?" says the booker. "What's in San Francisco? I show no booking for Philomena in San Francisco. In fact, I'm showing no bookings at all. She booked out. Told me she was taking the week off."

Connor feels a painful outward pressure on either side of his skull, above and behind the ears, as if he were growing horns.

NEUTRAL INFORMATION,
i.e, RAW DATA

Philomena Briggs, born Oklahoma City, Oklahoma, 13 July 1971. Height: 5' 10". Hair: auburn. Dress size: 4. Shoe size: 8. Measurements: 34-24-34.

INTERPRETATION

The above data come from her composite, the photo-illustrated business card distributed by Phil's modeling agency, and in fact is not raw at all but cooked to a turn. The actual birth date is 1969. The place of birth was a town too small to show up on any map. The measurements are obviously suspect. And the last time I bought her a dress I had to return the 4 to Barney's and get the 6. "The salesclerk told me they ran small," I noted helpfully as she tried it on, knowing that if she got upset with the way she looked in it, I might not get lucky for days. Not to mention the danger to nearby ceramics and glassware.

HOW I GOT MY JOB

The joke around the office is that Jillian Crowe, our beloved editrix in chief, gave me the celeb beat at *CiaoBella!* after she heard that I was living with a model named Phil. Another point in my favor was the suit I wore for my interview, a vintage Brooks Brothers gray-flannel hand-me-down from the Dad; Jillian thought I was fashion forward enough to have anticipated the return of the three-button sack suit. She has since discovered her mistakes, and observed my relative lack of starfucking passion. Also, I lost popularity throughout the office when I refused to get behind the seventies revival, my contention being that it's bad enough that many of us will have to look at snapshots of ourselves in those clothes, in those shoes, with those haircuts, every time we pull out the old family album for the rest of our lives. For entirely different reasons I am dreading the inevitable upcoming eighties revival. Big-shouldered knights in matte Armani.

At the mag, it is a source of collective shame that I possess not a single item of apparel bearing the Prada or Gucci logos. Flyers for sample sales are left on my desk with the notation *FYI*.

My contract is up at the end of the year, less than six weeks away. No one has approached me about renewal. My cubicle on the "editorial" floor has been gradually, inexorably, encroached by storage space; I am in the vanguard of the virtual-office concept, faxing in my copy via modem from my apartment. Each time I return bodily to the magazine I find that the partition defining my space has been moved yet again; there is now room for only my desk and chair. Perhaps I should read this month's feature, "The Nine Secrets of Office Life." For example, number 2: "Don't be a loner; the workplace is no place for rugged individualism, girlfriend!"

Our office is a tidal pool of feminine hormones. Svelte Harrison James, the only full-time male on premises, often volunteers his services as a fitting model for in-office shoots. As a straight male I am viewed as the urban equivalent of the village idiot—harmless, perhaps, but kind of a communal embarrassment. My only institutional credibility derives from my association with Phil, whose picture has several times graced both ad and editorial pages.

ENTER, PHIL

I met her in Tokyo, on the Ginza Line between Akasaka-Mitsuke and Shimbashi. For more than six years I had been seeking something in Japan. Maybe, after all, it was a girl from the American Southwest.

One pivotal morning in Kyoto I woke up feeling like a stranger on the planet, so peculiar and senseless did the previous course of my life seem to me. Having lost the faith necessary to maintain my arcane pursuit of Japanese literature, I embraced the ostensible simplicity of Zen. And then, after seven months of zazen in a Kamakura monastery, I decided that neither was I ready to leave behind the world of multiplicity and illusion. Spotting Philomena within two months of hanging up my robe struck me as a vindication of that sentiment. If not satori, it was nevertheless a lightning bolt of a sort.

I couldn't help noticing her, of course, the only other gaijin in the subway car, a head taller than the indigenous population, her black modeling portfolio clutched defensively to her chest. My impression, in that context, was that she was the embodiment of a kind of American beauty which I had almost forgotten the look of, and for the first time in many months I felt homesick, trying very hard not to stare. As pretty as she was, I also believed I could see more than anyone else could—a secret aspect to her beauty that spoke specifically to me. And I felt aggrieved imagining that she would soon pass out of my sight forever. "From the point of view of knowledge," says Kashiwagi the clubfoot in Mishima's *Temple of the Golden Pavilion*, "beauty is never a consolation." At that moment I felt like the cripple, staring at the golden temple. I looked away, embarrassed, after she suddenly met my riveted gaze.

"Excuse me? Do you know which stop is Ginza?"

I took my time, following an entire, meaningless line of print across the page of my *Cinema Nippon* before looking up. I wanted to say, "What makes you assume I speak English." After all these years in Japan I stupidly liked to imagine I blended in somehow. And I was still angry at her for the way she looked. But I was struck earnest by her expression, which seemed suspended between the poles of all-American ingenuousness and the wariness of the pretty woman.

ATTACK OF THE FIVE-
FOOT SALARYMAN

Somehow finding my voice, I told her Ginza was the next stop. She turned away, and I felt helpless to pursue my advantage, paralyzed by awe and shyness, forty seconds from losing sight of her forever when an unlikely hero came to my rescue. Stealthily glancing at the juncture of her skirt and her thigh, I saw a hand reach out and pinch her butt. She squealed, and I moved forward protectively. *"Anata no kobun shiteru,"* I said to the man, who looked at me agog—a talking gaijin. I took her arm, leading her away to a symbolically safe distance.

"What did you say to him," she asked, once we were seated in the coffee shop outside the station.

"I told him I knew his boss," I said. "Which is roughly the equivalent, cross-culturally speaking, of telling an American lech that you know his wife. The censure of wives not counting for much around here."

AN OKIE ABROAD

Refugee from a small town in Oklahoma, Philomena was in Japan trying to build up her modeling portfolio and savings account. She'd been in the country two months, sharing a flat with three other girls. Hers was a hardscrabble childhood at best. Something of a wimp myself, I admired her gutsiness. She was the kind of girl who could cut in line without pissing anybody off. *Hey, you don't mind do you, thanks a lot. See, I told you he wouldn't mind.* Not many guys would have minded being cut in front of by Phil. She had a look which made you feel you'd been physically touched, and she was not at all unconscious of her power. She'd learned to use what had been given to her.

THE FIRST TIME

Having already illustrated Philomena's drawbacks as a sexual partner, or rather as an intended sexual partner, I should give credit where it's due: the first night she went home with me I judged that everything I previously had called sex was a pale imitation of the Platonic form of fucking I experienced under Philomena's supervision. It started badly, or so I thought; sitting on the floor of my chilly apartment sipping tea, she told me about previous boyfriends, including one that she had "shared" with a friend.

"I used to see this guy at the gym," she said, "and he was so hot. We used to check each other out. But we never talked. One day we were leaving together. And without a word he just followed me home, threw me down on the bed. This happened a few times. And then one day I was eating lunch with my girl-friend Cindy, telling her about this guy—and there he was in the restaurant, looking at me. I got up to go the ladies' and he followed. Just followed me right into the stall and closed the door. What was so great was it was just sex. Nothing else."

I wanted her to stop and yet it was too late, it was like watching a car going slowly over a cliff; I felt powerless to intervene or turn away.

"It was too good not to share," she continued. "I told him to wait. And I went back to the table and told Cindy to go the ladies' room. It was like telling your best friend about a great sample sale."

True or not, this story so unmanned me that Philomena would have passed out of my life untouched if she hadn't carped the diem that night. But now I realize she knew exactly what she was doing. She had beaten me down only to raise me up again from despair—on her own terms. When we finally crawled under the sheets of the futon, chaste in our underwear, I was a quivering wreck. For a minute, perhaps five, we lay side by side in the dark. When she reached over and touched my cheek just beneath my ear, I went rigid; when she touched my thigh I had to suppress a sob. I was angry about the story, furious that she'd ever fucked another man, and then for rubbing my nose in it. But I couldn't hold out for long, and she knew it. When she touched my earlobe with the tip of her tongue I began to shake.

I finally lunged at her but she seemed to retreat, drawing away as if she had lost interest. Mad with lust, I attacked again and after a feint-yield she seized command again, rolled over on top of me and commenced torturing me with rhythmic and rationed delights, slowing, pausing just as I began to accelerate, slipping away at the precise moment it seemed that the friction of a single breath would have released me from the bondage of the exquisite filaments in which she had wrapped me.

Once it was finally over, I could have wept with relief and gratitude.

She stroked my hair. "Isn't it sad that it always has to come to an end?"

"The end," I said, "was the best part."

In the dim light of dawn I saw her shake her head. "No,"

she said. "Somewhere between the middle and the end is always the best part, but we never know exactly where it is until it's over."

Much later, I asked her why she had told me that dreadful story.

"It worked, didn't it?"

"Was it true?"

In response, she reached down and placed her hand on my cock.

WHAT SHE SAW IN CONNOR

Perhaps she was impressed with his knowledge, his fluency with the language. In that stranger-in-a-strange-land context, Connor cut a fairly striking figure, being able to fend off subway pinchers, order food right off the menu—without reference to the plastic models in the windows—count, ask directions and shout insults when necessary (this last no easy feat, Japanese being as impoverished in abusive and obscene words as it is overloaded with honorifics). Which is to say, he doubts she ever would have shacked up with him in the States. His previous amorous history had not been so spectacular as to inspire envy in the heart of his fellow man, and his success in Japan had largely been a function of his novelty: future housewives having a fling with a gaijin. But in the context of adult males known to Philomena, Connor was practically a saint, if only by virtue of having a reasonably pleasant disposition. Her father disappeared when she was three, and of her mother's many boyfriends she would only say that some had been less abusive than others; more than that, she says, whenever asked, he doesn't want to know. There is a room he cannot enter, and indeed he has been afraid to force the door. But in the middle of the night, she has awakened him, pleading with Duane, her stepfather, begging him to stop . . . not that he has ever let on. They live with Duane; he's right there in bed with them, though Connor has never let on that he notices.

After fleeing her mother's house at seventeen, she'd left Oklahoma altogether when her amphetamine-shooting boyfriend suggested that he was willing to share her with paying customers. Her next boyfriend, a photographer who helped her assemble her portfolio when she arrived in New York, had failed to tell her he was married.

Even when she began to speak of a future together, even when they jointly moved back to New York to pursue their shiny dreams, she remained skeptical of Connor's intentions. She found it difficult to imagine Connor might be different from others of his kind. Though prepared to cast her lot with him, she remained prepared for the worst. Her fatalism sharpened the edge of his yearning. To make her happy became his vocation. And yet the more he tried to convince her he was different from the men of her previous acquaintance, the more he worried that he might not be different enough.

Trying to prove himself worthy, he didn't stop to consider that what she doubted was her *own* worth.

MODEL PSYCHOLOGY

A beauty contest title had been her only ticket out of Oklahoma. Hadn't everyone always told her she could be a model? Hadn't Duane taught her that sex is currency? All the insecurities that she presumably hoped to conquer by exploiting her troublesome, God-given pulchritude were promptly exacerbated by a profession which judged her solely on the basis of those looks; because for every client that booked her, dozens of others found her wanting in comparison with some other girl, providing her with a steady diet of rejection. (*But what was your original face,* goes the famous koan of Huineng, *before you were born?*)

And now—acting. Jesus.

In his fortunate role as boyfriend-of, Connor exempts Philomena from his categorical skepticism vis-à-vis other members of her sorority, whom he occasionally is called upon to interview. ("Actually, I eat pretty much whatever I feel like. I'm like this real junk food junkie. Big Macs, potato chips. I just pig out all the time but for some reason I don't gain a pound"—CTRL, *Eat your hearts out, fat girls.* Or "I was a real ugly duckling as a kid"—ALT, *duck.*)

OFFICE HOURS

Finding the apartment oppressive, I repair to the midtown offices of *CiaoBella!* One message for me with the receptionist. "Check your e-mail from 'A Fan.' " Moments after I sit down in my tiny cubicle, it is invaded by Tina Christian, the advice columnist, our own Ms. Lonelyhearts. Tina is a perpetual-motion machine, a dervish of windmilling limbs and whippy blond hair.

"The big news around the office is the white T," she says, perching her skinny butt on the edge of my desk. "It's, like, a significant trend, the white T. Kate and Christy are wearing them, ditto the girls in the office, in case you haven't noticed. We're doing a spread, Armani is, like, giving a party tomorrow night at his new boutique to celebrate it. *The new simplicity.* The T-shirt. In white. This is what we do for a living."

Thinking of Philomena in a white T-shirt, I sigh.

Tina waves a photograph in my face. "Now, *him* I would like to see in a white T. Or preferably no T. Simplicity itself. The author—in the buff." Closer inspection reveals it to be Jeremy's publicity photo. "Reliable sources tell me," she says, "that you are acquainted with this Byronesque figure. Naturally I scoffed and jeered. 'Connor?' I said. But, hey, I'm willing to be convinced. If you, say, had his home phone number, that would prove that you actually know him, subject to me calling to verify and maybe meeting him for a drink just to make sure he's not a stand-in or impostor you use to impress innocent colleagues."

"Are we," I venture, "reviewing him?"

She cocks her head in dubious contemplation, straightening a paper clip she has plucked from my desk. "Apparently too depressing for our young, bubbly, ambitious, fun-seeking twenty-something readers. At least that's what Bonnie told me. Though I *could* see a possible feature in the well—with pix. What the hell is he so depressed about, anyway? I mean, he looks like a fucking Ralph Lauren model with a functioning brain. But that's okay, I don't mind depression, I love a project, I know I could cheer him up. Did I ever tell you I was cheerleader at Horace Greeley High? God, I am *so* hungover it's not even funny. Were you at the Versace thing last night—and if so can you tell me if I was? You don't have any Advil, do you?"

I hand her the bottle, which I just happen to have in my top drawer.

"So," she says after swallowing a handful, "can you introduce me or what? I could read his manuscripts, collect his Prozac from the pharmacy, fetch his slippers at night."

"Slipper fetching is a touchy subject with Jeremy."

"I suppose you're going to tell me I'm not intellectual enough? Hey, I read the classics at Smith. I own the complete works of Sylvia Plath. I understand symbolism and irony. Irony—advice columnist whose love life sucks."

"I thought you were going out with Kevin Shipley."

"Kevin's such a geek. Though he has his uses. He's, like, the only guy I've ever dated who's short enough to go *up* on me. Which is a good thing because *writer's* block is the least of his problems. I don't know, I just haven't gotten around to dumping him yet."

"Put in a good word for Jeremy before you dump the guy." Kevin being the book reviewer for *Beau Monde*.

"If *I* put in a good word for Jeremy, Kevin will definitely trash him. Poor Tom Beller. I flirted with him one night at a party. It actually didn't even occur to me that Kevin was reviewing his book that week. Whoa, brutality above and beyond the call . . . I mean, anybody under the age of, like, *eighty* who's actually finished a book already has a strike against them in Kevin's mind."

Craning to inspect the correspondence on my desk, she flutters her hand dismissively. "Dating, what a fucking nightmare. It's almost enough to make me stay with Kevin. I just lie back and pretend he's Tom Cruise." She sighs. "What *do* men want, anyway? Don't answer that. It's not like I don't put out. Plus I've been known to give a highly reviewed blow job. It's not like *we* don't want to get laid, too."

Having failed to spot anything interesting on my desk, she stands up and tosses her hair back. "So, are you going to help me out or what?"

"Jeremy is, well, let's just say difficult."

"All I want to know is, is he straight? After that I'll take my chances." Suddenly she jumps in my lap. "Pretty please." She puts her lips against my ear. "Since you refuse to sleep with me, I think it's the least you can do."

"I'll make inquiries."

She kisses me on the lips. "I'll name our firstborn Connor." Windmilling off, she asks, "How's Phil?"

Fortunately she doesn't wait for the answer. Later, I see that she has left behind a page from her latest column:

ADVICE FROM TINA C

To Frustrated: Sure, you and your guy have had a little spat. It's all part of having a RELATIONSHIP. Those twisted conversations that are one part spoken word, one part secret code, one part mind-reading, one part MALE DUMBNESS, and the next thing you know you're in your own private Bosnia. Here's a recipe that'll have him begging to surrender: give the Mouse Blouse to your little sis and check out the animal print Flirt Shirts in the GOTTA HAVE column this issue. . . .

TOKYO, AUTUMN 1993

She moved into my tiny flat in Roppongi after the first night. We slept on a single futon, which we laid out on the tatami floor each night and folded up each morning. When Philomena went off on go-sees, I practiced calligraphy and took notes for my Kurosawa book. Long enamored of the Japanese cinema, after leaving the monastery I had devoted myself to film, which seemed more Zen-like in its immediacy than literature. Meanwhile: teaching English; writing movie reviews for the *Japan Times* and *Tokyo Business Journal*; two evenings a week taking the train to Shinjuku to conjugate English verbs with Japanese businessmen: *I dump / You dump / He dumps /*

*We dump / You all dump manufactured goods below cost on
the American market in order to gain market share.*

Once while we were making love the tatami began to trem-
ble beneath us; the cookware and china came chiming to life
in the kitchen as a shelf of books in the main room toppled to
the floor, narrowly missing the futon.

"Damn, you *are* good," Philomena said, after the last
tremor had subsided.

On free nights cruising the outdoor market for mordant
pickled vegetables, anthropomorphic gingerroot, fat talc-y
sacks of short-grain rice, bug-eyed fish, skinny chickens with
feet. Starting the automatic rice cooker when I heard Philomena's key in the door. We made love when she returned
home, and sometimes again after we had rolled out the futon
for the night. (Up to now, I might add, the greatest privilege of
my uneventful life has been fucking Philomena.) Between
tumbles we packed our plastic washbuckets under our arms
and set off for the *sento*, the public bath down the street, kissing goodbye at the steaming door as she went in the ladies'
side and I in the men's, handing our two hundred yen to an
ancient crone whose booth straddled the two worlds. (Ah yes,
the public bath, the only place they didn't stare at my *face*.)

After six years I was fairly jaded, but Philomena was new
to Japan, and her curiosity and delight reinvigorated my own
sense of wonder. In particular, the inversions and ostensible
paradoxes delighted her. One day she came home thrilled with
the discovery that in Japanese an orgasm is a *going* rather than
a *coming*. She kept experimenting with the concept in English. "It's like—honey, don't go in my mouth please." And a
few days later: "Do you realize they wash their hands *before*
they go to the bathroom?" Every day a revelation for her, and
for me a refreshment of perspective.

This might have gone on forever, but within the year we
moved to New York—which is to monogamy what the chan-
nel changer is to linear narrative.

BREAKFAST ANYTIME

Our first year in New York, however, was as promising as the opening credits of a movie. In fact I wrote it up as a screenplay—though in the screen version we met in the city after arriving with separate and inappropriate partners. Philomena, newly signed to an agency, found everything fresh and excellent. She loved the BREAKFAST ANYTIME sign in the window of our local diner, with its implication that here in the great city you could make up your own schedule, that it was always the beginning of the day in New York. Once she started to get magazine work the Greek owner asked for a photograph, which he framed and hung over the counter among the photos of the soap actors, belly dancers, Matthew Broderick and other neighborhood celebs. *Best to all the gang at the Acropolis, Philomena.*

MAN ON THE WAVE

Sometimes I suspect that since I bailed on academia I have been a ronin, a man on the wave, storm-tossed and unaffiliated.

The role of the samurai was to serve his master. If necessary, to die for him. A samurai who lost his master, for whatever reason, was no longer a samurai but a ronin, his very reason for existence suddenly removed. A masterless samurai was a virtual contradiction in terms, a big-time lost soul.

E-MAIL

To: Jenrod@inch.com
From: Scribbler@aol.com
Subject: Reality
Dear Jennie:
Thank you for your letter. Unfortunately you are quite wrong about me being someone you would want to meet. And the photograph you seem to admire was the

work of a very artful dodger with a very expensive
camera. As are all the pictures in the magazine. Try not
to believe anything you see or read in our little rag, or
others like it, and you will be a wiser woman. Delusion,
the Zen masters tell us, is the fundamental sickness of
human beings. If it is not too late, try to get over "the
acting bug." Whatever you do, I wish you well.
Sincerely, Connor McKnight

PHYSICAL APPEARANCE

I suppose you've formed a picture of your protagonist by
now, though it occurs to me I haven't been much help in this
regard. But then, I've always found the minute portraiture of
nineteenth-century fiction fairly useless. For me, those precise descriptions of the hero's nose/mouth/eyes/moles/forehead
never come together as an actual face. Maybe it's a failure of
synthetic imagination on my part, but in my mind they always
end up jumbled, like a portrait in the analytic cubist mode. It's
always easier to visualize the minor characters, with their bes-
tial analogues, done in the broad strokes of caricature—Mr.
Fox, Mr. Rat, Miss Sheep. Then, too, as a reader I like to take a
certain amount of responsibility for filling in the details. I'd be
most grateful if you would endow me with rugged, slightly
tragic features.

I have actually heard it maintained that beauty is only skin
deep; Jillian Crowe, on the other hand, says that appearance is
destiny, which is probably closer to the truth. "It's not necessarily whether you win or lose, darling," she once said. "It's
how you look while you're playing the game." Something
only a born winner—and looker—could say.

Certainly you must have decided by now, for instance, that
I am not nearly ambitious enough to be short. Generally it's
the taller guys who have the confidence to be fuckups. Actually, until a late spurt of growth when I was fifteen I was small
for my age. This hormonal surge was accompanied by a bad
case of acne; at the exact moment when sex invaded and colo-
nized my imagination, I couldn't imagine anyone wanting

anything physical to do with me. I subsequently attained
something more than normal height and my face more or less
cleared, though in fact it retains a vaguely lunar aspect to this
day.

Several women have claimed that I am more attractive than
I think, which surely makes me an extremely rare instance of
my sex—men overestimating their physical appeal just about
as consistently as women underestimate theirs—and much of
the limited success I have enjoyed with women in my youth
had the aspect of a pep talk. By now I recognize that brand of
womanly pleasure that comes from cheering on the underdog,
the nurturing sex's delight in nourishing a pale case of confidence. This, I think, is more relevant than the color of my hair
or the shape of my nose.

CELEBRITY SEARCHES

From the office, Connor calls Celebrity Searches, a service to
which his magazine subscribes. "Can you give me a current
location on Ralston, Chip?"

After three minutes: "Still checking." Finally: "We show
him in his Malibu house up until Thursday last week, then we
pick him up last Saturday at the Mark in New York. Checked
out Monday and we're not showing anything since."

"Can you work on that for me?"

"Sure. Meantime, how about Brad Pitt? He's right here in
town. With Gwyneth."

"Who I really need to find is my girlfriend."

"Actress?"

"Model."

"Supermodel?"

"Just a model. Model slash actress."

"Model, nonsuper. Slash actress. Name?"

"Philomena Briggs."

After a search he tells me she's not in their database.

"Could you check the name Fabrizio del Dongo?"

"What, the fashion designer?"

"Protagonist, novel by Stendhal. *Charterhouse of Parma.*"

"Come again?"

WINE NOTES

Guy on the street tries to sell me a bottle of 1976 Lafite Rothschild. Sidles up to me on Eighth Street, wearing those knit gloves with the fingertips amputated to show off his cracked, striated nails, then walks alongside me cradling the bottle as if he were the sommelier at "21" presenting my selection. "Wine of the vintage," he says. "Robert Parker gave it ninety-six points. A quote 'Beautiful bouquet of cedarwood, spices and ripe fruit' unquote. Give it to you for thirty." I wave him off. Actually, I've never been a big Lafite fan. Plus I'm hungover today, for a change.

ANOTHER SPECIAL OFFER, THIS
TIME FROM THE PHONE COMPANY

Connor wants to believe in magic. He tells himself that if he can refrain from picking up the phone until the fifth ring, just before the machine picks up—if he can hold out that long he will be rewarded with the sound of Philomena's voice on the other end. But after five rings he is greeted by a nasal honk belonging to an employee of the phone company. The caller wonders if she might explain a limited-time offer—a service package combining call waiting, voice mail and caller ID.

"I have to get off the phone," he says. "I'm expecting a call."

"That's the beauty of call waiting," she says.

"I already have call waiting—wait, hold on a minute. What's this caller ID?"

"A very useful service. Whenever you receive a call your caller's number appears in the window of the special multi-feature phone which is free to our customers who sign up for this service before the end of the month."

"I'll take it," Connor says.

PUBLICATION DINNER

Dinner at Da Silvano with Jeremy Green, editor Blaine Forrestal, agent Rachel Salmanson: a celebration of the official publication of Jeremy's new collection of stories tomorrow. The first to arrive, I am shortly joined by Rachel, who does not recognize me. "Hi, it's Connor," I say helpfully. And then, when this fails to elicit a hearty greeting: "Jeremy's friend."

"Oh right," she says, scanning the room. She's wearing a white T-shirt under, if I'm not mistaken, a Dolce and Gabbana suit. She clearly doesn't approve of the table to which we are escorted, beside the front window, until she is informed that it's Anna Wintour's regular spot.

"The food's actually quite good," she informs me, as if I had disparaged it, or as if, more likely, she assumes I've never dined here before. Tiny and angular, with a permanent air of impatience, she displays the thin blade of her smile as Blaine joins us at the table. "Jeremy's always late," she explains, after the pleasantries have been exchanged.

"Really?" Blaine purses her ample lips. "I've always found him to be extremely prompt. But then I tend to run a little late myself. Hope *you* haven't been waiting long."

SECRETS OF THE LITERARY LIFE

Jeremy arrives direct from the course he teaches at the New School, complaining about his students.

"*You* should teach it," he tells Rachel. "Last week, I'm giving a talk at this community college in Long Island. Of the eight people in attendance: one fell asleep and snored, one left in the middle, and one asked if I could introduce her to my agent, so I did what I always do—since he rejected my first collection—gave her Mort Janklow's home number. And another asks, inevitably, where I get my ideas. I told him there was a 900 number we published writers call for ideas. That's why you need an agent, of course. The only way you can get the number in the first place is from an agent. It's true—you poor buggers—it's all connections! That's what they all secretly believe, anyway. So I tell them: fifty dollars, a hundred dollars and two fifty for a short story idea; two fifty, five hundred and a thousand for novel ideas. Coover's 'The Babysitter,' for example, that's your top-dollar story idea. Ditto Sontag's *The Way We Live Now*. This business of absorbing the tradition and struggling with the recalcitrance of language doesn't interest them. All they really want is an introduction to my agent."

"Just so long," says Blaine, "as you don't introduce them to your *editor*."

Even before Jeremy arrived the air was spritzed with the musky whiff of feminine competition between these two women, each of whom feels proprietary about the tortured, handsome young artist. (Reminding me, for some reason, of my very first literary party in New York, a *Paris Review* affair which I attended on Jeremy's coattails, when I watched two young men squabbling for the honor of carrying a comatose poet laureate down the stairs.)

LINEAGE

The slightly tardy star of the evening looks particularly Viking tonight, rampant blond hair hanging halfway down his back. One can see how he doubts his parentage. He refers to his family—his alleged family—as "those people in Oyster Bay." He suspects that a practical joke was played at the portal of his latest incarnation, that he was given the wrong parachute as it were, landing in the midst of a suburban Jewish family, heir to a discount mattress dynasty. Although he possesses a fabulously sensitive instrument for the detection of anti-Semitism—can sense an unspoken slur across vast distances, through closed doors and windows—he nevertheless imagines he should be Irish or possibly Cossack, in the latter case improbably identifying, like the great Isaac Babel, with the folks who tortured and slaughtered his ancestors. When he was twelve Jeremy began attending Catholic Mass, and at fourteen he took his first Communion. In fact the protagonists of his stories tend to bear

Irish names. Certainly he doesn't resemble his siblings, two amiable dark-haired fellows who sell mattresses. He keeps trying to get his parents to admit that they adopted him. This makes holidays at the Green household tense. I went there once for dinner and found myself apologizing and virtually translating for the putative eldest son.

A FASHIONABLE CROWD

Our collective attention is captured by movie stars Liam Neeson and Natasha Richardson, who arrive in the company of Sam Cohen, über agent. The volume of conversation drops almost to a whisper, then suddenly rises higher than before, as if it were remote controlled from a dial behind the bar.

"I love the way I'm just sitting here innocently," says Jeremy, "thinking that I'm living my own life, celebrating the publication of a destined-to-be-obscure collection of stories, and suddenly I get reduced to the status of audience."

"You're perfectly free," says Rachel, "to ignore them."

"That's a self-conscious decision in itself. I don't want to *have* to ignore them."

"I was just talking to Sam this afternoon," says Blaine.

"So?" Jeremy demands. "Maybe you should go over and say hi. To your good friend *Sam.*"

The arrival of my colleague Tina Christian at this moment seems a mixed blessing. Detaching herself from her own party, she immediately streaks over to our table and kisses me elaborately.

"Connor! I was just saying absolutely *everybody* comes here."

"And even a few nobodies," I say, before introducing her to my tablemates.

"Oh, you have such great taste," she says to Blaine. "You publish all my favorite books." This strikes me as a clever remark, seemingly diversionary as it is from the real focus of her interest.

"I'm just publishing Jeremy's," Blaine says—not news, obviously, to Tina.

"Oh, God, are you *that* Jeremy Green?" she burbles. "I just read the galleys of *Walled-In*."

"That makes you part of a very elite group," Jeremy says. "I think they only printed five or six."

"I thought it was brilliant."

Jeremy can't quite disguise his pleasure. We are all sluts of one sort or another.

"I can't stay, I'm with this group of losers," she says as she pulls up a chair beside me. "Unfortunately they're all my best friends."

VEGAN ACTIVISM

Tina seems to have more time than she imagined. After we have ordered, she tells Jeremy that she much prefers short stories to novels. "I mean, how many people have *time* to read novels?"

"Believe it or not," says Blaine, "there are a few of us left."

"Enjoying your charbroiled beef scab?" Jeremy asks the diner beside us, a young Wall Streeter who has been speculating about the size of his year-end bonus. Who, until moments ago, looked very satisfied with his lot, not least with his striped and succulent rib eye. Dining with Jeremy is always an adventure. Recently he was asked to leave an Italian restaurant on the Upper West Side after delivering a speech, from atop his chair, on the horrors of veal.

"Jeremy," says Blaine, "can't we, you know, just live and let live here? Do we *have* to make a scene?"

"Jeremy's always felt very strongly about this issue," counters Rachel, who has the prior claim on him and isn't about to relinquish it. "I don't think there's anything wrong with standing up for your principles."

"How does it feel," Jeremy asks Blaine, "to have an agent lecture you about principles?"

"Oh, *fine,* just because I try to look out for your interests, just because I try to beat up publishers for the best possible advance so that you can have the leisure to *write*—suddenly I'm *The Agent*."

Jeremy reaches over to embrace her. "It's true," he says. "Publishers come and go, but agents are forever."

Now Blaine's pissed, Rachel slightly mollified.

"Agents have feelings, too," says Tina, who would like, ever so much, to have one of her very own.

JEREMIAD

The appearance of a rottweiler outside the window on the sidewalk leads to the subject of Jeremy's beloved Sean. The negotiations have broken down entirely. "I offered three grand," he informs us.

"God," exclaims Tina, "what kind of dog *is* it?"

"Don't ask," says Rachel.

"Please," adds Blaine, finally finding a point of concord with the agent.

"A toast to *Walled-In*," Rachel says, raising her glass.

"Here, here," I say, raising my own.

"A book which," says Blaine, "I am as proud of as anything I have published in my entire career."

Jeremy raises his own glass. "A book which *Kirkus Reviews* has described as 'depressing and labored.' "

"*Kirkus* is a joke," says Blaine with Waspy hauteur.

"That's what the *New England Review* called my last collection," Jeremy recalls, " 'a joke.' "

"They did not," Rachel insists. "And anyway, whoever heard of the *New England Whatever.*"

"We just got a great blurb from Bret Ellis," says Blaine. "I meant to tell you."

"Oh, yeah, terrific," says Jeremy. "All the homicidal slackers will skateboard straight to Barnes and Noble for a copy of *Walled-In* and a latte."

"Not to mention," says Blaine, "the Auster and the Thom Jones quote."

"If I'm lucky somebody may think it's Tom Jones the singer. And fucking Auster had to write a movie before anyone got down on their knees."

"Let's not write off the audience for *Walled-In* just yet," Blaine says.

LIFE, PRO AND CON

Jeremy's malaise turns general. "Why did I come back this time? I wonder." A believer in reincarnation, he is referring to the mortal coil. "I mean, what was I thinking? Did I suddenly, in a weak moment, remember how good it feels to take a shower, the touch of warm water on the skin. Was that it?"

I can't help laughing. The literary posse glares at me.

Tina, on the other hand, tries to convince Jeremy to get high on life. "Don't you just want to see what happens next," she says. "I mean, I wake up every morning—well, noon, whatever—and it's a new day in the city, even when I'm hung-over I basically can't wait to run out my door to find out what's out there—"

"A knife-wielding crackhead."

"I mean anything can happen—"

"Run over by a cab, raped and left for dead."

"Like when I was on my way here tonight, I had no idea I'd meet one of my favorite writers. . . ."

"Puh-lease," says Rachel, lifting her martini while I stare longingly at my empty glass.

"They look perfectly happy to me," says Tina, glancing over at Liam and Natasha. "Except I keep hearing he still has a sneaker for Julia."

Jeremy rolls his eyes. "I was definitely born in the wrong century," he says. "It all comes down to whether you live in the kind of universe where *DV* stands for 'Diana Vreeland' or 'Deo volente.' "

"Who's Deo Valente?" Tina asks.

Jeremy, through gritted teeth: "It means 'God willing,' in Latin."

"There *was* a Dino Valenti who was some kind of folksinger," Rachel chips in helpfully.

THE CRITIC

Looking up, I find myself looking at Kevin Shipley, who is glaring at our table, his general aspect if possible even more crabbed and dyspeptic than usual. Though I barely know him, he is someone of whom you feel compelled to ask: Have you ever used the word *joy*? Are you familiar with the definition? Although Tina tells me he actually has a cat on which he lavishes affection. I once applied for his job, before he had it, but of the several clips I submitted—freelanced reviews for obscure publications and Japanese to boot—two were positive. Which any reader of that mag could have told me was the wrong note entirely for a book review. As opposed to a celebrity profile.

I look to Tina, who seems to be *too* unaware of Kevin's scrutiny, her arm draped casually around the back of Jeremy's chair.

NOTHING WITH EYES

With the arrival of our meat-free appetizers—no one has dared to order animal protein, unless you count my linguine alla vongole—Jeremy is once again fiercely scowling at the next table, where the waveringly carnivorous investment banker is trying to finish his rib eye.

"Do you eat fish?" Tina asks Jeremy.

"Nothing with eyes," Jeremy snarls.

I am relieved to learn that my clams will escape censure.

"What if," Tina says, "we wear shades."

"That slab of flesh on Mr. Hermes' plate over there was grazing happily in a pasture just a few days ago."

This hardly seems the time to explain to Jeremy about the aging of beef.

"Excuse me," says the man's companion. "But I think you're incredibly rude." Suddenly she is up, standing beside our table in her Ralph Lauren suit and her black-velvet hairband, matching Jeremy scowl for scowl. "You've been glaring at us, making me and my associate feel extremely self-conscious."

THE CASE AGAINST MEAT

"You know," says Jeremy, "quite aside from the cruelty and slaughter you're inflicting on the poor defenseless animals, there's also the far less important question of what you're doing to your own miserable bodies." Jeremy's voice expands to fill the dining room, which seems to be shrinking by the minute. "As a practicing carnivore, you can be certain that at this very moment some ten or fifteen pounds of undigested meat are lodged in your upper intestine, which might explain why you walk as if you had a Louisville Slugger three feet up your ass."

"Right on," Tina says. Then the woman takes a slap at Jeremy, her hand rebounding harmlessly from the ample mass of his hair. Even the luminaries at the front table who have so carefully avoided looking around the room can't help it at this point. Natasha, by the way, has very nice eyes.

"Typical blood lust," Jeremy sputters, as the captain rushes over to intervene. The woman's companion rises from his chair but seems at a loss as to his next move. "And *you*," says Jeremy, standing up himself and pointing at him, "you can just sit right back the fuck down unless you're looking for a Pellegrino high colonic."

The anal theme has become far too prevalent for my tastes.

RETREAT

Jeremy is finally persuaded by the captain and myself to wait outside while Blaine takes care of the check. Not before Tina slips him a card, in full view of Shipley, whom she has thus far failed to acknowledge.

From the sidewalk I watch as Rachel debates with herself whether or not to pay her respects to the high table. Fortunately for her, Jeremy is pacing farther up the street when she decides to risk it.

"Congratulations," Blaine says angrily when she joins us outside. "You managed to upstage the movie stars. You must be very pleased with yourself."

"Did anybody ask for my autograph after I left?"

Rachel sighs. "Grow up, Jeremy."

United at last in their irritation with the author, the women announce they're sharing a cab to the Upper East Side.

"The only reason you're upset," Jeremy shouts after them, "is because you don't think I'm famous enough to be difficult."

"What say to a nightcap at Mount Olympus," I suggest as we watch the cab join a lazy school of its yellow brethren finning up Sixth Avenue.

"I think I've had just about enough merriment for one night."

The world, I think, is evenly divided between those who want company in their misery and those who fret alone. Though Jeremy would probably insist that it's divided between those who cherish principles and those who favor decorum.

MESSAGE FROM PHIL

"Hi, it's me. You there? . . . Guess you're out. I'm rushing. We're actually in Santa Barbara at the director's house and now I'm headed to L.A. I'm not sure about the schedule. It's nuts. Call you when I know where I am. Big kiss."

This message is on my machine when I return from dinner. It's the tone of voice that's so disturbing. A false, heightened breeziness. The words strung together on a thin wire of nervous gaiety.

CONNOR'S REACTION

These past few days he has been able to suppress his anxiety about Phil. But hearing her voice, he knows his suspicions were well founded. He *knows*. His ribs seem to constrict around his lungs, making him acutely aware of the throbbing muscle which is his heart. Panting like a winded dog, he paces the living room, slapping his fist into his palm.

Santa Barbara?

Maybe it's not too late. If he can reach her in L.A., maybe he can stop her from doing what it is he fears she has already done.

MODEL SEARCH

Dialing the Chateau Marmont, the Sunset Marquis, the Four Seasons, the Bel-Air, the Bel Age and the Peninsula while searching the drawers for cigarettes—which he gave up a year ago. He finally finds a pack of horrible stale Newports that someone left in the apartment. Lights one from the stove and suddenly thinks—Wait a minute, who smokes Newports? No one *he* knows. And Phil has never smoked. Jesus, she's been entertaining black guys in the apartment. No wait, could be a girl, one of her friends. But what friends? Who *are* her friends, anyway? Does she have any? Who the hell can he call?

Finally he calls her sort-of-friend Patty in Santa Monica, congratulating her on her infomercial, trying to sound casual as he asks if she has heard from Phil.

"You guys having, like, problems or something," she asks suspiciously. The tone of sisterhood closing ranks against the infidel male. Nothing like that, Connor assures her in a reedy, unconvincing voice. It's just that Phil's in L.A. and he's lost her number, the machine ate the tape, he needs to talk to her right away.

"I haven't talked to Philomena in six months."

"Yeah, well, if she does call, tell her to call me, okay?"

Who else can he call? He realizes how strange it is that his girlfriend should have so very few girlfriends of her own, a sign he should have noted before. Suddenly it seems irresponsible, even dangerous, to have so few friends. To have almost no friends. After all, who is your boyfriend supposed to call when he can't find you? At first this lack of comrades seemed attributable to their expatriation, later to their mutual romantic absorption in each other—back when they were fucking every day and he didn't much care if he ever got out of bed again. . . .

WOMEN BEWARE WOMEN

Connor remembers something Brooke once said: "Beware the woman who doesn't like other women; she's probably generalizing from her own character."

MODEL BEHAVIOR

Sometimes Phil would become friendly with another model; they would spring up like daffodils in our lives, briefly, their long legs sheathed in ripped jeans, long arms around their dark Euroboys . . . dinners at Raoul's and B Bar . . . *Bonsoir, there's Linda and Kyle . . . How was Milan? So sad about Richard and Cindy. Cristal and cigarettes, maybe just a little snort of H—where's Kate? More cigarettes! Buccal fat pads removed, plus her eyes . . . Actually, I almost never do coke anymore practically. . . .*

Generally these acquaintanceships would trail off, or end badly. "Whatever happened to Veronica," Connor would ask, only to be told that she turned out to be a real bitch. Not that he missed these brilliant nights as the dimbulb boyfriend, the awkward beauty accessory, the anonymous companion. *So nice to have met you, Collin. . . . What is it you do, Cullen? You must be very proud of Philomena, Curran. . . . What do you write, Kiran? Of course, you must know Court?*

FLASHBACK

"Why don't we ask Katrinka and her boyfriend for dinner?" you proposed one fine spring day.

"*You* ask them. The three of you can go out. Or better yet, just the two of you. You and Katrinka."

"I thought you liked Katrinka."

"I used to. Till I found out she was a liar."

"What did she lie about?"

"Lots of things."

"Like what?"

"Like she said you were coming on to her."

"She said that?"

"Uh-huh."

At this point you were hard-pressed to speak up in Katrinka's defense. In fact, it did seem she once might have flirted with you a little, and you felt guilty that you had not actively discouraged it, this flirting, partly because you were grateful to be noticed at all. You would have to watch that kind of thing—you vowed to make Philomena feel more secure. She would realize eventually that you loved her, and in the meantime it was just the two of you, you and Phil, dining à deux.

There are worse fates, of course, than finding yourself alone for the night with Philomena Briggs. At this moment you would gladly give up your own few friends for the privilege.

PANIC

The cigarette tastes so bad he immediately lights another.

On a flash of inspiration he rushes back to the bathroom and searches the cabinet beneath the sink, the drawers in the bedside table, her cosmetics case, the oval Shaker box and the shagreen jewelry box he bought for her twenty-sixth birthday. Lingerie drawer, scattering panties and bras to the winds. Under the bed, back to the bathroom, the soap dish in the shower, everywhere that he has ever seen her diaphragm. Which is not in the apartment. He slumps to the floor of the shower stall, still wet from his evening rinse.

She *knew* he would be at dinner with Jeremy when she called tonight. Oh, yes, definitely. The night she left, Connor asked if she would be home in time for Jeremy's big dinner. Phil wrote it in her book, said she'd try. This little detail, barely noticed at the time, now looming enormous. She fucking *knew*. Waited until he was out to call.

Santa Barbara?

As a last resort he checks his e-mail with all the optimism of a camel essaying the eye of a needle.

MORE FAN MAIL

To: Scribbler@aol.com
From: Jenrod@inch.com
Subject: You are worthwhile!
Dear Connor:
It was GREAT to hear from you but I was totally amazed you sounded so DOWN on yourself. I think actually it is often the case that the best people are the hardest on them selves. How can you say your not a worthwhile person? LOOK AT YOURSELF! You are a successful writer for a national magazine!

I think you have been listening to the wrong people. It's important to surround yourself with people who build U up not tear U down. Like me, sometimes I think I'm hanging out with the wrong people. All they think about is Thank God Its Friday and Look at that Guy in the BMW. I guess you would call us a gang. In high school I felt lucky to be part of it because you can't just be on your own but now that I am out with a job I want to better myself. Its hard when your with people who don't have any ambition except to be with the hottest guy which is maybe somebody who is doing something illegal for a living. Like my friend Tina she's really cool but last year she slashed this girl with a boxcutter who was supposedly stepping out with Jimmy Ortega and she had to have fifty eight stitches to her face. And sometimes she says I'm stuck up when really its just I want a better future. Anyway I better go. If my boss catches me on line I will be in big trouble.

For what it's worth, I believe in you. REALLY! E me!

P.S. Do you like to dance? Do you ever go to Chaos? Or even the Latin Quarter? Maybe we could meet sometime. How about Friday night? Me and Tina will be there at Chaos at midnight. See you there!

SUCCOR FROM A MORE
CREDIBLE SOURCE

Connor signs off, dials his sister. Perhaps she can convince him that his fears are groundless, say something to ease the incessant, throbbing pain.

For once in her life, Brooke picks up the phone.

"She's gone, Brooke."

"Yes, you told me. San Francisco, as I recall."

"She took her *diaphragm*, Brooke. Jesus, I can't stand it. I can't sit down. I can't stand still. I don't want to be in the apartment another minute but I don't want to leave in case she calls."

"Why don't you come over here?" Brooke proposes. "You can leave my number on your machine." Thankfully, she does not remind him, as is her wont, that there are people far worse off than he.

In the cab, shuddering uptown, he drums the back of the seat in time to his desperate heartbeat.

"What are you, Gene Krupa? Relax already." Last of the old New York cabbies.

When Connor sees his sister's face he comes apart like a three-dollar umbrella in a gale. Brooke scoops up the wrecked metal ribs and shredded black rayon and walks the whole mess inside. Half a dozen soothing, empty—make that false—formulae are uttered. *It's all right*, et cetera.

When he has partially regained his composure she is hefting a steaming kettle in the kitchen.

"I didn't know you knew how to boil water."

"You're thinking of Mom," she says. "I learned this in the lab. Actually, it's not as difficult as it looks."

"Just please don't say I'm better off without her."

"Only because it would arouse your chivalrous instincts. I long ago learned that the quickest way to get a guy panting for more abuse was to run down the lady in question. I have no desire to provoke you into defending her." Brooke looks uncharacteristically competent in an oversize Middlebury sweatshirt which Connor gave her about twelve years ago, with her hair swept back in a ponytail, her thin, freckled hand with its striped scars resting on the kettle. If only he were allowed to fall in love with his sister. In fact, Phil thinks he *is* in love with Brooke. "Why don't you fuck your sister" being one of Philomena's late-night refrains. Connor has a sudden guilty insight: that his custodianship of Brooke has interfered with the care and feeding of his fragile girlfriend.

"Her *diaphragm*, Brooke."

"I thought you were the condom generation."

"I hate condoms. Swimming in a rain coat. Besides, we've been in a completely monogamous relationship for three years."

She raises her eyebrows at this doubtful assertion. "God, you smell like Lynchburg, Tennessee."

"I've been drinking."

"I'm *shocked*."

"It doesn't help."

"I wish you'd tell that to Dad."

"It just feels so goddamn bad."

"I know." Stroking his hip, she hands him a Beethoven mug full of steaming water on which floats a tea bag with pendant tag: Lapsang souchong. "What did you do, wet yourself?" she asks, removing her hand from his ass.

"I sat down in the shower."

"Let me get you a robe."

Connor slaps his hand against the wall. "I don't understand how she could be so eager to run off and fuck some other guy when I have to beg and plead just to get any once or twice a week."

"Shhh."

"It's not fair."

"I know."

FAIRNESS AND MATH

Brooke discovered injustice and the negative numbers on the same day. She was in Miss Tollitson's first-grade class at Winterhaven Elementary School, performing feats of arithmetic. Miss Tollitson was a fierce egalitarian of procrustean bent who felt that Brooke was a little big for her britches—Miss Smarty Pants, as she later complained to the principal. Brooke would have shined in any context, but nowhere quite so brightly as amongst the sons and daughters of intermarried dirt farmers, porch loungers and dead-machinery curators of Central Florida, from which stock Miss T herself was descended. One morning after Brooke had successfully answered an increasingly difficult series of additions and subtractions, Miss Tollitson snarled, "All right Miss McKnight, what's seven take away ten?" Arms folded high on her bony chest, a premature look of triumph (as Brooke tells it) suffusing her beaked, leathery visage. Of course, Brooke knew this was a trick question. But she was stubbornly determined not to be defeated by the old battle-ax. And suddenly, the answer seemed as obvious as if she had been Archimedes in his bath. She saw in her mind's bright eye a series of phantom integers, transparent abacus beads hovering in the void.

"Minus three," she announced.

Miss Tollitson's red-faced reaction verified her discovery. "We don't know about that yet," she sputtered. "That's sheer impertinence, Brooke McKnight. You just go right down to Mr. Brent's office and we'll see how smart you are."

And so Brooke was sent home from school for the crime of discovering the negative numbers before the Florida Board of Ed had planned for her to do so.

SUDDENLY, THE BUZZER

The door speaker crackles, announcing the arrival of Doug Halliwell, M.D.

"Oh, hell," says Brooke, smiling apologetically.

Possibly the last person in the world I would want to see at this moment.

"I'll get rid of him, I promise."

"I've been advising you to do that for months."

"*Please*, Connor."

"And don't you dare tell him my girlfriend has dumped me. I don't need his pity."

"Too late for that," Brooke mutters.

I retreat to the sofa to sulk, hoisting a copy of the *Mathematical Intelligencer* for a prop, hearing him at the door. . . .

"Just finished up at the, uh, hospital, and I thought you might, I don't know, want to get a bite, I mean we don't have to. Oh, I didn't . . . hello, Connor."

I wave absently in his direction, pretending to be absorbed in an article on knot theory.

"Connor and I are having a little family conference. But you're welcome to a cup of tea." I sneak a look in Brooke's direction in order to glare, but she's not about to let me catch her eye.

"I don't mean to . . ."

"No, no. That's all right."

I sense Mad Dog's presence at my back, hesitating to enter the room proper, standing politely in the foyer while Brooke rattles around in the kitchen. I can picture him, bobbing forward slightly from the waist, head deeply recessed into his shoulders, hair receding up his forehead. For some reason, his timidity offends me, though I'm not such a hardass as to snub him entirely. Perhaps it is my own timidity I see and dislike in his face, whose features I can never really remember from one meeting to the next.

But yes, that must be him, standing just as I imagined, in his khaki Sansabelt pants and his anorak. Now I remember what he looks like. With his forward-hunched posture, his bug eyes and Roman nose, he resembles a perched vulture.

"Have a seat," I suggest, as if I am the host, or the doctor.

He shrugs, moving tentatively into the room, examining its meager features. "How's the, uh, the writing going," he asks.

"I wouldn't know," I say. "You should ask the writers." His attempt to take my pretensions at face value further infuriates me. Dimly I perceive that Doug bears hardly any blame for the fact that I hate what I do for a living, and hate myself for what I have failed to do with my life, even as he returns from a sixteen-hour shift of plugging gunshot wounds and resurrecting gasping cardiacs. I know I'm behaving childishly—a glimmer of perception that only makes me meaner. It's seldom difficult to know how one *should* behave. The Golden Rule, the Categorical Imperative, all that. The former has been revised, of course: *Behave unto others as if they were about to become incredibly famous.*

THE DOCTOR'S VISIT

Brooke bustles in with a broken-handled mug, which Doug receives gratefully, grasping it as eagerly as if it were the answer, finally, to the nagging question of what to do with his hands outside of surgery . . . until he realizes how hot it is and searches frantically but quietly for a neutral surface on which to put it down.

"But you're still working for the, uh, the magazine, aren't you?" he persists, blowing on his scorched hands.

"Barely."

"How was your day, Doug?" Brooke chirps. I can't believe she perks up for this limp specimen.

"Not too bad." Thankfully he doesn't have to elaborate, being interrupted by his beeper.

"Use the phone in the bedroom," says Brooke, and then, as he disappears, she hisses: "Will you try for once not to behave like a total asshole, if only for my sake."

I'm stung. Me, an asshole? I remind her she said she was going to get rid of him.

Doug emerges to announce he's needed at the hospital. Someone at death's door. He seems relieved, actually, to be needed, to go back where he clearly belongs; God knows *I'm* relieved. He pauses just long enough to spill some tea down the front of his sweater. Brooke wipes him off and kisses him at the door.

"I don't understand what you see in that dork."

"He's sweet and kind and decent—three qualities nobody's going to pin on you. I've had a rotten year and I'm very grateful for Doug's interest."

"He has subzero personality."

"No, what he doesn't have is attitude. There's a difference."

I can't stand to see Brooke angry at me. We hardly ever disagree on anything, so I'm crushed by her failure to share my judgment of the good, the virtuous Dr. Halliwell. But I can see that she is mad, and to win her back I apologize. Knowing she wouldn't really appreciate the observation, knowing he can't probably help it, I won't even mention the funny way he wheezes instead of breathing.

A PARABLE

Later, sitting on the sleigh bed, Brooke strokes her brother's hair and, with another story from their childhood, his soul. A story about a Welsh terrier and a calico cat. "Remember old Rogue? How we could never get him to eat his dog food. Hated it. Tipped his bowl over and scattered food across the floor. But as soon as Clio stuck her whiskers in his bowl he'd go wild, barking and growling and running around in circles till she'd had her nibble. Then he'd rush in and devour every last bit of it."

Connor knows his sister too well not to take the point, but at the moment he is too unhappy either to acknowledge or dispute it.

"You've been with her three years. In all that time you've failed to demonstrate a commitment. But now that someone's got his nose in your bowl you're howling. I hate to say it, but this is kind of a guy thing. You boys think you want virgins, but I think what you really want is to put your peepees where the other peepees have been."

This somehow reminds me of the joke Philomena told in the cab en route to the Baby Doll Lounge the night before she left, and though it should be palliative it only makes me miss her all the more, thinking of the soft weight of her in my lap.

PHILOMENA'S JOKE

"So there's this guy," she begins, "—shut up and listen—this guy's shipwrecked on a desert island."

"Is this the one about the Doberman and the sheep?" asks Ralph, the hair genius.

"No it's not. Quiet!" She takes a whack at Ralph, and continues. "So this guy's wasting away on this desert island for weeks and months, till one day another big storm blows up, and another ship crashes on the reef. After a while he sees this body bobbing in the surf so he swims out and grabs this blond hair and pulls the body to shore. . . . *Quiet!* And it turns out to be Sharon Stone. Well, he gives her mouth to mouth—no, shut up. . . . He revives her and of course she's very grateful and all. No, she's *not* still naked, Connor, it doesn't matter. Okay fine she's naked. Anyway she's grateful and all but after a few weeks it's more than that. She realizes she's falling in love with the guy. And she's like, Isn't this great, if not for this shipwreck I never would've met the man of my dreams. Of course he's ecstatic—I mean, whoa, Sharon Stone's in love with him and he's in love with her and everything's great and they decide to get married if they ever get off this goddamn island but after a while she notices that he's getting moody, it's not quite the same. She tries to tell herself he'll get better but he just seems real depressed and finally she says, 'What's wrong? I'll do anything you want, just come back to me.' And he says it's nothing."

"Fag!" shouts Alonzo, self-described "powder fairy."

"Shut up, 'Lonz."

(And feeling Philomena in your lap, gazing at her close up, in profile, you felt painfully, irredeemably hetero.)

"But finally he says," she continues, " 'Will you really do anything I want?' and she goes, 'Of course,' so he says, 'I want you to dress up like a guy, there's like all these guys' clothes that've washed up on the beach—' "

"Told you!"

"Yes, I'm sure you can relate to that, 'Lonzo—and Sharon's thinking, Shit, I knew it was too good to be true, he's getting all kinky on me, but she loves him so much she'll do it. And then he explains that after she gets dressed up he wants her to walk around one side of the island while he walks around the other side and they'll meet halfway. 'And when you see me, pretend you're some guy who knows me and ask me how it's going.' So she walks around one side, and when they meet she says, 'Hey, Frank, how's it going?' And he says: 'Going great man. You won't *believe* who I'm fucking. . . .' "

BACK TO THE PRESENT

"Why can't I just marry you?" Connor says.

"I make a bad wife. Just ask Jerry."

"Fuck Jerry. Jerry's a dickhead. Tell me another story. Please. Anything that doesn't involve slaughter and cruelty in other parts of the world."

ANOTHER STORY

"Have I ever told you about strategies of the hunt for large primes."

"Oh, God, not that one."

"As you know, primes are only divisible by themselves and one—they're like building materials of number theory, like fundamental particles in physics or the basic elements in chemistry. All the other whole numbers can be written as products of these primes. There are an infinite number of primes, of course, so you'd think it would be fairly simple to find them."

Undoubtedly, you would. But I'm betting . . . it's *not*.

"But actually it's quite tricky, even with the help of computers." As she speaks, I glance at the thin scars beneath the sleeve of her nightgown. "They behave very perversely and they're hidden among the other numbers in very unpredictable sequences. Searching for the really big ones—I'm talking numbers like two to the, say, seven thousand six hundred and thirteenth power—searching for the big ones is kind of like trolling the surface of the ocean for giant marlin. You have to stake out a wide swath of territory and then kind of gradually close . . ."

This goes on for some time. Large primes aside, I'm wondering what the best strategy is for hunting petite models.

CONNOR'S MIND WANDERS

Random thoughts:

A yearning for Philomena's body as site-specific as that of the salmon for the patch of watery gravel in which he was hatched. The belief that he will always miss her, that no one else will come so close to filling his intense, recurring need to swim upstream. That he will be like those poor anadromous finny pilgrims stuck in a pool at the base of a massive hydro-electric dam, forever exiled from home.

Is Brooke right? That the male of the species needs frequent verification of the desirability of the love or sex object? The only absolute proof being the consummation of interest on the part of another male, which consummation forever robs the lover of his sense of possession, and drives him completely insane with jealousy.

Is Connor guilty, as charged, of enjoying his model girl-friend's trophy status? Instead of encouraging her to do something that wouldn't make her so crazy? Instead of, for example, marrying her? Practically inviting her to escape into the arms of some horny photographer or male model or whoever may be ramming it up against her missing diaphragm at this very moment?

Or does his evasion of commitment reflect his aforementioned sense of his own unworthiness? Should he give her credit for admiring those few qualities that he values in himself: his intelligence, his impractical education and his lack of malice? Or does he, out of self-loathing, despise her for admiring in him such qualities as count for nothing in the marketplace?

SEXUAL SURROGACY DEBATED

"Do you think it's weird that when I have sex with Philomena I'm always conjuring up another sexual encounter."

Brooke thinks about it. "I suppose you could say it's like a stereoscope, one of those old optical devices, where you view photographs of the same object from two slightly different points of view, your two eyes putting together the images to create the illusion of depth."

"What exactly," you ask, "are the two eyes? In this case?"

"But a more sinister interpretation would be that you're incapable of appreciating the actual intimacy you enjoy with Philomena and you have to distance yourself from the domestic Philomena with whom you shop for groceries and pay the bills by turning her back into the kind of sex object who is displayed in Hollywood movies and glossy magazines like the one you work for, and in which she frequently appears. But if it makes you feel any better I think all men do that. Except that most of them have to leave their own apartment in order to supply the image."

JEEVES RALLIES ROUND

Connor still can't sit still. He paces around the living room, stopping to examine any domestic objects he fails to recognize. Finally, Brooke resorts to Wodehouse.

There is a tradition in the McKnight family of sojourning in Wodehouse territory when life seems especially grim and real. Connor appreciates the gesture all the more since Brooke doesn't believe that it is either possible or desirable to escape the sorrows and horrors of this world (although he once heard her bat around the concept of Possible Worlds in connection with some conundrum of logic).

She reads aloud about Bertie's attempts to steal the silver cow creamer from Sir Watkin Basset, while attempting to avoid matrimony with Basset's moony daughter Madeline. After more than an hour he suddenly feels exhausted from his ordeal and admits he might be able to sleep.

CONNOR'S DREAM

Your repose is tortured and storm tossed until Brooke finally takes you in her arms. All at once you feel nearly at peace. In the familiar warmth of your sister's embrace you feel you have arrived at your destination after a long, arduous, unhappy journey. You kiss your sister and drift off toward sleep, and in your dream you are embracing a beautiful woman. Could it be Pallas? It is not Philomena, certainly, but someone very familiar. You kiss her mouth and burrow into her chest. Watching yourself in your dream you feel radiant. And you are just on the verge of becoming whole when Brooke says, "No, Connor, don't. Connor, stop!"

ANOTHER DREAM

You are sitting in a pastoral field when Philomena suddenly drops down by your side, her eyes alight with lust. You have never seen this expression on her face, a wanton mask. She reaches for your jeans and unzips you. You ask her where she's been. "Can't talk with my mouth full," she says wickedly, bending down, proceeding to fill it. "What about all these people?" you ask prudishly, just noticing the presence of others. "I've already taken care of them," she says, looking up. And then you see that all the men around you are lying on their backs in postures of satiation with their jeans around their ankles. A man walks past, fixing his fly, and winks at you.

You wake in a panic, sit up. Brooke is breathing lightly beside you. What is peculiar about the dream: Philomena claimed to be too self-conscious to enjoy you going down on her, and out of some deeply misguided sense of mutuality felt that you, too, could do without.

In the dream you are as aroused as you are jealous, turgid with grief and lust.

BROOKE'S DREAM

Brooke dreams of bodies floating down a river in Tanzania, mutilated bodies cascading over the Rusumo Falls onto the rocks below.

AN ITEM IN THE DAILY NEWS

Grazing my morning tabloids on the E train, heading home, I come across this:

> . . . Highrise heartthrob LIAM NEESON at DA SILVANO, taking a swing at novelist JEREMY (*Walden*) GREEN, who was apparently paying too much attention to wife NATASHA RICHARDSON . . .

AD ON A BUS SHELTER

CLUB MED—LIFE AS IT SHOULD BE: White sand, turquoise water, caramel flesh. Thanks very much for reminding us. A cold drizzle falling here in Manhattan; a malevolent cloud has swallowed the tops of the Trade Center Towers.

JEREMY GREEN, LITERARY DETECTIVE

Upon returning home I rush to the answering machine. I checked once this morning from Brooke's, but that was forty minutes ago. Difficult as it was to leave the refuge of her nest, I thought my chances of hearing from Phil were better if I was stationed at the phone—although I left Brooke's number on the machine last night.

Only one call, from Jeremy. "Damnit, McKnight. Call me." Disappointed as I am to find his voice in lieu of Phil's, I call immediately. I'm always expecting some terrible message from Jeremy, or about Jeremy, who not only presents himself as a character in the second act of a tragedy, but also rewrites his will every six months: currently I am his designated literary executor. As with my sister, my chief fear is that the third act may take place when I am out of sight.

"The *Times* review is running on Saturday."

"That's great." Apparently he hasn't seen the *News*. Far be it from me.

"How do you know it's great? Have you heard something?"

"I mean, just getting reviewed in the daily *Times* is kind of a big deal, isn't it?"

"Saturday is like going to Paris in August."

His call waiting clicks and he dumps me for Blaine.

Shortly he calls back. "I just reread *Goodbye, Columbus*," he informs me.

"Ah. Brenda Patimkin . . . underwater kissing . . . diaphragm." As soon as I've said it I feel the ache of loss and regret. *Diaphragm*—terrible word, obscene little Frisbees flashing across the edge of my vision, booby traps underlying the very path of my consciousness. I think that was the first time I heard of one, reading Roth's first novel. Had no idea what it was. Wish I still didn't.

"It's so *obvious*," Jeremy says indignantly. "It came to me like a goddamn lightbulb switching on over my head." More than a cliché, in Jeremy's case this sounds like a potential fire hazard. But I'm relieved, too, that he hasn't swallowed an entire bottle of Percocet, nor opened his veins in a warm tub after deciding that his talent—compared to the titans who were born of the sun who traveled a short while, et cetera—is too meager to justify his continued consumption of planetary oxygen.

"Salinger," he announces, cryptically. "Roth took Salinger's suppression of his own Jewishness, the phantom Jewishness of Salinger's faux Wasp characters, and made the subject matter explicitly Jewish. The social observation, the class consciousness, the hyperrealistic observation of the courtship rituals of postwar urban youth—and then he used the license that Bellow and Malamud had granted to speak explicitly of Jewish themes. Voilà—*Goodbye, Columbus*."

"The Glass family *was* Jewish, weren't they?"

"Half Irish, half Jewish," Jeremy says impatiently. "The faith passes through the mother, in this case Bessie, who's Irish. So, no. Salinger was probably unconsciously trying to cop some Irish-lit cred. But Roth—I mean, sure, *Goodbye, Columbus* is fucking great. I'm just saying it doesn't come out of nowhere."

"That's a relief," I say. "Now, how about a drink? A restorative . . . *cocktail*?"

"I've got my shrink in half an hour."

"Ah yes, the Celtic and the Hebraic approaches to sorrow and confusion, respectively."

"I need more meds to get through this fucking publication."

"Send me the book," I say in parting.

E-MAIL

To: Scribbler@aol.com
From: Jenrod@inch.com
Subject: Waiting on U
My friend Tina thinks I should send you a photo so you won't think I'm "a dog." You shouldn't judge a book by its cover I always say but let's face it in this business Plain Janes aren't exactly the flavor of the month except maybe Kathy Bates, no disrespect intended I think she's a major talent. I am sending U my "head shot" by "snail mail" which actually shows more than just my head. E me! I'm waiting with baited breath.

PREEMPTIVE STROKE

Monday: We're lunching with Pallas. Of course, we had to promise her a hundred dollars for her time. Plus the lunch. Why are we doing this? Trying, perhaps, in case it becomes necessary, to implement the plan called Life After Philomena? Just to assure ourselves of our essential fidelity we beat off before leaving the apartment, conjuring up a particularly juicy episode in which Philomena set aside her distaste for oral sex.

PALLAS BY DAY

Pallas arrives just a few minutes late. Conversation in the restaurant falls and finally rises again, a collective susurration. She is discreetly breathtaking in a white T-shirt (but of course!) and a simple blue silk jacket with matching trousers. Is it just my imagination, my insider's knowledge of her unclothed form, or is there a fine, invigorating tension between her natural abundance and the architectural strictures of the tailored suit? Or, then again, is it possible she actually looks kind of silly in clothes? I rise and hold her chair, brushing against her arm, inhaling an aggressive perfume.

"What do you know?" she asks.

"Less and less, Pallas. I'm in an epistemological recession."

"Do other people understand half the junk you say?" She doesn't seem worried, just mildly curious, head swiveling around the room. "Where are the celebrities," she asks. Apparently I'd promised her some.

Quick scan of the room. Somehow I doubt that the editor in chief at Farrar, Straus & Giroux qualifies in Pallas's book. So I decide to go on the offensive. "In what way would it improve your life if there *were*, say, a movie star in the room?"

"What?"

"Did you know that until relatively recently, historically speaking, actors were viewed as occupying a lower position on the great chain of being than, say, tapeworms or silverfish? They were viewed—and this is pretty hard to dispute when you think about it—as pretenders, poseurs, dissemblers; their moral character therefore highly suspect. I mean what explains this fucking international epidemic of thinking that people who are paid to simulate real life on-screen are somehow more *real* than the rest of us. We're suffering from a mass hysteria, an epidemic of surrogacy, vicariously living the lives of Pamela Anderson and Charlie Sheen."

Disinclined to lubricate the flow of conversation, Pallas seems to be searching the room again.

"So," I ask, "do you like your job?" A desperate conversational gambit.

After squinting for a long moment at a distant diner who turns out not to be famous, she glances back to me and shrugs her shoulders, thereby animating her chest in a mesmerizing manner. "Yeah, it's okay. It's kind of fun, I guess. The money's pretty great." She taps at the pack of Seven Stars I have absently removed from my pocket. "Hey, I didn't know you smoked. All the Japs at the club smoke that brand. We grow tobacco down where I'm from. Smokeless mostly. That was probably one of the reasons I left. Every time you make out with some stud you stick your tongue in the stuff. You'd reach down for a Coke or a brew and find yourself swigging some guy's spit."

Amazing—we are practically having a conversation. This is the longest speech I've ever heard from Pallas, replete with intimate glimpses of her past.

"What do you want to do with your life now that you're here," I ask cautiously. "I mean, you can't keep dancing forever."

"I want to be an actress."

"Ah, knock me over with a feather."

"How come you're so mean about actors?"

"Probably just jealous," I say.

"You should come to my acting class."

I wave to the waiter, who is surely in somebody's acting class, and point to my empty glass of Stoli Cristall.

"I think dancing's great training, you know, appearing before an audience and all, and it definitely helps with your inhibitions and all."

"Which inhibitions might those be, Pallas?"

"Do you know John Cusack?" she asks.

"Not personally. Why?"

"I was just thinking that guy over there kind of looks like him. A little."

"Have you heard from Chip Ralston?"

"Is that why you asked me to lunch?"

"I asked you to lunch because I'm tragically infatuated with you." Which is, oddly, somehow true, despite the fact that I'm even more desperately in love with Philomena than ever now that she has dumped me, despite the fact that everything that comes out of Pallas's mouth is a cliché or worse. This kind of love I could never explain to my sister.

"Somebody called from his manager's office. They made a date for dinner next week."

"Chip's manager's taking you out?"

"No, you dope. *Chip's* taking me out to dinner."

"I don't suppose you might tell me *where* Chip's feting you?"

"Actually, I don't know. Someone is going to call me that day and tell me."

The waiter comes over and recites the daily specials—all of which sound vaguely nauseating.

"How about a cocktail?" I suggest.

ONE OF MOM'S FAVORITE WORDS

Cocktail. One of the earliest of words I learned at my mother's breast. (In fact, had my mother breast-fed me I would have undoubtedly imbibed them with her milk.) *Shall we have a cocktail? . . . I think it's almost cocktail time.* I'd have my juice and she'd have hers, from which I was allowed a sip. And, afterward, the sweet-sour smell of her wet kisses and the sound of her laughter, like ice in a silver shaker. Whereas my father's word was *highball. I think I'll build myself another highball.* A word I'm less fond of, evocative as it is of masculine bluster, disputations and broken glassware. Then, once he'd built himself a highball and consumed it, he would pay himself a *dividend.* (This economic model seems to have fucked up my sense of capital formation and my chance of being an investment banker—the operative concept being that you got rewarded for consuming.)

Later in life, the word *cocktail* betokened a perpetual silvery Manhattan dusk when the night with its lurid promise was all ahead of you. A portmanteau of sorts, a sum of parts, a

word which seems to compound the two instruments of the
sex act, as practiced by heteros. . . . This thought turning rancid as I imagine Philomena splayed and impaled . . . and then I
recall last night's dream. . . .

Pallas orders a kir royale. I am drinking heavily, self-
consciously, though it apparently has no effect whatsoever.

A WAVE OF SADNESS

"Why should I tell you about Chip," Pallas pouts. "You could
be, like, one of those stalkers."

"I'm not crazy," I say. "I'm just . . . sad. I think my girlfriend's run off with someone else." I hadn't really intended to
tell Pallas, and I was not consciously trolling for sympathy.
Though I am gratified when she takes my hand and looks
directly into my eyes for what may be the first time in our brief
association.

"Poor, baby," she goes.

"I deserve it."

"She'll be back."

"I don't think so, Pallas." I haven't actually realized that I
believe this until I hear myself say it. I turn away from Pallas's
benign gaze, the lurid dream-image of Philomena poisoning
the air around me.

"Well, don't let any grass grow under your feet." She
reaches over and strokes my cheek.

"I can't blame her. I mean, look at me. Having lunch with
you, for instance. I mean, no offense, but."

"You're actually a pretty nice guy. Don't beat yourself up.
You never really even hit on me. Not really. I mean, do you
have any idea how rare that is? You wouldn't believe what I
have to put up with every night."

"Don't mistake timidity for virtue. Would you excuse me
for a minute?" Overcome with a sudden wave of grief, I lurch
downstairs to the phone, where I dial my machine and check
my messages.

Despite or even because of my appreciation of the lumi-
nous Pallas, all of Philomena's virtues have come crowding

back to claim my doting attention. The way she never returned from a trip without bringing me a present, for instance: a belt from Milan, a fucking beret from Paris, a pair of shades from L.A., an antique globe from the Upper East Side. The way she hid little notes in my luggage when I traveled. *Imagine me with you right now doing nasties all over your body.* Our first trip on ecstasy. Her childlike devotion to the rituals of Christmas. The fact that it was *possible* to have an interesting conversation with her, unlike certain other parties one might imagine oneself to be in love with, and despite the howling mindlessness of her so-called profession—certainly no more banal than my own.

TEMPORARY RELIEF

One message—from Jillian Crowe's office, asking me to call in immediately. Then, a hand on my shoulder—Pallas behind me, looking compassionate, concerned.

"You're crying," she says.

"I am?" She opens the door to the bathroom, which in fact is not equipped with a bath. "That's the men's," I say, as she peeks in. She nods, takes my hand and hauls me in behind her. She removes a Kleenex from her purse and wipes my eyes. Then she kisses me on the forehead. At which point I really fall apart. She embraces me, folding me into her soft contours, rubbing her hand across my back. "There, there . . . whoa, what's this? *Somebody's* feeling better."

Kissing my neck as her hands search for my fly, and then for the opening in my boxer shorts and then, Oh, God, as in: There is a . . . oh yes. I shouldn't be doing this—though I'm not really doing much of anything except submitting to the delicious friction. But it is already too late to contemplate resistance to the insistent rhythm of Pallas's ardent hand. . . . She releases me only long enough to (insert audible moan of pleasure here) lick her hand. And as she sets to her task it occurs to me that in sex, as in life, there is a delicate—and, in the current case, exquisite—balance between lubrication and friction. Facilitation and resistance.

"Pallas, *please*." Apparently this is my voice, with its urgent note of entreaty—though I am not sure what I'm begging for. More? Or perhaps I am asking her to promise that this flood of ecstatic sensation will never cease, or at least that the pain will not rush in again once it subsides. In any case, Pallas gently nibbles at my lips as her hands work their thorough wonders. I suspect she's had some practice. In fact she does it better than I do it myself.

But here's the really weird thing, as Pallas—God bless her—sinks to her knees: from that moment till the end, I am fantasizing about Philomena.

"Thank you thank you thank you," I groan, as Pallas spits discreetly into the sink and washes her hands.

"You needed that," she explains plausibly.

POSTORGASMIC DEPRESSION

Still thinking of Philomena, missing her more than ever as I hold the men's room door open for Pallas. And for a moment I hardly register the striking fact that Jillian Crowe is standing by the phone outside, very minimal and forbidding in a dark gray, probably Calvin Klein, suit, thirty blocks south of her usual lunchtime post at the Royalton. I am reminded of what someone once said about her: that she could have been beautiful if she hadn't decided to be elegant instead. Her eyebrows rise above the tortoise rims of her shades as she registers me and my companion. Unfortunately the pay phone is situated in such a way that it is difficult to squeeze past even someone as svelte as Jillian Crowe.

"I'll call back," she barks into the receiver. "*You* I've been looking for," she says to me.

I shrug. "Busy busy busy."

"Yes, I can see that."

"This is, uh, Pallas . . ." The Christian name, pagan as it is, hangs suspended in the air on a gust of rising intonation, for I realize I've never known her surname. "Pallas, Jillian Crowe." Jillian regards Pallas with that special condescension that thin women who look good in clothes reserve for voluptuous women who look best without them.

Turning to me, Jillian asks, "Where *exactly* do we stand on the Ralston piece?"

"I'm, well, still working on it."

"Ah, you two were discussing the article in the men's room, were you?"

"Chip?" Pallas inquires brightly. "We were just talking about him."

A sudden, stupid inspiration: "Pallas is Chip's girlfriend."

This has the desired effect on Jillian, who looks at Pallas with new regard, and Pallas seems to take it in stride, raising her shoulders. Jillian scrutinizes her more closely, as if remembering her dimly from another life and trying to figure out which one. "Weren't you at the Metropolitan Art Society benefit with Charlie Lapidus?"

Pallas shrugs. "I don't really recall."

This seems like a good time to leave. I slide past Jillian, towing Pallas, waving enthusiastically on my way up the stairs.

"Ralston by the end of the week, Connor."

"Ah, yes, well . . ." I dismiss her with a jaded flutter of my hand; somehow I have nearly convinced myself that the Ralston piece is well and truly under way.

Pallas for her part swans back to our table with the haughty bearing of a movie star's consort; upon resuming her seat she adopts the self-consciously oblivious celebrity mien, refraining from looking out around the room in order to avoid meeting the tedious stares of idolaters. She does it well, I must say. Even her manner with the waiter has a new callow intimacy. Laughing louder than necessary at my inane attempts to amuse her, she devours her steak while I ventilate my softshell crabs with my fork; how, I wonder, could I have failed to notice before now how much these crustaceans resemble the giant, unkillable water bugs that climb out of the drains in my apartment? Stabbing them again for good measure.

Later, I steer Pallas past Jillian's table and put her in a cab. "You're an angel of mercy," I say.

"You're sweet," she says absently, already gone, our adventure in the men's room ancient history for her, as she contemplates her future with Chip: the trips to Cannes, the Academy Awards, the pesky tabloid allegations.

HOME

I've been robbed. This is my first thought when I return to the apartment. The place is trashed, the contents of drawers and cabinets strewn across the floor and countertops. Or else my search for cigarettes and Philomena's diaphragm was more thorough than I realized.

No messages. One e-mail.

To: Scribbler@aol.com
From: Jenrod@inch.com
Subject: Photo
Dear Connor:
God I am *so* embarrassed, I shouldn't have sent you that picture but Tina talked me into it. It's like last year when she told us we had to beat down this girl she didn't like, I didn't want to but I did. Plus we'd been drinking and smoking and I wasn't really thinking too straight. If you haven't looked at it yet please don't, gotta go here comes my supervisor. . . .

TRUANT SISTER

A call from Brooke's psychopharmacologist:

"I'm sorry to bother you, Mr. McKnight, but I was a little concerned about your, ah, well, your sister. She's missed her last two appointments and she's not answering, that is to say she's not returning, my phone calls."

"I saw her last night," I say. "She seemed . . . okay."

"Ah," he says. "Well, I wonder if."

"You want me to have her call you?"

"Well . . ."

"Doctor, exactly how would you diagnose my sister's . . . problems."

"Well, I wouldn't want to, that is to say, there's no simple explanation. I would say that she manifests a complex of symptoms that I wouldn't want to——"

"Jesus Christ, Doctor. Is she clinically depressed? Would you say that? *Can* you say that?"

"She exhibits symptoms of depression, but I really can't . . . this falls in the area of doctor-patient—"

I hang up on the off chance that Philomena might be trying to call.

A CALL FROM MOM

"Hi, honey. How's every little thing with you?"

"Swell," I say. Mom has such a dreamy and ethereal disposition that I try never to puncture the bubble. The last, miraculous child of ancient parents, she grew up in an atmosphere of benign and privileged neglect in Charleston, then wafted through Bennington, till my father brought her to ground, briefly, after a mixer at Williams. When Dad graduated a few months later, they married and moved into my grandfather's house in Florida, where Mom resumed the life of her childhood—painting landscapes, tending the garden and riding. One hates to worry her. When Jeremy met her he declared that she was on her final incarnation, a nearly complete being making the final trip to earth.

"You sound tired," she says. "Are you all right, sweetie?"

"Just fine, Mom."

"I don't know how you do it," she says, "I swear you're going to work yourself to death up there."

"I'm okay."

"Your father sends his love. Is there anything I can bring you?" The annual Manhattan pilgrimage commences in a few days. I can't think of anything I want from Central Florida, except perhaps a sinkhole in which to disappear.

"Just your own sweet self," I say.

MAIL

Amidst the bills and magazines a letter for Philomena Briggs, addressed in handwritten block letters. No return address. The envelope, which has no watermark, is cheap enough that I can by holding it up to the light see a handwritten letter within, though unfortunately I can't really read it without tearing the envelope open. Which is the work of a moment.

Dear Bitch:
You think im a no body but well see about that. God made you pretty but I can make you ugly.

CONNOR TO THE RESCUE

Connor calls Philomena's booker, exhilarated by his legitimate fear for Phil's well-being.

"Liz, it's Connor. I've got to—"

"Sorry, Connor. Even if I knew where she was I couldn't tell you."

"She's in danger."

"Is that a threat?"

"There's a letter here from some nutcase—"

"Opening her mail, are we?"

"This guy knows where we live."

"Where *you* live."

"Jesus, Liz. I'm worried for her."

"If I hear from her I'll pass that on."

"But what about the letter?"

"All the girls get these things. What planet have you been on? If you send it along I'll put it in Phil's file."

"Please, Liz . . ."

"Goodbye Connor."

A SUMMONS

Call waiting clicks; Jillian Crowe's assistant is on the other line. "Jillian wondered if you would be available this evening to escort her to a dinner at the home of Christina Carlton and Jason Lentz."

Apparently my stock is up since I emerged from a restaurant men's room with Chip Ralston's alleged girlfriend on my arm and a shit-eating grin on my face. Christina Carlton is, of course, an actress: I once interviewed her, shortly before she married a music mogul.

"Jillian will be sending a car. Also an outfit."

"What, it's a costume party?"

"We have you down as forty regular. What size shoes do you wear?"

SARTORIAL AID

At seven-fifteen the town car arrives, glistening with sleety rain. The driver, a taciturn Irishman, hands me a garment bag and tells me he'll wait in the car. At least she didn't send someone to dress me.

I emerge stylishly from my apartment in my John Bartlett suit with navy-on-navy shirt-and-tie ensemble.

We drive uptown to pick up Jillian at her building off Madison. The doorman calls her while I stand in the lobby admiring the neoclassical architectural prints.

"You look wonderful," I say, admiring her tight, lime-green pants and black turtleneck.

She examines me, loosens my tie, shakes her head. "Lose the tie," she advises. "Always underdress a little, if only to make others worry that they're overdressed."

Satisfied, she takes my arm. "Anyway, we're going to the *West* Side."

BACKGROUND, SHALLOW AND DEEP

"They tried to get into 740 Park," Jillian informs me of our host and hostess. "Probably the best building in New York. Although the really secure residents use the other address, 71 East Seventy-first, which is the other entrance. But the board turned them down. I mean, what were they thinking? What was their Realtor thinking? Showbiz? CPW. A building like *that* doesn't want *show* folk. . . ."

"It's nice to know," I observe, "that there are still standards, somewhere."

She smiles, the first time in many moons that I have earned her approbation. "So tell me about your rest-room assignation. I'm quite impressed. Too bad you can't use it, it would make quite a nice little set piece: intrepid reporter emerging from the loo after a quickie with the oblivious star's concubine. Sad that we have such a morally upright editorial stance."

"Is that the stance where we try to convince young women to obsess about their appearance and weight while spending thousands of dollars on the clothing manufactured by our advertisers?"

"Is that supposed to be an original observation? Don't try to be cynical. You don't do it very well."

POLITE CONVERSATION
AT THE MAJESTIC

Jillian presents me to our hostess, Christina Carlton, a woman with extensive Broadway and Hollywood background who used to play sexpots but now is trying, reluctantly, to make the transition to playing somebody's mother. In the meantime marrying Jason Lentz, one of the many gentlemen who became rich by getting fired from one of Time Warner's music labels. Fortunately, surprisingly, she is pleased to see me.

"Oh, I remember you," she trills in a voice piercing enough to halt ancillary conversation. "I was so delighted with that lovely article you wrote, and I told my manager I wanted to do something nice for you, and he said, 'Well, darling, I'm sure he'd appreciate a nice blow job.' "

The room finds this a hoot, but what's more entertaining, I discover, is my reaction, exacerbated, perhaps, by the fact of Christina's suggestively puffed, chipmunk cheeks.

"Oh, look, he's blushing. He's actually blushing."

"I didn't know anyone knew *how* to blush anymore."

This remarkable talent of mine for showing embarrassment is remarked upon as I am introduced to the other guests, including my host, looking very much at home in jeans and a cashmere sweater; James Croydon, the editor of *Beau Monde*, in full Savile Row armor, who appears to be doing a Tom Wolfe imitation; and Todd Fulham, the decorator, in basic downtown black, who tells me he did the apartment, a ten-million-dollar penthouse disguised as an Adirondack hunting lodge. He takes me on a brief tour, pointing out the signed Stickley, the William Morris daybed, the Frida Kahlo canvas, the Hopi and Marblehead pottery. In the library, he hands me his business card on which he has also written his home number with the invocation *Anytime!*

"I'm afraid," I say, "that your talents far exceed my decorating needs."

"It's not your apartment I'm interested in."

"Well, I can't tell you how sorry I am to admit that I'm one of those poor bastards who's helplessly drawn to the opposite sex."

"Oh, come on," he says. "You're walking Jillian, you work for a fashion magazine for God's sake. Don't play straight with me." He strokes the sleeve of my borrowed suit as if to underline his point.

"Appearances can be deceiving."

"And deceit can be so appealing. Are you sure you're not just teasing me?" he says, as a liveried servant enters and announces dinner.

FAUX PAS

At the table I discover myself seated between Anne Sheridan, the designer, and a voluptuous young blonde whom I'm nearly certain I recognize as a dancer at Mount Olympus. She is the escort of Charles Lapidus, the grinch who owns airlines and cosmetics companies and a movie studio, and like me she is clearly out of place at this glossy gathering. She tells me she is a law student at NYU. When I ask her if by any chance we've met before she says coldly, "I don't think so," and ignores me for the rest of the evening. Anne Sheridan compliments me on my John Bartlett suit, and between courses remarks to our hostess: "Now, Christina, keep your head above the table at all

times." Everyone else seems to get the joke before I do. Blow
jobs seeming to be today's leitmotif. "Look," Anne says, "he's
blushing again."

I try to keep a low profile, which is fairly easy, since the
topics of chat are foreign to me, until the table starts in on the
O. J. Simpson civil trial.

"Can you believe Don Ohlmeyer is still friends with O.J.?"

"He actually believes he didn't do it."

"Oh, *come* now. The man isn't stupid."

"O.J. or Don?"

"Take your pick."

"I'd rather not, actually."

"And now he denies he ever beat her."

"There ought," I say, "to be a special circle of hell reserved
for any man who beats a woman." For some reason this comment seems to freeze the conversation. If I'd thought the sentiment was in any way controversial I would not have expressed
it. But those few people who bother to glance at me do so as if
I have just advocated some particularly egregious form of
child molestation.

Finally our hostess breaks the silence: "Can you believe,"
she asks, "that Whoopi Goldberg actually got past the co-op
board in the Forman's building?"

IN THE CAR, ON THE WAY HOME

"Was that your idea of a joke or were you *trying* to wreck the
evening?" Jillian asks as soon as the driver closes the door
behind her. "Don't tell me you didn't know that Charles
Lapidus beat the shit out of Samantha, his ex-wife. I mean,
you would have had to be living on the moon not to know
that."

"So *that's* why no one would look at me for the last hour."

"It was in every column in the city. My God. It's not
exactly like I can call him tomorrow and apologize. And what
did you say to his date to offend her?"

"I think she was upset that I'd seen her naked."

"You really are hopeless," Jillian says. "What ever inspired me . . . God, I'm so tense." She cocks her head from side to side, then slides over beside me. "Are you any good with your *hands*, at least? Make yourself useful and get this crick out of my neck." She turns in the seat, presenting me with her back.

As I tentatively knead her neck, she says, "Surely you can do a little better than that." I dig in. For all its outward grace and Nefertitian extension, her neck is as gnarled to the touch as an Alpine conifer clinging to a wind-scoured cliff. Philomena's neck would get this way; in order to facilitate the present task I pretend I'm unknotting her after a hard day in front of the cameras.

"I see your female fans are sending you dirty pictures."

"Beg your pardon?"

"There was a photograph going around the office today. Part of this morning's reader mail. Hardly suitable for publication. I must say you seem to be a very popular boy lately. I'm beginning to think you possess hidden talents." She places a hand behind my head and pulls me toward her; suddenly her tongue is probing my mouth like a plumber's snake.

"This is kind of awkward for me," I say when she finally releases my head and reaches for my belt.

"Worried about your girlfriend?"

"I'm not even sure," I say, "that I *have* a girlfriend."

She looks at me aghast. "What do you mean?"

"She's kind of missing at the moment."

"But she's coming back?"

I shrug. "I'd like to think so."

"God," she says, drawing herself away. "I didn't realize you were unattached."

"Is that . . . a problem?"

"I never fuck unattached men."

Not a moment too soon, we have arrived in front of Jillian's building.

"Don't bother, I can walk myself to the door. The driver will take you wherever you want to go." She kisses me on the cheek, her lips chapped as sandpaper, while the driver holds the door.

"If your girlfriend comes back, you can consider my offer open. And if she doesn't, well . . . I'm sorry."

The door closes. Jillian starts to walk to her door, turns and walks back to tap on the window, which I lower. "Next time you're shopping for steady companionship, I would advise you to avoid the narcissistic professions."

A TYPICAL MORNING
IN THE WEST VILLAGE

10 a.m. Wake. Headache. Remember that Philomena has abandoned you, and is probably waking up with someone else. Someone who in the first flush of new love gets to fuck her in the morning, as you once did.

Heartache. Back to sleep.

11:15 a.m. Waking again. Realize that Philomena is still gone. That some nutcase is out there stalking her. That he has obviously written to her before, yet she never even mentioned it to you. What else didn't she tell you?

Guilt-ridden at sleeping so late, you crawl out of bed and survey disorderly, depraved bedroomscape: shoes, socks, jeans, 'zines, empty Evian and Absolut bottles. Vow to clean up bedroom. Soon. For sure. Search top bureau drawer for the nude photo of Philomena that she gave you two years ago for Valentine's Day, for purposes of tormenting yourself, and possibly purposes of masturbation. Fail to find it. It, too, is gone. Consider what this means.

Could she have taken it back? Add this to your list of damning clues, along with her unpaid half of the rent and the missing diaphragm.

FURTHER CORRESPONDENCE

To: Scribbler
From: Lawgirl
Subject: Brooke
Bro:

Finally talked to Brooke which did little to ease my mind. Jesus, I feel bad about man's inhumanity to man, but not fulltime. Is she still seeing her shrink? Can't you take her out to see a movie, or something? She's not cutting herself, is she? Sorry about your girlfriend. Next time, try Black. You'll never go back.

REAL LIFE

11:20 a.m. Shower. No shampoo. Mental note: Buy some. File it next to yesterday's identical mental note. By this time your mind is as messy with untended business as your apartment.

11:45 a.m. Newsstand for the *Times* and the *Post*. The former because you're a serious guy and the latter because you're not.

11:48 a.m.–12:30 p.m. Acropolis Coffee Shop, consuming coffee, bagel and newsprint. Refugees in Zaire. Anna Nicole Smith redundantly in a coma. Whitney threatens to dump Bobby Brown unless he goes to the Betty Ford Clinic. A gang of schoolgirls in Queens slashing the face of one of their classmates with a boxcutter.

You look up at the framed photograph of Philomena, right between the big-haired soap star and Matthew Broderick. *Best to all the gang at the Acropolis.*

But what about me, Phil? What wishes for me?

Here in the far West Village, the midday coffee shop clientele is thankfully weighted in favor of goggle-eyed fast-breakers with pillow-pressed coifs sucking down coffee and staring suspiciously at their bagels, although there are a few early rising working folks tucking into their second meal of the day, devouring hamburgers and tuna melts. On the way out, a lingering look at the icon on the wall, your lost love smiling down on her public. *Best to all the gang. . . .*

12:48 p.m.—Safe at home, you sit at your desk examining mail, which comes complete with requests for money. Should you give to the Gay Men's Health Crisis, Amnesty International, your alma mater? "*Mr. McKnight,* won't you consider a gift of $1000 or more?" You would like to, but your bank statement shows some seven hundred less than that in your checking account. The phone and electric bills should certainly be paid. *Someone* ought to do that, some philanthropist perhaps, like that guy who died recently who used to award trust funds to injured cops and mugging victims. Second notice from the phone company, already ten days overdue. Picking up the receiver, you still get a dial tone! If only you could find your checkbook underneath all this paper. Here's something—a letter you received about two weeks ago:

CHAIN LETTER
With Love All Things Are Possible

This paper has been sent to you for good luck. The original is in New England. It has been around the world nine times. The luck has been sent to you. You will receive good luck within four days of receiving this letter provided you send it on. This is no joke. You will receive good luck in the mail. Send no money, send copies to people you think need good luck. Do not send money, faith has no price.

Do not keep this letter. It must leave your hands within 96 hours. An RAF officer received $470,000. Jon Eliot received $40,000 and lost it because he broke the chain. While in the Philippines, George Hish lost his wife 51 days after receiving the letter. He had failed to circulate the letter. However, before her death he had received $7,775,000.00.

Please send 20 copies and see what happens in four days. The chain comes from Venezuela and was written by Saint Anthony DeCrou, a missionary from South America. Since this copy must tour the world, you must make 20 copies and send them to friends and associates. After a few days you will get a surprise. This is true even if you are not superstitious. Do note the following: Constantine Dias received the chain in 1953. He asked his secretary to make 20 copies and send them. A few days later he won the lottery of two million dollars.

Dolan Fairchild received the letter and not believing, he threw the letter away. Nine days later he died.

Do not ignore this. It works.

Here perhaps is the source of your calamity and subsequent grief: like the hapless RAF officer you broke the chain. What if you had made twenty copies and mailed them out? *If only . . .* In your bereaved state this shrill imperative improbably strikes home; you are even prepared to believe in the omniscient narrator who has followed the exfoliation of this letter from Venezuela out across the planet, the last omniscient narrator on the planet, the others having retired or been fired from the good novelistic jobs, leaving this one poor slob to become a kind of ethereal gumshoe, a semiliterate detective shadowing the myriad incarnations of this barely grammatical letter into the office of Jon Eliot and the bedroom of Dolan Fairchild and up the brain stem of George Hish (which names, I might add, seem to me like the lumpy fabrications of an undergraduate creative writer) and on through your own mail slot into the hallway where you have planted your desk.

Oh, to be a character in an old-fashioned story. Or a big-budget romantic comedy, since Hollywood has taken over from novelists the business of wish fulfillment: Mixup unmixed, discord morphing to concord, misunderstanding understood. FADE TO: kiss.

In your pathetic, tenderized state you are almost prepared to believe in a capricious and personalized fate to which this innocent-looking piece of Xerox paper is attached as if by a rheostat. *Connor McKnight left the letter sitting on his desk. A week after receiving it his girlfriend packed up her diaphragm and disappeared. Two weeks later he was run over by a taxicab.* Maybe it's not too late. Maybe if you sent it out now. . . .

Looking for some business-sized envelopes in which to send out the chain letter you find the new issue of *Esquire Gentleman.*

A CALL TO THE COAST

1:05–1:32 p.m. *Esquire Gentleman.* Anyone for a bottle-green velvet dinner jacket?

1:33 p.m. Call Chip Ralston's scary publicist, Judith Viertel, in L.A. Secretary puts you on hold. And then over the receiver come the unmistakable strains in a Muzak version of Rod Stewart's "Do Ya Think I'm Sexy?" After you've listened to the whole song twice a voice breaks in—

"We're considering your request," she announces without preamble. You are astonished to be talking to her, Judith Viertel being the kind of publicist who practically has her own publicist—a fierce protector of the famous who is herself famously unavailable for bit players of the Fourth Estate like myself. "I'm faxing you a release specifying the parameters of acceptable questions and giving us approval of all quotations."

"I already signed, Judith. This was a done deal two weeks ago." Although you're not exactly proud of signing away your journalistic integrity, it's now standard operating procedure with the big stars, and it's not like we're talking about issues of national security here. Judith herself invented this particular form of prior restraining order a couple of years ago.

"Chip's in discussions with Tarantino right now, and then he's got to edit his documentary on the election. I can't be bothering him with this kind of shit. I'll have somebody get back to you in the next week or two."

And then, without further ado, she's gone. And you, my friend, are screwed.

1:45 p.m. Shuffle to the newsstand for a pack of Seven Stars and the *Daily News.* You haven't really started smoking again, just a temporary thing till you get through this crisis. It comes back to you, though, no question. Inhale, exhale. Like riding a bike. From zero right back to a pack a day. Light one right here in front of the store. Suddenly worried you might be missing a phone call from Philomena, you hurry back, dodging deranged panhandlers and weaving back through the oldsters bundled up in their wheelchairs in front of the nursing home, mummifying in the winter sunlight.

AN INTERLUDE OF SELF-DISGUST

1:51 p.m. No messages.

2:00–2:13 p.m. All around you the city hums with purposive activity and commerce while you wallow in a slough of sloth and despond. Your life has no purpose and no direction. No wonder Philomena left. The phone rings, thankfully abbreviating this line of self-flagellation.

"I can't write," Jeremy says. "I can't even read. The *Times* review's been postponed." God bless him, another unproductive citizen of the metrop. You can hear Todd Rundgren's "It Wouldn't Have Made Any Difference" in the background.

"Maybe you'll get one of the guys."

"You want to have lunch?" he asks. "Isn't that what what real people do, the civilians? Have lunch? Take lunch? *Do* lunch? What's the verb now? People with jobs and normal schedules. Correct me if I'm wrong, but don't they go to their offices and talk on the phone and go to meetings and save the world and then around about noon, twelve-thirty, they repair to coffee shops and restaurants to take on some well-earned calories, some charred mammal flesh on a bun or what have you, in the company of their *business associates*? I suppose," he continues, "that's one blessing about not having a real job. I don't ever have to use the phrase *business associates. Hello, this is Homer Lunchbox, my business associate. Shall we do lunch?*"

Many people might feel privileged to have Jeremy's schedule, to be the masters of their own time, but he often speaks as if he believes that his freedom and leisure are burdens inflicted on him by the lucky bastards who get to wake up to the alarm clock every morning and take a train to work, or for that matter to write mindless articles about empty-headed celebrities. This is what I love about Jeremy, his uncompromising unreasonableness.

I tell him I will be happy to try this crazy little thing called lunch, though truth be told I'm not very hungry.

AT THE EMPIRE DINER

"That tweedy asshole's staring at me."

"Why would he be staring at you?"

"I don't know, he probably hates Jews."

"Jeremy, you don't *look* like a Jew," I whisper. "Even your mother has her doubts. You look like a goddamn Swede. You look like Thor or Woden, for Christ's sake. Did you have a Scandinavian milkman when you were growing up?"

Whether or not the man in question, an aging prepster in Harris tweed, had any previous interest in Jeremy, he does turn toward us at this moment, revealing, it seems to me, a face that is more plausibly Semitic than my friend's.

"What's the matter?" Jeremy shouts. "You've never seen a Jew with long blond hair?" Holding up a hank of his blond mane.

An admirer of the sixties, Jeremy is still fighting the old battles, perhaps because he missed them at the time. Like the priest of a lost religion, he rails against the corruption of a society in which the Beatles' "Revolution" is used to sell sneakers.

"Is Lehmann-Haupt Jewish?" Jeremy asks.

"Actually," I say, "I have no idea."

"What's-her-fucking-name hates everybody except Anne fucking Tyler and Amy fucking Tan. I don't stand a chance. Wrong initials, wrong sex."

"When do I get a copy of the precious book?" I ask.

"You're on the list," he says. "Blaine's assistant's mailing the personal copies today."

We are sitting at the counter of this Platonic form of all diners, this chrome, black-and-white Art Deco photo stylist's wet dream of a beanery, waiting for our grilled cheese and tomato sandwiches. When we ordered a few minutes ago the counterman asked if we wanted them with bacon, and Jeremy erupted into a tirade about sulfites and nitrates, limited planetary resources and cruel and unusual methods of pig execution. I get nervous, therefore, when the man next to us orders a bacon cheeseburger. I am afraid that at the very least Jeremy will tell the man the story of his conversion: how, when he was eleven years old, he was driving with his parents and they passed a cattle truck on the highway, bearing a herd off to slaughter. Looking into the eyes of these cows, Jeremy had an epiphany, and pledged right then and there that he would never touch beef again. How Jeremy knew that these particular bovines were en route to the slaughterhouse I have never been able to determine. But he has stuck to his resolution for more than twenty years. Nothing with eyes.

While Jeremy would like to advise me about my problems, he has difficulty getting past his own. As a listener, he's like a man who can't ever quite seem to get out of the house; he keeps stopping at the door and turning back to get his scarf, checking to see if he accidentally left the stove on, and then suddenly the phone rings. . . .

Jeremy is too self-absorbed and tormented to spare much sympathy for others, but generally it is comforting to spend time with him because after getting an earful of Jeremy's inner life you feel blessed by comparison.

"When Natasha left me," he says, "I couldn't get out of bed for a month."

"You're *still* in bed, Jeremy."

"You're right," he says happily.

Natasha is the lost goddess of Jeremy's cult, the queen of a prelapsarian kingdom located in Middlebury, Vermont. They lived there together for six years, first as undergraduates and then as latter-day hippies, growing and eating vegetables, fucking and putting up fruit in Mason jars. As with Sean, the lamented Irish terrier, Jeremy didn't know what he had until it was gone, and he has been mourning it ever since. Although it has been seven years since Natasha left to find a room of her own, Jeremy speaks of their shared past, and the betrayal, as if it were yesterday. There have been other doomed romances, but Natasha is the primal wound, the pattern for all the others and for all his stories. In Jeremy's fiction, someone like Natasha is always leaving.

"Maybe she'll come back," I say.

"Natasha?"

"Philomena."

"She's gone, Connor. She's only coming back to get her clothes. Plus, watch, she'll take all the tapes and CDs you bought when you were together. They always do, even the ones they bitched about at the time. It doesn't matter that she absolutely hated *Led Zeppelin II* or *Louder Than Bombs*, it doesn't matter that she always told you to turn them down. She'll scoop 'em right up along with the complete works of the fucking Simon twins."

"You mean the Cocteau Twins."

"No, the Simon twins. Carly and Paul. Fucking *girl* music."

"For a vegetarian you're not very politically sound."

"Hey, do I look like a dork to you?"

Anyway, I think, I probably won't be able to listen to any of the old tunes, fraught as they will be with unbearable poignancy.

THE MAGIC OF TODD RUNDGREN,
THE REGRETS OF CONNOR

Jeremy listens constantly to the Todd Rundgren albums which constituted the soundtrack of his long idyll with Natasha. The ones he bought to replace the ones she took with her. As he reiterates between bites of his sandwich, he considers Todd the underheralded genius of recent times. Meanwhile, I am thinking about the ways in which I failed to keep Philomena happy:

- Withholding affection, perverse little gestures in the domestic struggle for dominance.
- Not kissing her as much as she wanted or perhaps needed to be kissed, gratuitous kissing somehow falling out of your repertoire after a year or so of living together.
- All the mornings you got annoyed when she tried to share something from the newspaper, acting put out about having your own reading interrupted.
- The Danish woman you made out with at Temple Bar.

- All the flowers you failed to bring home after the first few months.
- Pallas.
- Your unforgivable snobbery, most especially on the evening she tried to share her delight and wonder after reading Raymond Carver for the first time. "He's great," she said, and you said, "Hey, tell me something I didn't know."
- Being proud of the fact that she was a model.
- That actress in L.A.

No wonder she ran off with some other guy. What took her so long?

THE WISDOM OF PAI-CHING

"You haven't touched your sandwich," Jeremy points out, eyeing it with interest. Whatever his claims to sloth, he has already jogged five miles today, his standard practice, which presumably works up the appetite; I wouldn't know.

"Yeah, well." Charred and shiny with grease on my plate, it looks vaguely hostile. "The great Zen roshi Pai-Ching tells us, 'If one does not work for a day, one should not eat for a day.' "

"Zen, Schmen," says Jeremy. "The Chinese and the fucking Japanese, they're not real Buddhists. Any society that systematically indulges in wholesale whale killing, live monkey-brain eating, and the bloodthirsty harvest of endangered species for their alleged aphrodisiac body parts cannot call itself Buddhist. Plus Zen was what ruined Salinger. I mean, once he got into that one-hand-clapping shit it was all over."

"You want the sandwich or not?"

Jeremy switches plates while I stare balefully at a young couple smooching in a booth.

"Maybe I should just get in my car and drive," he muses. "Leave the state before the paper comes out, go someplace where they don't get the *Times*, where they hate New York."

CHAIN LETTER, CONT.

This letter has been around the world in a hundred and eighty days. Connor McKnight left the letter sitting on his desk. A week after receiving it his girlfriend packed up her diaphragm and disappeared. Two weeks later Connor discovered the letter on his desk. He sent out twenty copies and subsequently his girlfriend returned and said she loved him. It seems she had been hit by a taxicab in a foreign city and suffered a case of amnesia. The day after her boyfriend mailed this letter she regained her memory and came home. The day after her return, Connor found a paper bag on the street containing $2,830,520 in cash. They were married a week later and now divide their time between St. Bart's, Aspen and Tamarindo.

MISCEGENATION SPECULATION

Here's something I've been awaiting for about the last ten years: the first high-profile marriage of a Hollywood sex goddess to a Japanese billionaire. The fact that this hasn't happened already is inexplicable without reference to Japanese xenophobia. With a little help from good old American racism. These kinds of insights—and I have them all the time—could be worth money. Thinking that this particular area of inquiry nicely combined my underutilized background in Japanese studies with my beat as celebrity chronicler, I once tried to interest Jillian Crowe in an essay on this subject. Glasses on top of her head, Jackie style, she asked, "Connor, darling, do I honestly look like the editor of the *New York Review of Books* to you?"

OUR HEROINE CHECKS IN

Just leaving the apartment when I hear Philomena's voice on the machine: "Hi. You there? Guess not." Sounding none too eager to find otherwise, all too ready to hang up without a struggle.

As rapidly as any actor in Stetson ever unholstered a Colt Peacemaker I snatch the receiver from its cradle. "Where the hell are you?"

The silence lasts long enough for me to fear I've scared her off, like the fisherman who yanks his rod at the first flutter of the bobber. Finally, the line tightens from the other end: "That doesn't really matter."

"Come home. Please. No questions asked."

"I think I need some time to think."

"Phil, what are you doing? Where are you?" God, my voice sounds pathetic, tremulous, quavering between tenor and falsetto.

"Things haven't exactly been so great with us lately."

"I'll be better. I'll be so good you'll think I'm someone else."

"You're not so bad, Connor."

"Then why aren't you here?"

"Look, I've got to go."

"Who are you with?" I demand, desperately changing modes.

"I'm . . . not with anybody." I don't need a polygraph to confirm that the rhythm and tone of this response are all wrong.

"So why did you take your diaphragm?" I ask. "Who are you fucking while you're taking all this contemplative Virginia Woolf *Room of One's Own* time to think?"

A benighted sigh. "Goodbye, Connor."

"My parents are coming to town," I say, lamely. I believe this is called—in the terminology of logic—appeal to false authority.

"Say hi for me."

"That'll warm their hearts."

"I'll call in a few days," she says. And she's gone.

Deranged by jealousy and grief, I feel even worse—if such a thing is possible—when I realize I have forgotten to warn her about the letter, that she might be in danger. Furious at her for not allowing me to protect her.

E-MAIL

To: Scribbler@aol.com
From: Jenrod@inch.com
Subject: Chaos
Did you like the picture? I'll be at Chaos day after
tomorrow. Midnight. See U there? I'll recognize you
for sure.

To: Jenrod@inch.com
From: Scribbler@aol.com
Subject: Your Kind Invitation
My parents are coming to town, always an ordeal, and I
doubt that I will feel much like dancing. However, if I
haven't hung myself from the shower rod by then—
who knows? But you had better start without me.

INVENTORY

Between drinks I sift through Philomena's possessions, the
vodka bottle within reach. First her modeling portfolio, the
many beautiful moods of Philomena: funky in Sui; sultry in
lingerie; laughing amidst a clatch of gorgeous Merit smokers;
but more often blank, pouty, staring beyond the lens. The New
Model Demeanor, an expression beyond expression—the look
that says, *Not only will you never look like this, not only will
you never touch this, but I'm not even going to work for you.*
The exquisite boredom of the mannequin. *Let the actors act,
let them pretend to be something, I'm young and beautiful and
I desire nothing.* In these pix Phil looks so frighteningly like
all the other models—the way the saints in Byzantine mosaics
all look the same—that I can't always be sure it *is* Phil.

Dozens of pages of contact sheets. In her desk: a packet of
birthday and Valentine cards from yours truly, tied in a pink
ribbon, which I set aside, not presently feeling strong enough
to read them. The other cards and letters are revealing only
by virtue of their scarcity: a single letter from a model she

roomed with in Tokyo; infrequent postcards from her mother, chillingly newsy; a brief monogrammed note from my own mother congratulating her on her appearance in a Gap ad. A file folder with all of my published articles. Assorted amusing items from the *New York Post*, and a page from last month's *Vogue* on Chip Ralston with *FYI* scrawled over the headline— the gesture of a helpmeet. She was always saving items for me in her restless grazing of the glossies. Surely at the moment she so thoughtfully clipped this she wasn't thinking of leaving me. Finally, a draft of my lost and unlamented screenplay, *The Simple Life,* an offbeat romantic comedy about a writer and a model, inscribed on the cover page: *To Phil, my muse, leading lady of my heart.*

No secret journal. No trace of him—my enemy. Looking at the mirror she broke the night before she left, I wonder: How many years bad luck?

The clothes in her dresser are erotically mnemonic: here the skirt I pulled down in a frenzy one afternoon, here the sweater I was too impatient to remove on the same occasion. The generous, empty cups of her bras a painful synecdoche for her absence.

PSYCHOPHARMACOLOGY

"Maybe she's telling the truth," I say. "Maybe she just needs time."

After a sleepless night, I am in Brooke's apartment, watching her smoke a joint.

"You'd better have some of this," she says.

"You know I don't like drugs that make me feel stupid. I feel stupid enough to begin with. I like the drugs that make me feel incredibly smart, only I can't afford them."

"I *want* to feel stupid," says Brooke.

"You have more IQ to spare than the rest of us."

"Have you heard that song: *Don't want to get stoned, / But I don't want to not get stoned*?"

"When did you start keeping up with popular culture?"

"Some band called . . . the Melonheads? Is that right? Did

that guy die of an OD? I don't know." She examines the tarred, smoking roach as if it might tell her—I'm not about to, since she'll make fun of me for knowing. Finally she asks, "Have you tried any of these new smart drugs I hear about?"

"If you ever watched the boys and girls at a rave, you wouldn't hold out a lot of hope for the brain boost of putative smart drugs. I've always found, however, that if you add a couple shots of vodka, at least you *feel* smart."

"Connor, in your view, is there anything to which one doesn't add vodka?"

"Give me a sec. I'm thinking."

"Don't hurt yourself."

"Bourbon."

"What about it?"

"Something to which one doesn't add vodka."

"Jesus. You sure you don't want some of this? Little hit?"

"Only if you can guarantee it will bring Phil back."

"It's just an herb, not an industrial-strength toxin." She giggles. "What was the name of that band you liked?" she asks. "Retarded Youth?"

"Sonic Youth? Arrested Development?"

"Sounds like you either way."

The good thing about Brooke's smoking pot: maybe she'll get the munchies.

"Don't tell Mom and Dad about Philomena," I warn her as we head out to meet them.

TEA EN FAMILLE

"Geronimo," Brooke says when we bail out of the cab in front of the St. Regis.

And there they are—Mom and Dad, having a little chat with the waiter in the King Cole Bar. We sneak up and greet them awkwardly. Does everyone feel shy when they first see their parents again, or is it just me? The feeling being: Yes, of course I remember you, but I hope to God you've forgotten that thing I did with the cantaloupe when I was fourteen. My mother hugs me unreservedly, smelling faintly of sunshine and oil paint. My father and I have a special dodge-and-feint routine which results in a kind of brief, manly half-embrace. Unless he's drunk. So the good news is he's sober, or else he'd be clinging to my neck and telling me that he just wants me to know that he loves me in spite of everything and he really hopes—and he's not just saying this—that he hasn't been too really *awful* a father.

"Brooke, darling," says Mom. "Have you been sick?"

"Good God, Brooke," blurts Dad. "You look like you've been at Auschwitz."

"I do wish," Brooke says, "people would stop frivolously invoking one of the major horrors of the century for purposes of cheap physical analogies."

"She's had the flu," I say, instinctively covering for her.

"I thought," says Dad, "we'd gotten over this problem after Madeira."

"There's been a lot of flu this year," Mom says helpfully. "I think it comes from Hong Kong, like so many other things. Your father and I went there four or five years ago and it was really absolutely fascinating. All these Chinese people. Dad got me the most beautiful string of . . ." She drifts off for a moment, as is her wont, her attention snagged by something in the middle distance.

"String of teeth?" says Brooke.

"What a perfectly wonderful idea—a string of teeth," Mom says. "I used to save your baby teeth. I wonder what happened to them?" She seems stumped. "Let's have a drink, shall we? A festive cocktail?"

The waiter has rematerialized at this opportune moment.

"Tea for me," says red-eyed, righteous Brooke.

Mom starts humming "Tea for Two," pausing to order her own drink. "Do you think I might just have some Campari with a little bit of sweet vermouth and a splash of seltzer." The waiter raises his pencil from the pad with a flourish, as if to say it is his pleasure to entertain strange drink orders, but Mom isn't quite finished. "With a slice of orange . . . in a snifter." She shapes a big bowl with her hands. "And do you think could you float a little teensy bit of gin on top?"

The waiter is reeling.

"Basically," I explain, "my mom wants a negroni on the rocks with a splash of soda."

Brooke says, "I'm sure that clears things right up, Connor."

"Is *that* what I ordered?" Mom asks, smiling at me, her very bright child. "It sounds so sophisticated the way you say it."

Dad can hardly contain his impatience and barks his order: a Johnnie Walker Black with soda. Good manly stuff. He drinks Red at home, Black on special occasions. In his book, both are equally efficacious. With a cringe of apology directed toward Brooke, I order a Bloody Mary. Yes, I find it cheers up the tomato juice considerably, that little splash of vodka. These fucking potheads can get very self-righteous about alcohol, though it's true that no one in my family ought to be encouraged to drink. Not that Mom and Dad have ever needed any encouragement. Just point them at the bar and stand back.

"The city looks very festive," Mom says.

"We tried to fluff it up for your arrival," Brooke says. "Connor put up a humongous evergreen over in Rockefeller Center and I tied a giant red bow around Cartier."

"My clever ones."

"So, what do you think of your mayor?" Dad asks me. I almost get the impression that he imagines that I sit down every so often with Rudy and discuss the future of the metropolis over drinks.

"Actually," I say, "he kind of gives me the willies."

My father frowns. "Well, I'll tell you one thing. You could sure as hell use a Republican mayor in this crazy town."

Speech suddenly seems perilous with so many subjects to be avoided—Brooke's anorexia, Dad's drinking, politics.

"Let me give you just one example," he says. "Waldorf-Astoria. New York landmark, right? Classmate of mine, Billy Buxton, Billy was general manager when they renovated the place, must've been fifteen, twenty years ago. Endless delays, holdups, thefts of material. Just for instance, one day the carpenter's union gets mad at the plumber's union. So what do you think they do? Pour cement in all the drains in every last room. Little prank to register their unhappiness with the plumbers. Every single pipe in the building has to be ripped out to the tune of a few million smackeroos. Did the carpenters pay for that? I don't think so. The plumbers picked up double overtime to pull the pipes out and replace them. After the carpenters had ripped open the walls for them. That . . . ," he says, pointing a finger at my sternum, "that's a New York Story for you."

"Naked city," says Brooke.

"You look tired, Connor," says Mom. "Have you been just working yourself to death up here?" It is Mom's opinion that Yankees, and especially New Yorkers, work far too hard and long, thereby compromising their health and serenity. If she only knew.

"Connor's been making the world safe for celebrity," says my adoring sister.

"I just don't know how you-all do it," says Mom, her tone combining admiration and exhaustion.

"Some of us don't," Brooke replies.

"It's no wonder," Mom says, "you had to take a rest from that dreadful school of yours."

"What, exactly," Dad ventures, "is your status at the university?"

"I'm on basket-weaving leave," says Brooke.

"I mean to say . . ." But whatever Dad means to say is thankfully lost as the waiter arrives, as welcome as the mail boat pulling into a South Sea harbor.

"Cocktails," Mom announces brightly as she hoists the skewered orange slice from her drink and inspects it. "California," she concludes.

Dad signals for the waiter, who scurries over. "My wife would like a slice of plump, juicy Florida orange in her cocktail."

"Beg your pardon?"

"As opposed to this desiccated wedge of California . . . whatever. Could you forward that request up the chain of command?"

The waiter says he'll see what he can do.

"Bing Crosby," says Dad. "Remember that little piece of business? He takes our money, does the ads for Florida. Then turns around and puts his money into Sunkist. Makes a fortune on those dried-out California navels. It's an arid state, for Christ's sake. A desert. How the hell do they expect to grow a juicy delicious citrus product?"

Mom informs us that a near neighbor's orchard in Florida has . . .

THE SPREADING DECLINE

which comes from a worm—called a nematode—that feeds on the roots of orange trees (which in Florida are invariably grafted on the rootstock of lemon trees, but that's another story). The tree dies slowly, from the top down, while the yield steadily decreases. The spreading decline was frequently invoked by the male parent as the ultimate and inevitable judgment on those children who didn't appreciate just how lucky they were to have a large, watertight roof over their heads.

THE SILK ROUTE

Later, after the hospitality director has promised my father to inquire into the possibility of using Florida oranges for all the hotel's juice and garnish needs, we take a family stroll up Fifth Avenue, gazing glazily at the little gemlike Tiffany windows with their gingerbread Christmasy landscapes, then slice briskly through the bright crunchy air of late November over to Hermès to buy Dad his annual Christmas tie. With a pang I recall that last year I bought Philomena (among many other excellent presents I couldn't afford) a horsey, colorful Hermès scarf. As I recall she liked it, liked the vision it conjured of some future self as a respectable Park Avenue lady swinging her perfect shoulder-length coif across Seventy-fifth Street on her way to lunch at Mortimer's. Certainly she liked it better than the Marc Brouwer dress, with its formfitting clinginess and plunging neckline. "What are you trying to do, pimp me?" she demanded. No, God no, not that, though it occurs to me I might have been guilty of trying to show her off just a bit.

But I didn't want other guys to *fuck* her, *honest*. I just wanted other guys to *want* to fuck her. There's a big difference.

Disposed as I am at this moment to blame myself, I am also aware that it could easily have gone the other way last Christmas, depending on the sheerest of whims: Philomena might have been furious at the scarf, taken it as a sign that I saw her as aging and frumpy. . . .

Not that I'm complaining. Really, I'm not. Come home. All's forgiven.

"What do you mean there's no Christmas tie this time of year," Dad demands of the clerk. "There's *always* a Christmas tie."

"I'm afraid we didn't do an actual Christmas tie per se this year, sir."

"But I always buy the Christmas tie," my father says unhappily. "Every year." At this moment it is easy to imagine him as a small boy. Like me when I wanted the minibike for Christmas and got the deluxe chemistry set instead.

Mom and Dad go on to Brooks Brothers, the next stop on the McKnight New York circuit. Advent Stations of the Cross. Dad is irritated when I excuse myself. It's a family thing, going to Brooks, getting the big nod from the old-fart salesmen who have been waiting on Dad for years. I plead work at the office, agreeing to meet them later at Wally's and Joseph's.

"Oh, let's do see your office," suggests Mom. "Isn't it right near Brooks Brothers?"

"There's really nothing to see," I say truthfully. Although if she met my parents, Jillian might be inclined to cut me some slack. "Really, go on and enjoy the town. I'll catch you at seven."

DEUS EX MACHINA

Back at the apartment, I find a box from the phone company in the entry hall. Inside is my brand-new phone unit with digital-display window featuring caller ID. I connect the phone as per instructions and stare at it hopefully, but I'm no more successful in willing Philomena to call than I am at telepathically commanding Brooke to eat.

THANKSGIVING CHEER

Recently in the *New York Times* Frank Prial wrestled with that perennial question: what wine to match with your Thanksgiving turkey and traditional fixings. Some say champagne, some chardonnay. Frank leans toward zinfandel, and there's even a case to be made for a young cabernet sauvignon. Be advised that my father recommends Johnnie Walker Black, over ice, mixed with moderate amounts of club soda or seltzer water. Cuts right through the tart sweetness of the cranberry sauce which makes Thanksgiving wine matching so tricky. And none of these pretentious single malts, thank you very much.

Thanksgiving dinner at the St. Regis. Traditionalists that we are, Mom and I are working on a bottle of champagne. Mom has pronounced the bubbles "very festive."

Doug, old Mad Dog himself, is throwing back the Diet Cokes like there's no tomorrow. Brooke is sipping mint tea, like the hippie she once was, glaring at the food, or at least I think she is, though she has yet to remove her sunglasses, a detail which would hardly bear mentioning in the more fashionable precincts of New York, but Brooke is scrupulously untrendy. What I find most curious is that no one has decided to comment on Brooke's shades, not even my father, whose notions of pukka comportment and sartorial propriety are so severe.

"I love Thanksgiving," Mom says.

"I find it difficult to give thanks," Brooke mutters, "when so many people in the world are suffering tonight."

"Give thanks you're not one of them," says Dad, tucking into a fresh scotch.

"In Mogadishu a family of four doesn't see this much protein in a month."

"You must see a lot of suffering," Mom says to Doug. I still don't understand why he had to come. Doesn't he have his own fucked-up family to annoy?

Doug shrugs stoically, making himself appear for a moment even more neckless than usual.

TRAUMA, THEORY AND PRACTICE

"Is there a special season," Mom asks, "or a time of the month or anything when you get more traumas than other times?"

Dad snuffles at this question—that nasal exclamation of a man who is at once accustomed to, and yet never ceases to be amazed by, the eccentricity of his wife's questions.

"No, actually, that's a good question," Doug says, answering Dad's snort. "The full moon is the worst. Emergency rooms are always extremely frenetic the night of a full moon. We see more knife and gunshot wounds. I don't really know how to explain it scientifically, but the empirical evidence is fairly convincing. What's easier to account for is the fact that sick children, particularly from economically disadvantaged neighborhoods, tend to be brought to the emergency room after eleven p.m."

Mom looks happily perplexed. "And why is that?"

"Because that's when prime-time television ends."

"The children wait until after prime time to get sick?"

"I believe," Dad says, "Brooke's, uh, *friend* means that the *parents* wait until after their favorite shows are over before they bother to bring the little urchins in."

"That's dreadful." Mom turns to Doug. "Is that true?"

Doug nods sadly.

"I assume," Dad says, "we're speaking of the economically disadvantaged."

"The worst are the self-mutilators," says Brooke, rising out of her stupor to do a brief promotional spot for her beau. "Can you imagine having a ward full of desperately ill and injured people to tend to, and having to spend two hours on some guy who, well, tell them about that thing yesterday. . . ."

"Well," says Doug, "I wish I could say it was a unique case, but in fact we've seen it before. Patient arrived on the ward yesterday under his own power, clutching a towel to his groin, we estimate he lost more than thirty percent of his blood."

"Don't tell me," says Dad.

"Fortunately, his sister had recovered the, uh, penis, and put it on ice."

"He cut it off himself?" asks Mom.

"I'd think," I say, "you'd bleed to death."

"No actually, curiously enough, in a clean, perpendicular cut the veins tend to dilate and self-seal, as it were—"

"Doug spent ten hours in surgery," says Brooke.

"Now, on the other hand, if the penis were sliced diagonally, there would be a much greater danger of fatal blood loss since the veins—"

"Stop, for God's sake!" Dad shouts. "Is this any kind of dinner table conversation."

I don't know, I kind of agree with the old man, although I can't help feeling a healthy sort of morbid curiosity, not to mention a twinge of sympathy for Doug, the outsider, who draws his head down even farther into his shoulders like a scared turtle. I mean, it's a little unseemly, this skilled healer cowed by my elegantly useless father.

Brooke says, "God forbid a little reality with our happy repast."

"Doug," says Mom, "are you sure you wouldn't like a *teeny* bit of champagne? Or a nice cocktail? Something with a bit of fruit and fizz?"

MORE BEVERAGE NOTES

One factor Frank Prial doesn't take into account about holiday potables is their combustibility. When long-separated members of the same family are soaked in spirits and rubbed together, explosions almost inevitably result. Maybe the turkey is a catalyst of some sort. This year it happens after I ask Mom how she met Dad. It's a story I haven't heard in years, certainly never with the vivid dramatic detail she gives it this afternoon.

BOY MEETS GIRL, SPRING 1955

"We used to think Williams boys were so square," she says, sipping delicately at her champagne, the stem of the flute pinched lightly between age-spotted pointer and thumb. "And of course they were."

A curmudgeonly harrumph from my father here, who could almost pass for a square college boy, still dressed in the uniform of his preppy youth—blue blazer, blue oxford button-down shirt and regimental tie—his pink, pickled face unlined by the tussles of commerce or metaphysics.

"We used to think Bennington girls were artsy-fartsy dykes," counters my father, who, after all, was the captain of the debating team.

"And the Williams boys were so very tolerant of diversity," Mom continues, winking at us. "But we had to admit they were awfully good-looking." She smiles sweetly at my father, who pretends not to be interested in this story. Beneath her sun-and-nicotine cured skin, Mom's still girlish, her pale blue eyes childishly bright, her long hair worn just as it was at Bennington, the gold now ghosted with silver.

"I drove down with Cassie Reymond and some other girls. Cassie was an actress who later moved to New York and last I heard she was married to that actor who was in that wonderful play, what was it called, about the—it wasn't with Richard Burton but somebody like that?" She looks hopefully at my father, who coughs impatiently into his hand.

"*Camelot?*" Doug proposes.

Oh, *do* shut up, Doug.

Beside us, a silent Japanese family, oblivious to the feast of the Pilgrims, wraps itself around some steaks. Father, mother, two solemn preteen daughters in severe white blouses and pageboy haircuts.

"Anyway, we got there and it was awful, all these fierce, shy, hungry boys in their nice J. Press suits and their crewcuts, waiting to pounce. We drove down in Cassie's car, thank God, but there was a bus that arrived from Smith or somewhere like that, someplace frilly and proper, maybe Holyoke I don't know. Anyway, this bus came just as we pulled in and the boys were just waiting there. They formed a kind of gauntlet or gamut—what is it? I can never get those two things straight. Is gauntlet the glove that you throw down when you challenge somebody to a duel, or is that gamut? Anyway this was the other one."

"*Gauntlet* is actually the word you're looking for," says Doug. "I think," he hedges, for modesty's sake.

"And then there's *gimlet*," says Mom. Speaking of words.

Here at the St. Regis they serve the fancy, lumpy cranberry sauce with real berries, but I prefer the cheap jellied kind. It appears that I am the only one paying any attention at all to his food. No, actually—Brooke seems to be carving a mandala in her mashed potatoes. "So," she says, looking up wearily. "As far as I can tell nothing happened. Maybe you and Dad never actually met. Which would account for this feeling I have that I'm not *really* here. Which would account for this continuing ontological skepticism with regard to myself."

"Oh, we met, all right," Mom assures her. "I spotted your father hovering halfway through the dance. He was dressed exactly the way he is now—blue blazer and a blue oxford-cloth button-down shirt and the striped tie. Could be the same tie." My father looks down at the neckwear in question, pennant of some lost regiment of the king's army, and shakes his head. In fact he went to Brooks Brothers yesterday in order to stock up on these very items, these crucial components of the uniform which tell my father and the world who he is. "He was kind of cute square," Mom continues. "And, oh, I remember—he was wearing saddle shoes."

"Not I," my father says, but I could see he was enjoying this. "White bucks, maybe."

"You were. That was almost the cutest part about you, your nervous little brown-and-white feet."

"My feet are *not* little. Nine and a half C." He turns to Doug. "You call that little?"

"He kept making these circles around us, getting a tiny bit closer with each swing, all nonchalant and pretending not to notice me, though of course it was hard to tell which girl he was pretending not to notice, since there were four of us and he was so pointedly oblivious. Well, he panicked when they announced the last song—I think it was 'Smoke Gets in Your Eyes.' "

My mother breaks off her narrative to warble a bar: *"They asked me how I knew / My true love was true . . ."*

"What's the matter with you?" my father demands, noting my suddenly crumpled demeanor. Philomena and I used to love that song in its Bryan Ferry version. And now here I am, acting it out.

"And when another boy asked me to dance," Mom resumes, "I realized it was me he'd been pretending not to notice because his face just collapsed, he just wilted as this flattop boy with no neck trotted me off. I could feel those lovely sad blue eyes watching as we danced."

My father snorts in disapproval of this pitiful portrait. "Oh, come now."

"Well, I dragged my feet on the way out—if I'd walked any slower I think I would've taken root in the pavement like a big old cypress tree in a swamp—and I was just about to give up on him when I felt a hand on my shoulder in the parking lot."

"What'd he say," asks Brooke.

"He asked me if I wanted a tour of the campus."

Brooke hoots with laughter. "At least he didn't ask you to see his etchings."

Dad turns pink as a boiled shrimp. The Japanese family aims their solemn dark eyes at us, strange noisy gaijin. *Ah, so desu—this is typical American family.*

"I did *not* say that," Dad insists.

HOW TO GET YOUR BEAU
TO POP THE QUESTION

"Well, I didn't really need to see the campus, but I told him I'd love to go someplace where we could talk. So we ended up sitting in his roommate's Buick. And of course the talking led to kissing. I thought he was just a wonderful kisser, and after about ten minutes I realized he was just in agony, and so of course I wanted to help him. It seemed like the least I could do."

"Lillie!"

"And the poor sweet boy was so grateful he proposed to me right there in the back of the Buick."

"What," Brooke asks, "you gave him a blow job?"

"Young lady!"

"Heavens, no," says Mom, "I just, you know, used my hand."

DAD DEMURS

"This is not family conversation!" Dad thumps the table with his fist, making shimmery waves on our beverages.

"You got a proposal out of a hand job?" Brooke's impressed, Doug nonplussed. Meanwhile, I'm thinking back on my luncheon encounter with Pallas; perhaps I should've proposed, offered to take her away from all this. . . . But where? And once upon a time, when we were still mad for each other and conscious of it every moment, Philomena gave me a hand job in a cab. Why didn't I propose to her then? Why didn't I ever? God, I was stupid. If only I had, she'd be sitting here now, eating Thanksgiving dinner, comparing notes on postejaculatory proposals with my mom. *Well, when I jerked Connor off in that cab, right before the cabbie told us to get out, he just up and asked me on the spot.* What she'd be seeing at this exact moment, if she were here, is my father rising unsteadily to his feet like a booster rocket on the launchpad, wobbling, shrugging off the clench of gravity. He nearly tips over as he unexpectedly reaches full extension, but quickly regains the vertical. "This is not . . . I simply won't have it."

He slams his open hand on the table to get our attention, snaring that of our fellow diners as well.

The Japanese are agog. Is this a typical American custom?

The waiter dashes over. "Is everything all right, Mr. McKnight?"

"Oh, everything is just grand. Just marvelous. My wife wants the whole world to know about our intimate relations. A nice family discussion about hand jobs on Thanksgiving Day."

No question, he has the attention of the entire room now. The captain is edging over our way, and the other diners have turned away from their turkey and stuffing and their own pallid conversations. Dad notes this, and seems to start playing to the room. I recognize the look in his eye. He had the same look just before he launched the turkey across the dining room a couple years back.

"Splendid. Hand jobs in the old Buick. Maybe over Christmas dinner we can talk about oral sex. My daughter seems to favor that subject. Lovely. Why don't we just let it all hang out, as you kids say. Very modern. Silly of me to cling to these old-fashioned notions of decency and modesty. Behind the times. Nothing's taboo, nothing's sacred. It's on television every day now, people falling all over themselves to reveal their most intimate filthy secrets. Splendid. Tell America, tell your own son and daughter all about their father's sex life. Brooke, Connor, anything else you'd like to know? Anything your mom's left out? Maybe she'd like to tell you about my private . . . parts. We could go on TV. That would be very modern. Excellent. Why don't we just have a show-and-tell."

The captain has arrived just behind and to the right of my father's chair; he intervenes quickly, but not quickly enough, as Dad unzips his fly.

The two young Japanese girls at the next table simultaneously raise their hands to cover their mouths, though not their eyes. Their mother squeals—I can't help wondering if she's thinking about comparative anatomy—and then it seems to me the room falls silent.

Even *I* am stunned, accustomed though I am to our dramatic family gestures. When my father throws his arms open in a gesture of theatrical finale, the captain instinctively reaches down toward the exposed member, then snaps his hand back, just short of its apparent goal, as if he'd been bitten, judgment triumphing at the last moment over impulse. The problem, from his point of view, seems insuperable: how to conceal the offending organ without touching it. My father seems to grasp his dilemma, and to delight in it. His anger has metamorphosed, through the miraculous alchemy of alcohol, into perverse glee. The lawgiving patriarch has switched places with the anarchic child. Grinning impishly, he plants his hands on his hips in defiance of the would-be guardians of propriety.

The waiter, on a sudden inspiration, removes the serviette from his forearm and gingerly tucks it into the waist of Dad's gray flannels. And finally, after several eternities, the captain and the waiter together succeed in leading him off. "Just trying to catch up with the times," he tells them. "Trying to satisfy the curiosity of my loved ones. My beloved family, such a goddamn comfort to me in my declining years. . . ."

I sit grimacing at Brooke—who looks back at me with a kind of jaded chagrin—and try to pretend that I am not in this room, that my father did not just whip out his dick in Lespinasse in front of forty or fifty people, that they are not still staring at us, the family from hell, that Mad Dog was not here to witness this mortification so that on top of everything else I have to suffer a sense of familial embarrassment vis-à-vis Doug.

Here's what I'm thinking: If I had the choice of turning back the clock five minutes so that this never happened, or living through it all again and having Philomena back, faithful and happy, which would I choose?

"I thought it was a cute story," says Mom.

Of course I would choose Phil.

"It was, Mom." Brooke pats her papery, sun-speckled wrist. "I think we all really enjoyed it, except possibly Dad. Connor, you'd better go find him."

"No, actually I think I'll just rush down to City Hall and change my name, thanks."

"I'll go," says Doug, the helpful bastard.

"All right," I say. "I'm going, I'm going."

"He's never done that before," Mom notes for the record.

MORE WINE NOTES

Attn: Frank Prial: I am thinking, for next year's apéritif, maybe a nice glass of hemlock.

STILL OUT THERE, SOMEWHERE

Returning to the apartment, I flop down on the sofa, looking forward to some analgesic football. To someone from another country, this gnashing of bodies would appear chaotic, and yet there is a deep pattern here, helpfully illustrated by the commentators after each play. Even if there's no analogy with my own lurching progress, it's nice to watch some other guys get beat up for a change. And yet the choking melancholy seems only to mount within me. Finally I realize that the nubbly wool of the sofa is redolent of Philomena—the sweet smell of her soaps and unguents as well as the deeper, funkier scents— that my head is placed exactly where she usually sits, and I recall that the last time I saw her sitting in this spot she was gamely reading Faulkner's *Wild Palms*, looking up from her gorgeous trance to ask me vocabulary questions . . . and once again my eyes cloud over with tears. After at least a dozen tear-free years I have become a veritable artesian well.

Nose to the cushion, I am furiously attempting to masturbate when Philomena's phone chirps in the bedroom. Member in hand—his father's son—I walk over to the door to listen for the message, hoping for a clue, hearing only a series of clicks and beeps, the hiss of the answering tape. I'm already back on the couch when I realize that it's *her*—checking her messages from wherever she may be.

Racing back to the bedroom, tearing the receiver from its cradle. "Phil, hello, is that you? Please, don't hang up. Talk to me, will you? For Christ's sake. Where are you?"

"Hello, Connor," she says gravely, after a long silence. As though she knew of a terminal illness about which the doctors have not yet informed me, the patient. "I thought you'd be out with your family."

"I was."

"How are they?"

"Please. One sordid melodrama at a time. Phil, come home."

No response to this plea.

"Where *are* you?"

"I'm . . . it doesn't make any difference."

"Or should I say, with who?"

"Don't you mean *whom*?"

"What is this—levity?" I scream. "You wouldn't even know the difference if I hadn't taught you."

Another silence at the other end. I'm horrified at my own lack of charity, not only because I fear she'll hang up.

"I'm sorry, Phil, I didn't mean . . . I'm just sick with missing you and thinking about you fucking some—"

"Connor, don't. This is about you and me. It doesn't have anything to do with anybody else."

"Then why do I think it's about you trading up in the world?"

"Maybe you have low self-esteem."

"No shit."

Just when I can't think of what else to say I remember the threatening letter. I tell her about it, offer to go get it, though I'm glad when she tells me not to bother, since she'd probably hang up in the interval.

"It's this guy who saw me in *GQ*. He's mad because I didn't respond to his marriage proposal."

"What, you have a relationship with this fucking guy?"

"No. He's just written me some fan letters."

"How come I never heard about this?"

"I don't know."

"I guess there's a lot you haven't been telling me."

The silence stretches out. At least she's still on the other end, and we're not actually fighting. I'm loath to intrude on this hushed respite, and after a minute or more I begin to cherish it as a kind of intimacy. As an observer, I become curious about how long it will last, until I become fearful that she may break off before I've had a chance to state my case, whatever that might be.

"Do I know him?" I ask at last.

"The letter guy?"

"No, the diaphragm guy."

She sighs. "Maybe we should just focus on practical things," she says. "Can we do that, please? I'm sending a moving company over next week. Do you think you could be there to let them in?"

"Do you still love me *at all*?"

"Don't ask me that."

"Did you ever?"

"Don't be ridiculous, Connor."

The sound of my name on her lips is exquisite torture. "That's my role. To be ridiculous. That's the part I get to play in this little farce aspiring to tragedy."

"You're not ridiculous. Except when you talk like that." She laughs. "Who else would say 'this little farce aspiring to tragedy.' "

"Come home." My voice a pathetic birdlike squawk, its tonality undeniably ridiculous.

"Don't make this harder than it has to be."

"I don't quite see how it's been so terrifically backbreakingly hard on you. You haven't even . . . you haven't been willing to face me or even talk to me. Seems to me like you've made it pretty goddamn easy on yourself so far."

"You had three years to talk to me, Connor. You *don't* talk. At least not to me."

"I talk."

"Not about your feelings."

Could this be true? I don't think so. Well, maybe. I don't know, I thought there would be plenty of time for that later; I thought it was bad manners to yammer away about your problems. "I could learn," I say. "Okay? I could, you know, learn how."

"It's too late, Connor."

"Why is it too late? Don't say that." Tears are sluicing down my cheeks, leaking into the holes in the mouthpiece of the Princess-model phone. It might be simplest if I were suddenly electrocuted here, crying into Philomena's telephone. Except that I have one last desperate gesture to make: "Phil, I want you to marry me."

A year ago, six or even three lousy months ago, Philomena would have crawled through the phone to say yes. Not that I flatter myself with the idea that being yoked to me forever is so irresistible. But I do believe the idea of marriage seemed to her the perfect cure for a complex of yearnings and disappointments, most notably an imperfect childhood; and I was the logical candidate if only because I was *there*. We talked

about it, alluded to its eventuality in that sensible way of couples who have lived together a long time. And indeed, she was
waiting. She hinted, no, she actually stated outright that she
wouldn't wait forever. That there were other men who thought
she was pretty great, who would leap at the chance. Warning
me about this very moment, when it would be too late because
she would be gone. Yes, I remember now. But what the fuck
was I thinking about then? I don't know what I was doing.
Waiting for absolute certainty, I guess. I should've listened to
Brooke when she was trying to explain Heisenberg and Gödel;
apparently they don't even have that kind of certitude in math
and science anymore.

"We'll move out of New York, get a little house somewhere. Live the simple life."

Now it's Philomena's turn to cry when she finally sobs, in
response to my outrageously belated offer: "Connor, don't say
that."

"I mean it."

"It's too late."

"Why do you keep saying that?"

When she speaks again her voice is dispassionate. "I'm
moving out, Connor."

"Where will you move to?"

"Look, I've got to go now."

"Don't go. Wait. Call me on my line—just for a minute."

"Why?"

"I just . . . please."

"I've really got to go."

"Please, Phil—"

"Goodbye, Connor."

And she does go, back into that lurid void which I roam in
my sleeplessness where she trills her song of lust beneath a
man without a face.

DINNER AT "21"

Brooke couldn't handle the farewell repast, finding neither the
concepts of (1) eating nor (2) family irresistible. I have duti-

fully dragged myself to this final Station of the Cross: the
'rents are leaving in the morning. Dad is subdued and chagrined after his performance yesterday. His hands are shaking,
although he cheers up in the downstairs saloon after hearty
personal greetings from Bruce, the manager, and Joseph, our
waiter. He sips black coffee, spilling as much in his saucer as
he manages to bring to his lips. Doing my best to uphold the
family dishonor, I drink Bloody Bulls.

"Your grandfather used to sit at this booth." This statement
is directed at me, the young master, apparent heir to the high
regard of a third generation of "21" waiters and captains.
"Used to sit right in that corner banquette over there, they'd
beat him to the table with an extra-dry Beefeater martini,
straight up with three olives." My father's voice is full of sen-
timental masculine pride, as if spending half your life on your
butt drinking martinis were a tremendous dynastic accomplishment. "Whenever we couldn't find him, we'd call here
first. He took me here after I got into Williams and bought me
my first official drink."

Thoughts about my grandfather: smart enough to sniff the
crash of '29 coming and pull out with a couple million, which
really *was* a couple million in those days, but not smart enough
to realize that all his hard work, financial acumen and shady
dealing would result merely in his son's being debilitated by
the patrimony, which said cripple would pretty much squander.

"What's wrong, sweetie," Mom asks, after Dad wobbles
off to the bathroom. Ditsy as she is, I forget sometimes how
acute Mom can be. "Has she left you, Connor?"

All at once my chest is heaving. When she asked me about
Philomena earlier, I tried to dissemble cheerfully, chattering
about her trip, her career, our plans.

"I'm so sorry, honey." Sitting beside me on the banquette
my mother hugs me and wipes my face. "I haven't done a very
good job of preparing you for anything, have I?"

Even in this shattered mood, I'm able to laugh at the notion
of Mom as a trainer.

"I remember when you were born," she says, "just before
the big freeze. You wouldn't remember, of course, but the temperature hit twenty degrees. And your father was out working

through the night, spraying the groves when my contractions started. You were a breech birth, did I ever tell you? And it was a long terrible night for me and for your father out in the groves. And we were in the hospital almost a week. When I came home, all along the road I could see the damage—the leaves turning brown and falling off, but the fruit still hanging on the naked trees like Christmas-tree balls. And when we came around the corner from the Jenkses' to our land I saw the leaves were still green. The ice had saved the trees. And I suddenly realized it could have been different; that I might've lost you. And I remember at that moment wanting so much to be able to protect you from everything that was cold and unpleasant." She stroked my hair. Her eyes were glazed, but for once I felt she was truly looking at me. "And I'm so sorry that I can't." For just a minute, I find perfect sanctuary in the dark softness of my mother's breasts.

Then Dad returns, bringing the world and the sad distance of family life with him.

HOUSE CALL

The buzzer summons me from the blissful oblivion I have somehow achieved on the couch, my first real sleep in several days. Ignoring it is not a luxury available to someone like myself hoping desperately for a miracle. I leap from the couch and stumble to the door, rubbing my neck. Imagine my surprise and chagrin to discover Dr. Halliwell on my doorstep. It takes me a moment to recognize him, though. The green hospital scrubs under his anorak finally clinch it.

"I just happened to be, well, actually, I was over at St. Vincent's and I thought I'd drop by."

Unable to summon a defensive strategy, I usher him in. Despite the fact that I think he's a dweeb, I am mortified to look at the apartment through his eyes. Sent the cleaning lady away last week because I was trying to sleep and because I was embarrassed even for *her* to see the wreckage, with the result that it has grown and compounded itself as rapidly as the interest on an unpaid VISA balance. If I could wish away any one

element of the debris at this moment, it would be the dead sol-
diers, the beer, Absolut and Jack Daniel's bottles that suddenly
seem so very numerous indeed. I realize, of course, that dirty
clothing and towels do not belong in the living room, where
they detract from the air quality and overall ambience. And
how could any one person read, let alone own, so many news-
papers and magazines? Well, I am a literate slob, at least. The
best that can otherwise be said is that there aren't a lot of dirty
plates, since I haven't eaten much. Just a couple of pizza boxes
spread around the few available surfaces, like accent pieces.

"Little party last night," I mumble. "Few friends over to
watch the game."

"Oh, that's very, that must have been . . ."

"Listen, it's a little messy here. You want to step out for a
drink?" I grab my jacket from the back of the couch and push
him back out the way he came.

"I didn't mean to disturb you."

"Actually," I lie, "I'd just finished writing a piece."

"I enjoyed your article on . . . I've forgotten her name.
Actress."

"You must be thinking of my ode to Cortney Thorne
Smith." If Doug were anyone else I would know he was mock-
ing me. The sad thing is I believe he means it. Perhaps Doug
admired that poignant passage in which Cortney admitted that
she'd always been ashamed of her body and almost had
(gasp!) breast reduction. At any rate, he is reminding me however inadvertently of the absurdity of my existence, which
does not improve my general mood.

We pass a black transvestite in a silver-fox coat trudging up
Washington on his way to work. Blow jobs for the hubbies in
Cherokees; watch out for the baby seat. Doug looks back at
the trannie and I wonder if he is shocked.

"I think I treated him for hepatitis a couple of months ago."

I'm—what? Surprised, impressed. Small world, though
Doug's world is larger than I'd imagined.

Albert King's guitar piercing the frigid evening air outside
as I usher Doug into Automatic Slims, my local drinketeria,
which is sparsely populated at this early hour. What is this
hour? Whatever happened to my Swatch? And who was the

actor I once interviewed who confessed that the best thing about fame was that he no longer needed to wear an expensive watch to get respect?

Is the sun over the yardarm yet? My father, before he tucks into his first drink of the day, likes to announce that it is. I've never stopped to ask what this means. Should I ask Doug? But he doesn't look like a sailor. So I order a Bloody Mary, which is appropriate anytime, while Doug settles for a club soda and lime.

"On duty at eight," he explains. Otherwise, you know, he'd *really* be getting down, doing shooters and Mad Dogging all over the place. Maybe I should take him up to Hogs and Heifers, where Julia Roberts dances on the bar.

A SERIOUS TALK

"Listen, I don't mean to be . . . it's just that I'm a little, not worried, but let's say *concerned* about Brooke."

"In what way?" While I'm not unconcerned about Brooke myself—I'm terrified—I'm not necessarily prepared to confide in this relative stranger.

"Well, there's her . . . she doesn't really eat. I think she has a problem, a potential problem, in this area. And some days she can hardly drag herself out of bed." An awkward pause— as if remembering he has just awakened her brother in the p.m. Aha! A family trait. "I see some . . . let's just say, *depressive* tendencies." He sips his soda pensively. "And I thought maybe you could, I thought if we could just discuss it. . . ."

Part of me would like to reach out to this man, to tell him that I share his worries and it's breaking my heart. But it's *my* heart, and Brooke is *my* sister. "Brooke's always gone through these phases," I explain. "She gets a little weird, stops eating for a while, then she wakes up one morning and she's fine again."

"I think it's a little worse than that," he says, as forcefully as I've ever heard him say anything.

"She'll be all right," I insist.

"This may seem like, I don't mean to overstep any bounds, but is there any history of this kind of thing in your family?"

I could tell him about my paternal grandmother, who once tried to drown a certain evil spirit who by her account was in possession of my father's five-year-old body, and who was shipped up to a bucolic institution in Connecticut every couple of years for what they called nerves. As Irish Catholics, my father's side has done an excellent job of acquiring the neurasthenic traits of ancient Wasp pedigree while preserving the traditional failings associated with the old sod. And then there's Mom's Faulknerian family—completely batshit.

But I say, "Nothing particularly comes to mind."

"The family doesn't seem to be functioning . . . quite as supportively as it might."

"We can take care of ourselves."

"I hate to bring this up, but your father just exposed himself in public yesterday."

"I didn't say we weren't eccentric."

At least he didn't cut it off, like some of Doug's acquaintances.

He stares into my eyes for the first time that I can remember, his face hardening into a mask of judgment. "You're not the only one who loves Brooke."

I realize that I am being a complete asshole. And I am almost ready to yield, to try to behave like a decent person, when Doug stands up and lays a five-dollar bill on the bar. "Well, thanks," he says. "I better get up to the hospital."

"I'll see you," I say, hating myself just a little more than usual.

BROOKE CHECK

She's watching the Bosnian War Crimes Tribunal on Court TV.

"Let's go get a bite."

"I'll bet that's exactly what this murderer said right after he eviscerated a Bosnian Muslim in front of his family."

"It was just a thought."

She continues to stare at the screen, where the defendant, wearing headphones and penal pajamas, listens to the proceedings with an expression more bored than belligerent.

"Your boyfriend came to visit me," I say.

"You're always pissing and moaning about the fashionable people you claim you're forced to associate with," she says in an even, uninflected tone, still staring at the TV. "But I'm afraid you've become one of them."

"What does that have to do with Mad Dog?"

"You make fun of him because he's not cool, because he doesn't have an ego that sticks out six feet in front of him like an erection when he walks down the street." She directs at me a look of cool and brutal appraisal. "I hate like hell to say it, but right now Doug's a better person than you are, Connor. Last night at the end of Doug's shift an eighty-three-year-old woman came into the emergency room with her lungs full of fluid, and she said to Doug, 'I know I'm dying, don't tell me I'm not.' And he told her it was true. And she asked him if he would stay with her while she died and he said he would. And he did. He sat with that woman for two hours and talked to her and held her hand until she slipped away. . . ."

Which is what I do, eventually—slip away. Had I come to check up on her, or on myself?

LUNCH AT "44"

"Sorry I'm late. Listen, I was at Chaos this weekend and the weirdest thing happened." Tina Christian pauses and looks longingly at the distant row of banquettes upon which sprawl the dukes and duchesses of the periodical publishing realm. "Next time," she says, "let me make the reservation." Vis-à-vis our table, which is virtually outside the castle walls. I stand to hold her chair, the chivalrous McKnight.

"So this Latina babe comes up and starts schmoozing me. I thought she looked familiar. She's kind of cute in a Janet Jackson sort of way, but she was with some very tough looking chicks, they were like a pack or something. Then she starts asking me about you. At first it seems real innocent, but then she starts asking me if I'm your girlfriend and I get this funny vibe and finally I'm, like, whoa, wait a minute, this is that crazy bitch who sent you the naked picture. Which by the way we all enjoyed. But before I realize that's who she is I thought she was a friend of yours and we just kind of started talking. She seemed kind of suspicious about who I was so I was like 'Hey, I *wish*, Connor's a really cool guy but he's totally devoted to his girlfriend.' I mean, for all I know she could have been a friend of Philomena's. So then she's like 'Oh, yeah, I hear she's really great,' and I'm like 'Yeah, for a model she's actually okay.' If you really want to know, I said she was great. Which she is, I've never had a problem with Philomena except that it's kind of hard to be in the room with her because on her worst day she makes me feel like the basset hound standing next to a whippet. Anyway, I told this girl that you weren't a typical modelfucker and that you guys were like this old married couple, and she starts asking all these questions which eventually turn nasty. And finally I realize she's some kind of psycho, so of course I get out of there. I mean, who *is* this chick?"

"I don't know. She could be my next girlfriend." Thus you proceed to share your romantic woes with Tina, hoping for a little feminine advice.

"Not good," she says, worrying a breadstick with her teeth.

"What would you do?"

"I find in these situations the only thing *to* do is sleep with somebody else as soon as possible. Even if you don't really feel like it, at least you have the illusion of revenge. And having someone else's scent on you immediately makes you more attractive to the injuring party." Then, staring into the distance: "God, I've got to find out who's cutting Tina Brown's hair."

A FLAME

To: Scribbler@aol.com
From: Jenrod@inch.com
Subject: Modelfuckers
So now I know why you didn't even bother to show up at Chaos and why you are so high and migty about helping a person whose just looking for some career advice and a friendly shoulder to "lean on." Or even

maybe, who knows? See what develops between them?
Someone who might be a soulmate instead of just some
pretty face although not to blow my own horn lots of
people say I'm way prettier than most of the socalled
models in your stupid magazine. Just because your
girlfriend is a "top fashion model" I suppose you think
you're better than other people. Speaking of Swell
Heads I'll bet she has a real beach ball between her
ears—full of air! I suppose you don't know that most
models are really lesbians! What do you think they do
standing around halfnaked in dressing rooms all day?
You better believe their noses aren't so high up in the
air then! But maybe your one of those sickos who likes
to watch. Some day may be you'll learn the meaning of
the expression "beauty is only skin deep." And by then
it will be too late. There is another expression of
mine—be nice to the people you meet on the way up
because you will meet them again on your way down.
And may be that will be me waving to you from my
limo when you are drunken in the gutter. And where
will your anorexic PUSSYLICKING girlfriend be
then?

I'm not one of those people who believes everything
they hear I believe in giving people the benefit of the
doubt until proven guilty even OJ Simpson. So I'm
basically giving you one more chance to do the polite
thing and at least have the guts to say Hey sorry I stood
you up.

INTERVIEW WITH A VAMPIRE

Still no word from Chip Ralston, but I have scheduled an inter--
view with his friend Jason Townes. Chip's publicist booked it
through Jason's manager. Jason's staying at the Four Seasons,
in town to promote his new movie, and I'm slotted in for 10
p.m. By all accounts he is a night person. I consider calling to
confirm, but decide my chances might be better if I don't give
him a chance to reconsider. Sometime around 9 I fall asleep in

front of the television, waking up at 11:30 to the closing music
of an ancient *Cheers* episode. Running for a cab, I forget both
my notebook and my tape recorder, arriving in the lobby at 10
to 12. I pick up the house phone and ask for Stanley Kowalski,
the name under which Townes has registered, having waited
for someone to compare him to Brando since he was in summer stock.

"And who may I say is calling?" asks the house operator.
After many minutes she comes back on the line to say she's
sorry, Mr. Kowalski is not available. I have an appointment,
I insist: McKnight, Connor. Writer. Another interlude of
Muzak—not Rod, thank God—before she comes back on and
gives me a room number.

Upstairs, I knock several times. "Hey, what's up." The kid
who finally admits me looks like a midwestern collegiate athlete, closely shorn and blandly handsome, except for a prominent gold nose ring. He shakes my hand. "I'm Tab." My
comprehensive research indicates that Townes travels with an
entourage of high school buddies. This is sometimes taken, in
the popular press, as a sign of what a loyal, down-to-earth guy
he is—as opposed to, say, someone who needs a lot of help
lugging his ego around.

Inside, it's hard to see for the dimness, the atmosphere
thick with smoke and a vague menace. Jason Townes is sitting
on a couch in a white terry-cloth robe, staring at the television.
A plump, voluptuous brunette in a tiny pink negligee is beside
him, rubbing his shoulders. As I approach tentatively, Jason
rises and extends his hand, looking sincere, if somewhat
fucked up.

"Hey, how are you, dude? Catch a seat." Tab sits down
beside the young woman and squeezes her ample breast, then
leans over and uses an American Express platinum card to
separate a huge line from a pile of white powder on the coffee
table. He snorts the line through a hundred. All very eighties.

A buff young skinhead, who appears at first to be wearing a
loud, colorful Hawaiian shirt, emerges from one of the rooms,
towel wrapped around his waist. In fact he is shirtless, his
torso adorned with a mosaic of tattoos, the sweaty tesserae
composed of skulls, dragons and naked women. Toting his

own rolled bill, he leans over and snorts a line, clutching his towel modestly.

I introduce myself. Jason, watching himself on the screen, does not look up. The tattooed man nods and says, "Kirk."

"Kirk just got off the road," says he of the nose ring, "with the Red Hot Chilis."

"That was some wild shit," says Kirk. "Talk about pussy, this one chick offered to let us pierce her clit."

"Yeah, well," says Tab, "that's like, Jason, man—one time this rich bitch once offered him twenty-five big ones for a locket of pubic hair."

"No way."

"The raddest," says Jason, still looking at the screen, "was that kid who killed himself onstage when the Cure was playing in Brazil. Now that's fucking commitment."

Kirk says, "I know this dope dealer—"

"We're shocked," says Jason.

"This dealer claims he knows a guy who has Errol Flynn's dick in like a jar. Supposedly it was secretly cut off and preserved in like whatever you call it. Says the asking price is a million."

"See, I should be charging *you*," Jason says to the girl, who is surely someone's sixteen-year-old Sicilian cousin from Queens. "Mine should be worth at least a hundred large."

"Then you'd have to be nice to me," the girl says.

"That reminds me, somebody was telling me this story," Jason says, but he is distracted by his own image on-screen. "I love this part." He points. "Did that stunt myself."

"He did," Tab says. "Director says, 'Jason, get out of the car, let's put the double in.' J. says, 'No way man. Just watch this shit.' "

Howls of amazed appreciation are provoked as the car sails off an overpass and lands on top of another moving vehicle.

"That," says Kirk, "is some styling roadwork."

Without looking away from the screen, Jason says, "So what's the pitch? You got three minutes."

"Pitch?" I say.

"For the flick." He looks at me, finally. "Aren't you a writer?"

"Actually, I'm here to interview you about Chip Ralston."

"Speaking of morons," says Kirk.

"Chip?" The girl looks up. "I think he's sexy."

Jason raises his eyebrows, then suddenly shoots his hand up between her legs. She squirms and squeals like a child being tickled.

"Chip's all right," Jason allows. "Hell, he's my best friend. He's down with me. Nothing wrong with Chip that a personality implant wouldn't fix."

Tab laughs—a throaty, barking sound that Jason seems to appreciate.

"You shouldn't say that about your friend," the brunette whines.

"Personality implant," says Jason, "and an ego reduction."

"That's a good one, J."

"Fucking guy, he's so clueless, he can't even take a piss without calling his psychic. Wait, now I remember that story," says Jason. "Chip said in an interview he liked van Gogh. Like he'd probably just heard the name from whoever was directing his latest picture. A week later he gets a fucking ear in the mail. Some *ho* sliced off her fucking ear just to show her devotion to the great Chip Ralston. Jesus, I fucking hate the way he shot me in this scene," Jason concludes, pointing again. "Look at this, rewind it. Fucking guy couldn't direct a Pampers commercial."

Tab barks and wallops his thigh.

"All this is *off the record*," Jason says to me. "Everything so far. And all this—" He waves his arm around the immediate vicinity of the couch. "You want some food, something to drink?" He gestures toward the huge buffet table in the middle of the room: striped orange shrimp and pearl-gray caviar, pâtés and melting mousses, cheeses and breads, sushi and sashimi. Somehow it all looks hyperreal, as luridly unappetizing in the murky funk of the suite as the lacquered plastic models in Japanese restaurant windows. More than slightly nauseous making. The bar is more to my liking, Cristal and an '85 Montrachet chilled in silver buckets; a fine selection of white and brown liquors, with all the mixers.

I taste the wine, probably excellent if one hadn't been

smoking and drinking for five days straight and had something in the way of taste buds left. Instead, I pour myself a large tumbler of Absolut. Aiming for a chair, I almost step on something, which on examination turns out to be a used condom, glistening like something recently living and freshly killed and skinned on the shaggy savanna of the carpet.

"Ow, that hurts." The young lady exclaims, trying to extract the star's hand from between her legs.

"Show the nice man your tits," Jason says, withdrawing his hand, sniffing it absently.

Shrugging demurely, she caresses the straps of her negligee over her shoulders, down her plump arms, revealing an abundance, a positive surplus, of blue-veined, white breast meat and dark, protuberant silver-dollar-sized nipples. Like the buffet, it seems a bit much.

"Nice, huh?"

"Great," I say.

"Right on. So you're a fucking journalist."

"Not really. I'd hardly—"

"I thought you were this screenwriter my fucking agent was hooking me up with. He, like, won an Oscar a few years ago. He's pretty famous. What's his name?" Jason looks at Tab.

"Steve something," Jason's friend concludes after a long pause and another line. "Or maybe Victor."

"Something like that. Wasn't he supposed to come up and pitch? Maybe you guys could corroborate. Couple of wordjockeys and all." He chuckles, seeming to contemplate the absurdity and drudgery of the logocentric realm, where scriveners scribble and toil, huffing and puffing like stevedores as they lift and carry big Latinate verbs and portmanteau nouns while Jason and his kind get all the pussy. He takes the rolled bill and sticks it in the mound of white powder.

"Actually, I am kind of working on a screenplay." God, did I actually say that? Without even the excuse of having consumed drugs? Disgusted with myself even before I finish the sentence.

Jason moans. "So's the fucking guy who cleans my pool." He turns to the girl. "Hey, I'll bet *you're* working on a goddamn screenplay."

"I have these thoughts sometimes," she says. "I write them down in this journal."

He looks at me. "What did I tell you?"

A very nude young man suddenly appears in the hall from another part of the suite, his slick, semierect penis bobbing absurdly like a dowsing rod.

"My turn," says Kirk, rising eagerly from the couch. A beautiful woman in a white terry-cloth robe materializes in the hallway, wafting toward us like a dream.

"I need another five hundred if I'm staying," she says, seeing me a moment after I recognize her.

"Kirk, get the money from my dresser," Jason says. Then, "What, you two know each other?"

Pallas is actually blushing. All that I will salvage from this encounter is the notion that she, too, can blush. I don't know why I care; I don't know exactly what kind of faith I thought I had deposited in trust with this woman who never promised me anything except a dance and a good view of her excellent breasts for twenty dollars—who threw in a blow job, gratis.

I'm not quite shocked, just thoroughly deflated.

"You want to go first?" Jason asks me. "Kirk can wait. He's already been in there once tonight."

"Twice," Kirk corrects.

"Don't worry about the bucks, it's on me," Jason says. "She's good, dude."

"I'm sure she is," I say. "I just remembered I have to go home and finish reading Saint Augustine's *Confessions*."

"Yeah, well, whatever," says Jason. "Hey, Kirk, where's the remote? Rewind that part back to the two shot." For all his careless generosity Jason Townes has forgotten me long before I have reached the door.

"Hey, that's my bill," he tells someone. "That's how you get hepatitis, sharing rolled-up bills."

A RARE PERSONAL APPEARANCE

When I return to my apartment Jeremy is leaning against my door, pressing the buzzer. He appears uncharacteristically inebriated.

"Are you acquainted with any contract killers?" he asks.

Pacing my living room floor, he pauses to survey the rubble. "Jesus, I think you've been robbed."

"Actually, I have been."

"Join the fucking club." He fumbles in his pockets, hands me a note:

> *I'm afraid we've become far too fond of Ronald to give him up. But perhaps we might be persuaded at a later date. Our apologies for any inconvenience this may have caused you. Sincerely—Edie Jamison.*

"Taped to the fucking door. House empty. Nobody home." It seems, as he finally explains it, that Jeremy has just returned from a trip to New Jersey where, by prior arrangement, he was to exchange four thousand dollars in actual U.S. currency for the terrier. "And she has the gall, did I tell you this, to name Sean—who already has a name that he knows and responds to—she has the fucking temerity to rename him *Ronald*—like Ronald fucking McDonald!"

When I smash my fist into the wall, Jeremy stops to catch his breath. He ambles over to examine the indentation in the plaster. "That must have hurt," he says.

ANOTHER LITERARY MYSTERY SOLVED

Later, we're drinking at the Whitehorse Tavern amidst the usual collection of students, hard-core locals and tourists visiting the shrine where Dylan Thomas drank his last.

"I'm thinking of flying to L.A.," I say.

"Better you than me. Ever heard the joke, studio decides to make *David Copperfield*, studio head says, 'What about a script?' Exec says, 'We're thinking William Goldman, Robert Towne.' Studio head says, 'What about the author? He tied up on another project, or what?' " Jeremy halts drunkenly. "Actually, that's a true story."

"Actually, I don't even know if she's in L.A."

"Wait, quiet, this is my song," he commands, as the

lugubrious opening chords of "It Wouldn't Have Made Any Difference" ooze from the jukebox. Unself-conscious for once in his life, Jeremy sings along while the tears well in my eyes: *"It wouldn't have made any difference, / if you loved me . . . / You just didn't love me."*

Popular songs become profound when we are wounded in love. I fire up a cigarette. Smoke gets in your eyes.

When the song ends, Jeremy says, "It's not the same playing it at home as hearing it in a bar, on a jukebox. The smoke, the draft beer, the company of all these fucking losers, the tinny, low-fidelity speakers competing against the obnoxious voices of one's fellow drinkers. The gritty poignancy of it all. That's how certain songs are meant to be heard. Jukeboxes are time machines for the bereft."

Jeremy tosses his long mane, unconsciously evoking quivers from a table of NYU coeds on the other side of the room. It should be counted to Jeremy's credit that he is generally unaware of the interest he excites in the opposite sex, though an ill-wisher might chalk up this obliviousness to self-absorption.

"Listen," he says, "think about this." Pausing for effect.

"I'm listening."

"Holly Golightly and Sally Bowles."

"Please, enough sluts for one night."

"I was reading what's-his-name's biography of Capote when it came to me. Capote was a big admirer of Isherwood and they eventually became friends. So I picked up *The Berlin Stories* and then went back and reread *Breakfast at Tiffany's*. No question, Holly is an American clone of Sally Bowles, right down to the unconvincingly heterosexual pal. A total rip-off. I mean, it's practically plagiarism."

WHAT PHILOMENA BRIGGS
HAS IN COMMON WITH HOLLY
GOLIGHTLY AND SALLY BOWLES

When Connor fails to swoon with excitement, Jeremy asks, "What do you mean enough sluts for one night? Did Philomena come back?"

Connor has a sudden dark inspiration: "Do you know something about Phil that I don't?" By now imagining himself fully prepared for, even expecting, the worst. "Or are you just trying to cheer me up?"

"What would I know?"

"I don't know, is she giving blow jobs in the Lincoln Tunnel? Sleeping with quadrupeds? I mean, am I deluded in thinking that she was faithful, that we had a fairly decent relationship, that this latest . . . *thing* is, I don't know—*uncharacteristic*?"

Jeremy hesitates, inhales and exhales in the manner prescribed by the Zen masters. "Listen, I've been meaning to tell you. There's this story in the new collection called 'Model Behavior.' It's *fiction*, okay. A fictive narrative. But I wanted to tell you before you read it."

"Tell me what?"

"It's basically a story about illusion and reality, about the worship of false idols. Part of the overall metaphoric construct of the collection—the claustrophobic madness of the city." He looks at me hopefully, as if to say, *Who could dispute the validity of such a theme?* "It's kind of about a writer and a model." He sighs. "It's about this guy who has an affair with his best friend's girlfriend. Which could appear to you, in a paranoid moment, to be based on real events. But I swear to you it never happened. It's what Roth calls *The Counterlife.* Basically the what-if version, the might-have-been version. I just wanted to tell you that before you read it."

Sensing Connor's disbelief, he becomes indignant. "I mean, I don't even know why I'm explaining this, you know the difference between fiction and nonfiction. Okay, sure, hate me for my fantasy, but I just didn't want you to think . . . you know what I mean."

He takes a long swallow of beer, watching Connor over the top of his mug.

For all the discounts he has made in his own self-esteem in recent years, Connor never imagined Philomena to be interested in anyone but himself.

"What happened?"

"I told you—nothing. The story's just a projection."

"This is me, Jeremy. I know all about your so-called fiction."

"It's a possible world."

"Jesus, Jeremy."

"Nothing really happened. Sure, maybe I wanted to. . . . It was nothing." He sighs again, placing his mug carefully on its coaster. "You were in L.A. I don't know, a year ago. We just, I ran into her at the movies and then we went out for a drink."

"A drink."

"I was telling her about a book, I don't know, something in the movie reminded me of Jim Salter, and we went back to my place so I could give her the book."

"Oh, *right.* Salter. Nice. *A Sport and a Pastime,* perhaps."

He shrugs. "Yeah, well."

"I can't believe this."

"I'm not trying to make excuses, okay? I guess I knew . . . I guess I felt a certain amorous—"

"What happened?"

"We kissed. Once. That's it."

Connor is reeling. *"Kissed?"* He wants to see the picture clearly, in color, so he can suffer its every detail. "Who started it?"

"I don't know, it just kind of happened."

"What did?"

"One minute we're talking about *A Sport and a Pastime* and then we were . . . we kissed. For a minute. For less than a minute. I mean, we stopped before . . . you know. Before anything."

"No, tell me. I don't know. I wasn't there. Did she take off her clothes? Did you feel her tits? Stick your finger in her twat?"

Jeremy is trying to shush his friend while the bartender scrutinizes him with a constabulary air.

"Nothing happened. We *stopped,* okay?"

"Who stopped?"

"Who cares? I don't know."

"Who stopped? And who didn't want to stop?"

"Connor, give it up. You don't need this."

"Yes, I do. *You* give it up."

"*I* stopped, all right? Are you happy now? *I* did."

"My friend."

"That's right."

It is a curious dilemma Connor's impaled upon, trying to decide whether he would rather be betrayed by his best friend or his lover. His former lover. His lost lover.

"I'm sorry, Connor, I've beaten myself up till my conscience is black and blue. It would've been easier for me to tell you. Look, it could've been worse. It was nothing, really. We were drunk. It was just a kiss, that's all. And later out of guilt and speculation and because it's what I do as a writer, I embellished it into a story."

"A story which everybody will think is true."

A DAZE

Everything in the room seems to be wrapped in a skein of gauze. You feel dissociated from the physical environment, as if you were high. You feel Jeremy's hand on your shoulder, the first time you can remember him initiating physical contact. You always have noticed the little things—Jeremy's eccentricities, for instance, or your own little mood swings—but you now realize that you have failed to take note of the big things. You have suffered a chronic and massive failure of awareness. And it occurs to you that inattention might, cumulatively, spread over years, be as great a crime as infidelity.

"Don't worry about *everybody*," he says, regaining his customary belligerence. "I mean, who's everybody? How many readers do I have? For that matter, how many friends do you have?"

"One less." Even as you say this, you know it's melodramatic, and that you will forgive Jeremy. But for now you must follow the customary forms of indignation. You stand up, throw a twenty down on the bar, a radical gesture, given how few of them are left in your possession.

"She knew about that actress in L.A.," Jeremy shouts as you retreat.

Ah, that.

Outside, the cold air helps jar you into a belated sense of alertness. You start up the street, reflecting on each step you take, as in walking meditation. Such is your glowering sense of menace that a ragged mendicant starts to approach and then dodges away from you.

TINA TO THE RESCUE

You stalk west to Washington Street. You want to be in a small loud room full of strangers who can barely hear themselves speak above the music, consuming first- *and* secondhand smoke, all the fucking smoke you can wrap your lungs around. Back to Automatic Slims, jam-packed from the bar to the windows. Adding your own body to the fray, you can't help feeling that it is the oldest in the room. You might not have noticed last week, or even yesterday, but no one in the place looks much over twenty. And they all seem too fucking happy, as if they didn't know how shitty their lives were about to become, once they graduate from Columbia or Sarah Lawrence or NYU Law School and learn that the hang- overs only get worse.

When exactly did you lose that feeling of invulnerability and infinite promise, your belief in both yourself and the abundance of time? You didn't really notice its leaving, but tonight you can say with certainty that it's gone.

A blond flag on a black stick: Tina Christian emerges from the men's room, pinching her nose, wrapping you in a brittle embrace.

"Connor, I am *so* glad to see you, you look like shit. I'm just on my way to Spy Bar. You can be my date."

"I'm not very good company."

"I can't afford to be picky. At least you're taller than me." She tugs me toward the door. "Have you talked to Jeremy?"

"I just left him."

She stops to wave at someone behind you. "*Where?* Did he mention me? God, I have *got* to talk to him. I am *so* not proud of myself but I was, like, I couldn't help it. Kevin was being such an asshole and I was so pissed that I told him about sleeping with Jeremy. I think I must have been drunk. Plus I was a little pissed at Jeremy because he hadn't called me. I know, I know . . . I just feel *terrible* about it. . . ."

DAYBREAK

Sleep is out of the question. At five-fifteen the red light pulses through the blinds and I am sober despite my best efforts to stupefy myself, my virtue nominally intact despite Tina's best efforts. I sent her away when I finally realized she was making me feel worse instead of better. Now I sit up and spread the slats; they're loading a body in the back of the ambulance. The sheet stretches all the way over the lump of the head.

Earlier I had bobbed in Tina's frothy wake, following her first to Spy Bar, then to Chaos, because we heard from a friend of hers that Chip Ralston was supposed to show up there. Chip was not present, but Tina introduced me in the bathroom to a friend of hers who claimed that he'd sold him some ketamine last week and who offered to sell me a ring that used to belong to River Phoenix. "If you're really interested," he said, "I know a guy whose cousin worked at the funeral parlor. Dude scooped a handful of ashes from the urn, he's selling them by the gram." Searching the pocked face for a glimmer of irony, I listened to Tina puking in one of the stalls.

GOOD MORNING: A FAX!

Dear Connor:

Finally got hold of Brooke last night, told her about Christmas. She said she understood, but she sounded a little manic to me. What's going on? I'm counting on

you to look after the girl. If anything happens to her you
will wish I had drowned you back when you were six.

I have a meeting in New York a few days before
Christmas so maybe we can all go down to Florida
together and spend a day there before I go on to
Freeport.

Love,
Corvetta

WORD FROM RALSTON'S CAMP

Evening: I'm at my computer checking various Web sites—
http://www.starzzz.com; www.hollyword.com—when the
phone rings; my caller ID shows an incoming call from Los
Angeles.

"Hello?" I start jotting down the number, a 310.

"Hello, could I please speak to Colin McNeal?"

"Would you settle for Connor McKnight?"

"Oh, sure. This is Cherie Smith. Chip Ralston's assistant?
Chip just wanted me to tell you that he's changed his mind
about the article. He decided he won't be able to do it after all."

"Are you kidding?"

"He just told me to tell you is all."

"Excuse me," I say. "Do you think I could speak to him?"

"I'm sorry, but he's really busy right now."

"It's not that I'm dying to write this article, but I don't have
enough money in my checking account to pay my half of next
month's rent, let alone my missing girlfriend's half."

"I'm sorry, but I'm just doing my job. Well, have a nice
day. Bye."

I'm not about to give up that easily. Now I have the number.
Out to get a pack of smokes, practicing my imitation of Jason
Townes, trying to reproduce his famous dusky tone in order to
get past the assistant and speak directly to Ralston, my prey,
the bastard.

"Jason Townes here." No, not quite. "Hi, Jason calling. Can
I talk to Chip." Close. "Hi, it's Jason," I say, shivering at the
corner of Twelfth and Hudson. "Jason Townes."

"Yeah, and I'm Michelle Pfeiffer," says the young black woman walking her dog behind me.

Back in my apartment I smoke two cigarettes to abrade my voice, wait fifteen minutes, then call back the magic number inscribed on my notepad.

"Hello?" says the familiar voice. "Hello? Who is this?"

"Phil?"

"Connor?"

"What are you doing there," I ask, when I finally find my voice, though the answer seems obvious enough, if somewhat incredible.

"How did you—"

"Does that *matter*?" I say. "I mean, you're asking *me* how *I* . . . Jesus. I can't believe this is happening."

"I didn't want to hurt your feelings."

"You didn't want to hurt my feelings? *That's* why you're fucking Chip Ralston—to spare my feelings? What would you do if you actually *wanted* to grind me under your pointy little heel and crush my spirit beyond repair?"

"I mean, that's why I didn't want you to know."

"And *that's* why he blew off the stupid fucking interview?"

"Connor, you could hardly write objectively about him under the circumstances."

"I didn't *know* the circumstances."

"Well, you would have." After a pause she adds, "*Hard Copy* caught us leaving Morton's last night. It'll probably run tonight."

"I'm getting on a plane right now."

"Connor, don't. It's over. Anyway, we're going to Montana this afternoon."

"Montana?"

"Chip has a place outside Livingston. We're going to spend some time there."

"It must be just . . . *lovely*."

"I told you I wanted a simpler life."

"*Simpler?* You're going to Livingston fucking Montana with Chip fucking Ralston. Do you have any idea what a cliché that is? I've got it in my computer. 'CTRL, *Montana cliché*.' It's not simple. It's just stupid."

She is silent on the other end; as for me, I can hardly speak. Finally I say, "This is a joke, right?"

"Connor, these things happen. You know? It's nobody's fault."

"Chip Ralston?"

"I can understand your being upset."

"It's pathetic."

"Don't make me say things you don't want to hear."

"He's a fucking midget, Phil."

"Don't worry about that, Connor. Chip's a giant where it counts, thank you very much."

I slam down the phone and regret doing so immediately. Scooping up an Imari porcelain frog—one of Philomena's prized possessions—I hurl it against the wall, where it shatters predictably. We bought it at a flea market in Kyoto and I remember wondering what would happen to it, the first durable object we had ever purchased together: Would it become a stitch binding us together? Would we look at it ten years, twenty years, hence and remember? Afterward we went back to the Ryokan in the hills to the west of town, where the deep cedar tub was steaming in anticipation of our arrival, blue-and-white striped robes laid out on the black-bordered tatami mats. What would I give to go back, if I could? Would I relive it all to this moment, with foreknowledge? Or would I drown the bitch right there in the tub?

For the next twenty minutes I call the number on my pad, filling Chip's answering tape with expletives and entreaties. After the fifth call the number rings continuously.

I'm trying to imagine how to live with myself for the next thirty years when the buzzer goes off.

MORE GRIEF

Jeremy stands in the doorway. Wild eyed, he brushes past me into the apartment.

"You and your fucking girlfriend!"

"I just talked to her."

"Who?"

"Philomena."

"Don't even mention the name."

"What," I say. "What did you hear?"

"Read all about it." He's waving a newspaper in his hand.

"Philomena's in the paper?"

"Oh, she's in the paper all right."

To Connor it seems perfectly reasonable that his girl-friend's treachery should be exposed in the *New York Times*. With trembling hand, he takes it, folded open to the middle of the C section, and sees Jeremy's picture glowering hand-somely beneath the headline: GLIB DEPRESSIVES ON PARADE. Confused, he says, "It's a book review."

"It's not a fucking book review," Jeremy shouts. "It's a knife in my heart."

Connor reads further:

> Jeremy Green's first collection earned the author a solid if modest reputation as a literary craftsman possessed of a darkly humorous vision. Since then he has been pho-tographed at trendy gatherings in the company of fashion models and cavorting in the company of such movie stars as Liam Neeson and Natasha Richardson. "Walled-In," his new collection, seems less like the product of an original artistic vision than a self-conscious display of glitzy urban angst. . . .

"Three years of work, a lifetime's apprenticeship to my fucking craft . . ." A savage kick sends a sofa cushion flying across the room. "Does that count? Dragged kicking and screaming to *one* lousy party, thrown out of *one* celebrity watering hole—and now I'm a whore? 'Glitzy urban angst'? '*Cavorting*' with movie stars?"

Although Connor has difficulty concentrating, he can see that the rest of the review follows syllogistically from the lead. He asks himself, If given the choice of having Phil back or else rescinding Jeremy's review . . . and in so doing comes up against the limits of altruism. "She's run off with Chip Ralston," he says.

"Fuck Chip Ralston. And fuck Philomena. Fuck all of you."

Not knowing what else to do, Connor pours out two tumblers of vodka and places one of them in Jeremy's hand.

"I can imagine—"

"Nobody can imagine," Jeremy barks. "Nobody who hasn't been here."

"It's not that bad," Connor says. "I mean, I've seen worse."

Jeremy looks at the glass as if he'd never seen one before, then hurls it across the room. Rising and bolting for the door, slamming it for good measure, he leaves Connor with an early copy of the newspaper of record.

A FEW PARTING WORDS
FROM THE EDITOR IN CHIEF

The next morning, the other Manolo drops.

"Connor? Please hold for Jillian Crowe."

I tell her I can't hold, but suddenly Jillian is on the line: "Whatever you did to alienate Chip Ralston and his people is one—"

"What *I* did to Chip Ralston? That son of a bitch is fucking my girlfriend."

"Well, tit for tat. You can hardly fault him for that, Connor. After your little adventure with his concubine. In fact I think that's very democratic of him. Droit du seigneur and all. But I'm afraid Lapidus has pulled eight pages of ads from the magazine."

"What?"

"Charles Lapidus—"

"Who, the wife beater?"

"And while there was no official explanation I think we both know who's to blame. You know, I kept thinking, you've been hanging out for long enough that by now you ought to be dry behind the ears. I kept waiting. At any rate, I don't think your heart was ever in this enterprise. I'm sure you'll find a position more worthy of your talents elsewhere. Your contract is up at the end of the year, yes? Please keep in mind that it's a small world we live in and any scurrilous allegations would pretty thoroughly sabotage your future prospects, limited as they might be. Well, I think that covers it. Goodbye Connor."

TWO WEEKS LATER,
THEATER DISTRICT

Clustered around the side entrance of the Ed Sullivan Theater on West Fifty-third Street, home of *Late Night with David Letterman*, we are freezing our asses off, waiting for the stars. Two blue police barriers form a corridor from the curb, and a security guard hovers listlessly at the stage door. We press our crotches up against the barricades, autograph books and pens clutched to our chests, looking toward the street, stamping our cold feet for circulation. But we don't really mind the cold, which certifies our sincerity and our determination. (Besides which, some of us are just a *teeny* bit drunk.) The fair-weather fans are home on a day like this. The studio audience has already gone inside; while the standbys and the tourists are waiting at the front entrance. But these are amateurs, pallid enthusiasts, not like us. We're the real fans, the big fans. We are the biggest fans. As in "Hey, Clint, I'm your biggest fan."

Bearlike Clarence, for instance, with his huge, fur-hooded army-surplus parka, his scholarly thick black glasses, his ultra-professional mien, his unabashed air of a man engaged in an important pursuit at which he excels: "I just got Brooke Shields, man. She's a real nice lady. Real nice. Yeah, I got her over at NBC few minutes ago, she's on *Conan*. Not like that Geena Davis, man. Remember last week, she brush right past you, don't look at nobody, think she a fucking queen. Look like a drag queen, you ask me. Arnold, he's like that. Don't sign no autographs. Tell you who I like, I like Richard Harris. A gentleman, know what I'm saying? He be cool. Not like that Richard Chamberlain. Richard Chamberlain, he come through here he shake your hand, that sucks, man, what I'm gonna do with a handshake? Can't show your friends a handshake, you can't put it on your damn wall."

"Can't sell it," Charlie says, zipping up his Mets warm-up jacket. A plumber in Patchogue, Long Island, when he isn't here outside the Ed Sullivan Theater, or in the lobby of NBC headquarters in Rockefeller Center, he and his friend Tony are armed with unlined six-by-nine-inch index cards. They are fans, but their hero worship is tainted by mercenary motives. If they can get three cards signed, they will sell two to a dealer.

Clarence does not approve of Tony and Charlie. "I don't sell no autographs. I'm doing it for me, man, not like some of them. I ain't saying it's against the law, I'm just saying it don't reflect well on the rest of us, know what I'm saying? You got to have a certain respect for these people, right? Because they people too. You take the biggest superstar in the world, he's a person, same as you or me. Am I right? He got his life, he got his problems."

"Yeah," says Tony, "like, 'Gee, let's see, how often do I want my dick sucked today?' "

"Hey, fuck you, man. It's not all like that, you know what I'm saying?" Clarence speaks as if with the authority of one who has been a huge star in another, recent life, and who remembers it all too clearly. He addresses these remarks in part to the company at large and in part to his companion Vasya, whose blue eyes are foggy and slightly unfocused behind his thick glasses, the earflaps of his hunting cap askew, his chin spotted with lichenlike tufts of beard. Vasya carries an ancient Kodak Brownie camera which he holds up to his ear from time to time as if he expects it to say something.

Suddenly the throng goes taut and silent, congealing into a single quivering sensory organ, as a shiny black stretch fins up to the curb and stops, its cargo invisible behind the smoked glass. The uniformed driver marches officiously around the car to open the curbside door.

"Chip!" screams one of the photographers. "Over here!"

"Hey, Ralston!"

"I'm your biggest fan, Chip."

"How about an autograph, Chip?"

"Look over here! Smile!"

A CLOSE PERSONAL ENCOUNTER

The actor hesitates, framed in the open door of the limo, getting the lay of the land before launching himself toward the stage door, hunched, his head retracted as far as possible into the turtle shell of his jacket, moving quickly, but not quickly enough to dodge me as I slide under the police barrier and cut him off.

"Hey, Chip, I'm Connor McKnight." Savoring for a nanosecond the infusion of fear in his much admired and indeed very striking hazel eyes, I nail him with a headbutt aimed at the bridge of the nose which actually connects with his temple as he tries to duck away. Solid contact, nonetheless. Solid enough to hurt the shit out of my head.

"I'm your biggest fuckin' fan, Chip," I say.

He wobbles, clutching at the police barrier with one hand, his stunned skull with the other, then sinks to his knees just as the security guard tackles me and pins my face against the cold grainy concrete.

CONNOR FACES THE PRESS

After a couple of hours in the holding cell my name is called. Thankfully, the largest man in the cell, who'd just shot an associate of his over on Ninth Avenue, was no fan of Ralston's. When I announced the nature of my offense, he took me under his protection. Ralston had played cops in his last two outings and was pronounced to be a pussy.

Brooke is waiting for me out by the front desk. So is a reporter from the *Post*. A sallow man, ancient by tabloid standards—easily forty—he pushes back the bill of his NEW YORK IT AIN'T OVER cap and flips open his steno pad.

"Why'd you do it," he asks, as I finish signing out.

"I didn't like his acting choices."

"Is it true you've been stalking Chip Ralston for months?"

Brooke takes my arm and we bolt for the door. Outside, more reporters and photographers swarm up the steps.

"Connor, over here."

"Is that your girlfriend?"

"What's her name?"

"Hey, Connor."

"How about the two of you kissing for a picture?"

They pursue us as we race down the street. A reporter runs alongside of us, brandishing a tape recorder: "What about this rumor he owed you money on a drug deal?" Two paparazzi run up ahead of us and crouch down directly in our path on the sidewalk, clicking away.

"What rumor," asks Brooke.

"It becomes a rumor," I explain, "as soon as they quote you denying it. Just walk."

"Come on, Connor," says the reporter.

Incredibly, I can't help feeling strangely exhilarated by the attention of these men of the press and at the scrutiny of pedestrians. So this is what it's like, I think. My sordid little moment to shine. Not the limelight, exactly. More like the lemonlight, the reflected glory experienced by one-day sensations and the sexual partners of the stars. That yearning to exist, as they do, outside of themselves. Like Philomena, now. Brooke, however, is getting very upset.

After several blocks we duck into a Japanese restaurant. Japanese businessmen smoking at the bar. For a moment it's as if I've stepped back in time to Kyoto. Before Phil, before any of this.

To the reporter who follows us into the restaurant, I explain that Chip and I were lovers, that he had cruelly used and abused me. Which I figure should keep him busy for a while. Not to mention Chip's publicist. While he races back to the office I order up a gimlet.

"You can't keep drinking this way, Connor."

"You can't keep eating this way," I counter.

"I'm not eating."

"Precisely. You're anorexic, Brooke."

"*Me?* Are you out of your mind? I eat like a pig."

"Have you eaten today?"

"Sure, I've eaten."

"What?"

"I had some pretzels."

"You're sick, Brooke."

"And what are you?"

"I'm sad. I'm just incredibly fucking sad. Okay? Jesus. At least you haven't cut yourself recently."

"Please don't yell at me. I just really need you not to be critical right now, all right?"

"Okay." I take her hand, her thin, bony hand, until she pulls it away to light a new cigarette from the glowing butt of the old one.

"Are you missing her?" Brooke asks.

"What do you think?"

"Do you suppose," she asks, "you would've married Philomena if not for me?"

"What would you have to do with it?"

"I don't know—you feeling like you needed to take care of me?" Before I can think of how to respond, she adds, "I guess that's pretty self-aggrandizing."

"Unfortunately, I can't really blame anybody but myself. Would you eat a California roll if I ordered one?"

RITES OF THE SEASON

"So," Brooke says as we step into the limpid gloom of the midtown canyon, "what would you like to do? Go to Rockefeller Center, see the tree and watch the skaters?"

For some reason I find this hilarious. A boy and his sister taking in the sights. I'm laughing so hard I have to hug Brooke for support. "Then maybe check out the windows at Saks, catch the Christmas show at Radio City?"

She's laughing, too, patting my back.

"I don't know if they let felons in to see the Rockettes."

"What do we care? Back home there's oranges hanging on the trees. Can these fucking New Yorkers say that? You realize we're leaving tomorrow?"

"It's not going to be Christmas without Corvetta," Brooke says, her smile disappearing. Then under the influence of a new inspiration, she smiles. "I know, let's not go home. Let's go to the Bahamas. Get away from all these white people with their shopping bags and their family curses."

"We can't get away from them. We *are* them."

Seeing the sadness in her face, I hold her in my arms, the pedestrian traffic of Fifth Avenue surging around us. Me thinking of Philomena standing on a stool like an angel in a white robe, putting the star on the Christmas tree last year.

REVENGE FANTASIES

—Chip Ralston, gored by an elk in the hills outside Livingston, Montana. In the groin.

—Philomena betrayed by Chip, who runs off with Milla Jovovich. Major tabloid coverage of their Las Vegas wedding.

—Chip dying of a drug overdose on the sidewalk outside the Viper Room in Los Angeles as passersby pass by. Later, in the parking lot actress Christina Applegate mimics his spastic death throes for the amusement of her friends.

—Philomena, diagnosed with terminal illness, comes home to New York. Connor McKnight—a true, if agnostic, Christian—takes her back, against the advice of friends and family, and nurses her through her long illness. Her dying words: "Oh, Connor, I'm so sorry. You were the only man I ever loved."

PAJAMA PARTY

Understanding that I'm not eager to go back alone to my apartment, Brooke invites me to spend the night before we fly home. She agrees to eat if I agree not to drink—a difficult trade for both of us. Corvetta calls from the airport to say her flight was delayed, that she's going straight to her hotel and she'll see us after her meeting tomorrow. I'm just as happy to have the night alone with Brooke. When the food arrives she picks at the Szechuan vegetables, wielding the chopsticks like a jeweler, deconstructing emerald peapods, examining water chestnuts for color and clarity.

Brooke's in her pajamas—actually an old pair of Dad's flannels from, you guessed it, Brooks Brothers. "It's like when you were little," she says happily. "And you'd sneak into my room."

"Before you went away to school," I say, my voice betraying a resentment which catches even me by surprise.

Though she got straight A's in the "honors" program at the local high school, it was finally decided, after she'd been caught smoking pot in her bedroom, that Brooke needed to be finished at boarding school. While Mom and Dad tripped over themselves and tossed back an extra glass every day attempting to *avoid* knowing what she might be up to, my sister was finally caught in the act by Daisy, our fierce Baptist housekeeper of many years, who is a far more compelling authority figure than either of our parents, with much stricter notions of how a white girl from a good family should comport herself. Daisy made such a fuss on this occasion that my father was embarrassed into action. Brooke was resigned, as I recall, but I was devastated. And I was angry at her because it almost seemed as if she wanted to get caught; she knew Daisy was in the house, and Daisy's movements are never discreet, her advent inevitably presaged by huffing and puffing and a trembling of furniture.

"You ruined my childhood," I say, "all because you had to smoke a joint in the house."

"It wasn't pot," Brooke says.

"What do you mean it wasn't pot?"

"I was caught with Sandy what's-his-name, the housepainter. You knew that."

"I didn't know that."

"I think it was more a case of you didn't want to know it."

CONNOR McKNIGHT, TAXIDERMIST

"You were a funny kid," Brooke says as she strokes my hair. "We were so isolated out there in the groves and I was afraid you'd turn out really weird. Collecting stamps and coins and beetles and playing with lizards. Oh, my God! Remember your taxidermy phase? I'd almost forgotten that. When Vermeer the Parrot died and you decided to stuff him? You never were very good at letting go of things, now that I think about it. Dad took you to the taxidermist in town. And you started that correspondence course. All those peckerwoods coming to the back door with poached game and roadkill? I'd open up the freezer looking for a Creamsicle and there'd be a dead owl staring out at me. I think that was when I stopped eating on a regular basis."

CHIP RALSTON, PLUCKY
CRIME VICTIM

At eleven-thirty we watch *Letterman*, the very show that was taped only hours ago, in spite of an incident which host and guest thrillingly recount for the audience. Ralston's a big hit, carrying an ice pack, explaining how the martial-arts training for his new picture had come in handy when fending off his attacker—the crazed stalker—and commiserating with Dave about the way in which well-deserved adulation occasionally, in the case of a few warped individuals, modulates to dangerous obsession. "But, hey, Dave, it goes with the territory, doing what we do, being in the public eye, and I'm definitely not going to let an isolated incident like this cut me off from my fans or make me paranoid. Hell, this is the greatest job in the world, and you've got to take the rough with the smooth."

The studio audience roars its approval.

FURTHER REVENGE SCENARIOS

—Connor McKnight as Toshiro Mifune, in the movie *Yojimbo*, wrapped in ratty kimono, sword thrust in his obi, striding bandy-legged down a dusty street in a rural Japanese village. The burg eerily silent. Suddenly, men pour out of the buildings on either side of the street, swords raised. They rush McKnight, who slices them down one by one, until only their leader, evil Yakuza chieftain Chip Ralston, remains standing.

Terrified, Ralston tries to run, and then, finding himself in a
dead-end alley, pulls a gun from his kimono and fires it—a
dastardly violation of Bushido, the samurai martial code.
Grazed by the shot, McKnight advances fearlessly, to cut the
coward down. McKnight sheaths his sword and strides down
the street to the brothel, where he throws aside the mama-san
like a sack of grain and tells the courtesan Philomena-chan
that she is free. "Take me with you," she pleads, clutching his
knees. "I travel alone," he responds, shaking himself free and
striding off with stoic, bandy-legged nobility down the dusty
street.

   —Chip Ralston performing dinner theater in Winter
Haven, Florida, his last five movies having bombed, numbers
four and five going directly to video without benefit of theatrical release. Connor McKnight, visiting his ancestral home
with his beautiful wife, actress/model Milla Jovovich, takes
his grateful aging parents out for an entertaining dinner before
flying off the next day to the Caribbean on his private jet. After
the show, Connor graciously sends a drink to the former star,
along with his card, no address or title—just his name
engraved in Antique Shaded Roman on Crane's ecru notecard
stock; on the back of this card Connor has written down two
telephone numbers, one the extension of a junior agent at
William Morris, the other the toll-free telephone number of
the Hair Club of America, with the notation "Word to the
Wise."

THAT'S ME IN THE SPOTLIGHT

The next morning I wake up in Brooke's bed, alone. I can hear
her moving around in the next room. It's almost noon. Without
moving from the bed I check my answering service. Sixteen
messages—including interview requests from New York and
national tabloids, as well as *Hard Copy* and *A Current Affair*.
Also a call from a casting director who says she saw my picture and would like me to read for a part in a movie that starts
shooting next week.

   Erasing all of the messages, I crawl out of Brooke's bed,
and walk softly to the door.

SCENE FROM AN IMAGINARY SCREENPLAY

CLOSE UP ON *the edge of a razor blade which seems to be floating in space.*

Still CLOSE, *but drawing back we see that the blade is attached to a retractable paint scraper which is held by a feminine hand.*

REVERSE ANGLE ON

CONNOR MCKNIGHT, *standing framed in the doorway of the bedroom, looking on in horror.*

REVERSE ON

BROOKE MCKNIGHT, *a very pretty if somewhat haggard woman of thirty-five, whose hand is holding the paint scraper, staring at it intently.*

ANOTHER ANGLE *from which we see several scars on the inside of Brooke's bare left arm.*

CONNOR (*offscreen*)

Brooke!

She continues to stare at the blade, as if in a trance. . . .

DECORATING

Connor approaches cautiously, as she continues to stare at the dangerous tool in her hand. He kisses her cheek as he pries her fingers from the instrument. Which seems to break the spell.

"Good morning," she says brightly. Her hands suddenly free, she fishes for a cigarette. Now Connor notices that she's wearing a paint-spattered smock. Half a dozen cans of paint, lids removed, stand on a fan of newspaper; all of the books

in her bookshelf are stacked on the floor. The wall beside
the fireplace is mottled with peach- and salmon-colored
splotches, any one of which, on a normal day, might nicely
complement her own carroty complexion.

"Did I by any chance lend you my old paperback of Jim
Harrison's *Legends of the Fall*? Remember that cover? I can't
find it anywhere, it had that nice Santa Fe salmon kind of
shade in the background, I really think that would be just a
great color in here, don't you?"

"Brooke, what's with this sudden interest in interior decor?
We're supposed to be going home for Christmas in three
hours."

The smell of paint makes Connor nervous, signifying fresh
starts and bright expectations. He watches his sister virtually
spin around the room, pausing here and there to move a chair
or tap the ash from her cigarette.

"I was going through my drawers and I found this apricot-
colored pullover Mom gave me a few years ago from Lands'
End, then I thought about how depressing these walls were.
They look like the walls of some incredibly dreary municipal
office in some dying rust belt town. I mean, they're not even
white for God's sake, they're the color of smog or something—like the air on a depressing day in Los Angeles." She
scrutinizes the paint splotches on the wall. "Which one do you
honestly like the best?"

She asks this exactly as if Connor were very well known
for being cagey about revealing his favorite color.

"Brooke, can you hear me?" Having seen this dervishing
behavior before, he backs her against the wall, puts his arms
around her and squeezes gently. "We're leaving today.
Corvetta should be here anytime."

"I kind of like the smoky peach—of course I can hear
you—but it's hard to tell from just a little dab of it, when you
do the whole room it might be way too dark."

Connor increases the pressure of his embrace, crushing his
face into the coppery mass of her coconut-shampoo-and-
cigarette-scented hair. With his cheek pressed against her neck
he registers her monologue as a series of distant vibrations.
Suddenly it seems very peaceful here, within the thicket of her

semifragrant hair, an unexpected ambience of sanctuary reminiscent of childhood. As Brooke buzzes on, Connor could almost fall asleep. But she won't let him, becoming shrill in her defense of the ocher family of colors. He squeezes almost as hard as he can, until she finally stops babbling.

"We're going home, Brooke."

"Jerry's getting married again," she says in a tiny voice.

"When did you hear this?"

"This morning. He called to tell me so I wouldn't have to read about it in the press, as he so self-aggrandizingly put it. Not so that I wouldn't *hear* about it, which would have been a more than adequate locution. So that I wouldn't *have to read about it in the press*." She pauses to consume half a Marlboro in a single breath. "Like it'll make the cover of fucking *People* next week. Shit, it probably will. He's getting married on the beach in Bali. One of his students—surprise, surprise. I said, 'Jerry, I really don't think it behooves a scientist to be quite so predictable, so transparently and simplistically *determined* an entity.' "

"Do you still love him?"

She sighs and considers. "No. If I really loved him I'd want him to be happy, wouldn't I?"

Well, Connor thinks, this would seem to go a long way toward explaining the painting and the color chart and the razor blade.

"Look, if you promise to pack, I promise to help you paint when we get back."

It's not as if he's so eager to go home for the holidays. For the last few years Philomena had redeemed the tired rituals of Christmas with her bright childish expectations. Their first year in Japan she found a tiny bonsai tree and pinned stockings to the wall above the kerosene heater, and between this recollection and the sight of Brooke in her manic state it's all he can do to keep from taking the paint scraper to his own wrists.

THE SPOTLIGHT, CONT.

The flight leaves at four. Fearful of leaving Brooke alone, I convince her to come to my apartment and help me pack, more or less on the pretext that I'm afraid to be alone in the place. Which is more or less true. Fortunately Corvetta calls from her meeting; I tell her to meet us there.

We stop at the newsstand. A picture of yours truly on page 3 of the *Post* this morning, very soigné in my Patagonia ski jacket, pinned on the sidewalk beneath the security guard outside the theater, my expression that of the dazed psychopath. I recognize Vasya's calf-high vulcanized rubber boots in the background—a veridical detail which is more realistic and familiar to me than my own face, or the written account of the incident. KARATE KID CHOPS CHIP. The *Post* reporter somehow uncovered my Japan background and apparently concluded that I was a Karate Kung Fu Aikido adept, black belt in half a dozen deadly arts. The karate notion synergizes neatly with the promotion of Chip's latest flick, which has a ninja subplot. An unnamed spokesman reports that I had made numerous threatening phone calls to Chip's unlisted number which I presumably obtained in my role as a former celebrity correspondent for *CiaoBella!* and categorically denies that there was ever any romantic relationship between myself and the star. A spokesman for *CiaoBella!* citing "erratic behavior" chimes in that my contract is about to expire. An "associate" at the magazine confirms that I am "kind of a loner, a bit of a weirdo." Riding downtown, I pass the tabloids to Brooke and flip through *Beau Monde*, where I discover Kevin Shipley's review of *Walled-In*.

> At least Peter Benchley had the courage of his lowbrow convictions when he decided to rewrite Moby Dick. [*No, actually, but I saw the movie.*] The same cannot be said for Jeremy Green, the Brad Pitt of the Upper West Side lit set. After slogging through "Walled-In," Green's unspeakably pretentious homage to Thoreau, as in Henry David, I am bracing myself for Jay McInerney's take on *Leaves of Grass*.

I can't honestly say whether I would have read on or closed the magazine at that moment out of respect for my erstwhile friend, but in any case the cab pulled up in front of my apartment as I finished the first paragraph.

In New York City, particularly in the Village, it is not unusual to find people camped out on your stoop. Of the young woman sitting on my step I remember registering a purely visual sensation—that my landlady's Christmas wreath seemed from my vantage to form a green halo behind the springy mass of her dark hair. I placed a solicitous arm around my sister's shoulder as she stepped out of the cab.

When the stoop sitter stood up I assumed she was making way for us. Pretty, I thought, noting a resemblance to the actress Jennifer Lopez. She started down the steps, staring at me intently, as if she knew me. A cab shuddered to a stop beside us. Turning, I saw Corvetta climbing from the back, an expression of puzzlement crossing her face, as if *she* didn't recognize us after all. I followed her gaze, turning back in time to see the girl in the leather jacket raise her arm and hold it aloft, her curious stance—and perhaps the afterimage of the spiky crown of wreath—putting me in mind of Lady Liberty, clutching in her hand something which in the winter sunlight glittered like a tiny torch. . . .

ONE YEAR LATER

To: Scribbler
From: Philo
Subject:
Dear Connor:
I feel like so much has happened, I don't really know
where to begin. I wanted to write you after I heard
about Jeremy but I didn't really think it was my place.
God, it was such a shock. Coming so soon after I left it
must have been pretty devastating. I wish I had handled
it better. But it sounds like you have made the most of
adversity. I heard you were staying at the Chateau
Marmont a few months ago, but I thought the last thing

you would want is to hear from me. But if you feel like it, it would be nice to see you the next time you come out to L.A. But I will understand if you don't.
Love, Phil

CONCORD OUT OF DISCORD

December is the perfect month for a Florida wedding, warm evenings scented with orange blossoms—that strange moment when one crop is on the tree and another is blossoming beside it. Although in this case the epithalamia are tinged with melancholy, since Dad has been forced to sell the old homestead after mortgaging it to the hilt. But here we are, gathered beneath a tent beside the old white house, with its porches and gables, the groves spreading around us in orderly fecundity. Upstairs, the relics of my childhood—the taxidermied animals and juvenile poetry, the stamp collection, Marvel comics, baseball cards, certificates of merit and love letters—are packed in boxes for shipment to New York. In a few weeks a family from Ohio will try its luck here. Dad has been off the sauce for three months now, so chances are good that the ceremony will go off without any embarrassing incidents. My parents have bought a little condo just off the beach in Naples and with luck will have enough cash to last them. If not, Dr. Doug has pledged to help out. After all, he's family now. Despite my worst intentions I find it harder and harder to dislike him. I felt terrible when he asked me to be his best man. In fact, I'm about to deliver a toast to the groom. Among the sentiments I hope to express is my belief I'm at best the second best man, as Brooke told me over a year ago in New York.

Brooke is—dare I say it—happy, and that's miracle enough for me just now, unlikely as it has seemed for so many years. She has convinced Doug to take a year off from his practice to work with refugees in central Africa, where she will accompany him as a nurse's aide. Since last Christmas she's gained ten pounds; soon she'll be almost hefty enough to sign with the Ford Agency. A beautiful bride, crooked ear and all. I'm put in mind of that quaint nineteenth-century medical treatment—bleeding the patient. It´s as if, having dabbled at mutilating herself all those years, getting well and truly cut by a frenzied girl with a boxcutter seems to have removed the old ill humors. Her parotid gland may require further scrutiny, but the truth is she's perversely pleased, given her lifelong distrust of pulchritude, to sport a slight disfigurement: a raised pink crescent below her earlobe. Fortunately, she turned away at just the right moment.

At Brooke's insistence, her assailant, Jennie Rodriguez, is a guest at the wedding; her doctor felt her attendance would provide a sense of closure to the unfortunate episode. On two occasions I have participated in her court-ordered therapy, which has been successful at least to the extent of convincing her that slashing people with boxcutters is socially unacceptable, even under the influence of peer pressure. She's actually a very sweet girl. She feels particularly terrible that she attacked the wrong woman—my sister instead of my girlfriend. "Isn't it weird," she said just a moment ago, "the way it all turned out."

"Isn't it," I agreed.

Jennie loves Florida, at least what she has seen of it, and tells me she's thinking of moving to Miami.

Bob Jamison, of Flemington, New Jersey, remains free on bail, and seems, on the basis of his lawyer's statements to the press, to believe that he acted well within the rights of a homeowner when he shot an intruder in his kitchen at 3 a.m. The shooting occurred the night before *Beau Monde* hit the newsstands. Although some have suggested a link, it seems unlikely that Jeremy could have seen Kevin Shipley's review before he decided to drive to New Jersey in the middle of the night in order to liberate his dog; no copy was found in his possession. Subsequent reviews—and there were a lot of them, posthumously—were almost universally laudatory. *Time*'s reviewer found premonitions of early demise in both of the books, while another portrayed his death as the tragic surrender of a soul too delicate to survive the malicious and ill-informed judgment of a glib and inhospitable critical establishment. I think Jeremy would have been particularly pleased to see the word *glib* in that context. I was pleased when the *New York Post*'s page 6 reported that Kevin and Jeremy were rivals for the affections of Tina Christian. On the other hand, if his employers found this news disturbing, they have so far kept their chagrin to themselves.

As for me, I have a small scar on the palm of my hand where I grabbed at the boxcutter a year ago, which I cherish as the emblem of larger wounds. For months, my first conscious sensation on waking in the morning was the dull ache of loss, complicated almost immediately by feelings of guilt, as if I had to choose between mourning Jeremy and missing Phil— as if I was afraid that some genie would suddenly appear to offer me the choice of bringing back one or the other.

I managed to avoid seeing Chip Ralston's latest movie, in which Philomena had a small part. (I did catch Jason Townes's new flick—and was mildly surprised to see my old friend Pallas appear briefly on-screen.) I'm not unhappy to report that Chip's movie opened poorly and raced to video. According to *People* magazine, he's still dating Phil, though she has her own apartment. According to starzzz, an Internet gossip page, he's stepping out with a stripper, and Phil's recent communication leads me to credit the latter report. Every day for a year I checked my e-mail and my answering machine with the conscious if dwindling hope that I would hear from her. I shrieked with delight when the letter finally appeared on my screen, but I have not yet responded. The heart has its reasons, but they are seldom reasonable. If the concept of romantic love has any use, it is to denote that vast residue of inexplicable attraction which is not covered under the categories of blind lust and well-informed self-interest.

As soon as I finish the first draft of my screenplay—probably the *day* I finish—I am going to see her. But not until then. I'm waiting because I want to go to her in my moment of triumph. And because—could it be?—I'm afraid our actual reunion may be less shapely and conclusive than the version I am conjuring for the screen.

HOW CONNOR GOT HIS
START IN SHOWBIZ

In his will Jeremy named me his literary executor. It's a busy sideline, working with Rachel, his agent: requests for serial rights, reprint rights, movie options, translations. After all the lurid publicity, *Walled-In* sold briskly in hardcover and is about to be released in paperback. People for the Ethical Treatment of Animals—the sole beneficiary of his estate—stands to collect a handsome annuity for some years to come.

If I felt awkward about using my position as Jeremy's executor to champion my own cause as screenwriter, in the end I reasoned: Who better than me? The studio was amenable, partly on the basis of the screenplay I pulled out of my drawer, partly because it could hire me for scale—a negligible sum in its scheme of things. I'm currently adapting his story "Model Behavior," which was optioned by Fox. Someone who works at Brad Pitt's production company is said to have given him a copy of the book; based on his expression of interest, Rachel and I were able to make a respectable deal for the underlying rights as well as my first draft plus polish with an optional second draft on the screenplay. Brad's a long shot, of course; at our last production meeting, Chip Ralston was one of the names that came up. After pretending to consider this option, I said I didn't really think he was right for the part. At the moment the producers are pretending to be interested in my opinion.

ANOTHER HAPPY ENDING

We're pitching it as "a noirish romantic comedy," the story of a tormented writer's brief and tempestuous affair with his best friend's model fiancée. It's been impossible, of course, to remain entirely faithful to Jeremy's story, film and literature being different media, after all. But I comfort myself with the knowledge that infidelity is precisely the subject of Jeremy's story. In our early discussions the producer told me we needed a third act, and at the moment we all seem to be, as he put it recently, "on the same page."

It's weird, working on the third and final act, the part that wasn't in Jeremy's story. The part beyond this. But the final scene is already written. It wrote itself, as they say. I mean, there was never any question about the ending. That's one thing you can say for the movies.

In the end she comes back to me.

Stories

THE BUSINESS

I'd heard all the jokes before I moved out here. But still, you think Hollywood will be different for you. You say to yourself, Sure it's a jungle, but I'm Dr. Livingstone.

I graduated from Columbia with a degree in English lit and went to work for a newspaper in Bergen County, just across the river from Manhattan, keeping my cheap apartment on West 111th Street where I lived with my girlfriend. My thesis was a poststructuralist analysis of film adaptations of major American novels, and within a year I'd wangled the job of movie reviewer and entertainment reporter. I loved the movies, always have. The idea of being a screenwriter came to me during a group interview with a writer/director who was in Manhattan flacking for his new picture. It wasn't the fact that he didn't seem particularly bright, or that he made his ascent sound so haphazard and effortless, but something more visceral—the way he looked sitting there smoking a cigarette with the light coming through the window of the fortieth-floor corporate tower. I could see the pores in his skin and the stubble of his beard, and there was something green stuck between two of his teeth. And I suddenly thought, That could be me sitting there with two days' growth and a green thing on my teeth.

I didn't quit my job that day or anything, but I did start writing screenplays, renting films I loved and studying their

structure, thinking about what they had in common. I was
abetted in this by my aunt Alexis, who once had been a contract player at Paramount. She'd been in a couple of westerns
with John Wayne and was briefly married to a director. After
the divorce she moved to New York; the director had made her
quit the movies, she said, and it was too late to go back, but
she still talked as if she were a member of a warm extended
family called "the business." She claimed as friends some relatively famous folks, and she read *Variety* and the *Hollywood
Reporter* faithfully. I knew from our actual family that she'd
been somewhat badly used out there, but she wasn't bitter.
Now she gave acting lessons and occasionally did community
theater. When I moved to New York, she more or less adopted
me. My parents were divorced, fading into the orange sunsets
of Arizona and Florida, respectively.

Alexis lived in faded elegance in a grand prewar building
over near Sutton Place, a duplex she'd occupied for years, the
first couple with her third husband, and which she couldn't
have afforded if not for rent control. Even with a severely
depressed rent she'd had to sublet the more luxurious lower
floor, which was separated by two doors from her own quarters upstairs. The centerpiece of the downstairs apartment was
a spectacular canopy bed replete with rose-colored chintz
drapery. Alexis herself slept in the upstairs parlor on a pullout
sofa. The lower floor was occupied by the manager of a rock
group who was burning holes in all the upholstery. Alexis
knew because she snuck down and snooped around whenever
he wasn't home.

Alexis encouraged my screenwriting ambitions and read
my earliest attempts. She also provided the only good advice
I've ever gotten on the subject. "Dalton Trumbo once told me
the secret of a screenplay," she said, mixing herself a negroni
in the closet which served her as kitchen, pantry and bar. At
six in the evening the fading light was slicing through the mul-
lioned windows at a forty-five-degree angle—that second-to-
last light thick and yellow with doomed bravado—and making
the dust swimming through the apartment seem like movie
mist. "He was a lovely man, much misunderstood. That
McCarthy stuff—terrible. But as I was starting to say, Dalton

said to me one night—I think we were at the Selznicks', and I said, 'Dalton, what's your secret?' and he whispered something in my ear which I won't repeat. I gave him a little slap on the wrist, not that I really minded. I was flattered and told him so, but I was still married to the fag—before I found out, of course. So I said to Dalton, 'No, no, what's the secret of a great *screenplay*?' And he said, 'It's very simple, Lex. Three acts: first act, get man up tree; second act, shake a stick at him; third act, get him down.' "

When she was really in her cups Alexis told me she'd call Swifty Lazar or some other great friend of hers and fix me up, the exquisitely carved syllables of her trained speech softening, liquefying like the cubes in her glass. But the fact is she didn't have any juice in the industry. I didn't mind. I eventually landed an agent on my own, at which point I figured it was time to make the leap of faith. Plus my girlfriend announced that she was in love with my best friend and that they'd been sleeping together for six months.

I sublet my apartment and rented a place in Venice three blocks from the beach. This was in February, and I loved exchanging the frozen, rotten city for a place smelling of flowers and the ocean. At the same time, more than anywhere else in Southern California, Venice reminded me of New York with its general shabbiness. There were plenty of bums, just so I wouldn't get too homesick, and the crime rate was also pretty impressive. But basically I felt the same way about California that Keats did about Chapman's Homer. I quit smoking, ate plenty of fruit and vegetables, started sleeping regular hours.

One thing I didn't do was rush out to join AA, which was just then becoming really hip. If I had, I probably would've met some girls. But I was still under the thrall of the writer-as-holy-lush idea. Who could imagine Raymond Chandler sober? One of my favorite stories involved Joseph Mankiewicz, the other genius behind *Citizen Kane*, who arrived drunk one night—not uncharacteristically—at an elaborate A-list dinner party. He then got drunker, and finally evacuated the contents of his stomach all over the table. As the other guests looked on horrified, Mankiewicz turned to his hostess and said, "Don't worry—the white wine came up with the fish."

———

In Venice, my second-story studio had a little terrace off the back. I'd wake up early most mornings and take my computer out there, overlooking a tiny courtyard choked with cacti, palms and flowering bushes. Having grown up in the intemperate zones, I'm still a little thrilled by the sight of a palm tree. My landlady believed that nature should be allowed to take its course and just let it all grow. The couple across the way believed in nature too; they fucked at all hours with the shades up and I couldn't help seeing them, usually her bobbing up and down on top of him, facing me. I guess she was performing. Maybe she thought I was a casting director. . . . Anyway, I appreciated it, since that was as close as I was getting to carnal knowledge.

My second screenplay opens with this very long scene, close on couple making love, girl on top, camera pulling back out the window, pulling back, reverse angle on the guy watching from his terrace. Eventually the girl and the guy on the terrace—a writer, of course—meet and have this incredible affair. She decides to leave her boyfriend, but of course he turns out to be a coke dealer involved with some very heavy Colombians, and the girl knows enough about the gang to implicate them in a murder. Except she doesn't realize it until . . .

Believe it or not, this screenplay attracted the interest of a fairly important producer. That was when I first met Danny Brode. The producer had a first-look deal with the studio where Brode was the new vice-president of production. The meeting Brode scheduled for me was my first with a studio executive. I spent about three hours that morning trying to figure out what to wear and whether to shave. Finally I shaved and put on a white shirt, tie, blazer and jeans. Brode made me wait an hour, and when I was ushered into his dazzling white office he shook my hand and said, "What, you got a funeral or a wedding today?" When I looked baffled he said, "The tie, dude." So I knew I'd worn the wrong thing, and knew he knew I'd worn the tie for him.

Brode was wearing jeans and a work shirt which barely held him in. Standing about five foot six, the man weighed three hundred if he weighed an ounce. He had D cup cheeks, and his chin would've made another man's potbelly. Not exactly the guy to be handing out advice on appearances. Anyway, he told me he'd been running late all day and had to drive out to the Valley to check on a film in postproduction, could we take the meeting in his car?

We went out to the parking lot and got in his car, which was this four-door Maserati sedan. I didn't even know Maserati made sedans, but figured Brode was too big to drive around in one of the sports models. On the drive out to the Valley he spent most of the time on his car phone, but in between he listened as I pitched like crazy. Finally he said, "Instead of a writer, how about if this guy's an artist. We move the thing from Venice to San Francisco, and he's got a humongous studio filled with canvases—and right out the window he sees the couple screwing. The art thing's very hot right now and this way we'll get a lot more visuals." I don't know, I probably would've made him into a female impersonator. I was dying to get into the game, my savings were exhausted, my Subaru needed new brakes, and I had yet to meet a girl who wanted to go out to dinner with an unemployed screenwriter. My ex–best friend had just written to say he and my ex-girlfriend were getting married, and he hoped I didn't have any hard feelings. After pretending to think deeply about Brode's suggestion for a minute, I said, "I like it. I think I could make it work."

He dropped me at the gate of the soundstage and gave me a business card from a car service. "We'll work it out with your agent." I stood around baking in the sun for an hour before the car finally came to take me back to the studio. That night I bought a bottle of Spanish bubbly, which I knocked back on the terrace while my neighbors traded orgasms.

I called Alexis in New York, and she told me that I was part of the big family. We talked for an hour, and for once I believe I matched her drink for drink. Then I thought about calling my old girlfriend, imagining her chagrin when she realized what she'd given up, but passed out instead.

"Martin, darling, I'm going to make you a rich man," my agent told me a week later. She'd grown up on Long Island and had only been out here a couple years, but she talked just like something out of *What Makes Sammy Run*. They must give you a copy at LAX or something, I don't know why I never got mine.

The deal was two drafts plus revisions at scale, which if not a great deal was more money than I made in a year at the newspaper. And I was thrilled to have a foot in the door. "Danny Brode's really big," my agent said without a trace of irony. "That man is going places, and he can take you with him."

"I don't feel like going to the fat farm," I said.

"You better start watching your mouth around this town," my agent said. "It's a small community, and if you want to be part of it, you've got to play by the rules. Bo Goldman and Bob Towne can afford to be smartasses, but you can't."

"Could you send me a list of these rules?" I was so happy I couldn't help being full of myself. The next week she took me to lunch at Spago and introduced me to several people she described as important players, calling me "Martin Brooks, the writer."

Then I started writing the draft that would transform my hero into a painter. I flew up to San Francisco for atmosphere, talked to gallery owners and artists. Just dropping the studio's name opened doors, and I implied that a major star was interested in the lead. Back home I was able to get an interview with an LAPD narcotics detective who filled me in on the inner workings of the drug cartels.

Ten weeks after the papers were signed, I handed in my new draft. The next day I got a FedEx package with Danny Brode's card attached to a bottle of Cristal. Only his name—no title, studio, address or phone number—was printed on the card. *Danny Brode.* No need to wear a tie around here. Anyway, drinking that bottle of Cristal was the high point of the whole experience.

The hangover set in a couple weeks later when my agent called. "Basically they're thrilled with the script. Ecstatic. But they want to talk to you about a couple of little changes."

"No problem," I said. "We're contracted for two drafts, right? I mean, I make another ten grand or so for a rewrite."

"Don't worry your genius brain about it. Just take the meeting and we'll see what they want."

What they wanted was a completely different story. Having fallen in love with his idea of the art world backdrop, Brode now wanted a movie about how commerce corrupts artists. Columbia had an art project in development, and he was determined to beat its release. We could keep the drug element—the big-shot gallery owner was also involved in the coke trade. I sat in Brode's huge white office, trying to figure out where the white walls ended and the white-leather furniture began, trying to see the virtues of this new story and to recognize some shred of my own script.

Nodding like an idiot, I practically called him a genius and said I didn't know why I hadn't seen all this potential in the first place. Back home, though, I called my agent and screamed at her about the stupidity of studio executives and the way art was corrupted by commerce. She listened patiently. Finally I concluded, "Well, at least I get paid to be a whore."

She said, "Try and pick out the virtues in his concept. I'll work on the money."

"What do you mean, 'work on the money'? It's in the contract."

"Of course," she said.

I sat down again and tried to be professional about the whole thing, which is to say I tried not to give a shit. Three weeks later I delivered the new draft. I'd just bought a new car, a little Beamer, with my first check. When my agent called one morning to talk about another project, I said, "When do I get paid for my second draft?"

"We're calling that a polish instead of a draft."

"A *polish*? It was a *whole new story*, however stupid. I knocked myself out. Are you trying to tell me I'm not getting paid? What about the contract?"

"Look, Martin, you're new at this. Brode says it's a polish, and he wants you to do one more polish before he shows it to the head of production."

I was beginning to understand. "You mean I get paid for a second draft, but it's not a draft unless Brode says it is."

"Let's just say it behooves us to give Danny Brode some slack at this point. You don't want to get known as a difficult

writer. Give him one more polish and I promise you it'll be
worth your while in the long run."

When I threatened to go to the Writers Guild, she said
she'd hate to end our professional relationship.

Maybe you've heard the one about the devil who goes to
the agent and says, "I'll give you any client you want—
Cruise, Costner, Pacino, you name it, in exchange for your
immortal soul for all eternity." And the agent says, "What's
the catch?"

I stopped trusting my agent from that moment on, but I followed her advice. I wrote three drafts, got paid for one, and
the project was in turnaround within six months. Though I
didn't see Brode for a couple of years, in a sense my agent was
right. I was bankable because I'd had a deal, and that led to
other deals, and within a couple years I had my first movie in
production and moved into a house in Benedict Canyon. And
whenever I needed a villain for a story, someone rich and powerful to harass the protagonists, I had vivid impressions to
draw on.

Danny Brode became even more rich and powerful. He married into a Hollywood dynasty and shortly thereafter was running the studio his in-laws controlled. Consolidation of power
through marriage was established procedure in this particular
family. Brode's father-in-law was supposed to be affiliated
with a major crime family. In the film community it was whispered that in a premarital conference Brode had been made to
understand cheating on his wife would constitute his precipi-
tous fall from grace. This was considered slightly bizarre,
since everybody fucked around in proportion to their power
and wealth, most of all people who owned studios and casi-
nos. But the old boy was apparently overfond of his first
daughter.

"Some nice Faustian elements in this situation," I said to
the lunch partner who first filled me in on this story. I once
heard someone say there are only seven basic stories, but in
this business there's only one. In Hollywood the story is
always Faust.

"Some nice what?" he said.

I smiled. "I was just thinking of an old German film."

Brode got even fatter. In a town where everybody had a personal trainer and green salads were considered a main course, there was something almost heroic about his obesity. From time to time I would see him at Morton's or wherever, and after a while—once CAA took over my representation, for example, and I started dating actresses—he even began to recognize me. I heard stories. My first agent was right—the bitch. It's a small town.

One of the stories I heard was about a novelist I knew from Columbia. After his first novel made him famous he startripped out here to soak up some of the gravy. Success came on him pretty fast, and he ran so fast to keep up with it that he got out in front of it. He bought a million-dollar co-op on Central Park West and a beach house in Maine plus he had a little problem with the *C* word. He'd sold his book to Brode's studio outright, which is to say he got paid the same no matter whether it went into production or not. By the time the second payment was due, this writer was pretty desperate for money—he was overdue on both his mortgages, his girlfriend had an insatiable wardrobe, and his wife was socking him for a big settlement. Brode knew about this. So when it came time to pay off, he called the writer up to his house in Malibu and he said, "Look, I owe you a quarter mil, but at this point I don't know if we're going to go into production. Things are tight and your stock's gone down. Let's just say either I could give you seventy-five and we could call it even. Or I could tie you up in court for the next ten years." The writer starts screaming about the contract, his agency, the Writers Guild. And Brode says, "Talk to your agent. I think he'll see it my way."

Even in Hollywood this is not standard procedure, but the writer's stock had dropped; after being hot for a season, he'd cooled off fast, and the agency, after a lot of thought, decided to go with Brode and advised the writer to take the seventy-five and shut up.

By the time I heard this story I wasn't even surprised. I'd learned a lot in three years.

I was doing well by local standards, and that I found myself doing business with Brode again wasn't really surprising. Several production companies were tracking an idea of mine when Brode told my agency he wanted to work with me. CAA packaged a deal with me, a director and two stars for a story about—well, let's just say it was a story of betrayal and revenge. This was the one I'd been wanting to do from the beginning. "A Yuppie *Postman Always Rings Twice*" was the one-liner devised by my agent. For a variety of reasons, some of them aesthetic, it was important to me that the movie be shot in New York. Brode wanted to do it in Toronto and send a second unit to New York for a day. Toronto was far cheaper, and thought to resemble Manhattan. I knew I couldn't change any producer's mind when two or three million dollars were at stake, so I worked on the director. He was a man with several commercially successful films behind him who was dying to be an auteur. He couldn't understand how the kind of respect that Scorsese and Coppola got had thus far eluded him, so it wasn't hard to convince him that New York's critical fraternity would take his film much more seriously if it was *authentic*; that is to say, if it was shot in New York. You couldn't fake these things, I said, not even in the movies. You think Woody Allen would shoot a movie in Toronto, or that they'd publish him in *The New Yorker* if he did? Or consider Sidney Lumet, I reminded him.

That did it. Though Brode kicked and screamed, the director was adamant and very eloquent; besides, his clout far exceeded mine, commercially. In the end, after I'd handed in the third draft, they headed off to New York with long lines of credit and suitcases full of cash for the friendly local Teamsters, who for all I knew were distantly, if not disinterestedly, related to Danny Brode.

I went along for preproduction, since the director'd decided he liked having me around; so long as I didn't ask for a consulting fee, the studio was happy to pay my expenses.

Brode's assistant, a woman named Karen Levine, would be on location, while he would fly out once in a while to check in. Levine was so petite, blond and terribly efficient that at first I hardly noticed her. In Los Angeles one can become accustomed to thinking of beauty as something languid, sexiness as a quality that adheres only to the slow-moving, self-conscious forms of actresses and professional companions. And while Karen was no odalisque, I began noticing her more and more. Despite the legendary informality of Southern California—the indiscriminate use of first names, the gross overextension of the concept of friendship—it was unusual to encounter someone who could sail straight between the whirlpool of craven servility and the shoals of condescension. Karen did, and I liked her for it. That she was doing more than working for Brode had occurred to me, but my discreet inquiries suggested they were strictly business and that Brode was living up to the contract with his father-in-law.

Then I heard Karen say she was looking to rent an apartment for the three months of filming. I thought of Alexis, who had finally thrown the rock manager out, losing several thousand in the process. I figured the studio would pay a rent bloated enough to make up some of what Hollywood had taken out of her in the old days. Alexis would be thrilled by her renewed proximity to "the business," and I liked the idea of doing Karen a favor.

We were both staying at the Sherry-Netherland, and one afternoon I walked her over to Sutton Place. She'd grown up in Pasadena and was a little nervous about Manhattan, so I wanted her to see the city at its best. On a cool day at the end of April, the air was crisp and swept clean by a light breeze. Across the street the Plaza glowed white in the sun. The daffodils on Park Avenue were blooming in the center median, and the doormen stood guard at the entrances of the grand old buildings. Karen looked casually tremendous in an Irish sweater and jeans; I felt like a boy returning to his own country after making good in the colonies.

Alexis greeted us in a flowing caftan, kissed Karen on both cheeks and ushered us into the upstairs parlor where she'd laid out a tea service that would've done Claridges proud. She then took us on a tour, pointing out pictures of herself with the Duke, and Bogie, a signed first edition from Faulkner, a set of candlesticks given to her by Red Skelton, the love seat on which she'd traded confidences (here she winked) with Errol Flynn. Some of this stuff even I hadn't heard before. She was laying it on a bit thick, but Karen seemed both attentive and relaxed. When we went downstairs I knew Karen was hooked as soon as she saw the big canopy bed floating in the middle of the big paneled bedroom, wreathed in rose-colored chintz. Before Alexis had mixed her second negroni—"I don't usually drink in the afternoon, but this is an occasion, are you sure you won't have one?"—it was decided that Karen would move in for the three months and that Alexis would introduce her to the landlord as her niece; the rock manager had been her "nephew."

When we finally left at six, I asked Karen out to dinner. She said she had a lot of work to do but would love to some other night.

When shooting started, I hung around and visited the set every couple days. Brode flew in most weekends, which surprised me, though he seemed to be taking an excessive interest in the project. Each of his visits managed to make someone miserable. Three weeks into shooting it was me. Having decided he didn't like the ending, he wanted an upbeat rewrite. I kicked and screamed about the integrity of the story. Then I tried to go through the director; but Brode had worked on him first, and he was impervious to my warnings about what *The New Yorker* would think of the new ending. Apparently he was more concerned about his two points of the gross.

"It comes down to this, Martin," Brode said as he sawed into a veal chop one night at Elaine's. "You write the new ending or we hire somebody else. I'll give you another twenty-five, call it consulting." I watched him insert half a pound of calf's flesh into his maw, waiting for him to choke on it and die. It occurred to me that he was too fat for anybody to successfully perform the Heimlich maneuver, so I could say to the police officers, *Hey, sorry, I tried to get my arms around him, but no go.*

I rewrote the ending. For me it ruined the movie, but the

American public bought sixty million dollars' worth of tickets, a big gross at the time.

I visited Alexis frequently and used these occasions to knock on Karen's door. One night she finally allowed me to take her to dinner. I told her what I'd never told anyone before, about how my ex–New York girlfriend ran off and married my best friend. Karen was appalled and sympathetic. By now she'd adopted the Manhattan uniform of nighttime femininity, looking very sexy in a small, tight black dress. At her door we exchanged an encouraging kiss, but when it began to develop into something else she pulled back and announced she had to be up at five.

A week or so later I went over to visit Alexis. As she was mixing the negronis she said, "Who's Karen's boyfriend, anyway? I take it he's some big shot."

"I don't think she has a boyfriend," I said, somewhat alarmed.

"I can't understand how someone as pretty as Karen could let that fat man touch her."

I felt relieved. "That wasn't Karen's boyfriend, it was her boss."

Alexis snorted. "Call it what you want. I know all about girls and their bosses."

"It's not like that with Karen."

"Don't tell me what it's like," she said. "I have to listen to them. And now I have to buy a new bed."

"What're you talking about?"

She put a finger to her lips, walked over to open the stairway door and listened. Then she motioned for me to follow her down.

The canopy bed was wrecked. The box spring and mattress which had previously floated a couple feet off the floor were now earthbound, the bedposts and chintz draperies tangled and splayed.

"I've had bosses like that," Alexis said. "But thank God I never had that one. The poor girl's risking her life every time she climbs into bed with that whale."

———

Brode had flown back to the West Coast that morning, so I had a whole week to plot my strategy. I called a meeting as soon as he got back to town. The only time he could meet me was breakfast: the Regency, at seven-thirty.

When I arrived at eight he was just finishing off a plate of ham and eggs. "I'm just leaving," he said. "What's up?"

"I have another movie. You might like this one."

"What's the pitch?" he said. "I've got exactly three minutes."

"It's a mob story."

"That turf's pretty well worked," he said.

"You'll like this one," I said. "In my story, a young mobster's career takes off when he marries the don's daughter. But there's a catch: if he ever screws around, the don tells him, he'll be a piss-poor scuba diver, fifty feet under without oxygen. At first the son-in-law does very well. However, a young wise guy within the organization happens to live in the same building as this very attractive girl, and there's a farcical scene involving this broken bed. The broken bed leads to very dire consequences for some of the parties concerned."

Brode's face turned dark red as he listened. At the end of the pitch he looked into my eyes to see if he might've misheard me. Then he said, "What do you want?"

"I want another movie with you. Okay, maybe not this one, but something else. And I want to coproduce."

"I could have you . . ." He didn't finish.

And that's how I became a producer, on terms that were highly satisfactory from my point of view. I don't think Danny felt it was the best deal he'd ever made, and I knew I'd have to watch out for him. But the project I eventually developed made money for both of us, which made me feel a little safer when falling asleep at night.

A year after this breakfast I flew back to New York for Alexis's funeral. One of ten mourners, I cried when they lowered her coffin into the ground out in the cemetery in Queens. The last time I remembered crying was on a day that should've been one of my happiest. I'd just gotten a call from an agent in Los Angeles who'd read my script and decided to represent me. I waited two hours for Lauren, my girlfriend, to come home from work. I bought flowers and champagne and called everyone I knew. Finally Lauren got home and I almost knocked her over. We'd talked about moving to California together if anything happened for me. I poured champagne and talked about our future in the promised land. "We can live near the beach," I said, following her into the bathroom, where she rubbed a pink towel back and forth across her dark hair. "We'll drive up to Big Sur on weekends." That was when she told me. One minute I've got champagne streaming down my face, and tears the next. I thought about that as I listened to the words of the minister at the cemetery, and felt the wetness on my cheeks. I remembered that day years ago in a one-bedroom apartment on West 111th Street as being the last time I cried. I don't think it will happen again.

CON DOCTOR

They've come for you at last. Outside your cell door, gathered like a storm. Each man holds a pendant sock and in the sock is a heavy steel combination lock which he has removed from the locker in his own cell. You feel them out there, every predatory one of them, and still they wait. They have found you. Finally they crowd open the cell door and pour in, flailing at you like mad drummers on amphetamines, their cats' eyes glowing yellow in the dark, hammering at the recalcitrant bones of your face and the tender regions of your prone carcass, the soft tattoo of blows interwoven with grunts of exertion. It's the old lock 'n' sock. You should have known. As you wait for the end, you think that it could've been worse. It has been worse. Christ, what they do to you some nights. . . .

In the morning, over seven-grain cereal and skim milk, Terri says, "The grass looks sick."

"You want the lawn doctor," McClarty says. "I'm the con doctor."

"I wish you'd go back to private practice. I can't believe you didn't report that inmate who threatened to kill you." McClarty now feels guilty that he told Terri about this little incident—a con named Lesko who made the threat after McClarty cut back his Valium—in the spirit of stoking her sexual ardor. His mention of the threat, his exploitation of it, have the unintended effect of making it seem more real.

"The association is supposed to take care of the grass," Terri says. They live in a community called Live Oakes Manor, two-to-four-bedroom homes behind an eight-foot brick wall, with four tennis courts, a small clubhouse and a duck pond. This is the way we live now—on culs-de-sac in false communities. Bradford Arms, Ridgeview Farms, Tudor Crescent, Wedgewood Heights, Oakdale Manor, Olde Towne Estates—these capricious appellations with their diminutive suggestion of the baronial, their faux Anglo-pastoral allusiveness. Terri's two-bedroom unit with sundeck and Jacuzzi is described in the literature as "contemporary Georgian."

McClarty thinks about how, back in the days of pills and needles—of Percodan and Dilaudid and finally fentanyl—he didn't have these damn nightmares. In fact he didn't have any dreams. Now when he's not dreaming about the prison, he dreams about the pills and also about the powders and the deliquescent Demerol mingling in the barrel of the syringe with his own brilliant blood. He dreams that he can see it glowing green beneath the skin like a radioactive isotope as it moves up the vein, warming everything in its path until it blossoms in his brain stem. Maybe, he thinks, he should go to a meeting.

"I'm going to call this morning," Terri continues. "And have them check the gutters while they're at it." She will, too. Her remarkable sense of economy and organization, which might seem comical or even obnoxious, is touching to McClarty, who sees it as a function of her recovering alcoholic's battle against chaos. He admires this. And he likes the fact that she knows how to get the oil in the cars changed or free upgrades when they fly to St. Thomas. Outside of the examining room McClarty still feels bereft of competence and will.

She kisses his widow's peak on her way out and reminds him about dinner with the Clausens, whoever they might be. God bless them and their tchotchkes. Perversely, McClarty actually likes this instant new life. Just subtract narcotics and vodka, and stir. He feels like a character actor who, given a cameo in a sitcom, finds himself written into the series as a regular. He moved to this southeastern city less than a year ago, after graduating from rehab in Atlanta, and lived in an apartment without furniture until he moved in with Terri.

McClarty met her at a Mexican restaurant and was charmed by her air of independence and unshakable self-assurance. She leaned across the bar and said, "Fresh jalapeños are a lot better. They have them, but you have to ask." She waved her peach-colored nails at the bartender. "Carlos, bring the gentleman some fresh peppers." Then she turned back to her conversation with a girlfriend, her mission apparently complete.

A few minutes later, sipping his Perrier, McClarty couldn't help overhearing her say to her girlfriend, "Ask *before* you go down on him, silly. Not after."

McClarty admires Terri's ruthless efficiency. Basically she has it all wired. She owns a clothing store, drives an Acura, has breasts shaped like mangoes around an implanted core of saline. *Not* silicone, she announced virtuously, the first night he touched them. If asked she can review the merits of the top plastic surgeons in town. "Dr. Milton's really lost it," she'll say. "Since he started fucking his secretary and going to Aspen his brow lifts are getting scary. He cuts way too much and makes everybody look either frightened or surprised." At forty, with his own history of psychological reconstruction, McClarty doesn't hold a few nips and tucks against a girl. Particularly when the results are so exceptionally pleasing to the eye.

"You're a *doctor*?" Instead of saying, *Yes, but just barely,* he nodded. Perched as she was on a stool that first night, her breasts seemed to rise on the swell of this information. Checking her out when he first sat down, Dr. Kevin McClarty thought she looked like someone who would be dating a pro athlete, or a guy with a new Ferrari who owned a chain of fitness centers. She is almost certainly a little too brassy and provocative to be the consort of a doctor, which is one of the things that excites Kevin about her; making love to her, he feels simultaneously that he is slumming and sleeping above his economic station. Best of all, she is in the program, too. When he heard her order a virgin margarita he decided to go for it. A week after the jalapeños, he moved in with her.

The uniformed guard says, "Good morning Dr. McClarty," as he drives out the gate on his way to work. Even after all these years he gets a kick out of hearing the honorific attached to his own name. He grew up even more in awe of doctors than most mortals because his mother, a nurse, told him that his father was one, though she refused all further entreaties for information. Raised in the bottom half of a narrow, chilly two-flat in Evanston, Illinois, he still doesn't quite believe in the reality of this new life—the sunshine, the walled and gated community, the smiling guard who calls him Doctor. Perversely, he believes in the dream, which is far more realistic than all this blue sky and imperturbable siding. He doesn't tell Terri, though. He never tells her about the dreams.

Driving to his office he thinks about Terri's breasts. They're splendid, of course. But he finds it curious that she will tell nearly anybody that they are, as we say, surgically enhanced. Last time he was in the dating pool back in the Pleistocene era, he never encountered anything but natural mammary glands. Then he got married and, ten years later, he's suddenly back in circulation and every woman he meets has gorgeous tits, but whenever he reaches for them he hears: "Maybe I should mention that, they're, you know . . ." And inevitably, later: "Listen, you're a doctor, do you think, I mean, there's been a lot of negative publicity and stuff. . . ." It got so he avoided saying he was a doctor, not knowing whether they were genuinely interested or just hoping to get an opinion on this weird lump under the arm, *Right here, see?* Despite all the years of medical school and all the sleepless hours of his internship, he never really believed he was a doctor; he felt like a pretender, although he eventually discovered that he felt like less of a pretender on one hundred milligrams of Seconal.

The weather, according to the radio, is hot and hotting up. Kevin has the windows up and the climate control at sixty-eight. High between ninety-five and ninety-eight. Which is about as predictable as "Stairway to Heaven" on Rock 101, the station that plays all "Stairway," only "Stairway," twenty-four hours a day—a song which one of the M.D. junkies in rehab insisted was about dope, but to a junkie everything is about dope. Now the song makes McClarty think of Terri marching righteously on her Stairmaster.

After a lifetime in Chicago he likes the hot summers and temperate winters, and he likes the ur-American suburban sprawl of franchises and housing developments with an affection all the greater for being self-conscious. As a bright, fatherless child he'd always felt alien and isolated; later as a doctor he felt even farther removed from the general populace—it's like being a cop—which alienation was only enhanced when he also became a drug addict and de facto criminal. He wanted to be part of the stream, an unconscious member of the larger community, but all the morphine in the pharmacy couldn't produce the desired result. When he first came out of rehab, after years of escalating numbness, the sight of a Burger King or a familiar television show could bring him to tears, could make him feel, for the first time, like a real *American*.

He turns into the drive marked MIDSTATE CORRECTION FACILITY. It's no accident that you can't see the buildings from the road. With homes worth half a million within a quarter mile, construction was discreet. No hearings, since the land belonged to the state, which was happy to skip the expense of a new prison and instead board its high-security criminals with the corporation that employs Dr. Kevin McClarty. He drives along the east flank of chain-link fence and triple-coiled concertina wire.

These guards, too, greet him by name and title when he signs in. Through the bulletproof Plexi he sees the enlarged photo of an Air Jordan sneaker a visitor just happened to be wearing when he hit the metal detector, its sole sliced open to show a .25-caliber Beretta nesting snug as a fetus in the exposed cavity. *Hey, it musta come from the factory that way, man, like those screws and syringes and shit that got inside the Pepsi cans, I ain't never seen that piece before. What is that shit, a twenty-five? I wouldn't be caught dead with no twenty-five, man, you can't stop a roach with that fucking popgun.*

Dr. McClarty is buzzed through the first door and, once it closes behind him, through the second. Inside he can sense it, the malevolent funk of the prison air, the dread ambience of the dream. The varnished concrete floor of the long white hall is as shiny as ice.

Emma, the fat nurse, buzzes him into the medical ward.

"How many signed up today," he asks.

"Twelve so far."

McClarty retreats to his office, where Donnie, the head nurse, is talking on the phone. "I surely do appreciate that . . . thank you kindly. . . ." Donnie's perennially sunny manner stands out even in this region of pandemic cheerfulness. He says good morning with the accent on the first syllable, then runs down coming attractions. "A kid beat up in D last night. He's waiting. And you know Peters from K block, the diabetic who's been bitching about the kitchen food? Saying the food's running his blood sugar up? Well, this morning they searched his cell and found three bags of cookies, a Goo Goo Cluster and two Moon Pies under the bed. I think maybe we should tell the commissary to stop selling him this junk. Yesterday his blood sugar was four hundred."

Dr. McClarty tells Donnie that they can't tell the commissary any such thing, that would be a restriction of Peters's liberty—cruel and unusual punishment. He'd fill out a complaint, and they'd spend four hours in court downtown, where the judge would eventually deliver a lecture, thirdhand Rousseau, on the natural Rights of Man.

Then there's Caruthers from G, who had a seizure and claims he needs to up his dose of Klonopin. Ah, yes, Mr. Caruthers, we'd *all* like to up *that* and file the edges right off our day. In McClarty's case from zero milligrams a day to about ten, with a little Demerol and maybe a Dilaudid thrown into the mix just to secure the perimeter. Or, fuck it, go straight for the fentanyl. No—he mustn't think this way. Like those "impure thoughts" the priests used to warn us about, these pharmaceutical fantasies must be stamped out at all cost. He should call his sponsor, catch a meeting on the way home.

The first patient, Cribbs, a skinny little white kid, has a bloody black eye, which, on examination, proves to be an orbital fracture. That is, his eye socket has been smashed in. And while McClarty has never seen Cribbs before, the swollen face is familiar; he saw it last night in his sleep. "Lock and sock?" he asks.

The kid nods and then winces at the pain.

"They just come in the middle of the night, maybe five of them, and started whaling on me. I was just lying there mind-ing my own business." Obviously new, he doesn't even know the code yet—not to tell nobody nothing. He is a sniveler, a skinny chicken, an obvious target. Now, away from his peers and tormentors, he seems ready to cry. But he suddenly wipes his nose and grins, shows McClarty the bloody teeth marks on his arm. "One of the sonsofbitches bit me," he says, looking incongruously pleased.

"You enjoyed that part, did you, Mr. Cribbs?" Then, suddenly, McClarty guesses.

"That'll fix his fucking wagon," says Cribbs, smiling hideously, pink gums showing above his twisted yellow teeth. "I got something he don't want. I got the HIV."

After McClarty cleans up the eye, he writes up a hospital transfer and orders a blood test.

"They won't be messing with me no more," Cribbs says in parting. In fact, in McClarty's experience there are two approaches to AIDS cases among the inmate population. Many are indeed given a wide berth. Or else they are killed, quickly and efficiently and without malice, in their sleep.

Next is a surly, muscled black prisoner with a broken hand. Mr. Brown claims to have smashed, accidentally, into the wall of the recreation yard. "Yeah, playing handball, you know?" Amazing how many guys hurt themselves in the yard. Brown doesn't even try to make this story sound convincing; rather he turns up his lip and fixes McClarty with a look that dares him to doubt it.

So far, in the year he has worked here, McClarty has been attacked only in his dreams. But he has been threatened several times, most recently by Lesko. A big pear-shaped redneck in for aggravated assault, he took a knife to a bartender who turned him away at closing time. The bartender was stabbed fifteen times before the bouncer hit Lesko with a bat. And while Lesko did threaten to kill McClarty, fortunately it wasn't in front of the other prisoners, in which case he would feel that his honor, as well as his buzz, was at stake. Still, McClarty makes a note to check up on Lesko; he'll ask Santiago, the guard over on D, to get a reading on his general mood and comportment.

Dr. McClarty makes the first official phone call of the day, to a pompous ass of a psychopharmacologist to get an opinion on Caruthers's medication, not that McClarty doesn't have an opinion himself; he is required to consult a so-called expert. McClarty thinks Peganone would stave off the seizures just as effectively and more cheaply—which after all is his employer's chief concern—whereas Caruthers's chief concern, quite apart from his seizures, is catching that Klonopin buzz. Dr. Withers, who has already talked to Caruthers's lawyer, keeps McClarty on hold for ten minutes, then condescendingly explains the purpose and methodology of double-blind studies, until McClarty is finally forced to remind the good doctor that he *did* attend medical school. In fact, he graduated second in his class at the University of Chicago. Inevitably they assume that a prison doctor is an idiot and a quack. In the old days McClarty would have reached through the phone and ripped this hick doctor's eyeballs out of his skull, asked him how he liked that for a double-blind study, but now he is content to hide out in his windowless office behind these three-foot-thick walls and let some other fucker find the cure for cancer. "Thank you very much, *Doctor*," McClarty finally says, cutting the old geek off midsentence.

Emma announces the next patient, Peters, the Moon Pie–loving diabetic, then slams the door in parting. A fat man with a jellylike consistency, Peters is practically bouncing on the examining table. Everything about him is soft and slovenly except his eyes, which are hard and sharp, the eyes of a scavenger ever alert to the scrap beneath the feet of the predators. The eyes of a snitch.

McClarty examines his folder. "Well, Mr. Peters."

"Hey, Doc."

"Any ideas why your blood sugar's up to four hundred?"

"It's the diabetes, Doc."

"I guess it wouldn't have anything to do with that stash of candy found in your cell this morning?"

"I was holding that stuff for a friend. Honest."

Another common refrain here in prison, this is a line McClarty remembers fondly from his drug days. It's what he told his mother the first time she found pot in the pocket of his jeans. The guys inside have employed it endlessly; the gun in the shoes or the knife or stolen television set always belongs to some other guy; they're just holding it for him. They never cease to profess amazement that the cops, the judge, the prosecutor, didn't believe them, that their own court-appointed lawyers somehow sold them out at the last minute. They are *shocked*. It's all a big mistake. *Honest. Would I lie to you, Doc?* They don't belong here in prison, and they are eager to tell you why. With McClarty it's just the opposite. He *knows* he belongs in here. He dreams about it. It is more real to him than his other life, than Terri's breasts, than the ailing lawn outside these walls. But somehow, inexplicably, every day they let him walk out the door at the end of his shift. And back at Live Oakes, the guards wave him through the gate inside the walls of that residential oasis as if he really were an upstanding citizen. Of course, technically he is not a criminal. The hospital did not bring charges, in return for his agreement to resign and go into treatment. On the other hand, neither the hospital administrators nor anybody else knew that it was he, McClarty, who had shot nurse Marcia DeVane full of the Demerol she craved so very dearly less than an hour before she drove her car into the abutment of the bridge.

Terri calls just before lunch to report that the caretaker thinks the brown spots on the lawn are caused by cat urine. "I told him that's ridiculous, they're not suddenly peeing any more than they used to—oh, wait, gotta go. Kiss kiss. Don't forget about the Clausens, at seven. Don't worry, they're friends of Bill." She hangs up before McClarty can tell her he might stop off at Unity Baptist on the way home.

Toward the end of the day McClarty goes over to Block D, to check the progress of several minor complaints. He is buzzed into the block by Santiago. "Hey, Doc, what chew think about Aikman's straining his ankle? Your Cowboys, they gonna be hurtin' till he come back." Santiago labors cheerfully under the impression that McClarty is a big Dallas Cowboys fan, a notion that apparently developed after the doctor mumbled something to the effect that he really didn't pay much attention to the Oilers. McClarty has never followed sports, doesn't know Cowboys from Indians, but he is happy enough to play along, amused to find himself at this relatively late stage in life assigned to a team, especially after he heard the Cowboys referred to on television as "America's team." Like eating at McDonald's, it makes him feel as if he were a fully vested member of the Republic.

"Hey, Doc—that strain? That, like, a serious thing?"

"Could be," McClarty says, able at last to offer a genuine opinion on his team. "A sprain could put him out for weeks."

Santiago is jovial and relaxed, though he is the only guard on duty in a cell block of twenty-four violent criminals, most of whom are on the block this moment, lounging around the television or conspiring in small knots. If they wanted to they could overpower him in a minute; it is only the crude knowledge of greater force outside the door of the block that keeps them from doing so. McClarty himself has almost learned to suppress the fear, to dial down the crackle of active malevolence which is the permanent atmosphere of the wards, as palpable as the falling pressure and static electricity before a storm. So he is not alarmed when a cluster of inmates moves toward him, Greco and Smithfield and two others whose names he forgets. They all have their ailments and their questions and they're trotting over to him like horses crossing the field to a swinging bucket of grain.

"Hey, Doc!" they call out from all sides. And once again, he feels the rush that every doctor knows, the power of the healer, a taste of the old godlike sense of commanding the forces of life and death. This truly is the best buzz, but he could never quite believe it, or feel that he deserved it, and now he's too chastened to allow himself to really revel in the feeling. But he can still warm himself, if only briefly, in the glow of this tribal admiration, even in this harsh and straitened place. And for a moment he forgets what he has learned at such expense in so many airless smoky church basements— that he is actually powerless, that his healing skills, like his sobriety, are on loan from a higher power, just as he forgets the caution he has learned from the guards and from his own experience behind these walls, and he doesn't see Lesko until it is too late, fat Lesko who is feeling even nastier than usual without his Valium, his hand striking out from the knot of inmates like the head of a cobra, projecting a deadly thin silvery tongue. McClarty feels the thud against his chest, the blunt impact which he does not immediately identify as sharp-instrument trauma. And when he sees the knife he reflects that it's a damn good thing he is not Terri, or his left breast implant would be punctured. As he falls into Lesko's arms he realizes, with a sense of recognition bordering on relief, that he is back in the dream. They've come for him at last.

Looking up from the inmate roster, Santiago is puzzled by this strange embrace—and by the expression on McClarty's face as he turns toward the guard booth. "He was smiling," Santiago would say afterward, "like he just heard a good one and wanted to tell it to you, you know, or like he was saying, *Hey, check out my bro Lesko here.*" Santiago told the same thing to his boss, to the board of inquiry, to the grand jury and to the prosecutor, and he would always tell the story to the new guards who trained under him. It never ceased to amaze him—that smile. And after a respectful pause and a thoughtful drag on his cigarette, Santiago would always mention that the doc was a big Cowboys fan.

SMOKE

That summer in New York everyone was wearing yellow ties. The stock market was coming into a long bull run; over plates of blackened redfish, artists and gourmet-shop proprietors exchanged prognostications on the Dow. And on the sidewalks noble dark men from Senegal were selling watches, jewelry and fake Gucci bags. No one seemed to know how or why these Africans had come to town—certainly not the police, who tried with little success to explain in English the regulations governing street vendors and finally sent out a special French-speaking squad, who received the same blank smiles. It was a mystery. Also that summer, Corrine and Russell Callahan quit smoking.

Russell Callahan was not one of those wearing a tie. He had worn a tie to work his first day at the publishing house and sensed suspicion among his colleagues, as if this had signaled aspirations to a higher position, or a lunch date with someone already elevated. The polite bohemian look of the junior staff suited him just fine, and abetted his belief that he was engaged in the enterprise of literature. On clear days he saw himself as an underpaid hack in a windowless annex of a third-rate institution. After two promotions he presided over a series of travel books composed of plagiarism and speculation in equal parts. The current title, *Grand Hotels of America,* was typical: he and his associates plundered the literature in print, sent letters

requesting brochures and then wrote colorful and informative
descriptions designed to convey the impression of eyewitness
reporting. Certain adjectives became severely dog-eared in
the process. The words *comfortable, elegant* and *spacious*
encountered outside the office made Russell feel queasy
and unclean. In May, a month after the current project had
been launched, two years after he'd started work, he'd been
assigned a college intern, an eager young woman named
Tracey Wheeler. As a mentor, he found himself assuming the
air of a grizzled veteran, and Tracey's enthusiasm helped to
focus his cynicism about his job.

Corrine worked as an analyst in a brokerage house. If she
had been a man, she would've had an easier time of it her first
year. She nearly quit on several occasions. But once she
became comfortable with the work, she found that the men
around her were vaguely embarrassed by the old cigars-and-
brandy etiquette, and vulnerable to the suspicion that she and
her female colleagues possessed a new rule book. Gifted with
mathematical genius and a wildly superstitious nature, she
found herself precisely equipped to understand the stock market. She felt near the center of things. The sweat and blood of
labor, the rise and fall of steel pistons, the test-tube match-
making of chemicals and cells—all the productive energies of
the world, coded in binary electronic impulses, coursed
through the towers of downtown Manhattan, accessible to her
at any moment on the screen of her terminal. Corrine came to
appreciate aspects of a style that had at first intimidated her:
she started playing squash again, and began to enjoy the leathery, wood-paneled, masculine atmosphere of the clubs where
she sometimes lunched with her superiors, under the increasingly benign gaze of dead rich men in gilt frames.

Corrine and Russell had met in college. They were married
the summer of graduation, and in New York their East Side
apartment became a supper club for former classmates. As a
married couple, the Callahans were pioneers of the state
of adulthood, but they were also indulgent hosts. They put
out crystal with dinner and weren't appalled if a piece of

stemware got smashed toward morning. Men who had found Corrine daunting in college, when she was an erotic totem figure, could now flirt with her safely, while women often confided in Russell, drawing him into the bedroom for urgent conferences. He had been known as a poet in college, his verse tending toward the Byronic. Now people who'd hardly known him at school fished up from the yearbook file of their memories words like *sensitive* and *artistic* when his name was mentioned.

A Memorial Day party had reached the stage at which the empty glasses were becoming ashtrays when Nancy Tanner drew Russell into the bedroom. As she tugged him by his fingers, he watched the thick tongue of blond hair licking the back of her shoulders and the edge of her red dress, and remembered again something he'd thought of earlier—that he'd actually slept with her one night in college.

"I guess you've noticed I haven't exactly been myself tonight."

She sat down on the bed and looked up at Russell, who thought that Nancy had been exactly herself, trolling her scooped neckline under the eyes of his friends, her laugh audible from any corner of the living room.

"My stepfather just went into the hospital with cancer. It's really got me down."

"That's rough." Russell didn't know what else to say, and Nancy seemed to be bearing up anyway.

"He used to take me to the Museum of Natural History. I always wanted to see the Eskimos, and I'd think how nice it would be to live in a little round igloo. I was a pretty ugly kid, but he'd call me his beauty queen." Actual tears were welling in her eyes, and Russell began to believe that she was genuinely upset, and to feel guilty for doubting it.

"I haven't told anybody," she said, reaching for his hand, which he surrendered. "I just wanted you to know."

"I find it hard to believe the part about your being an ugly kid," Russell said, finally summoning some conviction. She wasn't nearly as good-looking as Corrine, he reminded himself, impressed with his own loyalty.

She stood up and dabbed at her eyes with her free hand.

"Thank you, Russell." She leaned forward and kissed him. In temperature and duration it was a little beyond what the situation called for.

"Do you have a cigarette," she asked when she drew away.

In the hallway Bruce Davidoff was pounding on the bathroom door. Seeing Russell, he said, "Twenty minutes they've been in there." Back in the living room Corrine was talking with Rick Cohen, cupping her hand in front of her to catch the ashes from her cigarette, nodding vigorously, her smoky exhalations dissipating like contrails of her rapid speech. He liked to watch her at parties, eavesdrop on her conversations with other men. At these times she seemed more like the woman he had proposed to than the one with whom he watched the eleven o'clock news.

"Symbols work in the market the same way they do in literature," Corrine was saying.

Frowning earnestly, Rick Cohen said, "I don't quite follow you there."

Corrine considered, taking a thoughtful drag on her cigarette. "There's, like, a symbolic order of things underneath the real economy. A kind of dream life of the economy that affects the market as much as the hard facts, the stats. The secret urges and desires of consumers and producers work up toward the surface. Market analysis is like dream interpretation. One thing stands for another thing—a new hairstyle means a rise in gold and a fall in bonds."

Rick Cohen nodded to mask his incomprehension. Russell moved toward the kitchen to check out the wine situation. Except for Corrine, the perfect hostess, who was splitting the difference, it seemed to him that the publishing people were all talking about the stock market and the financial people were talking about books and movies. By the end of the night everyone would be talking about real estate—co-ops, condominiums, summer rentals in the Hamptons. Igloos on West Seventy-ninth Street. *Spacious, comfortable, elegant.*

After the last guest had been shoveled into the elevator, Corrine and Russell sat on the couch in the living room and had a cigarette before turning in. Russell put a side of Hank Williams on the stereo to wind them down. Corrine said, "God, I'm tired. I don't think I can keep this up."

"Keep what up?"

"Everything." She stubbed out her butt and winced at the ashtray. "We've got to quit smoking. I feel like I'm dying."

Russell looked down at the cigarette between his fingers, as if it might suddenly show overt signs of hostility. He knew what she meant. It was a nasty habit. They had talked about quitting before, and Russell had always believed that someday they would.

"You're right," he said. "Let's quit."

To mark the end of the smoking era, Corrine insisted, they should hunt up all the cigarettes in the apartment and break them into pieces. Russell would just as soon have waited till morning, but he got up and joined her in the ritual, leaving one pack in the pocket of a blazer in his closet for insurance.

As they were loading the dishwasher, she said, "Phil Crane was hitting on me tonight."

"What do you mean—'hitting on you'?"

"I mean he made it pretty clear that if I was interested, he was too." She sounded sad, as if she'd lived in a world where until tonight infidelity hadn't existed.

"That son of a bitch. What did he say?"

"It doesn't matter." She then added she was sorry she mentioned it, and made him promise he wouldn't say anything to Phil.

Later, in bed, she said, "Have you ever been unfaithful?"

"Of course not," he said, and then remembered Nancy Tanner in the bedroom.

Russell had first caught sight of Corrine at the top of a fraternity-house staircase, leaning forward over the banister with a cigarette in her fingers, looking down at a party that until that moment had seemed to Russell the climax of his recent escape from home and parents. He'd been drinking everything in sight, huddling with his new roommates, getting ridiculously witty at the expense of girls he was just working up the courage to talk to. Then he saw Corrine at the top of the stairs. He felt he knew her, everything essential in her character, though he'd never seen her before. He stifled his first impulse, to point her out to his roommates, not sure that they would see what he saw. Russell believed in his own secret aristocracy, a refinement of soul and taste which he had learned to keep to himself, and which much later he would almost cease to believe in. Later he would realize that most of us believe in our ability to read character from physiognomy. But now, while she ignored him from her aerie atop the staircase, he read intelligence into her eyes, breeding into her nose, sensuality into her lips, self-confidence into her languid pose. As he watched, a boy he recognized as a campus icon appeared on the landing behind her, along with another couple. She turned, and though he couldn't see her expression, though they didn't touch, the air of familiarity and possession between the two was unmistakable; and then both couples disappeared from view, retreating to the real party, the actual center of the world, an action that suddenly revealed the event on the lower floor to be a beer brawl, a congress of the second-rate.

The social and academic accomplishments of his first semester, unknown to Corrine, were committed in her name. He didn't have to sleuth hard for news of her, since she formed part of the group everyone talked about, which made her seem more desirable and less accessible, as did her liaison with Dino Signorelli. Signorelli was a basketball star and a druggie, a formidable combination. Tall, lanky and slightly bowlegged, he was alleged to be good-looking, although Russell disputed this judgment as he bided his time. He had four years.

Second semester Corrine was in his English class, and without ever actually meeting they became acquainted. At registration the next fall he ran into her coming out of the administration building and she greeted him as if they were friends. It was a hot September day. Russell admired the tan slopes of her legs, imagined that he could feel radiant heat from the waves of her long, dark hair. He kept waiting for her to say goodbye. She kept talking.

They talked through lunch at the Inn, filling the ashtray

and emptying beer mugs. They talked about everything, but he couldn't stop thinking about her mouth, her lips on a cigarette, the clouds of smoke that she exhaled seeming to him the visible trace of inner fires. Still smoking and talking, they found themselves in Russell's dorm room, where they suddenly fell on each other—a crisis of lips and tongues and limbs which somehow stopped just short of the desired conclusion. She was still going with Dino, and he was involved with a girl named Maggie Sloan.

Their romance fell dormant for almost two years, till Corrine called up one night and asked if she could come over. She said she'd broken up with Dino, although she had failed to make this clear to Dino, who began calling up and then coming over to shout drunken threats across the quad soon after Corrine holed up in Russell's room. Although he was worried about Dino, Russell savored the atmosphere of siege, which lent an extra dimension of urgency, danger and illegitimacy to their union. He broke up with Maggie Sloan over the phone. Crying, Maggie appealed to the weight of tradition—the two years they'd been going out. Russell, with Corrine at his side, was sympathetic but firm.

Outside the dorm it was a prematurely cold New England fall; red and yellow leaves slipped from the trees and twisted in the wind. For three days they left the room only to get food, staying in bed most of the time, drinking St. Pauli Girls, smoking Marlboros and talking. Russell had been a party smoker before, but Corrine smoked heavily, and Russell gradually caught up with her. They smoked before bed, after making love and then in the morning before they got out of bed, while Corrine told Russell her dreams in minute detail. Her imagination was curiously literal. She remembered everything—what people were wearing, inconsistencies and illogic that seemed to surprise and annoy her a little, as if she expected dreams not to be so dreamlike. Her view of the waking world, though, was somewhat fantastic. Certain dates and names were fraught with unlikely significance for her, and, much more than Russell, the class poet, she believed in the power of words. When, after a week, Russell asked her to marry him, she made him solemnly promise never to use the word *divorce*, even in jest.

He might have taken her acceptance of his proposal to be impulsive, her renunciation of Dino to be precipitate, but he'd been in love with her for two and a half years.

The campus seemed to split down the middle over the issue. Some sided with the new couple, some with Maggie Sloan and Dino, whose senior basketball season was visibly affected. He became a loud and dangerous regular at the pub, and one night, while Corrine and Russell were at a movie, watching French people smoke cigarettes and cheat on each other, Dino trashed Russell's room. Corrine and Russell developed a repertoire of Dino jokes. The day of their wedding, in June, two weeks after graduation, Dino was in a car wreck that landed him in the hospital for three weeks. Two years after graduation they heard that he was working as a representative for a feed-and-grain distributor in South Dakota.

The morning after the Memorial Day party Corrine reminded Russell of their resolution, and for the first time since they'd known each other they had coffee without cigarettes. Russell left his first cup unfinished.

Corrine was staring wistfully at her blue Trivial Pursuit coffee mug. Somebody had given them a set of four for a wedding present—Russell tried to recall who it was. "Remember that Campbell's soup commercial?" she said. "Soup and sandwich, love and marriage, horse and carriage?"

Russell nodded. "They forgot caffeine and nicotine."

"I've heard it helps to drink a lot of water the first few days," Corrine said. "Cleans out the system."

Russell got half a glass of water down before he had to leave for work. "We've got to buy you some new shirts," Corrine said, fingering Russell's frayed collar when they were in the elevator.

"I've got plenty of shirts," Russell said.

"We can certainly afford a few more," Corrine said.

One of us can, Russell thought.

At a little after eleven Corrine called him at the office.

"How are you holding up?"

"All I can think about is cigarettes."

"Me too."

Talking about it made it easier. Or else it made it harder. They weren't sure, but agreed to call each other whenever they were feeling weak. Tracey Wheeler, Russell's intern, came over with a set of galleys she had proofread, smoking a cigarette; she must have seen him looking at it longingly.

"Do you want one?"

"No," he said. "I've quit. At least I'm trying." He felt sad hearing himself. The words seemed to mark the end of a chapter in his life, and made him feel older, relative to Tracey, in a way he didn't like. It sounded fussy, not at all in keeping with the swashbuckling air he assumed whenever she was around.

After Corrine hung up the phone, Duane Jones, an analyst, who'd gone through training with her, came into the office and sat down. Corrine and Duane had made a habit of stealing a midmorning break together. This ritual had developed in part because they had been the only smokers in the training program. The first day of orientation she had done mental caricatures of the faces around the seminar table. Duane was *GQ subscriber, Dartmouth class officer, boxer shorts and jockstraps, lacrosse and skiing.* The fact that he smoked made him seem less buttoned-down. Now they often had lunch together, to the point that Russell was a little jealous. Russell always referred to Duane as "Dow Jones, Industrious Average." Duane called him "the Poet." This morning Duane sat down on the edge of the armchair across from the desk and adjusted one of his socks.

"Got any brilliant hunches this morning? Any dreams that might have a bearing on the Exchange?" He took out a new pack of Merits and slapped it against his wrist.

"Put out a heavy sell call on tobacco issues. We quit smoking."

"Say it ain't so. *You?*"

"Me and Russell both," she said, not certain whether she was being loyal or laying off part of the blame on her husband.

Duane stood up and straightened his yellow tie. "I won't

tempt you," he said. At the door he turned and winked. "But if you change your mind . . ."

That night Corrine cooked a deliberately bland meal of chicken, peas and rice. It was the first time they'd eaten at home in weeks. Corrine had read somewhere that red meat and spicy food aggravated the craving to smoke.

"I think we should try not to go out so much for a while," Corrine said, as they ate in front of the television. They were watching a rerun of *M*A*S*H*; Hawkeye was wooing a recalcitrant nurse.

"Have you noticed that on television hardly anyone smokes?" Russell asked.

Corrine nodded. "Moratorium on French movies."

"Absolutely."

"And it wouldn't hurt us to cut down on our drinking."

Russell agreed in principle, even as the ice shrank in his third drink of the evening. After ten hours of not smoking he had arrived home feeling like he'd been beaten up, and had reached immediately for the vodka.

Russell said, "The old soup-and-sandwich theorem."

"The thing we've got to realize," Corrine said, "is that you can't have 'just one cigarette.' If you break down once, you'll do it more easily the next time."

"Right." Russell was trying to watch *M*A*S*H*. Corrine had absolutely no television etiquette. She would talk through the first twenty-five minutes of a show and then ask Russell to explain what was going on. Her questions were a little maddening at the best of times. Tonight he was ready to hurl her out the window. Either that or grab the pack of smokes he'd left in his blazer in the closet.

"Russell?"

"Yeah?"

"Please listen just for one minute. This is important."

He looked at her. She was wearing her earnest, small-girl-wanting-to-know-why-the-sky-is-blue expression. He normally found this look devastating.

"Did you ever," she said, "when you were a kid, pretend that something really bad would happen to you if you did or didn't do something? You know, like if you didn't stay underwater till the far end of the pool, then somebody would die?"

"All the time," Russell said. "Thousands died."

"I'm serious. Let's pretend, like that, that something really bad will happen to us if we start smoking again."

"Okay," Russell said, turning back to the TV.

The next day Corrine screamed at Russell for leaving his dirty socks in the bathroom sink. He got mad at her when he went to the kitchen and found the cupboards bare: How was he supposed to quit smoking if he couldn't have some toast or cereal to keep his mouth busy? She said the shopping wasn't her responsibility—she certainly brought home her share of the grocery money. Corrine stormed out of the house without saying goodbye, forgetting her briefcase. At the office Russell bummed a cigarette from Tracey and almost smoked it out of spite, as a way of getting back at Corrine. He finally broke it in half and threw it in the wastebasket.

That night, when Corrine got home, their fight was not mentioned; they were both shy and solicitous, as if helping each other through a tropical illness. They cranked up the air-conditioning and collapsed into bed at ten. Russell woke up at seven with a keen sensation of guilt. Corrine was not in bed; he heard the shower running in the bathroom. Gradually he began to recall a dream: He'd been at a party, and Nancy Tanner was beckoning to him from the door of an igloo. The purpose of the invitation was unclear. Russell walked toward the open door. It was surprisingly distant, and with each step he told himself he should turn around and run. When he finally reached her, she held out a cigarette and smiled lewdly.

Corrine came into the bedroom wearing a towel twisted around her head and another secured beneath her arms.

"We've got to do something about this water pressure," she said, sitting down at the vanity. Lying in bed, Russell could see her face in the mirror as she began to apply her makeup. She caught his eye and smiled. "What are you so serious about?"

"Nothing."

"I had the weirdest dream last night," she said.

"What else is new," he said, glad that she was accustomed to his not remembering his own dreams.

"I dreamed about cigarettes. Sneaking a smoke, like when I was a kid."

Applying a tool shaped like a miniature toothbrush to her eyebrow, she said, "Have you dreamed about it?" Her eyes zoomed in on his for just a moment, and reflexively he answered. "No."

"I guess I'm just perverse."

The next night Corrine dreamed that she was standing on the sidewalk, waiting for someone. The street was entirely deserted, though it was Park Avenue. Not another soul on the sidewalk, not a car on the street. A black limousine appeared several blocks down, cruising toward her slowly, finally pulling up and stopping by the curb in front of her. The glass was smoked; she couldn't see inside the car. The back window slipped down; a man's hand emerged from the open window, holding out a pack of cigarettes. She looked up and down the street, and then climbed into the limo. She couldn't make out the figure beside her in the backseat, but as the car pulled away from the curb, she saw Russell looking down from a window in an apartment building high above the street.

In the morning she didn't mention the dream. Getting Russell's attention had been difficult lately anyway.

That week was the first real scorcher of the summer; the humidity brimmed to the verge of rain, without breaking. Walking to the subway the next morning, Corrine could feel her damp blouse sticking to her shoulderblades. In the station the men in yellow ties looked wilted, the women in their tailored suits defensive, as if they sensed that on days like this the subterranean violence of the city was likely to boil to the surface. She had forgotten to buy a paper, and as her gaze wandered idly around the platform, she suddenly met the eyes of a ragged man staring back at her with malevolent intensity. She turned away, staggered by that look, her mind unreeling images of carnage: muzzle flash, neon blood, filthy hands at her throat, boldface headlines. As the train rattled in, she couldn't help looking again; this time she saw a blank face and lusterless, unfocused eyes behind a tangle of matted hair.

A little after ten Duane Jones stuck his head into her office. "Still being virtuous?"

She motioned him in and whispered, "Close the door."

He raised his eyebrows and pulled the door closed.

"Let me have a couple of drags."

"All this secrecy for a couple of drags?"

"Just light it, will you?"

He shook a Merit out of his pack and held it out to her.

"No, you light it."

Duane was enjoying this. He lit the cigarette with his lighter and held it out to her. "The idea being that if I light it, you won't have actually smoked a cigarette?"

"Humor me." She took the cigarette and inhaled deeply, held the smoke in her lungs. "Funny, it doesn't taste like I thought it would."

"You look great with a cigarette."

She took another, strictly experimental drag. This was more like what she had anticipated, a reunion clinch with a former lover. But she wasn't going to hop into bed. She just wanted to remind herself that she could live without this one passion. Corrine held the cigarette out to him, fortified with a new resolve. "Take it."

"I've got more."

"Take it."

"Okay." Duane noted the faint peach impression of Corrine's lips on the filter. He took a drag.

Corrine was sorting papers on her desk, suddenly all business. "I'm going to be here till midnight if I don't get moving," she said.

"You know where to find me," Duane said as he left.

The stock market was getting hot; Corrine was working twelve- and fourteen-hour days. With the advent of Tracey, Russell's workload was considerably lighter, but because of Corrine's job they couldn't get out of the city much. At first he enjoyed being able to meet friends for drinks, watch TV or read at home without interruption, though as the summer wore on, he began to resent her scrupulous fidelity to her job. One hot night when she arrived home after midnight, he made insinuations, mentioning Duane Jones.

At the office he read the *Times* front to back before settling into his official chores, and sometimes composed fake guide entries for his own amusement. One morning, as the temperature climbed toward ninety and the air-conditioning became less and less a source of relief, he was writing one of these when Tracey came in with a new batch of her own vivid compositions.

"I think I've finished Michigan," she said. "What state are you working on?"

He read: " 'The Yukon Sheraton: charming, individual guest cottages constructed by native craftsmen of local materials; cozy interiors, domed ceilings, blubber heat. Year-round winter sports.' "

She forced a faint, nervous chuckle, and then became pensive. "Do you mind if I ask you something? Don't you think what we're doing is kind of, uh, unethical?"

"Think of yourself as a fiction writer."

"I just feel funny about it."

"Why do you think most of the senior staff is alcoholic?" This hard-boiled manner had become reflexive when he was talking with Tracey. He couldn't seem to be straightforward.

An inner struggle was working havoc on Tracey's normally cheerful demeanor. Russell couldn't help admiring the contours of her sleeveless top. "It's just, you're so talented," she gasped, as if delivering a horrible confession. She looked down at the floor. "I'm being a baby." She turned and walked out of the office. Russell stared at the door long after she had gone, then left early for lunch.

Lately Russell had felt a great shroud of gauze enveloping him, preventing him from touching life and getting hold of it. He felt torpid and cloudy, but didn't know whether this was a function of the oppressive weather, his decision to quit cigarettes or some subheading under Changes of Life.

Nicotine withdrawal seemed to dull his mind and sharpen all his senses. The rancid smells of the summer streets had never seemed so acute. The vapors curling from mysterious apertures in the city streets were cruel reminders. Where there's smoke, he thought. He ate four or five times a day. Even his hearing seemed sharper: noise bothered him, as if he were suffering from an extended hangover. And the women in their summer dresses on the sidewalks excited fantasies more detailed than any he'd experienced since adolescence.

On the way back from the coffee shop he walked two blocks out of his way to follow a redhead in a yellow halter top. He entertained the notion of striking up a conversation, but then she walked out of his life, slipping smartly into the revolving door of an office building.

"What the hell is wrong with you?" he said aloud, standing in the middle of the sidewalk, drawing scrutiny from several pedestrians who seemed ready to offer opinions.

He absolutely had to have a cigarette.

Outside the newsstand he stopped and reminded himself that he had already betrayed Corrine once today, if only in his imagination. He walked on, smokeless and repentant.

Waiting for a traffic light on the way back to the office, he looked over the display of a sidewalk vendor, one of those West Africans he'd read about in the *Times*, and spotted among the wares a cigarette case made out of python skin. Tracey would be leaving soon to go back to school. He bought the case for ten bucks and took it back to work. Tracey was at her desk, eating a bowl of cottage cheese.

"It's beautiful," she said. "You're so thoughtful."

"It comes with strings attached," Russell said.

She looked up warily.

"Give me a cigarette, for Christ's sake, before I die." He smoked it in her cubicle. They talked about her courses for the fall. Russell wished he were going back to college, wished that he were embarking on some open-ended adventure, as he savored what he told himself would be his last cigarette.

One morning toward the end of August, Corrine woke up at 5 a.m. in a terrible state. She'd had a dream—the apartment had gone up in flames. Her breath was short, and she was trembling. At first she wanted to stay home from work, and wanted Russell to stay with her, but Russell pointed out that if the fire were in the apartment building, they were both better off in their offices.

She called after lunch to see if he was okay. As he was leaving the office, he called to remind her about a cocktail party that night. The theme was *La Mort d'Été;* for some reason all the parties had themes that year, as if conviviality were no longer its own reward.

"I won't be able to make it," she said. "You should go."

"Got a previous engagement?" Russell suggested.

"Don't be an idiot, okay? It's been a bitch of a day already."

"What should I wear?" Russell said.

"Wear a tie. They won't recognize you."

"Remind me what you look like, so I'll recognize you when you get home tonight."

"I'll be the girl with dark circles under her eyes."

After a moment Russell said, "How's old Dow Jones?"

"The market's up four points."

"I mean the stiff with the starched boxer shorts."

"Duane is very busy, like the rest of us."

"I don't hear you denying my surmise about his undershorts."

"Would you like me to check?"

"No, that's okay."

"I'll see you when I get home. And no smoking."

Russell planned to make a quick appearance, but after two hours the party was just hitting optimal cruise altitude. The invitation said *Cocktails six to eight,* but food and booze were plentiful and everyone was canceling dinner reservations. Rick Cohen had some blow that he let Russell in on. By ten Russell had bummed three cigarettes. He felt guilty about the first. The second came after he visited the bathroom with Rick, and obviously that didn't count. Smoking the third, he decided that he was glad Corrine wasn't with him: he could be weak without spoiling her resolution.

Nancy Tanner arrived wearing one of her strapless dresses.

She was flashy in a way that reminded him of stewardesses—a stylized, overly wrought femininity that he associated with the service sector. Her obviousness made him feel virtuous. If Nancy were a film, she'd be *Superman II*. Corrine was, say, *Hiroshima, Mon Amour.*

Nancy spotted Russell and winked, then caught up with him at the bar. "Behaving yourself?" she asked.

"Trying."

"Haven't seen you since . . . you remember."

For a moment he thought she meant the dream. "How's your stepfather?" he said.

"My stepfather?" She looked baffled for a moment. "Oh, he's fine. He's better. Where's Corrine?" she asked, the way one asks after a tagalong sibling who has finally been given the slip. He felt that if he didn't challenge her tone in some way, he would be implicated in a developing conspiracy.

"Working," he said.

"All work and no play . . ." She arched her eyebrows and then escaped before he could register his indignation. That was going a little too far. He got a drink and plunged back into the crowd.

"We were just wondering what happened to Dino Signorelli," Rick said when Russell joined his circle.

"Last I heard, he was selling seeds in South Dakota."

"Spilling seed, you mean," Tom Dalton said.

"That guy could fake a guard like nobody's business."

"He could bend an elbow, too," Russell observed.

Russell was listening to Skip Blackman's girlfriend—who had never looked so good—talk about her incredibly boring job when Nancy touched his shoulder.

"Got a cigarette?"

Russell was about to say he'd quit, but deftly turned the reflex into a negative monosyllable.

"Let's find some," she said, her eyes sparkling in a way that seemed to make this simple notion witty and daring.

She took his hand and he followed her, feeling crisp and purposeful in his movements, negotiating the tight throng of bodies and the carpeted floor like an expert skier rounding the poles of a hazardous slalom course.

"I think I've got some in my coat," she said, leading him into one of the bedrooms. She closed the door behind them. He reached for her and drew her face to his, his feeling of precision and control dissolving, the ski slope giving way to a free fall through the clouds.

Shortly before midnight Russell reeled toward home. His legs were wobbly, but this was a transparent defensive strategy, a white lie on the part of the body on behalf of the guilty mind. It didn't work. His head was utterly clear, an acoustically perfect amphitheater for the voices of accusation. He told himself that it could have been worse; they hadn't closed the deal, those few minutes in the bedroom. But they might have. They were well on their way when somebody came in looking for a coat.

He took off his shoes in the hallway, eased the keys into the locks. The apartment was dark. He crept to the bedroom, which was empty. He tried to feel relief, told himself he had a second chance. He couldn't have faced Corrine tonight. She would have seen right through him.

Russell was in bed when he heard the stealthy tick of keys and tumblers. With one eye half open he watched the door of the bedroom. The hallway remained dark. Eventually he heard her tiptoe into the bedroom; accustomed to the dark, he could see that she was carrying her shoes.

He pretended to be asleep as she undressed and slipped into bed beside him. He wanted to take her in his arms.

Corrine lay very still beside him. He waited for her rapid breathing to resolve itself into the rhythm of sleep; she could fall asleep on a dime. Instead her breath became shorter, more irregular, until he realized that she was crying. Somehow she knew. Russell cursed himself for violating this intimacy, which over the years had become so finely tuned that she was able, even in the silent dark, to sense a change in pitch. Then he decided that was absurd. He began to wonder where she'd been all night.

"Oh, Russell," she said. "I'm sorry."

He lifted himself on an elbow and tried to see her face in the dark.

"What do you mean, you're sorry?"

She began to sob. Her back was heaving. She was trying to say something, but her words were muffled by the pillow.

"What?" he said.

When she finally spoke, it was in a dull, featureless voice that he had never heard before. "Tonight," she said, "tonight I had a couple of cigarettes. . . ."

She said more, but the sound of her voice was already fading away as Russell lay back on his own pillow, feeling the chill blast of the air conditioner on his face, imagining himself henceforth as a wanderer of frozen landscapes, and in searching for a suitably tragic picture of himself he came at length, unexpectedly, upon the image of Dino Signorelli, standing alone on a treeless prairie, hatless, leaning into the cold wind.

GETTING IN TOUCH WITH LONNIE

Jared let his parched eyes slide across the soothing green lawns, watched the impeccable houses sail past the cab window. Colonials, mostly—the indigenous style here in Protestant-refugee country—some dating all the way back to the exodus from the Old World. The twisty roads, paved and widened deer paths, the old stone walls, the deep green shade of oak and maple—all this was second nature to him. After two years, he wondered if he would ever become comfortable with palm trees and the architectural miscegenation of Los Angeles. In fact, he was thinking of moving back East. A town like this, maybe. He didn't have to live in Manhattan any more than he had to live in L.A. They would come to him now. Send a car (with a bar and a phone, please). He regretted not hiring a car and driver in Manhattan for the round-trip, but had thought Laura would consider it ostentatious. He could've made some calls on the way up. One thing he had to do was call Lonnie. That was one thing you got used to in L.A., car phones. The phone he could live without, but this cab he'd picked up at the train station seemed to date back to the Frank Capra era. Jared felt he was suffering some kind of serious chiropractic malpractice, between the springs sticking through the backseat and the potholes whose regular shocks seemed to travel directly up his spinal column without being even faintly absorbed.

Laura had tried to persuade him to move out to Connecticut

a few years back, to the kind of place they'd both grown up in. And now she's finally made it back to the suburbs, he thought, feeling clever for just a moment, then guilty.

The cabdriver kept looking up into the rearview mirror. Jared was becoming familiar with, but by no means tired of, that particular look.

"Hey, excuse me—but aren't you that actor?"

Jared nodded, his manner at once shy and weary.

"Yeah, I thought you were. Don't tell me. What's your name?"

Jared told him.

"Right, that's it. All *right*. You were in that movie."

"Been in a few," Jared noted.

"How about that? This is great. I woke up this morning, I had a feeling something was gonna happen today. You know what I mean?"

"I had the same feeling," Jared said.

"So, you checking into the Valley," the driver asked.

It took Jared a minute to understand the question. Then he said, "Me? No, I'm not checking in. I'm just visiting my . . . I'm visiting someone."

"Hey, no offense. Lots of famous people come through here. In fact, this place is kind of famous for that. Of course, they come here so they can, you know, have their privacy. No publicity. I could tell you some names, man."

"Well, I'm afraid I'm just visiting," Jared said.

"Okay, sure. Listen, do you think you could sign your autograph for my kid?"

They pulled up a long, tree-lined driveway to a cluster of buildings which once might have composed the estate of a prosperous gentleman farmer, or a small New England prep school—a Georgian mansion surrounded by white clapboard satellites on several acres of blue-green lawn. Hard to believe this haven was just over an hour from the city. After only a day and a half back in Manhattan he remembered how compressed and accelerated life could be. Exhausting. Living in New York was like being on location for a movie that never wrapped.

God, I'm wiped, he thought, which reminded him that he

needed to call Lonnie. Of course he wasn't sure if Lonnie was even in town.

Signing his autograph on the back of a taxi receipt, he heard his name called out. Laura was waving from the door of one of the houses, a large black woman beside her. Jared strode across the striped lawn, the two women coming out to meet him. Thinner than ever, Laura threw her arms around him and squeezed as hard as she was able. When she finally came up for air, he saw that the worry creases across her forehead had deepened. It had been four months since he'd seen her. She was still beautiful in her distress, a tall and elegant if rather too angular brunette. Her eyes fastened onto his, tugging at him, asking for answers to all of her questions. As a kid Jared had been terrified by an old, supposedly bottomless quarry near his house, and that image often came to mind when he thought about the depth and vastness of Laura's need. She required so much love, her childhood stunted by some sort of emotional malnutrition, and he'd grown more and more unhappy and, finally, angry as he discovered his inability to deliver enough of it. Somehow, the worse he felt, the worse he behaved.

"This is Dorene," Laura said, drawing back to indicate the companion at her elbow. "Dorene's my special."

"Your what?"

"She's like my nurse. She stays with me."

Jared shook Dorene's hand, then glanced back at Laura. "All the time?"

"No, of course not. She's with me from seven to three, and from three to eleven another nurse comes on. Then there's the night shift."

"You have somebody sleep with you?"

"She sits in the chair beside the bed."

"This is all so . . ." Jared halted, then nodded and tried to smile.

Laura nodded and shrugged. "They think I'm still suicidal. I don't know. Some days I am." She looked down at the ground. "Sorry," she said. "I know it's tremendously expensive." Though her face and her voice had been animated for a moment with the excitement of seeing him, she spoke now in the barely audible monotone he had come to know over the phone this past month.

"Forget it," Jared said, happy that there was something he could feel noble about. The fact he was paying for this made him feel a little less guilty about everything that had happened. She had said it wasn't his fault, really, that all of the demons of her childhood had broken out of their cages at once, that it went back way before him. Her sadness over the dissolution of their marriage was just one more thing—not the sole cause of this acute depression which had finally required hospitalization. Meanwhile, his friends told him that no one can be entirely responsible for the happiness of another human being. Still . . .

Jared felt he should lighten the mood, particularly with a stranger hovering a few feet away. "You know, Dorene," he said in a phony-sounding drawl, "ever since I was a kid I always thought I was kind of special. But it must be nice to *know* you're a special."

It was weak, he knew, but she rewarded him with a smile anyway.

"You want to see my room," Laura asked.

"Great," he said, and together the three of them started across the grass back to the house. Suddenly remembering, Jared reached into the pocket of his jacket and handed Laura a small, gift-wrapped package.

"I'm afraid I'll have to open that," Dorene said, reaching for it quickly. Suddenly she smiled a little sheepishly and returned the box to Laura. "Sorry, it's just rules. But I don't suppose just this once . . ."

"Thanks," Jared said, looking her in the eyes.

"I sure liked that movie of yours."

Laura stopped walking, bringing them all to an abrupt and awkward halt. "Take it," she said, holding out the box to Dorene. "Go ahead, take it. Rules are rules." Reluctantly Dorene reclaimed it.

"This is my tiny little part of the world," Laura said to him. "It's not much. But the funny farm's all I've got right now. You have the rest of America. So please don't try to charm everyone right off the goddamn bat, okay?"

———

Laura had decorated the room with her old stuffed animals, a number of framed photographs, including two of Jared, and several painted baskets he'd never seen. Two windows over-looked the woods and a stream. A hospital bed with metal rail-ings provided the institutional note.

Sitting on the bed beside Jared, Laura opened her gift, a bottle of Chanel perfume. "It's Number Nineteen," she said.

"Your fave," he said.

"I can't stand Nineteen. It's Number Five I like."

"Are you sure?"

"Of course I'm sure. I hate Number Nineteen." She threw the bottle down, and Dorene quietly retrieved it from the carpet.

"I'd swear it was Nineteen you liked," he said.

"One of your other girls," Laura said.

Jared had bought her the stuff for years, and couldn't believe he would forget. But there had been several Chanel purchases since he and Laura were together.

"Wait a minute, for Christ's sake. Remember a week ago, when I told you I was flying to London for that awards thing and we discussed how I should call Tony and Brenda and Ian and Carol and on and on, and when I called a couple nights later you said, 'What are you doing in London?' After we'd talked about it for half an hour?"

"So? I'm sorry, my short-term memory's not so hot. The doctors said it was a symptom of the depression."

"So maybe you forgot what number perfume you like."

"Jared, you're unbelievable. You could talk yourself off death row and steal the warden's wife on your way out."

"Never worked on you," Jared said, wondering if the nurse was used to witnessing these sorts of scenes.

"Unfortunately it still does," Laura said. "I want you back."

"What are you, crazy?" he said, unsure if he were trying to deflect the sudden seriousness of this meeting by hamming it up.

She held out her palms, indicating the room. "It would appear so."

———

, "This is Wharton House," Laura said, stopping in front of one of the largest houses in the complex. "The substance-abuse facility."

Jared nodded.

"I wanted you to see it. It's modeled on Hazelden, and supposedly it's a really successful program. You'd like a lot of the people in there. Writers, actors, professors. There's this one guy I really want you to meet. Rob—amazing guy. He's made a fortune on Wall Street—"

"Why in the world would I want to meet a *stock*broker?" Jared said, gently tugging at Laura's elbow in hopes of accelerating their tour of the grounds.

"I don't know, I just thought of you the minute I met him. He's got these eyes like yours. Anyway, he's in for cocaine. Used to deal to all these stars besides running his own investment firm. He's had an incredible life, lived with that model who's on the cover of *Cosmo* all the time and then—"

"You hate people like that, Laura."

"Eventually he started going to Colombia to buy quantity himself, so he gets busted and put in jail in Cartagena. But within two weeks he has these mercenaries blow up the jail and smuggle him out of the country. Anyway, *I* think you'd like him. He's really smart."

"If I told you about this guy, you'd say he sounds like an asshole."

"He's charming. And besides, I admire his courage in coming here. That takes even more guts than breaking out of jail."

"Sounds like love."

"No," she said. "Except insofar as he reminds me of you."

"That's one of the things I've missed about you," Jared said. "The way you use *insofar as* in conversation. Or *ergo*. We don't get that out in L.A. much. Anyway, I've never been to jail or Cartagena, either one."

" 'Bout time we headed up for lunch," said Dorene.

On the walk up the drive to the main house, they were joined by some of Laura's housemates. Eric, whom Laura had mentioned several times on the phone, was a gentleman of sixty and a professor of religion at Yale. He was not visibly depressed or sedated.

"Has Laura told you she's our best basket maker," Eric asked.

"I'm an arts-and-crafts hero," Laura said. "I'm thinking of opening up a crafts boutique after I get out of here. Call it the Basket Case."

After they moved through the cafeteria line, Laura introduced Jared around the table.

"Just arrive today?" said Tony, a young man with a scimitar-shaped scar across his throat.

Jared nodded, his mouth full of cold, tough veal.

"Where are you, Wharton House?"

"I'm just visiting," Jared said.

"He's my husband," Laura explained.

"Oh, I see."

Jared wondered if the man was perhaps making a point by pretending not to know who he was.

The talk around the table was of the food and pharmacopoeia—prescribed dosages of antidepressants and lethal dosages of self-administered medication. Connie, a recently admitted middle-aged housewife—blond and seemingly cheerful—had tried to kill herself with Valium, thirty of the five-milligram yellows. But she threw up, and everyone told her it wouldn't have done the trick anyway.

"Thirty of the blues might possibly have done it," Jared added, eliciting a fairly general agreement around the table. "Thirty Seconals would do the trick. But for real sledgehammer results, Dilaudids are your best bet. Thirty of those would kill you and your two best friends plus their household pets." That got a laugh. "Three thousand in the water supply would take out a medium-sized city." Then in Ronald Reagan's voice, he said, "The hell with nuclear weapons, you damn Commies, we got the neuron bomb."

Everyone laughed except Laura, whose eyes he avoided.

Jackson, a Unitarian minister, told how he had closed his garage door, climbed into the Oldsmobile, inserted a tape in the cassette player and hit the ignition. When the tape turned over for the second play and he found himself still conscious, if nauseous, he gave up and went back into the house.

"It was a new car, a 1988," he said. "The new emissions-control systems are so good you can't even kill yourself."

"What was the tape?" Laura said.

"Pachelbel."

"Good choice. I love the Chaconne."

"Thank you, Laura."

Laura's approach to the world had always been slightly skewed. Was that a function of the imbalances that had landed her here, or just her charming eccentricity? Jared loved her, was still unable to divorce her after almost two years of separation. Sometimes he suspected he was afraid to let go because she was the only person who wouldn't allow him to reinvent himself completely, into something bright and shiny and superficial. So many old friends had been replaced by new ones. Laura was perhaps his last chance to remember and preserve the best of what he had been. On the other hand, was success such a crime? Everybody changes, so why did she insist that he was both selling and destroying his soul? At worst he was just visiting Babylon on a round-trip ticket. Which reminded him.

"Gotta make a quick call," he told the company. "Keep the veal patties cold for me, guys. I'll be right back."

Jared was directed to a phone booth, where he used his credit card to call Lonnie's New York number. He listened through ten rings, then another ten. Strange, he thought, that Lonnie didn't have his machine turned on, but he probably was still asleep and had the phone unplugged.

"What was the phone call," Laura asked as they were walking back to her house, Dorene trailing behind.

This, he remembered, was one of the things he hated—the suspicion.

"My agent," he said, "and I can never get right through to him."

"Just try and give me these few hours, Jared, will you? You'll be back in the world soon enough."

"You're right. Okay, I'm sorry."

She took his hand and squeezed it. "I'm sorry Rob wasn't at lunch," she said. "I really wanted you guys to meet."

"Who?"

"Rob. The ex–drug dealer."

"Next time, then."

"Can you come back soon?"

"Real soon. I gotta be in L.A. for a week or so, but I can get back right after that. It's for a part," he added, seeing her disappointment.

They sat on lawn chairs in front of the house, and Jared feared a Serious Talk was coming on. But Dorene's presence made that unlikely. Laura reached out to take his hand again, and looked into his eyes as tears welled up in her own.

"Oh, Jared, I feel like I'm just this insignificant speck on this rock that's spinning through cold space. If nobody cares about any of us, why should I keep on living?"

"I care."

"Not enough. Not more than anything. Not enough to come back."

"Your hand's trembling," Jared said.

"It's the lithium." She withdrew her hand and looked at his arm dangling over the arm of the lawn chair. "So's yours," she said. "I noticed earlier."

He looked at it skeptically. "Jet lag."

"Oh, come on, Jared."

"I'm working too hard to be abusing myself," he said.

"You always tap your foot when you tell a lie."

"I'm trying to help with *your* problems," he said. "I'm functioning quite well out there, thanks."

After a sullen silence they began to talk again, about her doctors and her therapy and eventually, as the sun dropped in the sky and Jared became used to Dorene's presence and the suburban lawn came to resemble other suburban lawns, they talked about their families and the old friends, the people who'd been at the wedding five years before in her parents' backyard.

For a moment Jared imagines that he and Laura might make a nice life of it, buying one of these big old white houses with fireplaces everywhere, starting a garden, cruising into the city for the theater and dinner. In a way, to surrender to the gentle yoke of domestic life would be such a relief. He knows Laura wanted children—and he does too, before very long. And she'd told him about some decent fly-fishing water somewhere in the vicinity. But even now another world is calling out to Jared, from beyond the stone walls and shaded lanes. Down the railroad tracks, south across a river, he can almost hear the buzz that begins anew every night—the brassy clatter of silverware and female voices busy with his praise. . . .

Laura's asking him a question—repeating a question, in fact—about when he will be back. But just then he sees a man coming across the lawn. And when Laura turns to look at the man, her face lights up. He is tall, a younger man, although his posture seems weary, his gait heavy. The face is familiar, yet in this unfamiliar context it takes Jared a moment to identify it.

He stands up. "Lonnie?"

"Hello, Jared," the man answers.

"Lonnie? No, this is Rob," Laura says. "The guy I wanted you to meet."

"We've met," Rob says. And it's true. Jared's impulse is to flee across the lawn, but he doesn't feel he can move.

And the man he knows as Lonnie and has met many times, this man says, "Welcome."

HOW IT ENDED

I like to ask married couples how they met. It's always interesting to hear how two lives became intertwined, how of the nearly infinite number of possible conjunctions this or that one came into being, to hear the first chapter of a story in progress. As a matrimonial lawyer I deal extensively in endings, so it's a relief, a sort of holiday, to visit the realm of beginnings. And I ask because I've always enjoyed telling my own story—our story, I should say—which I'd always felt was unique.

My name is Donald Prout, rhymes with *trout*. My wife, Cameron, and I were on vacation in the Virgin Islands when we met Jack and Jean Van Heusen. At our tiny, expensive resort we would see them in the dining room and on the beach. Etiquette dictated respect for privacy, but there was a quiet, countervailing camaraderie born of the feeling that one's fellow guests shared a level of good taste and financial standing. And the Van Heusens stood out as the only other young couple.

I'd just won a difficult case, sticking it to a rich husband and coming out with a nice settlement despite considerable evidence that my client had been cheating on him with everything in pants for years. Of course I sympathized with the guy, but he had his own counsel, had many inherited millions left over, and it's my job, after all, to give whoever hires me the best counsel possible. Now I was taking what I thought of as, for lack of a better cliché, a well-earned rest. I'd never done much resting, going straight from Amherst—where I'd worked part-time for my tuition—to Columbia Law, to a big midtown firm, where I'd knocked myself out as an associate for six years.

It's a sad fact that the ability to savor long hours of leisure is a gift some of us have lost, or else never acquired. The first morning, within an hour of waking in paradise, I was restless, watching stalk-eyed land crabs skitter sideways across the sand, unwilling or unable to concentrate on the Updike I'd started on the plane. Lying on the beach in front of our cabana, I noticed the attractive young couple emerging from the water, splashing each other. She was a tall brunette with the boyish body of a runway model. Sandy-haired and lanky, he looked like a boy who'd taken a semester off from prep school to go sailing. Over the next few days I couldn't help noticing them. They were very affectionate, which seemed to indicate a relatively new marriage (both wore wedding bands). And they had an aura of entitlement, of being very much at home and at ease on this very pricey patch of white sand, so I assumed they came from money. Also they seemed indifferent to the rest of us, unlike those couples who, after a few days of sun and sand in the company of the beloved, invite their neighbors for a daiquiri on the balcony to grope for mutual acquaintances and interests—anything to be spared the frightening monotony of each other.

In fact I was feeling a little dissatisfied after several days, my wife and I having, more rapidly than I would have thought, exhausted our meager store of observations about the monotonously glorious weather and the subjects which we imagined we never had enough time to discuss at home what with business and the social schedule. And after a relatively satisfying first night, our lovemaking was not as inspired as I had hoped it was going to be. I wanted to leave all the bullshit at home, rejuvenate our marriage and our sex life, tell Cameron my fantasies, pathetically simple and requitable as they were. Yet I found myself unable to broach this topic, stuck as I was in a four-year rut of communicating less and less directly, reluctant for some reason to execute the romantic flourishes—candlelight and flower petals in the bath water and such—she considered so inspiring. And seeing her in her two-piece, I honestly felt that Cameron needed to do a bit of toning and cut back on the sweets.

But the example of the Van Heusens was invigorating. After all, I reasoned, we were also an attractive young couple—an extra pound or two notwithstanding. I thought more highly of us for our ostensible resemblance to them and when I overheard him tell an old gent that he'd recently passed the bar I felt a rush of kinship and self-esteem, since I'd recently made partner at one of the most distinguished firms in New York.

On the evening of our fifth day we struck up a conversation at the poolside bar. I heard them speculating about a yacht out in the bay and told them whom it belonged to, having been told myself when I'd seen it in Tortola a few days earlier. I half expected him to recognize the name, to claim friendship with the owners, but he only said, "Oh, really? Nice boat."

The sun was melting into the ocean, dyeing the water red and pink and gold. We all sat, hushed, watching the spectacle. I reluctantly broke the silence to remind the waiter that I had specified a piña colada on the rocks, not frozen, my teeth being sensitive to crushed ice. Within minutes the sun had slipped out of sight, sending up a last flare, and then we began to chat. Eventually they told us they lived in one of those eminently respectable communities on the North Shore of Boston.

They asked if we had kids, and we said no, not yet. When I said, "You?" Jean blushed and referred the question to her husband.

After a silent exchange he turned to us and said, "Jeannie's pregnant."

"We haven't really told anyone yet," she added.

Cameron beamed at Jean and smiled encouragingly in my direction. We had been discussing this very topic lately. She was ready; I didn't feel quite so certain myself. Still, I think we both were pleased to be the recipients of this confidence, even though it was a function of our very lack of real intimacy, and of the place and time, for we learned, somewhat sadly, that this was their last night.

When I mentioned my profession, Jack solicited my advice; he would start applying to firms when they returned home. I was curious, of course, how he had come to the law so relatively late—he had just referred in passing to his recent thirtieth birthday celebration—and what he'd done with his twenties, but thought it would be indiscreet to ask.

We ordered a second round of drinks and talked until it was fully dark. "Why don't you join us for dinner?" he said as we all stood on the veranda, hesitant about going our separate ways. And so we did. I was grateful for the company, and Cameron seemed to be enlivened by the break in routine. I found Jean increasingly attractive—confident and funny— while her husband was wry and self-deprecating in a manner which suited a young man who was probably a little too rich and happy for anyone else's good. He seemed to be keeping his lights on dim.

As the dinner plates were cleared away, I said, "So tell me, how did you two meet?"

Cameron laughed at the introduction of my favorite parlor game. Jack and Jean exchanged a long look, seeming to consult about whether to reveal their great secret. He laughed through his nose, and then she began to laugh; within moments they were both in a state of high hilarity. To be sure, we'd had several drinks and two bottles of wine with dinner, and excepting Jean, none of us was legally sober. Cameron in particular seemed to me to be getting a little sloppy, particularly in contrast to the abstinent Jean; when she reached again for the wine bottle I tried to catch her eye, but she was bestowing her bright, blurred attention on our companions. "How we met," Jack said to his wife. "God. You want to tackle this one?"

She shook her head. "I think you'd better."

"Cigar?" he asked, producing two metal tubes from his pocket. Though I've resisted the cigar fetish indulged in by so many of my colleagues, I occasionally smoke one with a client or an associate, and I took one now. He handed me a cutter and lit us up, then leaned back and stroked his sandy bangs away from his eyes and released a spume of smoke.

"Maybe it's not such an unusual story," he proposed.

Jean laughed skeptically.

"You sure you don't mind, honey?" he asked.

She considered, shrugged her shoulders, then shook her head. "It's up to you."

"Well, I think this story begins when I got thrown out of Bowdoin," he said. "Not to put too fine a point on it, I was dealing pot. Well, pot and a little coke, actually." He stopped to check our reaction.

I, for one, tried to keep an open, inviting demeanor, eager for him to continue. I won't say I was shocked, though I was certainly surprised.

"I got caught." He smiled. "By agreeing to pack up my old kit bag and go away forever I escaped prosecution. My parents were none too pleased about the whole thing, but unfortunately for them, virtually that week I'd come into a little bit of Gramps's filthy lucre and there wasn't much they could do about it. I was tired of school anyway. It's funny, I enjoyed it when I finally went back a few years ago to get my B.A. and then law school, but at the time it was wasted on me. Or I was wasted on it. Wasted in general. I'd wake up in the morning and fire up the old bong and then huff up a few lines to get through geology seminar."

He pulled on his stogie, shaking his head ruefully at the memory of his youthful excess. He didn't seem particularly ashamed as much as bemused, as if he were describing the behavior of an incorrigible cousin.

"Well, I went sailing for about a year—spent some time in these waters, actually, some of the best sailing waters in the world—and then drifted back to Boston. I'd run through most of my capital, but I didn't feel ready to hit the books again and somehow I just kind of naturally got back in touch with my suppliers from Bowdoin days. I still had a boat, a little thirty-six-footer. And I got back in the trade. It was different then—this was ten years ago, before the Colombians really moved in. Everything was more relaxed. We were gentlemen outlaws, adrenaline junkies, sail bums, freaks with an entrepreneurial streak."

He frowned slightly, as if hearing the faint note of self-justification, of self-delusion, of sheer datedness. I'd largely avoided the drug culture of the seventies, but even I could remember when drugs were viewed as the sacraments of a vague liberation theology or, later, as a slightly risky form of recreation. But in this era the romance of drug dealing was a hard sell, and Jack seemed to realize it.

"Well, that's how we saw it then," he amended. "Let's just say that we were less ruthless and less financially motivated than the people who eventually took over the business."

Wanting to discourage his sudden attack of scruples, I waved to the waiter for another bottle of wine.

"Make sure it's not too chilled," Cameron shouted at the retreating waiter. "My husband has very sensitive teeth." I suppose she thought this was quite funny.

"Anyway, I did quite well," Jack continued. "Initially I was very hands-on, rendezvousing with mother ships out in the water beyond Nantucket, hauling small loads in a hollow keel. Eventually my partner and I moved up the food chain. We were making money so fast we had a hard time thinking of ways to launder it. I mean, you can't just keep hiding it under your mattress. First we were buying cars and boats in cash and then we bought a bar in Cambridge to run some of the profits through. We were actually paying taxes on drug money just so we could show some legitimate income. We always used to say we'd get out before it got too crazy, once we'd really put aside a big stash, but there was so much more cash to be made, and craziness is like anything else, you get into it one step at a time and no single step really feels like it's taking you over the cliff. Until you go right over the edge and then it's too late. You're smoking reefer in high school and then doing lines and all of a sudden you're buying AK-forty-sevens and bringing hundred-kilo loads into Boston Harbor."

I wasn't about to point out that some of us never even thought of dealing drugs, let alone buying firearms. I refilled his wineglass, nicely concealing my skepticism, secretly pleased to hear this golden boy revealing his baser metal. But I have to say I was intrigued.

"This goes on for two, three years. I wish I could say it wasn't fun, but it was. The danger, the secrecy, the money . . ." He pulled on his cigar and looked out over the water. "So anyway, we set up one of our biggest deals ever, and our buyer's been turned. Facing fifteen to life on his own, so he delivers us up on a platter. A *very* exciting moment. We're in a warehouse in Back Bay and suddenly twenty narcs are pointing thirty-eights at us."

"And one of them was Jean," Cameron proposed.

I shot her a look, but she was gazing expectantly at her counterpart.

"For the sake of our new friends here," Jean said, "I wish I had been." She looked at her husband and touched his wrist and at that moment I found her extraordinarily desirable. "I think you're boring these nice people."

"Not at all," I protested, directing my reassurance at the storyteller's wife. I was genuinely sorry for her sake that she was party to this sordid tale. She turned and smiled at me, as I'd hoped she would, and for a moment I forgot about the story altogether as I conjured up a sudden vision: slipping from the cabana for a walk later that night, unable to sleep . . . and encountering her out at the edge of the beach, talking, both claiming insomnia, then confessing that we'd been thinking of each other, a long kiss and a slow recline to the soft sand. . . .

"You must think—" She smiled helplessly. "Well, I don't know what you must think. Jack's never really told anyone about all of this before. You're probably shocked."

"Please, go on," said Cameron. "We're dying to hear the rest. Aren't we, Don?"

I nodded, a little annoyed at this aggressive use of the marital pronoun. Her voice seemed loud and grating, and the gaudy print blouse I've always hated seemed all the more garish beside Jeannie's elegant but sexy navy halter.

"Long story short," said Jack, "I hire Carson Baxter to defend me. And piece by piece he gets virtually every shred of evidence thrown out. Makes it disappear right before the jury's eyes. Then he sneers at the rest. I mean, the man's the greatest performer I've ever seen—"

"He's brilliant," I murmured. Baxter was one of the finest defense attorneys in the country. Although I didn't always share his political views, I admired his adherence to his principles and his legal scholarship. Actually he was kind of a hero to me. I don't know why, but I was surprised to hear his name in this context.

"So I walked," Jack concluded.

"You were acquitted?" I asked.

"Absolutely." He puffed contentedly on his cigar. "Of course, you'd think that would be the end of the story and the end of my illicit but highly profitable career. Alas, unfortunately not. Naturally, I told myself and everyone else I was going straight. But after six months the memory of prison and the bust had faded, and a golden opportunity practically fell into my lap, a chance for one last big score. The retirement run. The one you should never make. Always a mistake, these farewell gigs." He laughed.

"That waiter's asleep on his feet," Jean said. "Like the waiter in that Hemingway story. He's silently jinxing you, Jack Van Heusen, with a special voodoo curse for long-winded white boys, because he wants to reset the table and go back to the cute little turquoise-and-pink staff quarters and make love to his wife the chubby laundress who is waiting for him all naked on her fresh white linen."

"I wonder how the waiter and the laundress met," Jack said cheerfully, standing up and stretching. "That's probably the best story."

My beloved wife said, "Probably they met after Don yelled at her about a stain on his linen shirt and the waiter comforted her."

Jack looked at his watch. "Good God, ten-thirty already, way past official Virgin Islands bedtime."

"But you can't go to bed yet," Cameron said. "You haven't even met your wife."

"Oh, right. So anyway, a while later I met Jean and we fell in love and got married and lived happily ever after."

"No fair," Cameron shrieked.

"I'd be curious to hear your observations about Baxter," I said quietly.

"The hell with Baxter," Cameron said. When she was drinking, her voice took on a more pronounced nasal quality as it rose in volume. "I want to hear the love story."

"Let's at least take a walk on the beach," Jean suggested, standing up.

So we rolled out to the sand and dawdled along the water's edge as Jack resumed the tale.

"Well, my partner and I went down to the Keys and picked up a boat, a Hatteras Sixty-two with a false bottom. Had a kid in the Coast Guard on our payroll and another in customs and they were going to talk us through the coastal net on our return. For show we load up the boat with a lot of big-game fishing gear, these huge Nakamichi rods and reels. And we stow the real payload—the automatic weapons with nightscopes and the cash. The guns were part of the deal, thirty of them, enough for a small army. The Colombians were always looking for armament, and we picked these up cheap from an Israeli who had to leave Miami real quick. It was a night like this, a warm winter starry Caribbean night, when the rudder broke about a hundred miles off Cuba. We started to drift, and by morning we got reeled in by a Cuban naval vessel. Well, you can imagine how they reacted when they found the guns and the cash. I mean, think about it, an American boat loaded with guns and cash and high-grade electronics. We tried to explain that we were just drug dealers, but they weren't buying it."

We had come to the edge of the beach; farther on, a rocky ledge rose up from the gently lapping water of the cove. Jack knelt down and scooped up a handful of fine silvery sand. Cameron sat down beside him. I remained standing, looking up at the powdery spray of stars above us, feeling in my intoxicated state that I was exercising some important measure of autonomy by refusing to sit just because Jack was sitting. By this time I simply did not approve of Jack Van Heusen nor of the fact that this self-confessed drug runner was about to enter the practice of law. And I suppose I didn't sanction his happiness either—with his obvious wealth, whether inherited or illicit, and his beautiful and charming wife.

"That was the worst time of my life," he said softly, the jauntiness receding. Jean, who had been standing beside him, knelt down and put a hand on his shoulder. Suddenly he smiled and patted her arm. "But hey—at least I learned Spanish, right?"

Cameron chuckled appreciatively.

"After six months in a Cuban prison, my partner, the captain and I were sentenced to death as American spies. They'd kept us apart the whole time, hoping to break us. And they would've, except that we couldn't tell them what they wanted to hear because we were just a couple of dumb drug runners and not CIA."

I sat down on the sand, finally, drawing my knees up against my chest, watching Jean's sympathetic face as if her husband's tawdry ordeal, reflected there, would become more compelling. I couldn't feel very sorry for him—he'd gotten himself into this mess. But I could see she knew at least some of the ghastly details that he was eliding for us, and that it pained her. And for that, I felt sorry for her.

"Anyway, we were treated better than most of the Cuban dissidents because they always had to consider the possibility of using us for barter or propaganda. A few weeks before we're supposed to be shot, I manage to get a message to Baxter, who flies down to Havana and uses his leftist cred to get an audience with fucking Fidel. This is when it's illegal to even *go* to Cuba. And Baxter has his files with him, and—here's the beauty part—he uses the same evidence he discredited in Boston to convince Castro and his defense ministry that we're honest to God drug dealers as opposed to dirty Yankee spies. And they release us into Baxter's custody. But when we fly back to Miami"—he paused, looked around at his audience— "the Feds are waiting for us on the tarmac. A welcoming committee of G-men standing there sweating in their cheap suits. They arrest all four of us for violating the embargo by coming from Cuba. Of course, the Feds know the real story—they've been monitoring this for the better part of a year. Out of the fucking *fritada* pan—"

"The *sartén*, actually," Jean corrected impishly.

"Yeah, yeah." He stuck his tongue out at her, then resumed. "I thought I was going to lose it right there on the runway. After almost seven months in a cell without a window, thinking I was free and then—"

"God," Cameron blurted, "you must have been—"

"I was. So now the FBI contacts Havana to ask for the evidence which led to our acquittal as spies so that they can use it to bust us for a smuggling rap."

I heard the sounds of a thousand insects and the lapping of water as he paused and smiled.

"And the Cubans say, basically—*Fuck you, Yankee pigs.* And we all walk. And Lord, it was sweet."

To my amazement, Cameron began to applaud. She was, I now realized, thoroughly drunk.

"We still haven't heard about Jean," I noted. As if I suspected, and was about to prove, Your Honor, that in point of fact they had never actually met at all.

Jean shared with her husband a conspiratorial smile that deflated me. Turning to me, she said, "My name is Jean Baxter Van Heusen."

I'm not a complete idiot. "Carson Baxter's daughter," I said, and she nodded.

Cameron broke out laughing. "That's just great, I love it."

"How did your father feel about it?" I said, sensing a weak point.

Jean's smile disappeared. She picked up a handful of sand and let it slip through her fingers. "Not too good. Apparently it's one thing to defend a drug dealer, prove his innocence and take his money. But it's quite another thing when he falls in love with your precious daughter."

"Jeannie used to come to my trial to watch her father perform. And that, to answer your question, finally, is how we met. In court. Exchanging steamy looks, then steamy notes, across a stuffy courtroom." Pulling her close against his shoulder he added, "God, you looked good."

"Right," she said. "Anything without a Y chromosome would've looked good to you after three months in custody."

"After I was acquitted we started seeing each other secretly. Carson didn't know when he flew to Cuba. He didn't have a clue until we walked out of the courthouse in Miami and Jean threw her arms around me. And except for a few scream-and-threat fests, he hasn't really spoken to us since that day." He paused. "He did send me a bill, though."

"The really funny thing," Jean said, "is that Jack was so impressed with my dad that he decided to go to law school."

Cameron laughed again. At least one of us found this funny. My response took me a long time to sort out. As a student of the law you learn to separate emotion from facts, but in this case I suffered a purely emotional reaction I cannot justify in rational terms. Unfairly, perhaps, I felt disillusioned with the great Carson Baxter. And I felt personally diminished, robbed of the pride I'd felt in discussing my noble profession with an acolyte only a few hours before, and cheated out of the righteous condescension I had felt only minutes before.

"What a great story," Cameron said.

"So what about you guys," said Jean, sitting on the moonlit sand with her arm around her husband. "What's your wildly romantic story? Tell us about how you two met."

Cameron turned to me eagerly, smiling with anticipation. "Tell them, Don."

I stared out into the bay at a light on the yacht we'd all admired earlier, and I thought about the boy who'd been polishing brass on deck when we walked up the dock on Tortola, a shirtless teenager with limp white hair hanging on his coppery shoulders, bobbing his head and humming, looking forward, I imagined, to a night on the town.

I turned back to my wife, grinning beside me in the cold sand. "You tell them," I said.

THE QUEEN AND I

As the tired light drains into the western suburbs beyond the river, the rotting pier at the end of Gansevoort Street begins to shudder and groan with life. From inside a tin-roofed warehouse, human beings stagger out into the steamy dusk like bats leaving their cave. Inside the shed, one can make out in the dimness a sprawling white mountain, the slopes of which are patched with sleeping bags, mattresses, blankets, cardboard and rafts of plywood. An implausible rumor circulates among the inhabitants of this place that the white mesa is made of salt which was once, when there were still funds for municipal services, spread on the icy city streets in winter; at present the rusting warehouse serves as a huge dormitory and rat ranch. At dusk the inmates rise to work, crawling out into the last light to dress and put on their makeup. Down on the edge of the highway along the foot of the pier, the shiny cars of pimps and johns wait alongside the beat-up vans from the rescue missions and religious organizations, ready to compete for the bodies and souls of the pier-dwellers.

I watch as three queens share a mirror and a lipstick, blinking in the slanted light. One of them steps away a few feet, creating a symbolic privacy in which to pull up his skirt demurely and take a torrential leak. A second lights up a cigarette and tugs on a pair of fishnet hose. The third is my friend Marilyn, queen of Little West Twelfth Street. It's my first night on the job.

I ran into Marilyn in the emergency room at St. Vincent's a couple days before. I went in for gingivitis, my gums bleeding and disappearing up the sides of my teeth from bad nutrition and bad drugs. It's a common street affliction, another credential in my downward slide toward authenticity. Marilyn had a broken nose, three cracked ribs and assorted bruises from a trick tormented by second thoughts.

"I thought you had a pimp, Marilyn," I said, watching a gunshot victim bleeding freely on a gurney.

"The pimp, he get killed by the Colombians," said Marilyn. "He never protect me anyways, the bastard. He punch me hisself." Marilyn laughed through his nose, then winced. When he could speak again he said, "Last time my nose got broke it's my papa do the breaking. He beat the shit out me when he find me dressed in Mama's wedding gown. I'm holding the lipstick and he opens the door of my room. Smack me good, scream at me, call me a dirty little *maricón*, he don't want no *maricón* for a son. The boy last night, he was like that, this big bulging muscle New Chursey boy. After I do him, he start hitting, calling me faggot. A lot them like that, they don't like what they want. Hey, man," he said, scrutinizing me with new interest. "Why don't you be my pimp? I give you five dollar every trick."

It was a measure of my prospects that I thought this was a pretty good offer. In fact, I'd been unemployed by another Colombian murder and was sleeping in Abingdon Square Park. I was dealing halves and quarters of coke out of a bar on Thirteenth when my man got whacked and I was left without a connection. Before that I'd been in a band, but the drummer OD'd, and the bassist moved to L.A.

When I first met Marilyn I was living in a cellar in the Meat District. Marilyn worked all night, and I was up jonesing on coke or crack and trying to write. I'm a songwriter, you see, a poet. There is beautiful, ugly music inside me, which plays in the performance space deep in my mind. Walking the streets, doing the bars, I hear snatches of it in the distance, above the subliminal bass line of the urban heartbeat. I am most attuned to it in moments of transport, when I'm loaded on cheap wine or crack. Sometimes I'm dead certain that with one more drink, one more hit, I'll grasp its essence and carry it back with me to the other side. An aesthetician of ugliness, I am living here in the gutter like Prince Hal, biding my time, waiting to burst forth like a goddamn sun.

A refugee from the western suburbs, I used to skip school and take the bus into the city. I hung out on St. Mark's Place and the Bowery, copping the look and the attitude of punk, discovering Bukowski and the Beats in the bookshops. Returning to the subdivisions of Jersey was an embarrassment. The soil was too thin for art. No poetry could ever grow in the grapefruit rinds of the compost heap. Ashamed of my origins, neither high nor low, I dreamed of smoky bars and cafés, steaming slums. I believed that the down and dirty would lead me to the height of consciousness, that to conceive beauty it was necessary to sleep with ugliness. I've been in that bed for several years now. So far nobody's knocked up.

Like Dylan says, *Someday everything is gonna be different, / When I paint my masterpiece.* I'll be rich and famous, photographed with models who will suddenly find me incredibly attractive—my goodness, where have I been all their short naughty long-legged lives?—and I will do a lot of expensive designer drugs and behave very badly and ruin my promising career and end up right back here in the gutter. And I'll write a song cycle about it. It'll be excellently poignant, even tragic.

Marilyn grew up in Spanish Harlem, where he was christened Jesùs, a delicate boy with a sweet face who is a plausible piece of ass as a girl. He wants to get married and live the kind of life I grew up in. Except he wants to do it as a woman. At night he looks longingly out over the Hudson at the dim glow of suburban Jersey the way I used to look over from the other side at the lights of Manhattan. He wants a three-bedroom house he can clean and polish while awaiting a husband who works in the city. There's a huge Maxwell House sign across the river from the Gansevoort pier, and he told me once that when he wakes up at the end of the average American workday he remembers the tuneful Maxwell House commercials he saw as a kid, dreaming about percolating a pot of coffee for a sleepy hubby.

The doctor who gives Marilyn his hormone shots says that

more than half the—what shall we call them?—the people who get the operation get married, and that more than half of those don't tell their husbands about their former lives as men. I personally find this just a teensy bit hard to believe. But Marilyn doesn't, and he's saving up for the operation.

Poor Marilyn with his broken snout. In this business he needs to be able to breathe through his nose. I decide to give it a shot. Could be a song in it. Plus I'm stone broke.

So as the sun goes down beyond the river into the middle of America where the cows are heading back to their barns and guys with lunchboxes and briefcases are dragging ass home to their wives, I'm trudging toward the Meat District with Marilyn, who is wearing fishnet hose under a green vinyl miniskirt and a loose black top. The Queen and I.

"How I look, honey?" Marilyn asks.

"Looking bad, looking good," I say.

"This my Madonna look. Those Chursey boys—they love it."

By now I'm sure you've guessed that Marilyn is currently a blond.

The smell gets worse as we approach Washington and Gansevoort, which is Marilyn's beat—the warehouses full of dead meat, the prevailing smell of rot inextricably linked in my mind with the stench of urine and excrement and spent semen. A sign reads: VEAL SPECIALISTS: HOT HOUSE BABY LAMBS, SUCKLING PIGS & KID GOATS. Whoa! Sounds like that shit should be illegal, know what I'm saying?

With darkness falling, a slow and funky metamorphosis is taking place. Refrigerated trucks haul away from loading docks while rough men in bloody aprons yank down metal shutters and padlock sliding doors. The suffocating smell of rotting meat hangs over the neighborhood and, when the breeze blows east off the Hudson, infiltrates the smug apartments and cafés of Greenwich Village—which is the only good thing I can say about this stench.

As the trucks disappear toward New Jersey and upstate, strange creatures materialize on the broken sidewalks as if spontaneously generated from the rotting flesh. Poised on high heels, undulant with the exaggerated shimmy of courtship—a race of lanky stylized bipeds commands the street corners. They thrust lips and hips at any cars that pass this time of night, the area not exactly being on the direct route to anywhere except hell or Hoboken. Motorists that find their way here cruise slowly down the unlit, cobbled streets, circling and returning to scout the sidewalk sirens. Sometimes a car slows to a stop near one of the posing figures, who then leans toward the driver's window to consult, haggle and flirt, sometimes to walk around the car and slip in the passenger door, reappearing a few minutes later.

The "girls" of Washington Street come in all sizes, colors and nose shapes; and in this light not all of them are hard to look at. One lifts a halter top to expose a pair of taut white breasts as a red Toyota with Connecticut plates crawls past. It's just barely conceivable that some of these sports who transact for five minutes of sex believe they're getting it straight. But ladies, I wouldn't count on it. I mean if your fiancé gets busted down here you might think about canceling the band and the tent and the cake. Or maybe not. They're probably good family men, most of them. And so long as clothes and makeup stay in place, no one needs to start parsing his proclivities. Sometimes the cops sweep through to meet arrest quotas; johns who find their pleasure interrupted by a sudden, official rap on the window almost always act shocked when the cops expose the gender of their sexual partners with a playful tug of the waistband or the not-so-playful rending of a skirt.

The clientele is nothing if not diverse, arriving in limos and Chevies, Jags and Toyotas. Whenever a certain homophobic movie star is visiting New York—a comic renowned for obscene stand-up routines which outrage the gay and feminist communities—his white stretch limousine is bound to linger on Washington Street in the small hours of the morning.

I take up a post beneath a sagging metal awning, half concealed in the shadows, while Marilyn takes out his compact to check on the goods. He frowns. "That salt is terrible for my skin. Suck the moisture right out, sleeping every night on a big pile of salt. Even the rats don't like living on the salt." Is that because the rats are worried about their complexions? I wonder. Meantime, near the curb, Marilyn strikes a pose he has borrowed from a Madonna video. Just up the street is Randi, who claims he used to play with the Harlem Globetrotters. Wearing a leather mini and a red halter, Randi stands six foot eight in heels beneath a sign that reads FRANKS SALAMI BOLOGNA LIVERWURST KNOCKWURST STEW MEATS & SKIRT STEAKS. Truth in advertising.

Down Gansevoort, at the edge of the district, the neon sign of a fashionable diner emits a pink glow. So very far away— this place where the assholes I went to college with are tossing back colored drinks and discussing the stock market and interoffice gropings. Like my former best friend George Bing, who wanted to be a poet and works for an ad agency in midtown. We roomed together at NYU, which I dropped out of after two years because I was way too cool. After George graduated we'd meet for drinks at the Lion's Head or the Whitehorse, where he thought he was slumming and I felt like an interloper among the gentry. So excited when he first walked in as a freshman—with a fake ID from a store on Forty-second Street—that Dylan Thomas had died practically where we were sitting, but gradually, over the years, he decided that the Welsh bard had wasted and abused his talent. I mean, sure, George admitted, he was great, but what was so bad about being comfortable, taking care of your health, eating sensibly and writing copy for Procter and Gamble in between cranking out those lyrical heart's cries? And I'm on my best behavior, nodding like an idiot coming down off something I smoked or snorted and hoping the bartender won't remember he threw me out three months before. And eventually, I think it became too embarrassing for both of us. I stopped calling, and Lord knows I don't have a phone, except maybe the open-air unit on the corner of Hudson and Twelfth. Actually, it's been a relief to quit pretending.

Farther down Washington Street a trio of junkies builds a fire in a garbage can, although the night is hot and steamy— the heat of the day, stored up in the concrete and asphalt, coming off now, cooking everyone slowly like so much meat.

These old guys, after they've been on the street a few years they never really get warm again. The winter cold stays in your bones through the long stinking summer and forever, like a scar. The old farts wear overcoats and boots in August. That way you don't have to change clothes for winter. One style fits all.

I'm just fine in my black T-shirt and denim jacket, which doubles as a blanket, thanks. Be off the street before that happens to me. When I paint my masterpiece. Franks salami bologna.

A red Nissan slows to a stop. Marilyn sashays over to the car and schmoozes the driver, turns and waves to me. I come out of the shadow to reveal myself in all my freaky emaciated menace, moon-white face and dyed black hair, my yellow teeth in their bleedy gums. Marilyn zips around to the passenger side and climbs into the car, which makes a right and slows to a stop a half block down the street, where I can still see it. Farther on, a bum in an overcoat parks his overflowing shopping cart on the sidewalk and peers in the window at the brightly lit diners eating steak *frites*.

Eventually Marilyn comes back from his date, adjusting his clothes and checking his makeup in a compact, like a model. That's what he calls it—a date. He hands me a damp, crumpled fiver. I don't want to think about the dampness at all. I want to scrape the bill off my palm and throw it into the stinking street, but Marilyn's all excited about being back at work and planning for the future. He's talking about how it will be after the operation, when he gets married and moves to New Chursey. I want to slap him and make him understand that it's the land of the living dead. It's not real, like this fabulous life we're living here on Gansevoort Street. The flesh they grill on their Webers out in Morristown comes out of the very warehouses against which we bravely slouch.

At least Marilyn will be spared the ordeal of having a rotten suburban brat who will grow up to resent and despise him for being a boring submissive housewife.

As the night deepens, business picks up, and I nearly become accustomed to the layered stench, the several octaves of decay. The old men sharing a bottle around the fire pass out and the fire dies. I skulk over to Hudson and buy myself a bottle of blackberry brandy to keep my motor running. A dealer strolls by offering coke, crack and smoke. At first I think, No, I'm on duty, but the second time he comes by I have twenty dollars in my pocket from Marilyn, and I buy a little rock and fire it up, tickling my brain, making me feel righteous and empowered—I'm here, I'm cool, I'm feeling so good, I'm back on my feet and the future is mine, if I can just smoke a little more of this I'll keep from slipping back, just a little more to maintain, to stop this fading, this falling away from the perfect moment that was here just a minute ago, to hear that perfect tune in my deep brain, that masterpiece.

Franks bologna et cetera.

The buzz has slipped away like a heartbreakingly hot girl at a bar who said she'd be back in a minute, promise. Leaving me oh so very sad and cranky. Where is the goddamn dealer?

The traffic in and out of the diner picks up around four when the clubs close, yellow cabs pulling up to dispense black-clad party people like Pez, the hip boys and girls who are not yet ready for bed. I buy a so-called quarter of alleged toot and snort it all at once thinking it will carry me farther, slower than smoking rocks.

Marilyn gets eleven dates for the night, a cavalcade of perverts representing several states, classes and ethnic groups, including a Hasidic jeweler with long Slinky sidelocks that bounce up and down as he bucks to fulfillment in the front seat of his black Lincoln, a construction worker with Jersey plates in a Subaru still wearing his hard hat and a stretch limo where the guy tells Marilyn he's in the movie business and tips twenty.

The Lambs of God van cruises up, pulls over beside us. The priest says, "Top of the morning, Marilyn." He looks surprised, not necessarily happy, when I slink out of my vampire shadow.

"Hello, Father," says Marilyn. "You looking for some fun tonight?"

"No, no, just checking to see that you're not . . . needing anything."

"Fine thanks, Father. And you?"

"Bless you and be careful, my child." The priest guns the engine and pulls away.

"Very nice, the father, but shy," says Marilyn, a note of disappointment in his voice. "I think maybe you scare him off."

"The shy shepherd," I say.

"I stay at that Lambs of God shelter one night and he didn't ask me for nothing," says Marilyn, as if describing a heroic feat of selfless ministry. "That day he just cop a little squeeze when I'm leaving. Food pretty decent, too." We watch a car go by, slowly, the driver looking us over from behind his sunglasses. He seemed about to stop, then peeled out and tore down the street. After a long pause Marilyn said, "My very first date was a priest, when I was an altar boy. He give me some wine."

"Sounds very romantic," I say, recalling my own altar boyhood in another life. In awe of my proximity to the sacred rituals, I didn't smoke or swear and I confessed my impure thoughts to the eager priest behind the screen until my thoughts transmuted themselves to deeds on Mary Lynch's couch one afternoon, which I failed to mention at my next confession, suffering the guilt of the damned as I slunk away from the confessional booth. When lightning failed to strike me through the days and weeks that followed, I began to resent my guilt and then the faith that was so at odds with my secret nature and, finally, to exult in my rebellion. And as I turned away from my parents and Church, I created my own taboo-venerating cult. Which perverse faith I am stubbornly observing here at five in the morning at the corner of Gansevoort and Washington.

Another car cruises by slowly, a junkyard Buick with two guys in the front seat. Twos are potentially dangerous, so I decide I'll show my flag and talk to them myself. I tell Marilyn to stay put, then I saunter over to the car. The driver has to open the door because the window won't roll down. Two small Hispanics in their fifties. "Twenty-five apiece," I say, nodding toward Marilyn. "And you stay on this block." Finally we agree on thirty-five for two.

I wave Marilyn over and he climbs in the backseat, and I'm just leaning back against the building lighting a smoke when

Marilyn comes howling and tumbling out of the car, crawling furiously as the car peels out, tires squealing on the cobblestones. Marilyn flings himself on me and I hold him as he sobs. *"Es mi padre,"* he wails. *"Mi padre."*

"A priest?" I say, hopefully.

He shakes his head violently against my shoulder and suddenly raises his face and starts apologizing for getting makeup on me, wiping at my jacket, still crying. "I ruin your jacket," he says, crying hysterically. It's all I can do to convince him that I don't give a shit about the jacket, which started out filthy anyway.

"Are you sure it was . . . him?" I say.

Gulping air, he nods vehemently. "It's the first time I see him in three years," Marilyn says. He's sobbing and shaking, and I'm more than a little freaked out myself. I mean, Jesus.

Finally, when he calms down, I suggest we call it a night. I make him drink the rest of the blackberry brandy and walk him back to the dock in the grainy gray light. As the sun comes up behind us, we stand on the edge of the pier and look out over the river at the Maxwell House sign. I can't think of anything to say. I put my arm around him and he sniffles on my shoulder. From a distance we would look like any other couple, I think. Finally I suggest he get some sleep, and he picks his way across the rotting boards back to the salt mountain. And that's the end of my career as a pimp.

A year after this happened, I went back to look for Marilyn. Most of the girls on the street were new to me, but I found Randi, the former Globetrotter, who at first didn't remember me. I do look different now. He thought I was a cop, and then guessed I was a reporter. He wanted money to talk, so I finally gave him ten, and he said, "I know you, you was that crackhead." Nice to be remembered. I asked if he'd seen Marilyn and he said Marilyn had disappeared suddenly—"Maybe like, I don't know, seems like a year ago." He couldn't tell me anything else and he didn't want to know.

About a year after that I spotted a wedding announcement in the *Times*. I admit I'd been checking all that time—perusing what we once called the women's sports pages—like an idiot, occasionally rewarded with the picture of a high school or college acquaintance, and then one fine morning I saw a picture that stopped me. Actually, I think I noticed the name first—otherwise I might not have stopped at the picture. MARILYN BERGDORF TO WED RONALD DUBOWSKI. It would be just like Marilyn to name himself after a chic department store. I stared at the photo for a long time, and though I wouldn't swear to it in a murder trial, I think it was my Marilyn—surgically altered, one presumes—that married Ronald Dubowski, orthodontist, of Oyster Bay, Long Island. I suppose I could have called, but I didn't.

So I don't really know how that night affected Marilyn, if it changed his life, if he is now officially and anatomically a woman, or even if he's alive. I do know that lives can change overnight, though it usually takes much longer than that to comprehend what has happened, to sense that we have changed direction. A week after Marilyn almost had sex with his father, I checked myself into Phoenix House. I called my parents for the first time in more than a year. Now, two years later, I have a boring job and a crummy apartment and a girlfriend who makes the rest of it seem almost okay. I'd be lying if I said there weren't times I miss the old days, or that I don't breathe a huge sigh of relief when I climb on the train after a few hours spent visiting my parents, or that it's a gas being straight all the time, but still I'm grateful.

You think you're living a secret and temporary life, underground, in the dark. You don't imagine that someone will drive up the street or walk in the door or look through the window—someone who will reveal you to yourself not as you hope to be in some glorious future metamorphosis but as you find yourself at that moment. Whatever you are doing then, you will have to stop and say, "Yes, this is me."

REUNION

The early morning silence of the graveyard is broken by the approach of a car. I duck behind a stone as the sound of the engine rises toward the gate and falls away among the streets of the town. Sitting on a flat marble slab, Tory continues cutting pieces of masking tape, which she attaches to the back of her hand. The cemetery grass is brown and worn, as if it has been grazed by sheep. The last shreds of morning haze cling to the old stones, which tilt at eccentric angles.

I stand up again but remain hunched, feeling conspicuous among the squat headstones, while Tory seems right at home, though she has warned me this is illegal. The old cemetery is surrounded by the town; although it is wooded and occupies a rise, I feel exposed. A seagull cruises overhead with an inquisitive squawk. My eyes are dry and itchy from waking too early.

"Stretch this as tight as you can across the face of the stone," Tory says, holding out a big sheet of newsprint from the tablet we picked up at a hobby store last night. I kneel as Tory directs me to raise and lower the paper until finally it's just where she wants it, and she secures it with masking tape. Then she rubs the crayon across the paper. Crayons, drawing tablets, masking tape. I find it strange that we have come to visit the dead with children's art supplies. "Not too hard," she says. White, archaic letters rise to the surface of the paper. The

letters gradually become words. HERE emerges, then BODY
OF. I think of it as ghost writing. The inscription states the
facts: name, age and parents. The stone is a triptych, the outer
tablets bearing images of a grinning skeleton on one side and
Father Time on the other. A skull appears under Tory's crayon,
then ribs. "This guy was very rich," she says. "The stone-
work's amazing. Look at these details—you can even see the
anklebones on Father Time." Tory nods toward the tablet of
newsprint. "Give it a try," she says.

I stalk the uneven avenues for a likely stone. In the corner
near the savings bank I find one dated 1698, with the name
NATHANIEL MATHER. A winged skull presides over the
inscription AN AGED PERSON WHO HAD BEEN, BUT NINE-
TEEN WINTERS IN THE WORLD. I sit down on the grass and
touch the stone. What does it mean? I once read about a disease that accelerates the aging process so rapidly that its vic-
tims die of old age in their teens. Or is it just a metaphor? A
young man worn down by troubles.

"Michael, come here," Tory calls.

I get to my feet and look around. "Where are you?" I ask in
a loud whisper.

"Over here." She raises her hand and waves from behind a
cluster of stones. I watch the cemetery gate as another car
passes, then scuttle over.

"Look at this." She points to a lichen-covered stone. The
engraving has a crude, homemade look. THE CHILDREN OF
CHARLES AND SARAH . . . The surname is unreadable.
EMILY, TWO YEARS. CHARLES, SEVEN MONTHS. ETHAN.

"There's no age for Ethan," I say.

Tory looks up at me. She doesn't say anything at first. She
holds the crayon like a cigarette and touches it to her lips as
she stares at me. Finally she says, "He died in childbirth." She
says this as if she holds me responsible.

"Where are the witches," I ask.

"They didn't bury them in the cemetery. This is hallowed
ground. They put the witches in unmarked graves on Gallows
Hill in Danvers."

"I wanted to rub a witch's stone."

"You can do the guy who sentenced them to death. Judge

Hathorne's right over there. That would be a good one for you to get. A fellow pillar of the legal profession." Tory is on her third rubbing of the children's stone. The first two were black. This one's red. I pick a stone near hers, keeping an eye on the entrance.

"There was one man named Giles Corry, who refused to confess or to implicate anyone as a witch, so they put a beam on his chest and started piling rocks on top to force a confession. But he refused to speak. They piled more rocks on. His ribs broke and finally he died."

"That's a lovely story," I say.

Tory's a little morbid these days. But she says this grave rubbing is something she has been doing since she was a kid. This is the first time we've come up here. Though we've been living together in New York for over a year, Tory hasn't been eager to go home for a visit. Her parents separated shortly before she and I moved into our little apartment. Her mother hung on to the house, but things are strained between her and Tory. I suspect Ginny's unable to live up to the high standards that Tory sets for those she loves, although I'm not sure, because we seldom talk about it. Tory is furious with her father for leaving with another woman; yet she also seems to blame her mother for letting him do so, for not being the kind of woman that no man would ever walk out on.

Shortly after we arrived, Tory gave her mother a lesson in makeup. Ginny submitted patiently as Tory demonstrated the uses of blush and mascara. Ginny has the skin of a tennis player and the hair of a swimmer; the makeup seemed to disappear without a trace moments after it was applied. Later, Tory worked on her mother's taxes; Ginny has an antique shop that was operated for years on the principle of losing money to write off her husband's taxes. But with the division of property hung up in the courts and two years of taxes due on the house, Ginny now is faced with the new and baffling imperative of making money.

The family, sans patriarch, has ostensibly gathered for Bunny's graduation. There are four sisters, spread over ten years, all conspicuously blond. Carol, her new husband, Jim, and her daughter by a former marriage are here from California. Carol's pregnant. Jim's a Christian. Under his tutelage, Carol has been born again. She is the oldest, and according to Tory she has been exemplary, doing all of the stupid and illegal things that her younger sisters might've been tempted to do. Bunny, who just turned twenty-four, is able to seem merely adventurous by comparison. She started Radcliffe but dropped out to marry a cocaine dealer. When the marriage broke up, she moved back in with her parents. In two days she'll graduate from a local state school, where she's dating a married professor twice her age. Tory is the third child. Mary, the youngest, still lives at home and mostly is into cars and boys. I'm not sure whether she likes the boys because they have cars, or the cars because the boys have them. She speaks confidently about horsepower, engine displacement, biceps and pectorals. She doesn't think much of me—I drive a Toyota and wear a thirty-eight regular. Last night at the supper table she noticed me long enough to ask if I would make a lot of money now that I've graduated from law school.

This family reunion might be the last one in the old house. Ginny can't afford to keep it. I'd love to live in a house like this one, an old post-and-beam matchbox core that has been added to in various directions over the last couple hundred years, jammed with primitive furnishings of scarred, fragrant wood; crude iron implements; cloudy bull's-eyed blue-green glass. I like the outbuildings, the sagging, disused stables and greenhouse; even the pool, cracked and covered over with a green scum, has the aspect of an ornamental pond.

I grew up in houses that were vague, standardized descendants of those in this neighborhood. Since arriving yesterday I've conceived an indeterminate fantasy of saving the old homestead with my legal skills, distinctly featuring the gratitude of this family of attractive females.

But for several weeks now I have felt helpless in the face of Tory's medical problems. She has been bleeding erratically. Her gynecologist in New York has several hypotheses. In two days she will check into Mass General for tests, and I'll drive back to New York to start an associateship at Cravath, Swaine & Moore.

———

On the way home from the cemetery we stop at a package store. Tory waits in the car. A red Camaro is idling in the parking lot, heavy metal blasting from the open windows. Inside the store, a kid with an Iron Maiden T-shirt hefts three cases of beer up to the counter. His denim jacket has the sleeves ripped out, BILLY embroidered above one pocket, HEAVY CHEVY over the other. He asks for three bottles of Jose Cuervo tequila. The clerk checks his ID doubtfully. "Frank Sweeney?" he says.

"Yeah, right," the kid says. The clerk sighs and hands the ID back. Coming out of the store, I spot Mary, Tory's younger sister, inside the Camaro. She waves. The kid with the ID is loading the stuff in the trunk.

"How do you like my wheels?" Mary says. "Don't tell Mom you saw me, okay? I'm supposed to be at Laura's house." The kid comes around the side of the car and looks me over. Mary doesn't introduce anyone. They leave in a roar of exhaust.

Back in the car, I describe the scene for Tory, who has been reading. "She's young," Tory says. She goes back to her magazine. Mary is the only member of the family who escapes Tory's censure. Tory's still able to see her as the baby. It seems to be something she clings to, this idea that there's still a baby in the family after all that has happened.

In the kitchen, Carol and her daughter, Lily, are playing with Barbies. Carol has four months to go on her next, but she's already huge. Between her religion and her fertility, she's bursting with contentment. Ginny, the aproned matriarch, is fixing lunch. Lily lifts her Barbie toward me and waves it from side to side as she speaks in a high, squeaky voice.

"Look, Barbie, it's Ken."

"That's not Ken," Carol says. "Who is that?"

"That's Michael," Lily says in her own voice, hiding her face in her mother's arm.

"You like Michael, don't you?" Carol says, doing a Barbie voice.

Lily shakes her head back and forth. She won't look up.

"Don't teach her to be a dumb blonde, Carol," Tory says.

"And who's that?" Carol says, directing Lily toward Tory.

Tory kneels beside Lily's chair and points her finger at herself. "Do you remember my name?"

Lily shakes her head and hides it again in her mother's shoulder. She can't remember Tory's name but has the others down cold.

"That's Tory," Carol says. "Isn't that a pretty name? *Tory* rhymes with *story* and *glory*, doesn't it?"

Tory says, "And *gory*."

"Do we have a kiss for nice Aunt Tory?" Lily shakes her head against her mother's shoulder. Tory stands up and leaves the room.

"Sandwiches are ready," Ginny says. "Grilled cheese, tomato and bacon." Ginny's one of those people who believe that there is very little that can't be fixed by putting a meal on the table.

"Jim doesn't eat bacon," Carol says.

"I thought he was a Christian. Isn't it Jews who don't eat bacon?"

"We eat low cholesterol."

Ginny puts the hot tray down on the counter. She takes off the oven mitt and lights a cigarette. "You eat low cholesterol. You don't smoke. You don't drink. You don't swear, and you don't like it when other people do. Is there anything else I should know as your innkeeper? Would you maybe like some more hay in your manger?"

"Jesus loves you, Mom."

Jim, the born-again husband, comes in, looking sleepy. "Is that bacon I smell?" he says.

"I was going to do fishes and loaves," Ginny says, "but I couldn't find a good recipe."

I find Tory in her room, lying on the bed with a stuffed tiger in her arms.

"I brought you a sandwich," I say.

She shakes her head. I sit down beside her on the bed. A framed grave rubbing hangs over the headboard. HERE LYES THE BODY OF. The bedside table displays a collection of handmade dolls. I pick up a porcelain doll in peasant costume, then put it back.

"This was my room all the time I was growing up," Tory says.

"Maybe one of these days we'll buy ourselves a big old house like this," I suggest. I wish I hadn't said "maybe," but I feel uncertain of the future. Tory and I have talked about marriage, though everything seems to be changing. I don't really know what I want. Everything has become so gloomy and difficult lately.

"I don't want a big old house," Tory says. "A big old house needs kids in it."

"Don't be so pessimistic. The doctor said that was a worst-case scenario."

"Doctors have been treating women like children for centuries."

There's a knock on the door, and Bunny comes in.

She throws herself down on the bed beside Tory. "And now the graduate, exhausted from rehearsal in the hot sun, takes a load off her feet," Bunny says. "Also, by avoiding her own room, she hopes to escape interrogation at the hands of the mother of the graduate."

"What interrogation?" Tory says.

"She wants to know whether Bill's going to be at the ceremony."

"Is he?"

"Of course."

"You could introduce him as the father of the graduate," Tory says. "He's even older than Dad. Is he going to bring his wife with him?"

"He's not older than Dad. They're the same age."

"That makes it perfect."

"He's in terrific shape. He works out and plays tennis every day."

"You're going to ruin the graduation for Mom if she sees him there."

"She won't see him."

"Is Dad coming?"

"I didn't invite the bastard."

The sisters fall silent, both bouncing lightly on the bed, as if responding to some signal I can't hear. The resemblance of the two sisters lying on the bed is eerie and exciting. They seem to lend each other beauty, their juxtaposition creating a context for appreciation. In silence, they exercise a lifetime of intimacy. Outside I hear the clop-clop of a horse on the road. Dust swarms in the wedge of sunshine coming in through the curtains; a shaft of yellow light catches the edge of Bunny's hair and appears to ignite it. Both women have their eyes closed. I watch them. They seem to be asleep.

I go downstairs. Ginny is sitting at the kitchen table, reading a magazine. The TV is on, a game show. Ginny looks up and smiles. "My *Gourmet* arrived so I'm happy," she says. "I hardly ever cook anymore, but I love to read the recipes." I take a seat at the big round table that is the hub of family activity. The house has dens, living rooms and I'm not sure what else, but everyone hangs out in the kitchen. I wonder if it was always this way.

Ginny closes the magazine and looks up at the television. Then she looks at me. "Do you think in this day and age it's possible to win an alienation of affection suit?"

"I believe it's very difficult," I say. "But I'm afraid it's not my area." I wish I could tell her something encouraging, save the farm, stay the execution. I imagine myself flat on my back while a hostile jury piles stones on the beam across my chest. I went into law school with a vague notion of righting wrongs. "I don't know much about divorce law," I say. "Corporate marriages are my field. But I could look into it for you."

"No, that's okay. I've got a lawyer. I shouldn't be bothering you for advice." She reaches over and pats my hand. "It's good to have you here. I'm so pleased that Tory has someone like you to take care of her. You're great together." She lights up a cigarette. "Carol—I'm just relieved that she's not in jail or the nuthouse. If Jesus is what it takes, fine. Although I must say having those two around makes me want to curse and smoke and drink just out of spite." She looks at her watch.

"How about a drink, Ginny? I picked up a bottle of vodka."

"Well, I suppose, since it's the weekend. . . ."

"It's an occasion," I say. "I think we're well within our rights here." I fix the drinks. We were pleased to discover, last night, that we both like vodka on the rocks with a splash. Tory was less pleased. She thinks her mother drinks too much.

"I'm so glad you're a sinner," Ginny says. "I can't tell you what a relief it is. Carol and Jim were here for two days before you arrived, and it felt like two weeks. Cheers."

The phone rings. Ginny jumps up and catches it on the second ring. She says hello three times and hangs up. "That could've been one of three people," Ginny says after she's back at the table. She raises her hand and holds up a finger. "It could've been my husband, calling to see if I was out so he could sneak over and steal the silver. He tried one afternoon, but Bunny came home and caught him." She lifts a second finger. "It could've been Bill, Bunny's aging lover. He hangs up if I answer because he knows I won't let him talk to Bunny. Can you tell me what a young girl would want with a fifty-five-year-old man? And he's married. He keeps telling her he's going to divorce his wife, but he certainly hasn't told the wife yet. Although she knows all about it." Ginny raises a third finger. "Bill's wife is the other mystery-phone-call candidate. She calls sometimes when she doesn't know where her husband is, to see if Bunny's home. She disguises her voice when she asks for Bunny."

Ginny takes a long sip of her drink. "You know, I almost feel relieved when I think of Mary drinking beer with boys her own age."

While I freshen our drinks, Ginny starts dinner. Mary calls to say she's having dinner at Laura's house. I wonder if Ginny knows about Heavy Chevy Billy. I feel uneasy, vaguely responsible for her. What if she's in an accident tonight? Lily cautiously enters the kitchen, without parents, self-conscious and pleased when Ginny and I compliment her on her new dress. She tells us her mommy made it. "Your *mommy* made it?" Ginny says.

Lily nods.

"Christ really does work miracles," Ginny says.

Tory comes down. "Why didn't you wake me up?" she says.

"For what?"

"I don't know. What have you been doing?"

"Saying bad things about you," Ginny says. "Want a drink?" I can tell Tory's looking her mother over to see how much she's had.

"I'll have a beer."

The phone rings again and Ginny grabs it. She says hello several times. Then she says, "I know it's you," and hangs up.

"Who?" Tory says.

"I don't know," Ginny responds.

Supper is chicken Kiev, cranberry muffins and asparagus. Carol and Jim take turns scolding Lily for her table manners. Jim seems very uncertain of his surroundings, and his discomfort makes me feel more at home. Although he has been here two days longer, I feel he's the outsider, the rude interloper. I hate his clothes and his mustache. I also hate the way he snaps at Lily. She's not even his kid. I wink at her across the table. Bunny announces she isn't going to eat anything and makes good on her threat, though she filled her plate to stop the argument. She's upset because her mother yelled at her about the phone calls. The news is on TV. A group in Boston is in front of a hospital protesting abortion.

"Jim and I belong to a right-to-life group back home," Carol says.

"A woman should have the right to do whatever she wants with her body," Bunny says.

"No one has the right to murder the unborn."

I find it annoying the way everyone bandies around the concept of *rights*.

"It would be nice if you people were as concerned with living women as you are with fetuses," Bunny says.

"Murder," Carol says. "That's what you're talking about."

"Is this dinner-table conversation," Ginny asks.

Tory stands up and excuses herself, then leaves the room.

"That was lovely, girls," Ginny says. "Tory's going into the hospital on Monday."

"Excuse me," I say. "I'll go see if she's all right."

Tory's in her room, lying facedown on the bed. I sit beside her and stroke her hair. "It's going to be all right."

She flips over to face me. "All right for you. You don't want children. You're glad about all of this."

"That's not fair."

"I wouldn't even be having these problems if it weren't for you. I'd be a mother already if it weren't for you."

"We weren't ready yet. It would've been a mistake."

"Carol is right. It's murder."

"You don't believe that."

Carol's inside the room before she knocks on the open door. She stands beside the bed. "I don't mean to barge in," she says. "But I thought maybe I could be of help." She lowers her ponderous form onto the bed. "None of us is strong enough to bear his burden alone."

"All of us are strong enough to bear the misfortunes of others," Tory says.

"Jesus wants to lighten your load. All you have to do is ask." Carol stretches out her hand to Tory, who examines it and its owner with mild distaste. "Do you love Jesus, Tory?"

"Do I look like a necrophiliac to you?"

I expect Carol to be shocked, but her smile is indelible. "You can run from Jesus, but you can't hide."

Tory says, "But can you get a restraining order, is what I want to know."

The evening passes in the kitchen in front of the TV. The women are skilled at dividing their attention between the television and one another, so while never seeming to watch they will suddenly comment on the action on the screen. The conversation has a casual, intimate rhythm. I listen from outside the circle, a privileged observer. I enjoy studying Tory on her home ground, and am eager to pick up the family lore. I feel a renewed interest, seeing her in this context. More than bone structure and habits of speech, I can see aspects of character I was never quite able to bring into focus suddenly illuminated and framed in their genetic setting. I feel like someone whose appreciation of an artist has been based on a single painting but then is suddenly admitted to his studio.

My role of licensed connoisseur is compromised by the presence of Jim. Awkward and out of place, he butts into the

conversation to ask who or what. He looks resentful, worried
that a joke is being perpetrated at his expense. Mercifully, Jim
heads up early after yawning pointedly at his wife. She tells
him she'll be up soon. Bunny is up and down. At one point she
disappears for most of a sitcom. I find myself sharing Ginny's
anger at the old bastard who's stealing her youth.

Ginny keeps saying how nice it is to have everyone home,
until, with her fourth drink, she begins to foresee the end of
the reunion and slips into sullenness. "Mary's been out every
night since she got her license," she complains to Carol and
Tory. "She's no company. She doesn't have time to sit down
with her old mom. She's always coming or going, and everything's a big secret. She doesn't tell me anything. And then
Bunny. She hates me because I don't want her to throw her life
away."

"She doesn't hate you," Tory says impatiently.

"Of course she doesn't," Carol says. "She *loves* you. We *all*
love you."

Ginny looks at Carol through tears and says, "Spare me this
indiscriminate love. The trouble with you religious types is
that you're promiscuous. Love, love, love. But then, you
always *were* a cheap date."

"Stop it," Tory says. "That's no way to talk to your daughter."

"That's all right, Tory," Carol says. "I understand Mom's
anger."

"No you don't," Ginny says, slapping her palm down on
the table. "You can't begin to understand my anger."

I feel I should leave, but right now that would only make
my presence more blatant.

"Between your sloppy el-you-vee and Tory's Ice Queen
judgment, I'm dying for a little daughterly affection." She
shakes her head. "What a brood. And Bunny. As if I need to be
reminded about old leches and young bimbos."

Ginny lights a cigarette. "And where the hell is Mary?
She's supposed to be in at eleven o'clock." We all turn to the
clock above the range: it says ten-forty. "All right," Ginny
says, "so she's got twenty minutes." They all laugh at the same
moment, like synchronized swimmers executing an abrupt,
graceful maneuver, their anger dispersed.

"Do you think she's still a virgin?" Ginny asks suddenly.

"Of course she's a virgin," Tory says.

"Mary's a sensible girl," Carol says. "She's not going to let herself be talked into anything."

I remember Tory told me that Carol had her first abortion when she was fifteen.

"She's only sixteen," Tory says.

"She's so cute," Carol says.

"She is," Ginny says.

Tory turns to me and says, "Isn't she a cutie?"

I could get very inspired on this subject. Instead I just say, "She sure is."

Carol says, "Remember that time she stuck the key in the electrical socket?"

At eleven o'clock Tory announces she's tired. "You don't have to come to bed yet," she says to me. I would like to stay up with the others, to sit quietly and listen to three women talk, but I say I'll come up with her. Ginny lets us share a room. Everyone kisses goodnight. Bunny, who has come back down, presses close enough for me to feel her breasts as she kisses me. Carol's breath smells chemically sweetened. Ginny folds me in a long, motherly hug. She says she's going up, too.

After she takes off her shirt, Tory points to the small protuberance on her left side. It is the size of a BB, only slightly darker than the surrounding skin. "Do you know that this would have been enough evidence to convict me of witchcraft in the seventeenth century?" she says.

I do know, because she has told me several times, but I say, "Really?"

"It's what they call an auxiliary nipple. A devil's teat. Proof that I've been suckling demons."

"Rules of evidence have advanced a little since then," I say cheerfully.

"Wouldn't it be strange if in former lives you were a prosecutor at the witch trials and I was a witch."

"I'm on your side, Tory," I say, putting my arms around her. As her face disappears against my chest I see that she is looking not at me but at some region inside herself. "Everything will be all right," I say. I can still see the sadness in her eyes and mouth. "We'll have children together." Maybe I say it because I want to sleep with her sisters and I feel guilty about it, or because she thinks that like her father I'll leave and I'm afraid she's right.

Lying there after Tory has fallen asleep, I conjure up the image of Bunny and Tory sleeping side by side on this same bed, and think about how I felt then, how I wanted to crawl between them and have both. What I really imagined, seeing these two women who look so much alike, was a single woman who was Tory leavened with Bunny's careless grace. As I drift toward sleep, I superimpose Mary's face, which seemed to me in the liquor store parking lot to be fearless and flushed with sexual anticipation, and to that I add Carol's womb. Then I see Ginny alone in the bed in which the four of them had been conceived. And I think of my own mother, who is dead, and my father, whom I haven't seen in eight months, and imagine myself as a pinprick of life, floating whole in the dark, before all of these divisions and divorces and separations.

ACKNOWLEDGMENTS

Once again, I am deeply indebted to Gary Fisketjon and Amanda Urban. I would also like to thank Jenna Lamond, Rob Grover, Susan Betz, Chip Kidd and Daniella Amini and to propose a toast to Bill Buford, who first published quite a few of these pages and who helped revive *Model Behavior* when my own enthusiasm was waning. I was also encouraged and abetted by my friend and longtime UK editor, Liz Calder. Alice Turner and Rust Hills improved several of these stories. Many thanks and cheers are owed to Ken (the financial wizard, not the witch-hunter) Starr, Michael Cantor and Cathie de Lorme. Kisses to Helen for knowing when to judge and when to reserve judgment. I'm indebted to Morgan Entenkin and Grove Atlantic for a room without a view. Finally, thanks to the New York Society Library, the Writer's Room and all the women who left me.